Her...
W...

Price:

HER

H46 361 092 5

BY WILLIAM HORWOOD

The Duncton Chronicles

Duncton Wood
Duncton Quest
Duncton Found

The Book of Silence

Duncton Tales
Duncton Rising
Duncton Stone

The Wolves of Time

Journeys to the Heartland
Seekers at the Wulf Rock

Tales of the Willows

The Willows in Winter
Toad Triumphant
The Willows and Beyond
The Willows at Christmas

Other works

The Stonor Eagles
Callanish
Skallagrigg
The Boy with No Shoes (Memoir)

The Hyddenworld Novels

Hyddenworld
Awakening

AWAKENING

WILLIAM HORWOOD

PAN BOOKS

First published 2011 by Macmillan

This edition published 2012 by Pan Books
an imprint of Pan Macmillan, a division of Macmillan Publishers Limited
Pan Macmillan, 20 New Wharf Road, London N1 9RR
Basingstoke and Oxford
Associated companies throughout the world
www.panmacmillan.com

ISBN 978-0-330-46169-6

1 3 5 7 9 8 6 4 2

A CIP catalogue record for this book is available from
the British Library.

Typeset by SetSystems Ltd, Saffron Walden, Essex
Printed and bound by CPI Group (UK) Ltd, Croydon, CR0 4YY

Visit **www.panmacmillan.com** to read more about all our books
and to buy them. You will also find features, author interviews and
news of any author events, and you can sign up for e-newsletters
so that you're always first to hear about our new releases.

For Joseph, Rachel, Joshua, Alice,
Oliver and Maxfield,
with love

AWAKENING

I

BIRTH

It was a hushed, still night and a million stars and a rising moon shone down upon White Horse Hill in Berkshire, England. Their light picked out the sinewy lines of the prehistoric horse carved into the chalk beneath the grass.

It was so clearly visible from the Vale below that two people had stopped awhile in the hushed and magical dark beneath the hill, on the pilgrim road that ended there.

'It looks as if it's about to gallop off across the Universe,' said one of them softly, 'or maybe it's just showing us the way home.'

The one who spoke was eighteen, more man than boy. His name was Jack and he was stocky and strong, with a forward thrust to his head that suggested purpose and intent.

The other was his partner Katherine, who was the same age, as tall as he but fair-haired. She was tired and in pain, her head bowed. She held one of her hands to her belly, the other rested on Jack's arm. She stood with difficulty.

Katherine was pregnant and very near her time.

'We're nearly home,' he said.

She raised her head wearily and nodded, too tired to speak or even smile.

The trees and bushes that lined the old way were silver and shimmery in the night. Somewhere from across the Vale a church clock began to strike midnight.

'April's over,' said Jack. 'Summer's begun.'

The White Horse looked down on them and the stars and moon lit their path as they continued on their way.

'Home' was Woolstone House in the village of the same name. It was no more than a few hundred yards on, off the ancient way and to their right, over a stile, across a stream, and up the sloping pasture to the great garden where Katherine played as a child.

Less than two years before they had begun their journey here, going out into the Hyddenworld, a place as real as the human one. Jack's coming had been long prophesied and Katherine was thought to be the Shield Maiden, a fierce warrior woman who rode the White Horse in service of Earth and Universe at times of great danger and sacrifice.

But the Hyddenworld was wrong about Katherine. She was just a girl who somewhere along her journey with Jack became a woman. It was not she who was the Shield Maiden, but the child she was carrying.

Now they had returned along the pilgrim road, passed through one of the henges which are the portals from the Hyddenworld to the human one and had come home to have her child.

With each passing moment her progress grew harder and she stumbled more, gasping from pain and for breath as her hand tightened on Jack's arm. Tall though she was, he was by far the stronger of the two.

'Take it slowly, one step at a time,' he said, 'we're nearly there . . .'

'Jack, I'm scared.'

'The White Horse is with us,' he said, his voice deep and calm.

He himself was of both worlds, or neither. He came from Germany as a rare 'giant-born', a hydden with the attributes of both hydden and human races, regarded with suspicion for his size and warrior powers. His kind were usually put to death before they reached maturity, but when he was six he had been rescued from that fate and the White Horse had carried him to England to be raised among humans for his own safety.

They reached the pasture and began the final climb. Halfway up she gasped suddenly, leaned on him more, but did not stop.

'Breathe deeply,' he said.

'I am breathing deeply,' she replied with spirit, 'if I wasn't the baby would have been born way back there . . . but I want . . . to . . . get home.'

The night was so clear that they could see every blade of grass on the path and finally the rise of great trees ahead of them where the garden began.

'Hold me close,' she said, 'help me on.'

Each step was a struggle, her body wanting her to stop and lie down, the first sharp pain she had felt earlier coming again.

They knew their baby was a girl even though no human doctor had examined Katherine. They knew as certainly as they knew their own names. They knew their child would be unusual, perhaps unlike any child before. She had a name, she had a role, and the moon and stars shone bright that night because they wanted to light her way to where she needed to be born.

'J . . . Jack . . . it's . . . I . . .'

She leaned into him and moaned and whispered, 'How far now because I don't think—'

She moaned again and let out another cry.

The slope eased as they reached the edge of the pasture and a single loose strand of barbed wire was all that separated them from the trees beyond. It looked like a wood but they knew it was not.

These were some of the trees of a living henge, a circle of life. There was no breeze low down but above their heads a wind played between the high branches and ran lightly among the fresh young leaves.

It was a whisper of welcome, a sighing of relief, an assurance they were wanted and they were loved. It was the Earth's own voice that spoke and the eyes of the Universe, which were all the stars, saw and winked in the black sky . . . as they had watched for nine months past, from the moment that the Shield Maiden was conceived in love and Jack and Katherine began their long walk back home, to bring her safely into the mortal world.

Jack reached out a hand, grasped the wire, barbs and all, and raised it high.

'I can't bend . . .'

'I think you can,' he said.

Sideways on, propped up by him, groaning, grimacing, floundering, she got under and then upright once more.

They went between two of the henge trees and began to cross the great circle of grass to the other side when she stopped, gasped and said, 'I think . . . Jack . . . she's coming now, she wants to be born.'

He looked through the henge up to Woolstone House, where all was darkness. It was too far to get there now, too late.

The wind above whispered more urgently and Jack said, 'Here, you'll have to have her here.'

He helped Katherine a few paces to the nearest tree.

'Hold on to that,' he said, 'and I'll fix you something to lie on. I won't be a moment.'

'Hurry!' she said.

He heaved off the great, heavy pack on his back and opened it, working by feel alone as he had learnt to do in the Hyddenworld for other emergencies than this, the greatest of them all. He laid out something for her to lie on.

'Jaaa . . . aack!'

As he went to her she grabbed him.

'Oh God it hurts,' she said, her hands and fingers digging into his arms, 'oh . . .'

He backed her to the makeshift bed, helped her down, put the pack in place for her head.

He looked in the direction of the house.

'I could try . . .'

She let out a little cry, laughed and squeezed his hand.

'You sound more scared than I . . . I . . . am . . . ooohh!'

'I *am*,' he said as he knelt over her, holding her, stroking her, giving her his strength. 'I am.'

The pain briefly passed, she breathed deeply again and said, 'So . . . what now?'

'I think it's pretty clear what happens now,' he said matter-of-factly, 'but we need light . . .'

She shook her head.

'There's light enough from the moon and stars,' she said, her tired eyes filled with love and fear, her hands holding on to him for reassurance.

'Well then . . .' he said, 'this isn't such a bad place for—'

'Jaaaack . . . !'

'I'm here,' he said, holding her protectively. 'I'm here . . .'

And then she screamed and screamed and cried and shouted and groaned and wept as the moon rode across the circle of the swaying henge above their heads.

'Push,' he said, 'push!'

'Jaaack . . . she's . . . *help* . . . *me!*'

His great, strong hands mingled with hers as they felt the baby, slippery and warm, in the shadow between her legs. 'Oh Jack . . . she . . .'

She cried out, their baby did, her thin first cry across the Earth and out into the Universe. Then another.

'Jack, help me . . .' whispered Katherine.

He helped her bring the child to her bare stomach, then to her breast, to hold, and hold, and hold ever tight, to never let her go.

As for Jack, exhausted too, he held them both.

Eventually . . .

'You know what to do . . .' she said.

They had prepared for him to do what he must if it came to a birth in the open air. He had the knife, already sterilized with fire, wrapped up in clean plastic.

But when he took it out he said, ever practical, 'I don't think so.'

He got some matches and a candle, and sterilized the knife again . . .

'Jaaa . . . ck!'

She pushed once more and the placenta came out and lay there, large and black in the dark.

A sleepy calm came over them as the baby snuffled at Katherine's breast.

Jack tied the cord in two places with twine, waited a little and then cut through in-between. No hesitation, no messing about, that was Jack. He put the placenta to one side and then checked that the baby was covered, and Katherine too.

He listened with satisfaction to the baby's thin cries and said softly, 'She's born, our child is born.'

'Is she all right?' whispered Katherine, a mother's oldest fear.

'I haven't even checked to see if she's a she!' he said lightly, 'but if she's who we think she is then the Earth herself will have seen she's all right. Any . . . anyway . . . anyway . . .'

He held them both.

'Anyway what?' she whispered, a hand leaving their child to touch his face.

He was weeping the deep beautiful tears of relief a father sheds for the safe birth of a child.

He had got Katherine home.

She had borne their child.

They were safe . . . and all was well.

The moon shone still above them as the White Horse galloped through the stars towards the first dawn of a new Summer.

2

PILGRIM

That same night, and at that same hour, the birth of the Shield Maiden in the shadow of White Horse Hill had repercussions in the Hyddenworld.

That this might be so had long been predicted in stories handed down the hydden generations for the past fifteen hundred years. But myth and legend are one thing, reality quite another, and a great deal more perilous for those caught up in it.

While Jack and Katherine were tending their newborn child in the henge at Woolstone, their close friend and recent travelling companion Mister Bedwyn Stort, a harmless scholar and scrivener, was in real and present danger of losing his life as a direct consequence.

Whatever the reasons for this, he found himself alone in the dark facing a situation from which he might very easily fail to extricate himself.

'This is not good,' he told himself as he realized the scale and nature of his difficulties, 'not good at all!'

And he was right.

Stort had left his friends some days before at the Devil's Quoits, a stone henge that straddled the same hydden road from which they had journeyed southward.

Of all the great pilgrim ways in the Hyddenworld none is as ancient or as hallowed as that, because it connects two places of great power and holiness.

The first is where the immortal White Horse, which serves the

Universe, came into being, in whose great shadow the Shield Maiden had now been born to a human mother.

The second is Waseley Hill, seventy miles to the north, where the legendary gem of Spring, which holds life's fire, was lost and never found.

Sadly, human roads have displaced this hydden way, while their settlements and factories have encroached and polluted it. For these reasons pilgrims rarely take the old route now. It is, in any case, very hard to find, especially at its northern end, where it runs among the southern suburbs of Birmingham, the great industrial city of central England. The city lies athwart what, in better days, was the Kingdom of Mercia, but that was fifteen hundred years ago, when human and hydden lived in harmony with each other.

Times changed and the little folk, as the humans thought of them, became 'the hydden'. They faded from human memory and found themselves turned into superstitious stories of elves and sprites, fairies and goblins.

Such fancies were always far from the reality. Hydden were – they *are* – three feet high when full grown and in every way as enterprising, intelligent and philosophical, or lazy, stupid and dull, as any mortal can be. But threatened as they were by their giant counterparts they learnt the art of hyddening, staying unseen.

They did this so well that humans, no longer expecting to see them, forgot how to. Until in time and to this very day, when humans glimpsed them, as they often did, they had no idea what it was they saw.

As a result the hydden realized long ago that they had no need to flee the human race and live in rough, wild places.

Instead they have long since done the sensible thing and taken up residence in human cities. There an easier and more fulfilling life was to be had along the abandoned rail tracks and sidings, by forgotten canals, in redundant sewers and around the built-over water courses and the interstices between old factories and inaccessible warehouses.

Today there is not a human city in the world that does not have a thriving hydden city deep within it.

Naturally some are more important than others because of their location, their history and their wyrd, or destiny. Most retain their human name among the hydden, like Bochum in Germany, infamous capital of the Hyddenworld which underlies the human city of the same name.

But a few, through time and usage, gained a hydden name all of their own. Such a one is Brum, the most feted city in the Hyddenworld and the home of liberty, individuality and common sense. And *where* is Brum?

Right in the deep, shadowy heart of old Birmingham, no more than a mile or two from the northern end of the old pilgrim road that leads to Waseley Hill.

Jack and Katherine reached their destination as the clock struck midnight on the last day of April, in the hours after which Spring gives way to Summer and brighter days begin.

But every hydden knows that those dark hours of the season's turn are not a good time to be out after nightfall. Strange things happen, time shifts oddly, children disappear – and Shield Maidens are born! – while the barriers between the past, present and future grow thin and frail and occasionally break.

In short, a very bad time indeed for a lone hydden to be walking the old pilgrim road near Waseley Hill, enshadowed as it is by dreams unfinished, yearnings unfulfilled and spirits unsatisfied.

Better to stay at home, lock the door, let no one in, make merry, make conversation, make love if that seems right, *but do not go outside*.

But that, unfortunately, was not the happy situation in which Mister Bedwyn Stort had found himself earlier.

After leaving his good friends to return to the human world and have their child, a chill and fretful rain-filled wind had harried him northward, as if to say *Mister Stort you must get to Brum quickly, danger looms!*

At first he had heeded the implicit warning of wind and rain and hurried along. But the youthful Stort – he was twenty-three – was by nature easily distracted and not the speediest of travellers. Tall and clumsy, he was inclined to allow his legs to become entangled with his stave, or to set off impulsively and leave something important behind, so that he had to retrace his steps.

Because he could never decide what not to take on a journey, he always took too much. As a result his portersac was weighed down with things for which no one else but he could possibly have found a use – black bin liners, lengths of twine, an extra chipped enamel mug, blackthorn twigs, burnt corks and the like.

Worse still, he often forgot where he was meant to be going, frequently got lost, and fell into such mishaps and misadventures that his friends would have preferred that he stayed safely at home in Brum with his books.

But that he could never do. The inventions he made he liked to try out in the real world, the languages he spoke he wished to practise with real people, and his abiding curiosity about all things hydden and human put into him a permanent wanderlust.

But one more thing about Stort, perhaps the most important thing of all, which made up for his many failings.

Despite the risks he took and the mistakes he made he showed great courage in all he did and – as his good friends pointed out to doubters – he always got back home in one piece, wiser than when he left and having made some discovery, physical or spiritual, which benefited hyddenkind.

However, the hard fact was that as twilight fell on the last day of April, Stort had realized that he wasn't going to make it to the West Gate of Brum until the early hours. So when he reached Beacon Hill, the penultimate rise on the pilgrim road, he stopped to ponder his situation.

From that vantage point he could see Waseley Hill to his left and Brum ahead and to his right, stretching away into the growing night, a vast and beautiful twinkling carpet of light.

Sensible travellers would have known at once that the best thing to do was to make camp immediately, preferably one that was well camouflaged. Then they could crawl into their bivvy bags, cover their eyes, block their ears and remain immobile until May Day was truly begun. That was the hydden way to survive a season's turn if stuck alone outside.

Failing that, the next best thing would have been for Stort to hide his heavy portersac in thick undergrowth for later recovery, and bypass the Hill to make a dash for Brum, trusting that the guardians of its gates would open up when they heard his urgent hammering.

Not ideal but far better than what Bedwyn Stort actually did, which was the most foolhardy thing a hydden *could* have done: he set off towards the shadows and darkness of Waseley Hill.

His reasons for taking this startling course of action were not simple and they had a history.

The first thing most pilgrims visiting Waseley Hill do is to seek out the source of the River Rea and imbibe its pure, cool waters. That ritual over, they dwell a little on the memory of Beornamund, founder of Brum, maker of artefacts of power and beauty and probably the greatest CraftLord who ever lived.

Few doubt that somewhere on the banks of the Rea, perhaps quite near its source, he had his forge. The roaring of his furnace and bright ringing of his hammer as he worked precious metals for the Mercian kings and lords, and their ladies, must have been often heard.

It was on the banks of the Rea that Beornamund met Imbolc, which in the old language means Spring, and fell in love with her. But when she died in a freak flood upon the hill – a strange, perverse happening indeed – the CraftLord blamed the gods.

Every hydden knows what happened next. Beornamund made a sphere of crystal and precious metals of such perfection that when he hurled it into the sky over Waseley Hill in angry defiance of the gods it attracted to itself the fires of the Universe and all the colours of the seasons.

The gods thought that if they let the sphere fall back to Earth and be destroyed all would be well. They had forgotten that the Universe is as one and that to break or sully even a small part of its perfection was to endanger all.

Fortunately, four fragments of the sphere remained: small stones or gems, each of which held the fires of life and the essence of one of the seasons: Spring, Summer, Autumn, Winter.

Great Beornamund guessed their importance at once and understood the trouble and danger he had caused. He found all the fragments but for Spring, search though he might. Eventually he made a pendant with four settings, leaving one empty against the day when Spring was found. It is said that at his death the White Horse carried Imbolc to Beornamund in spirit form. He was granted immortality for his services as a CraftLord, but for Imbolc to earn her place at his side for all time she must first wander the Earth as the Peace-Weaver, or bringer of harmony, until such time as she had lived out the centuries of her spirit life.

Learning this, Beornamund wrought the pendant anew, such that the gems would fall from it down the centuries and be scattered across the Earth, marking off each season's passing and giving his love strength to continue her journey. When Winter was gone she would know her journey was over. Only then, and after a mortal had found the lost gem of Spring, would Imbolc be allowed to take her rightful place at Beornamund's side.

But that would presage a darker and more dangerous time for the Earth. In place of the Peace-Weaver, her sister the Shield Maiden would be born: angry, frightening, a seeming curse on all who knew her.

If she was to be pacified the finder of the gem of Spring must give it to her, and afterwards find the gems of Summer, Autumn and Winter, wherever they might be, and give those to her too. Then, with the gems reunited and the fires of the Universe as one, the Shield Maiden and her mortal helpers would be able to regenerate the broken sphere and peace and honour between gods and mortal kind would be satisfied, harmony return, and the balance of the Universe restored . . .

But what had such a story to do with Mister Bedwyn Stort of Brum, a traveller incapable of getting from A to B without mishap, let alone one capable of traversing the Universe in search of lost gems?

This . . .

The many stories and prophecies surrounding the gem of Spring told that it would be found by an extraordinary hydden, and brought to the Shield Maiden with the help of a giant-born, a hydden who must learn to live in both worlds before he can live safely in either.

The path of the White Horse and its Rider, Imbolc the Peace-Weaver, had already crossed that of Bedwyn Stort twice. On both occasions Imbolc had seen in Stort a hydden of great power.

His own path had crossed that of Jack, a giant-born, and Katherine, a human girl of considerable resource and courage.

Stort was too modest and self-effacing to imagine that *he* was the 'extraordinary hydden' of legend who would find the gem. But what did seem quite certain to him was that the baby Katherine was pregnant with was the Shield Maiden and most likely to be born that night. Which meant in turn that the gem of Spring must be found that night too, as the myths made clear. These were the thoughts that made Stort take the risk and set off for Waseley Hill as night fell.

He did so with a memory that gave him comfort and strength. A few weeks before, Katherine had shyly taken his hand and placed it on her swollen belly that he might feel the child move. From that moment Stort had felt a loyalty and a love such as he never had before. It filled his heart, it brought joy to his lone spirit and it made his pulse race with hope and excitement.

If she was indeed to be born that night, and if she was the Shield Maiden, then perhaps there was no better pilgrim than Bedwyn Stort to be upon the old Road and hurrying on to Waseley Hill in the dark. Innocent and wise, fearful and courageous, faithful but questioning – perhaps these had always been the qualities the gem-finder would need.

But what he would do on the Hill, Stort as yet had no idea.

What dangers he might face he could not know.

What courage and purpose he might find he could not possibly imagine.

But there he was, the wind now a hurricane filled with rain, trees bending, creaking and cracking all about, and the very ground beginning to shake with an earth tremor.

Up ahead, the Hill itself to where he now walked.

To his left, and flowing down from it, the River Rea.

Right behind . . .

Behind?

He heard a roaring sound like a great wave churning on a steep shingle beach, readying itself to drive forward and destroy all in its path.

But surely, he told himself, *water cannot flow up a hill!*

Stort decided to stand his ground.

Let this flood of water come, if that's what it is! he cried aloud into the rain and wind, to give himself courage.

To no avail.

The roaring from lower down the hill grew louder still and put into him a fear like no other he had ever felt.

Not for the first time in life Stort had a sense of his own imminent destruction. He trembled, his knees shook and he felt himself unable to breathe.

But suddenly the rain stopped and the river ceased to flow, its waters uncertain, shaking, trembling, as if in the grip of a force far beyond an earthly one. Though everything was silent and most dangerous, a sense of peace came over Bedwyn Stort.

His fears slipped away, his courage returned, and with it a new certainty and a sense of wonder.

What he heard, what he felt, what he knew as he stood alone on Waseley Hill, was that great change was in the air that went far beyond the season's turn.

'Now is the hour and the moment!' he told himself, adding aloud, as if it were an invocation, 'Now will the gem of Spring, the first and the lost gem, finally be found! If that be true then assuredly I shall know that the Shield Maiden has been born!'

This was the way in which the wyrd of Bedwyn Stort was entwined that night with that of Katherine and Jack and of their child.

3

OFFERING

J ack's eyes snapped open, his mind and body instantly alert.

He did not move, not sure if it was danger that threatened or simply some change in the environment he sensed.

It was still dark but dawn was not far away. Katherine and Judith were asleep, his arms were still around them.

No movement, nothing near but . . . he relaxed.

It was the rank odour of a fox that had woken him.

Jack's eyes went from right to left, slowly. The wind was slight, coming from a little to his right, so not quite straight through the two great conifers that marked the entrance to the henge.

His eyes made the return journey and that time he saw it, in the undergrowth to the left of the conifers, its eyes silver orbs that caught the moon above and the beginning of dawn.

The fox was hunting and it was hunting them, its head moving cautiously out from the shadows, its front paw hesitating. For the briefest of moments Jack felt the fight response in a way he never had. Total protection of his young and her mother, zero tolerance of anything that threatened his family. But a *fox* . . . ? Even a fox.

Jack knew it had found them by scent, as he had first found it. Its purpose plain: it wanted something whose scent had an appeal that transcended the fear foxes felt when they ran into humans and hydden.

But this one wasn't interested in them, or the baby. It had scented the blood and the placenta. Jack stayed still, waiting with interest to see what the fox did while he enjoyed the new raft of feelings into which parenthood had thrust him: pride, wonder, responsibility, purpose, maleness, being the protector. He had felt that before in all the long weeks and months past, getting Katherine safely home. Now the feeling was multiplied. Katherine was an adult and could protect herself. His child was not, and could not.

Not yet anyway. Later, in the years to come, when she had grown a bit and was on her way to being a Shield Maiden, things would be different. But for now she needed them.

Everything had changed for him. The world had reorientated itself. The fox stood poised, head slightly to one side, listening, then moved forward again, still scenting the air.

Jack reached a hand to touch the beautiful curve of Judith's back, and Katherine's cheek. He did it gently, with infinite tenderness, but even so Katherine stirred and murmured.

The fox retreated at once but its eyes remained watching from the shadows.

Then he himself stirred because suddenly there was something he had to do. Where the impulse came from he did not know, but it felt deep and visceral and came from some ancient, ancestral part of him, from the very beginning of his kind.

They had been given a gift, and it was time to give one back and thank the White Horse for getting them home.

He often had such feelings and knew they were of a different nature and came from a different place than the instinct that Katherine sometimes had.

'It's because you're giant-born,' she would say. 'One day you'll take pride in that!'

It was a hydden expression to describe a genetic freak whose blood carried something of both human and hydden genes. Born a hydden but condemned to grow to human size and become giant, an outcast in the world to which he truly belonged.

That was why, when he was six, someone – he could not remember who – had sent him to be raised as a human for his own protection. In Germany, the land of his birth, he would have been a monster deserving only to be killed before maturity. In tolerant and enlightened Brum his presence was the fulfilment of a prophecy that turned on the finding and bringing together of Beornamund's four gems of the seasons.

Only when he learnt by accident that henges could be used as portals between the two worlds had he realized he might exist in both because he changed in the transfer to normal hydden size.

He knew none of this until he travelled into the Hyddenworld with Katherine. Only then did the feelings for hydden ways and unseen danger, the fast reactions, the profound reverence he felt for the Earth and Universe, his ability to hydden or hide himself and even his flair for hydden music, make sense.

So he knew now that the fox had come deliberately, sent by some hydden god or spirit, that he might make an offering of thanks to the White Horse. The fox was friend not foe, though he was hunter still.

'I'm going to clean you up,' he said quietly to Katherine, 'and then there's something I must do. Stay as you are, Judith's asleep. She'll need these hours close to you, skin to skin, more than a normal child . . .'

He knew it was so but not how or why he knew.

Katherine stirred with worry at the word 'normal'.

'Ssshh,' he whispered, 'she's fine, she's fine . . .'

He sat up straight and turned round slowly to check the fox was watching. It was and he was glad. Jack needed it to be.

He took the leather water bottle from his 'sac and washed his hands. Katherine had been very particular about them having water and clean cloths.

'Just in case it happens outside and there's only us . . . you'll have to . . .'

He knew what to do. Only when he was satisfied that she was clean and dry did he do what instinct told him to do afterwards. He reached his hands to the placenta he had put nearby. It was cold now and because of the water on his hands it was slippery again.

He knelt by her, got it in his palms, stood up carefully so as not to drop it and went to the very centre of the henge, the moon now almost on the edge of the circle of its trees, the last stars and planets shining in the sky.

'It's May Day,' he whispered, 'the start of Summer. More importantly the Shield Maiden has been born and the lost gem will soon be found.'

He held the placenta up towards the stars, turned a deasil circle three times, whispered words of Earth and Universe, and finally placed it on the ground in the circle of grass he had trampled.

Then he went back to Katherine and whispered, 'I need to take her for a moment, I need to give thanks and ask the White Horse to help her on the journey she's now started . . . it's all right . . . sshhh . . . I'll be just over there. It's something I have to do . . .'

He took the baby in his arms, sleeping still.

Seeing her beauty his eyes filled with tears that caught the dawning light.

'Come on, Judith,' he said, 'time for you to say hello.'

He went to where the placenta lay on the ground and stood astride it. Then, looking up at the circle of sky above him, at the last of the moon and the first of the dawn, his eyes on the few remaining stars, and finally looking between the trees to the dark wall of the escarpment that was White Horse Hill, the Horse invisible in the dark, he raised Judith up and made a plea that from that moment on, to the end of time, they would watch over her benignly. As he did so he knew without needing to be told that he was doing as parents had done, both human and hydden, through all the millennia of mortal life, where they were left to their own devices.

'Accept her,' he said, 'give her help when we no longer can, guide her as you guided us, bring her love as you brought it to us.'

As he spoke, his body stilled, so did Judith's and so too did Katherine's.

But the fox moved and came out into the open, its coat silvery in the dawning light.

It took another step forward, scenting the air towards where Jack stood with Judith raised to the skies. Then another step and another . . .

Until, all fear gone, it came to him, scenting the placenta, sensing utter safety, despite the humans being so near.

It barked, it licked, it took up what was there and ran with it back to the edge of the henge, but stayed out in the light.

Jack cradled Judith back into his arms and turned to watch it take the offering and eat it.

Jack murmured to his child.

The fox ate as if on the Earth's behalf.

When it had finished it looked back at Jack, turned tail and was suddenly gone.

'Jack . . .'

She needed help.

He went back to her, put their baby back between her breasts and covered her to keep her warm. Then the rays of the rising sun came among the trees and lit them all. Judith finally woke.

'I'm going to remove this towel and my jacket and cle . . . clean . . .'

Her cries were sudden and sharp, louder than a baby's only a few hours old ought to be.

Katherine tried to put her to the breast but she refused, her tiny crying mouth sliding over the nipple and ignoring it.

Jack did the best he could, liberal with water and the clean cloths Katherine had ready in plastic bags.

'I'm getting cold.'

The crying persisted.

'Jack . . .'

'She must be hungry.'

But the cry was pitiful and born of pain, it seemed, not hunger. Continuing to refuse the breast she cried still more; and even more when Jack took her in his arms again, wrapped tight in a towel and his jacket, and walked a few steps with her.

Katherine was exhausted and her clothes still a mess; so was he. Judith too, with dried blood and mucus on her arms and head.

'What do we do?' he asked Katherine, because he had no idea.

'You'd better go up to the house,' she said. 'I think we need help.'

And they did.

Katherine was getting cold and their baby was crying again. But now her hands had turned to fists and her eyes were screwed up and shut tight . . . as she gave herself up to cries of such pain that they knew something was terribly wrong.

4
DISCOVERY

As the sense of silence deepened about Bedwyn Stort there occurred one of those shifts in time which had often been noted as something that happened at the seasons' turn.

He had left Beacon Hill not long after twilight fell, only an hour or two before, but his chronometer showed it was midnight. The rain clouds above his head sucked away to north and south, east and west, as if time had speeded up. Then they circled round the horizon like a halo, in the centre of which, revealed in all its wonder and glory, was the Universe itself: the deep unknowable black of space the setting for a hundred million stars, the moon soaring bright, the cold air taking his two hands in its clean grasp and stretching them above his head in reverence and in welcome.

The ground trembled beneath his feet and he heard again the roar of the advancing wave and guessed that his life was more than ever in danger. But he knew that he must stay calm, stay firm and have faith that his courage and purpose would hold and see things through.

He realized it was in this same place, when he was a boy of eleven, that he had first met Imbolc the Peace-Weaver. Now, as then, a chill ran through his body which hollowed and aged him. His knees gave way and he felt his life begin to flee.

When Imbolc came before she had been near the end of her great journey down the centuries, the passing of each season of her spirit life marked with the loss of that season's gem until the last, that of Winter, had been lost.

Since then she had been Peace-Weaver on borrowed time, waiting for the coming of the Shield Maiden.

Stort felt the blizzard cold, and realized that destruction was almost on him. He could only hope that Imbolc would come again, her journey over and the time for her to go to Beornamund's side finally come.

He tried to speak, but could not.

He tried to keep his arms and hands raised to the bright Universe, but could not.

He tried to keep his eyes open to the world he loved, but felt them beginning to close.

Help me, he whispered to the gods.

Help me! he cried out to the Mirror-of-All in which mortals live their brief lives.

Help me, he asked of Imbolc in the silence of his dying mind.

'Help me,' said Bedwyn Stort.

The silence fled.

The wall of water raging up the hill mounted so high that it blocked out the lights of the sleeping city below and the star-filled clouds on the far horizon.

'Help me,' he whispered a final time as he waited for his body and his life to be torn apart and lost for ever in what now began to reach him.

It was then she came, standing between him and the raging dark water that would kill him, a woman so old she seemed part of the Earth and the Universe as well, a crone, her legs thin sticks, her wrists and hands no better than bleached twigs, her hair white gossamer, her body so bent and frail that the slightest puff of wind would break and scatter it.

Imbolc had reached the last moments of her great and lonely journey down the years since the gods sent her on her voyage as Peace-Weaver to the Earth, with only the White Horse to keep her company and a pendant with her life's seasons in the form of gems having to be lived and lost down the centuries.

Horse and gems all gone now, Beornamund nowhere to be seen, just a mortal on his knees whose name she knew and in whom she had known for twelve long years the hope of Earth and Universe would lie.

She had heard his weak cry and come to him, his faith her final strength. She showed no fear of the wave advancing up the hill towards them.

She went to Stort, reached out her old hand and said, 'Rise and stand by me and you'll be safe as you see what you must.'

Stort did so.

'Hold my hand,' she said, which he did fearfully, for Stort was afraid of her touch. It had nearly killed him twelve years before.

She smiled and said, 'Never fear, you survived it once and have proved yourself most worthy since. No harm shall ever come to you from a touch such as mine, only love.'

So he held her hand and took strange comfort from it.

'Now listen carefully,' Imbolc continued. 'My sister is born this night and that means my time is run. Yet I have strength left for one last thing but I need your help to do it! But . . . *hold fast!*'

Her voice was drowned as the water tore into them and round them, leaving them untouched, unmoved even as it ripped the earth from around their feet.

Then it was gone on up the hill, sucking the riverbed dry as it went.

For a moment all was still again but for the muted roaring of the water that was now above, turning, falling, boiling at the river's source before . . . before . . .

'It's coming back down!' he said.

He might well at that moment have finally run for his life, but something in the mud of the river bed, so briefly sucked dry, caught his eye. A glinting of sorts, a dull glow, a light not quite obscured.

He went to the river bed, Imbolc with him.

'It's a great boulder,' he said, 'and there's a light shining from beneath it.'

'No,' said Imbolc, 'that is Beornamund's old forge, exposed for a few moments of time before the water that now returns will carry it to oblivion. You have not time to seek out what it is that shines beneath.'

But Stort ignored her.

He went on his knees in the mud and reached under the old forge. Forcing his hand through mud and gravel, he sought the source of the light. All he could find was what felt like a small stone, but when he touched it with the tips of his fingers it moved first to one side then to the other before slipping beyond his grasp.

'It must be the gem of Spring,' he cried out desperately, 'but I cannot reach it . . .'

The Earth beneath him trembled as the wave of water rushing back down the hill towards him gathered strength.

'Come back,' Imbolc called out to him, 'I cannot protect you if you stay there. Come back!'

But Stort would not.

Again and again he thrust his hand and arm under the stone, sure that if only he could reach far enough and grasp tightly enough the gem of Spring and all its mystery would be found at last.

The Earth shook more, Stort reached too far, and the forge, great and heavy, shaken by the approaching water, slipped a mite and then a mite more until, feeling the pressure on his arm, Stort tried to move it out and found he was pinned down where he lay, even as his hand found the gem and held it fast.

'I touch it, I see its beautiful ambient light,' he cried, 'but I cannot free myself! At least I shall die having touched the stone the great CraftLord who loved you made and lost!'

Brave words of a brave hydden, but not the truth.

Far above him the sky cracked open and in that great crack the fires of the Universe shone forth for a moment before a vast shadow came and blocked out the brightest light to form the silhouette that seemed mortal but was as great as the sky above.

A hand reached out of the shadow and, grasping the edge of the forge, heaved it off Stort's hand and arm.

Stort looked up in surprise and relief and found himself staring at two great stars and knew he looked into immortal Beornamund's eyes.

The wave hit them then, but Beornamund stood guardian to Stort and Imbolc both, the water flying safely over their heads. The roaring slowly abating until all was still again and the crisis over.

Stort, sitting in mud, his clothes half torn from his back, opened his fist and saw therein, nestling in his palm, the lost gem of Spring in whose deep depths shone the light of bright new life.

'Give it to me,' commanded Beornamund.

Which Stort willingly did, for such a thing should never be held for long by mortal hand.

Then Beornamund turned to Imbolc, who seemed now to tower above Stort as well, her head among the stars, and he put the gem into its proper place, which was in the old pendant that hung around her neck.

Immediately her youth returned and she was as radiantly beautiful as in the springtime of her life when Beornamund first met her.

She took the pendant from her neck and knelt by Stort, or so it seemed to him, and placed the pendant with its gem safely inside his jerkin.

'Bear this for the Shield Maiden who has been born this night. Give it to her when she is ready for it. Keep it secret and safe. Bear the burden as only you can, bear it for her with the same love you have for Mother Earth and all things in her and on her. Will you do this for my sister and for me?'

'I will,' said Bedwyn Stort, his eyes beginning to close with fatigue, 'I will . . .'

'Sleep not, Bedwyn Stort, not here . . . Rise now, go home to Brum, let your friends care for you through the days ahead, for you have journeyed further this night than on a mortal pilgrim road. Be careful, for the floods rage back and forth and the season's turn is with us still.'

Stort rose and stumbled down the hill, pausing only at the bottom to look back.

He saw the clouds begin to close in again, swirling and turning in the sky until, filled with the light of stars and moon, they took the form of the White Horse which galloped across the Universe to Waseley Hill.

Beornamund raised his Imbolc into the saddle and mounted it too and then they were gone on the night wind, into the stars from which they came, a reflection that rode right across the Mirror-of-All.

Briefly, utterly exhausted, Stort slept. But then he felt himself borne along as if by the flooding river itself, bumping, bashing, bruising as he went, trying to stay awake, reaching towards the city he loved, trying to keep hold of the memory of what had happened, bewildered, amazed, astonished and, finally, unable to do more than stop and rest.

'I must not sleep,' he muttered, 'but I fear I will . . . and if I do I trust I shall awake after daybreak, see where I am, and trek the last part of the journey to Brum without more difficulty.'

5

IN THE DARK

But if Stort hoped he would arrive home in Brum without
further difficulty he was mistaken. He fell asleep again on the
way down, perhaps several times, until when he finally woke
properly he found himself to be wet, muddy, battered and bewildered
and standing in a daze caught still in the pitch of night.

'Strange to find myself in this condition,' he muttered to himself
before, memory returning, he cried out, 'Oh no! I cannot have lost it!'

He turned about in the darkness, encumbered by the enormous
portersac on his back, his legs tangling with his stave, while he
frantically searched the many pockets of his trews and jerkin. Then,
with great relief, he found what he thought he had lost: the pendant
into which Beornamund had placed the gem of Spring.

For the first time he allowed himself to feel all the excitement and
elation that came with realizing again exactly what it was he had
found in the previous wild hours of the night, up on nearby Waseley
Hill. He had succeeded in doing what generations of hydden had
failed to do for fifteen hundred years. There were few hydden who
knew better than he that of the four gems, Spring was the most
important of them all. Why? Because the whole point about Spring is
that it's the start of things.

But quite what the implications of his discovery were he was
unsure.

What the gem's power was, he dreaded to think.

What the consequences might be, goodness only knew.

'Bit odd really,' he mused aloud, as he often did, 'finding Spring tonight, considering this is the first day of Summer, technically speaking. On the other hand . . . maybe it isn't odd at all. You can't very well have Summer without first finding Spring, which means . . .'

A new and rather terrifying thought occurred to him.

'. . . which means that it may not be long before the gem of Summer shows itself as well. Like . . . well . . . very soon!'

One thing was certain, he told himself; *he* was not going off to look for the next gem in a hurry. He would leave that to someone else to find. Yes, most definitely! For if one of the gems could shift the moon and stars above his head, goodness knew what two together might do, let alone the whole lot of them. No, one was quite enough for now, and the best thing he could do was tell no one he had it for the moment. Not even his friends. He was tired and needed sleep. Beyond that he no longer wished to think.

In such a circumstance most sensible travellers would have moved away from the river bank, dug about in their portersac for some dry clothes, and hunkered down until first light. Then, and *only* then, would they proceed further.

Not Stort, as events earlier that night had shown. 'It is a long time since I rested my head upon my own pillow, in my own bed, in my delightful humble,' he told himself. 'It is not far. So . . . now that I am recovered, onward I shall go!'

So off he went, floundering on through the pitch-black night, rain in his eyes, wind in his hair, stave firmly in his hand and thinking that so long as he kept the sound of the angry river to his left he would, eventually, get to the West Gate of Brum. Logic dictated it.

'If I continue thus, I must get home! Nothing can stop me now!'

But logic is not always the best of guides on a dark and stormy night when the seasons are turning.

Moments later he walked straight into a large and very solid wooden post that towered above him in the dark, erected by humans some years before, on which were painted words he could not even see. Had he been able to he would have read this: DANGER, DEEP WATER.

It marked a dyke that ran into the river to his left, and the footbridge that gave safe passage over it.

Bang!

He started back in a daze, veered to the right instead of the left, entirely missed the little bridge over the dyke below, lost his footing and fell headlong in.

Splash!

A new and more permanent darkness descended upon him as his heavy portersac dragged him beneath the surface and cold, muddy water filled his lungs. His hands and fingers scrabbled uselessly at the bottom and the sides of the dyke.

His feet drifted away from him one way and then his body in another. As for his mind, it drifted in a different direction altogether. An already strange and terrifying night had brought him to something worse. As the cold intensified and his mouth filled with water and the pain in his chest increased still more, Stort knew that he was drowning.

I must not . . . the gem . . . the Shield Maiden . . .

He reached about until he caught hold of what felt like the root of a tree or bush. He pulled himself towards it, found the bottom of the dyke with his feet and pushed himself upward as hard and fast as he could.

He broke the surface of the water, was wheeled round by its flow, and had he not been holding the root might easily have been swept into the river he could hear but not yet see.

He scrambled up the side of the dyke, water pouring from his clothes and portersac. He lay on the muddy ground and caught his breath, spitting out mud and leaves.

When he opened his eyes again the night had lightened and dawn was finally on the way. He saw the post into which he had bumped on the far side of the dyke, the bridge he had missed and his stave that lay on the ground.

He got up shakily, retrieved his stave, crossed the bridge once more and set off along the river bank. He checked for the thousandth time that the gem was safe, he paused again to take a look at it, knowing even as he did so it might be a mistake. He did so anyway.

Suddenly the pendant turned and twisted in his hand, the chain slithered about like a snake and a bright and blinding light shone forth, suffusing everything it touched with the bright green of Spring, even him. Stort felt suddenly that he wanted to sing and dance and fancied he heard lovebirds in the branches of the trees overhead and the happy plash of fishes leaping for joy in the river nearby.

He felt a surge of energy, of delightful madness, and stirrings of a Springlike kind. However, his natural instinct for survival overcame any desire he felt to run, jump, dance and sing.

With a commendable effort of will he stood where he was, stowed the troublesome gem and its pendant away again and set off once more.

'That was a close thing,' he told himself, 'because I nearly . . . I mean I might have . . . I . . .'

The events of the night, the gruelling experience he had had, and the curious and disconcerting influence of the gem itself, finally got to him.

He stopped, he started, he seemed to see the sun rise faster than usual, and the river's waves appeared to reach up towards him like watery hands.

'It wants to steal the gem!' he told himself.

The stalks of bulrushes poked at his shins.

'They want to steal it too!' he cried.

A deep puddle appeared before him, across the path.

'It wants me to fall in and the Earth Herself will take the gem.'

He began to run, to creep along, to look behind him, to wave his stave about aggressively, to fear everything.

'I shall not yield to any who try to steal it from me!' he cried out aloud.

He saw a hawthorn tree ahead and the West Gate of Brum some way beyond it.

'Nearly home,' he muttered, 'but who can I now trust? And yet . . . this tree . . . a hawthorn . . . a benign, friendly sort of tree . . . perhaps I could, just for the briefest of moments . . . just lay my stave down, and my portersac and sit . . . yes, rest my back . . . so I can think what to do . . . just for a second or two . . .'

Bedwyn Stort sat down, closed his eyes and knew no more.

6
REALITY

Whatever hopes and dreams Katherine and Jack had about their coming baby, they were shattered by the reality of what they faced as the sun began to rise in the first hours of Judith's life.

Her crying was like no other sound either had ever known. It cut through their ears, their heads, their hearts and their bodies. It was like the threat of a red-hot knife: utterly demanding of immediate attention.

It seemed to be worse for Katherine than for Jack, weak as she still was.

She held Judith, she tried the breast, she petted her, she whispered to her, but still the crying came, wave after wave, never stopping, and an absolute demand for attention and help. *Wah wah wah wah wah wah* . . .

'I don't know what she wants . . .'

Worse, she was so clearly in distress, her cries so filled with pain, that even had Katherine been suffering the hot knife herself, she would have preferred to find out what was wrong and deal with it.

For Jack it was only slightly less painful to hear. He had to attend to sorting things out, getting help, keeping them warm, and those demands softened a little the need to see to Judith.

Wah wah wah wah wah wah . . .

'Jack . . . I don't know what's wrong . . .'

Worse still, as Judith cried in her arms she curled up, she grew red and hot, her mouth, so beautiful at birth, grew ugly with pain.

'Can't you . . .' began Jack, as filled with horror and panic as she was.

Can't you *what*!?

He had no idea.

A window opened up in the house, then the conservatory doors.

Astonishingly Judith stopped crying, turned her mouth to Katherine's breast and, for the first time, began suckling.

Katherine gazed down at her, all panic gone, and whispered, 'Ooohh' and smiled.

Tears came to Jack's eyes.

'You're a softie after all,' said Katherine, reaching a hand to him, her mood switching from utter despair to total elation.

'I think they've heard us up at the house . . . they're about to have the shock of their lives . . .'

Moments later Katherine's adoptive grandparents, Margaret and Arthur Foale, appeared. They looked the part: in their late seventies, grey-haired, a little stiff, dishevelled with sleep.

Margaret came first, drawn by the baby's cry.

Arthur was close behind, holding a hockey stick because whatever was going on might be dangerous. Travellers maybe, trespassers certainly, these days one never knew . . .

They peered timidly across the henge, which Arthur had formed by clever felling of existing trees and some planting of others decades before.

As Jack turned towards them their eyes widened in alarm and Arthur's grip on the stick tightened.

They had last seen Jack two years before and did not recognize him. He was bigger now and powerful-looking in a hulky, looming way.

His sudden broad smile was their only clue, but it was the best.

'J . . . Jack!?' whispered Margaret.

'Katherine!?' said Arthur.

'Hello,' said Jack, moving to Katherine's side where she sat on the ground, the baby still suckling.

'*Katherine!*' cried Margaret, rushing forward and kneeling in front of her.

'It happened last night . . . we . . .'

'There wasn't time,' said Jack.

'But . . .' began Margaret, panic in her voice.

'It's fine,' said Katherine. 'I just . . . we just . . .'

'Oh Katherine,' whispered Margaret putting her wrinkled arms around her and the baby.

Arthur, true to his upbringing and the moment, reached out a hand and shook Jack's rather formally.

'Well done!' he said.

Jack laughed and hugged him.

'Oooph!' exclaimed Arthur, 'but you're strong now . . .'

Margaret was crying, Katherine too, and the baby beginning to disengage.

'Welcome home my dears,' she said, 'oh welcome home . . . Come on now and we'll sort you out.'

It was a brief moment of sweetness and light, a moment in time to cherish.

They got Katherine up, Jack supporting her.

'Leave all that stuff,' said Jack, 'let's get them both inside.'

They walked slowly from the henge, arms around Katherine, she holding the baby, out between the two conifers.

Jack looked back.

His backpack lay on its side, Judith's 'sac as well.

The leather bottle, a blanket, a bloody jacket, a towel.

In more than a year of travelling it was the first time they had ever left a mess behind them, because in the Hyddenworld, from which they had returned, it is a cardinal rule of travellers that the Earth is left as She is found.

The sun caught the trees all around, their early Summer leaves shimmering with its morning light.

Beyond, up on the chalk escarpment, the White Horse galloped still.

Jack turned from that world to the reality of his new one.

'Let's get you sorted,' he said.

Judith, awake now, began her crying again, more desperate than before despite having fed, and the moment of quiet was gone and a different darkness beginning.

'Why! She does make a noise!' said Margaret brightly. 'When we're settled I think I'll . . .'

. . . *make a pot of tea*, Jack mouthed at Arthur, who smiled.

'Some things haven't changed,' he said.

While others had changed for ever.

7

RETURN

The sun was well risen and the damp fields and paths around Brum steaming with its warmth before the West Gate of the old city was finally opened for May Day morning.

Eight or nine hydden came cautiously out. They were armed with staves and wore thick boots to protect them from puddles and mud. Their strong arms and stolid builds showed them to be a working party of stavermen or civic guards sent to check things out and give the all-clear.

Already crowds of pilgrims were impatiently standing by the gate, eager to make the trek to Waseley Hill to pay homage to Beornamund and visit the source of the River Rea.

The tradition was centuries old but had declined forty years before when the Empire's army, the Fyrd, took control of the city in Slaeke Sinistral's name.

But a year ago, Marshal Igor Brunte, a disaffected Fyrd, had led an insurrection and declared Brum independent of the Empire. His timing was clever: he knew the Emperor had been 'resting' for many years and guessed that in his continuing absence no one else in Bochum would dare take so great a step as attacking Brum.

Brunte had reinstated Lord Festoon, the city's popular High Ealdor, and together the two had both military and popular support. No one expected this state of things to last for ever, and since the Emperor had gone into his sleeping retreat eighteen years before there were constant rumours that he had woken.

Meanwhile pilgrims had taken the opportunity to visit Brum and

Waseley Hill while they could, even coming from as far as the Continent. The green roads to Brum from the hydden ports of the Channel and North Sea were busy with travellers once more and the coffers of the city were brimming with the gifts and offerings, as well as the trade that such pilgrims bring.

All of them knew and loved the legend of the lost gem, which they had heard at their mothers' knees in many different versions from storytellers and wise folk.

But after the strange weather and frightening tremors of the night before, Lord Festoon had commanded his stavermen to set forth and check the path, clearing debris as they went and marking out diversions from the river bank where it showed signs of damage or imminent collapse.

It was this small group of responsible citizens who came upon the first obvious casualty of the events of the previous night. They did so soon after setting out from Brum.

They saw a sorry and bedraggled figure slumped against a hawthorn tree near the bank of the River Rea and covered head to foot in mud.

His face was battered and bruised beyond recognition, his hair mucky, his hands lacerated, and his nails torn.

It was a pity that the chief staverman of Brum, Mister Pike, was not among them, for despite Stort's state he would most certainly have recognized his good friend. As it was, the stavermen thought the casualty was a lone traveller, perhaps of dubious origin and intent, who had been caught out in the night by the extreme conditions and had fallen in the river and been lucky to get back out again.

'He looks more of a rascal and vagabond than an honest pilgrim!' said one of them.

'Aye, he does,' said another. 'Still, 'tis May Day after all and we'd best fetch him to the pilgrims' infirmary where a goodwife can be found to tend to him and Mister Pike can question him.'

One of them went closer.

'Do you know your name? Can you remember it?'

The stranger opened his eyes again, shook his head, looked puzzled but finally spoke.

'Unhand me!' he cried. 'Take me at once to Master Brief, with whom I have urgent business.'

Stort might have had trouble remembering who he was, but the name of his beloved mentor came readily enough.

'What business?'

'Business that is not your concern, you villains! Tell him . . . tell him that . . . I need to see him . . .'

They looked at each other doubtfully. Brief was the Master Scrivener of Brum and one of its most respected citizens. His door was generally open to all who came in a spirit of genuine scholarship and spiritual guidance, but it seemed unlikely that he would want a visit from a common traveller on a day like this, especially one so unpresentable.

The stranger tried to speak once more but he seemed lost in a world of his own, one of confusion and worry, one of despair. Only mutterings came out, and vague protests, as he clenched his fists and tried to fend off imaginary enemies. His pallor increased and his breathing grew shallow and desperate.

Any attempt on their part to examine his person or portersac for clues to his identity, or what he was about, provoked him into a violence that bordered on madness.

Despite his protests they used their staves for a makeshift stretcher to carry him into Brum at once.

May Day morning was not the best of times to be portering a litter burdened with a reluctant patient through the narrow medieval streets and lanes of Brum. The luckless stavermen found themselves jostled by shoppers, cursed by traders and objects of the idle curiosity of pilgrims. Though at times he seemed so poorly he was near death, at others their patient roused himself angrily and tried to rid himself of the straps that bound him to the litter, cursing his helpers as he did so and generally making himself a nuisance.

'Soon be there!' said one of the bearers heavily.

'He'll be given an opiate and he can sleep it off,' said another.

'But I don't want to "sleep it off"!' cried the hydden angrily. 'It's Master Brief I need to see, not a goodwife wielding a sleeping potion.'

The crowds got thicker, the difficulties greater, until the bearers could hardly move together, those on the right side being stuck fast, those on the left dragged suddenly forward.

It was then that the litter tilted dangerously. As they struggled to right it someone in the crowd thought it would be a laugh to give it a shove and suddenly it tipped right over. The straps broke and its occupant tumbled to the ground at their feet.

'Get 'im up or he'll run off,' cried one of the stavermen.

But it was too late.

The fall put new life into the traveller. Unable to rise up into the pressing throng and unwilling to put himself back under the control of those who were trying to help him, he scrabbled off among the legs and feet of the crowd, dragging his portersac behind him. Moments later they glimpsed him on the far side of the street, staggering down an alley, through a doorway out of sight.

They only caught up with him some time later as he stumbled up the steps of the Great Library to an annexe in which Master Brief lived. 'You're under arrest!' cried one of them.

'Anything you say, any protest you make and any further attempt to fight the officials of the law will go hard against you, so be still!' roared another.

They hauled him to his feet. But as they began dragging him off to the infirmary the doors of the Library crashed open.

Master Brief himself stood there, dishevelled but impressive, for though getting on in years he was well built and stood tall.

He was still clad in his nightshirt, with a large tome in one hand and a pair of spectacles in the other. His white hair was untidy, his beard tousled and he looked ill-pleased indeed.

'What is this?' he roared. 'It's bad enough that I have been kept awake all night by those rumblings in the city's foundations, but to have one of my few rest days of the year disturbed by ruffians is going too far!'

The stavermen explained what had happened.

Brief's glance fell upon the portersac and stave they had found with the prisoner, which one of them was now carrying.

'Where did you find those?' he demanded at once, his fury replaced by astonishment.

'With this ruffian.'

'Humph!' said Brief very ominously.

Despite his state of dishabille he came down the steps, put on his spectacles and examined the portersac and looked dumbfounded. There was only one hydden who packed his 'sac so badly.

He went at once to the hydden and peered closely at him.

'But . . . but . . . *but* . . .' he spluttered, 'do you not know who this is? The whole of Brum has been awaiting his return and you . . . you . . .'

A crowd had gathered. It now pressed closer.

'This hydden who you have harried hither and yon,' cried Brief, 'who has tried to run to me seeking sanctuary from your rough hands and violent staves, who was dragged down the steps of the Library bumpety-bump even as he tried to summon my aid . . . this excellent hydden . . . why he is . . .'

'Who am I?' said Stort sitting up and peering round, as bemused now as before and staring at Brief in puzzlement, 'and who are you? Another villain from this most villainous of cities! Let me be free. Lead me to Master Brief!'

'I *am* Brief, Master Scrivener of Brum, and you, sir, who seem quite literally to have forgotten yourself, are, if I am not mistaken . . . my one-time best and ablest student, Bedwyn Stort.'

'Am I?' said Stort.

'You are,' said Brief.

'And you claim to be Brief?'

'I do, and dammit I *am*.'

Then turning to the stavermen he said, 'Take him to my quarters in the Library, lie him down and hold him still, fetch a goodwife worthy of the name, and let us get to the bottom of all this . . . and another thing, fetch Master Pike as well as the High Ealdor, Lord Festoon. And Marshal Brunte too! Fetch 'em all at once to the Library!'

'But, sir!' said the stavermen, for Brief's instruction to summon the most important people in Brum there and then went beyond their competence and perhaps even his own.

'Do it!' thundered Master Brief, climbing back up the steps to prepare himself for what promised to be a very trying first day of Summer.

The news that Bedwyn Stort had returned to Brum in an injured and demented state spread through the city like wildfire and brought his friends and acquaintances hurrying to the Library, the crowd outside increasing. It barely dispersed overnight and grew larger still the following day.

He had to be restrained all night and any attempt to clean him up, to feed him, even to loosen his clothes, met with a crazed and violent resistance so ferocious that anyone trying to minister to him soon stopped.

There were one or two attempts to place efficacious drugs in his mouth, but he spat them out. Others tried soothing words, but these too were of no avail.

Marshal Brunte, de facto commander of Brum, and a tough, thickset hydden used to getting his own way, failed utterly to get any sense from Stort who, as the second day wore on, grew wilder and weaker at the same time. 'Inform me if death threatens him,' said Brunte, 'or if he recovers his sanity. Meanwhile we must fear the worst and set in motion plans for a military funeral or a ceremony and will present him with posthumous honours . . .'

Stort might not look much of a military hero, but only his quick thinking at the time of Brunte's insurrection against the Fyrd had saved the life of Lord Festoon. Without him it was unlikely that the irascible citizens of Brum would have ever given the Marshal the support they had.

Lord Festoon, High Ealdor of the city, was still wearing his chain of office from a function he cut short when he heard a new rumour that Stort was dying. He was an admirer and friend of Stort, at once authoritative and kindly. His prematurely grey hair gave him a magisterial air.

'If only he would let us examine and tend him properly,' he said sadly. 'He once saved my life at considerable risk to his own and I cannot understand why he will not let us help him now.'

Brief could not but agree.

'It is odd, is it not, that he seems to gain strength without our help but will not let us so much as wash or feed him? If it did not defy all reason I would suggest that something apart from ourselves is affecting him.'

Finally, it was Ma'Shuqa, daughter of Old Mallarkhi, wizened owner-proprietor of the Muggy Duck, the finest and most historic hostelry in Old Brum, who broke the deadlock.

Her affection for Stort, who had lodged with her in his youth, ran deep. She asked for a goodwife she knew well to be sent to his house and told Brief that he should be taken home at once.

'Goodwife Cluckett is strict but fair,' she said. 'She'll sort him out.'

These words, spoken as if Stort was not in the room, appeared to have a sobering effect on him.

He opened his eyes, sat up and said, 'I do not like goodwives. They frighten me and in any case I am rapidly getting better.'

Ma'Shuqa said, 'That's as maybe. But I bain't stopping her now. We'm taking you home and Cluckett will have you spright as a sparrow in no time!'

Half an hour later, by the light of a dozen lanterns, Stort was carried through the narrow lanes of Digbeth to his home. By the time they arrived he had so perked up that he was able to stand, with a little support, and dig about in his pockets for his key.

He opened the door himself, his strength returning even more. Someone lit a fire, someone else fetched water, a third some sweetmeats and provender of the kind that tempts jaded palates. Candles were lit and all made as comfortable as was possible in his dusty, untidy, cluttered home. Then everyone was sent packing but for his closest friends, Brief and Mister Pike and Barklice, the city's Verderer and in the past a frequent travelling companion of Stort's.

'Promise you will not leave me in this goodwife's hands when she comes,' he implored. 'Look! I am well after all! She will be the death of me.'

They no sooner promised than there was a sudden and peremptory knock at the front door, the kind of solid, heavy *knock-knock-knock* that people who expect to be admitted at once generally make.

Brief opened the door.

Stort took one look at the female standing there with a formidably large leather bag at her feet and an impatient look in her eye. He fled into his parlour and locked the door.

'You are?' she asked Master Brief.

'Me?' said Brief, taken aback.

'Yes, sir. You, sir. Who are you?'

'Well, I'm Master Brief and this is Mister Pike . . . we . . .'

'Where is my patient?'

'In the parlour,' said the mild Barklice, 'behind that door!'

She glared at the door, tried the handle, shook it and said, 'The key if you please. It is very bad practice to lock patients in.'

Pike smiled grimly.

'It's we who are locked out,' he said.

Goodwife Cluckett's eyes bulged and her cheeks flushed dangerously as she muttered, 'Absolutely unacceptable!'

She rat-tat-tatted on the door and said, 'Open this door this *instant*, sir.'

There was a sliding of bolts and Stort opened the door and eyed her.

She eyed him.

Then she turned to the other three and said, 'Please leave at once, I can handle this gentleman quite without your further assistance.'

'But . . .' began Stort, whose day had been a very hard one and now looked like it was going to get harder. 'Cannot my friends stay? In fact they promised they would. They must! I cannot be left alone with . . . with . . . with a female.'

'They cannot stay and you cannot go,' she said, 'and that's an end to it.'

She sniffed and then sniffed again and as good as stuck her nose into his chest and sniffed a third time.

'You are whiffy, sir, and whiffy will not do for someone in my care. To your bedroom at once and remove your clothes that they be fumigated and your person washed.'

'Me washed?'

He looked with ghastly appeal over her shoulder towards his friends.

'They are leaving, are they not?' she said, turning on them, her eyes narrowing.

Barklice backed away towards the door.

'You cannot,' said Stort, 'you promised . . .'

But as she eyed them beadily, one by one they began to leave.

'Please,' bleated Stort after them, 'do not desert me, dear friends, do not leave me in her hands!'

But they had fled.

The goodwife closed the front door, locked it, removed the key and added it to several already attached to the vast metal ring that hung from the girdle round her waist. Then, for good measure, she shot the bolts at the top and bottom of the door.

Stort stood in his own corridor looking at her with all the desperation of one who knows that all possibility of escape is gone and he must submit to his punishment.

She advanced upon him, her keys clinking, her shiny forehead dazzling, her bosom like the prow of a warship about to engage the enemy.

'Well, Mister Stort,' she said, 'and what exactly is it that you're waiting for? We have work to do! Disrobe at once!'

8

CRY FOR HELP

'We should take her to the doctor,' said Margaret for the hundredth time. 'There's obviously something wrong. Please, Katherine, it'll be for the best . . .'

It was five days since Judith's birth and a chaos of emotion, disorder and now disharmony had descended on Woolstone House. They would all have coped better with the crisis had they had more experience of babies.

They had none.

The Foales were childless and both came from families which had few children or lived so far away that contact was rare. Nor had their professional lives as university academics prepared them for the day-by-day realities of infants, least of all a unique one.

Katherine had no experience either. She was an only child and had never done the round of babysitting that her peer group had as a way of earning money. Her role had been helping her bedridden mother. As for Jack, he had lived only briefly in a children's home before making the car journey with Katherine and her parents which had ended in tragedy for them and third-degree burns for him. From then on all he had known was hospitals and young people's institutions. Babies were not part of that scene.

Only experience might have prepared them for the fact that a newborn infant can easily reduce a house and the adults living in it to disorder and constant stress.

The slightest cry seems a signal of danger.

A failure to feed, a sign of illness.

A moment's choking, a cause of worry and guilt.

A sleepless night . . .

Then there's the fatigue that sets in with the constant worry and lack of sleep.

Soon normality is fractured and relationships grow fraught as tempers rise and rationality flees.

This was what five days of Judith's terrible crying had done to the residents of Woolstone House.

'At the very least he'll give you reassurance, Katherine,' said Margaret, who had been worn to a frazzle dancing attendance on mother and child.

'I suppose . . .' said Katherine, who was hollow-eyed, 'that it does make sense, doesn't it, Jack?'

It was a plea as well as a statement. She was so tired, she just wanted someone to tell her she wasn't doing everything wrong.

'I must say, Jack,' added Arthur, 'there does come a point where the sensible thing is to admit that one needs help and maybe that point has been reached . . . and anyway, we do have a legal obligation to register a child's birth, even if she's . . . well . . . whatever she may be. Even then.'

Judith cried loudly, a thin scream, and Jack winced at the sound of it. He too was desperate.

He heard what they said but something told him no.

'Give her to me,' he said, taking her gently, 'I'll take her round the garden and we'll think about it together. Give you a break, Katherine.'

'I don't want a break, Jack, I want Judith to be happy.'

He stood with her by the kitchen door and stared back at them, all tired, all worried, all desperate for a solution to something none of them could understand. He had never thought about babies before, apart from the romantic idea he had after Katherine conceived. So far as he had thought about it at all, babies woke up, they fed, they needed cleaning and washing, they slept and then they woke up again.

It did not seem so simple any more and he knew Katherine was desperately worried.

He looked at them and breathed deeply as he felt Judith's hot mouth at his neck and then, despite everything, he felt gratitude. They were his family, his only family. The Foales had accepted him into their home and now Judith as well, and they were trying, as he was, to find a way through the confusion and doubt that had descended on them all.

'Maybe you're all right . . . I don't know . . .'

Then: 'Come on, Judith, let's go for a walk . . .'

'Don't be too long, she'll need a feed.'

'Okay . . .' he called back.

That was one thing that seemed all right, her feeding.

'Come on, my love . . .'

He chose to go round the house first because when he did, climbing up and down the stairs, backing into rooms to open doors when she was in his arms, moving to windows, his feet sounding on the wooden floorboards, it seemed to quieten her a little.

The house in which Katherine had been raised was large and rambling. The Foales had lived there for fifty years and were now in their seventies. Arthur was a former professor of Astral Archaeology at Cambridge University, Margaret a specialist in Anglo-Saxon literature.

Their home dated back to Elizabethan times and had been added to over the centuries in a piecemeal way, with innumerable rooms, three different staircases to the first floor and enormous attics. The areas on which Margaret imposed herself – the study she shared with Arthur, the conservatory and the kitchen – were tidy. So too was Katherine's bedroom, which she now shared with Judith and Jack. It overlooked the garden with a view towards White Horse Hill.

Since their return with Judith it had become a tip by Margaret's standards: hard to clean, impossible to keep the nappies and all the other things in order. They might have used one of the many spare rooms as a nursery, but Katherine wanted Judith with her through the night.

Disordered their lives might temporarily have become, but there was nothing untidy about the minds of Arthur, Margaret and Katherine. They were all mentally sharp, Jack knew that. If they had a fault it was that they were too intellectual, lacking the instinctive feelings Jack displayed, though free of the impulsiveness and stubbornness that sometimes got him into trouble.

In fact Katherine might easily have been mistaken for their real grandchild. She was taller than they were, but most of her generation were taller than their parents and grandparents. Her mother had been tall and dark before the tragic accident that brought them all together. It happened after Katherine's father, a doctor, had offered to give Jack, then six years old, a lift from the North to London. The weather was atrocious, roads were blocked, there was a diversion, and her father not only lost his way in the dark but lost control of the car as well.

It crashed and burned.

Katherine's father died rescuing her mother, who was so badly injured that she later became bedridden. Katherine herself, strapped to a back seat in the flames, was rescued by Jack, whose unusual strength and courage brought her out unharmed, but he suffered terrible burns to his back and neck which required years of painful treatment. Ten years later they got together again, fell in love and found a way into the Hyddenworld. They came to Brum, made friends with Bedwyn Stort, and only Katherine's pregnancy and her desire to come home made them return to the human world.

Jack stood at an upstairs window, staring out over the garden towards the two conifers that marked the entrance to the henge.

'Come on,' he said again, 'let's go and see where you were born.' He knew that if she wasn't crying as loudly as normal it was probably because she was exhausted and needed sleep. That didn't mean she slept, but perhaps being rocked in his arms as he walked would do the trick.

He passed Katherine on the stairs.

'I thought you were outside . . .'

'Just going . . .'

'Jack, I do think seeing a doctor would be best.'

'I know you do and you're probably right. Give me ten minutes; let me breathe some outside air. I just feel . . .'

'Take as long as you like. She looks like she might even sleep.'

He went on down, she up.

'Jack,' she called down.

'Mmm,' he said softly, looking up towards her.

'I love you both,' she said. 'I'm sorry that—'

'There's nothing to say sorry about, not now, not ever,' he said. 'We made her together, we're going to fight for her together. Now, you have a rest, her miserable ladyship and I will perambulate the garden . . .'

He was trying to make the best of it but it wasn't easy. Outside, her cries persisted, but in the Summer breeze were less claustrophobic, more tolerable.

Like the house, the garden was big and rambling, the rough lawn he was walking across one of many once formal now dilapidated features. The garden had been made in the late nineteenth century, maintained until after the First World War when gardeners became hard to find, and after that it had been one long, slow decline and more than a match for Arthur. The old rockeries, the terraces and stairs with cracked urns and occasional sculptures, and a formal rose garden behind which a rhododendron shrubbery extended, all spoke of a time when Margaret's family had money and status. All gone. It was a battle to pay the maintenance bills.

Until Jack came there had not been a young, strong pair of male hands working in the garden for years. He had grown to love it; Katherine already did.

Before that Arthur made the henge, explored the world beyond the human one, believing that if only its secret could be found there was a way that a henge – any henge – could be used to access a world other than their own. He had found it, and later so had Katherine and Jack – the one abducted into it, the other her rescuer. One way and another Jack and Katherine had fallen in love in the garden and during their summery walks up on the Berkshire Downs, along the Ridgeway and by the White Horse.

As he wandered across the lawn and Judith cried and cried he felt her distress as his own.

He stopped near the henge, with the shrubbery to his right, and whispered, 'If only you could say what's wrong, Daddy could try to help. What is it? Mmm? Find a way to tell me.'

Jack was as tired as everyone else, though he wasn't going to admit that. But out there in the garden, where no one could see, with Judith inconsolable, he could admit it to the trees and the grass and the skies.

He began to weep. He wept for Judith and for them all. He wept because he didn't know what to do. He wept because it felt like nothing was right, everything was wrong, and there was no help he could give.

Then, as suddenly as she always started, she stopped.

Just like that.

She even raised her head a little, which in a five-day-old was difficult if not impossible. Maybe, too, she looked off to their right.

Jack looked the same way, and for the first time in a long while, he heard the chimes. They were pieces of glass, or what looked like glass, on threads, tied to the bushes of the shrubbery, which caught the wind and tinkled away, night and day, soft and loud, falling completely silent only on the day that Katherine's mother Clare had died.

Clare had put some of the chimes there when she could still get out, so Margaret said. She believed they gave them protection against ... *them*, whoever they were. Malign little people, spirits and mischievous sprites.

Margaret half believed it too, or felt it was unlucky not to. She said that the chimes were already there when she was a child. Examining them, Jack concluded that a few were very old, the glass stained with rain and residue from plants. He also noticed something else. They never looked exactly the same, as if they came and went, the old as well as the new. Arthur doubted that, but being superstitious never went near them, though he liked the sound.

Now, it seemed, the chimes had made Judith stop crying.

He carried her to them, stood in the breeze that held their sound, closed his eyes, felt her body and its life.

'A baby's not weak,' he murmured, 'but strong, and you're stronger than all of them. Now, tell me ... what's wrong?'

She let out a cry again, a scream, most terrible, which carried on the breeze, along with the sound of the chimes, up and away into the henge, spiralling off into the sky. It was a cry for help.

Standing there, arms about her, Jack suddenly felt her pain, really felt it.

'No!' he said. '*No!*'

An image of when he was nine had come to him.

In bed, a skin graft to his back just completed, the pain unbearable and doctors and nurses and people standing around looking down at him. Not one of them touching him or holding him. Just adult eyes staring as he heard someone say, 'Of course, he'll need another . . .'

'No!' he had screamed. *'No!'*

That was the beginning of his battle with medical authority and the welfare services, and he had always wished he had someone to fight his corner for him. He never did.

But Judith did.

'You've got me, and Mummy and Arthur and Margaret . . .'

He held her tight and wept again until he felt a hand on his shoulder. It was Katherine.

'I'm not going to let them do to her what they did to me,' he said.

'Sssh,' she replied, 'ssh, my love . . .'

'My instinct says the best thing is for us to keep her warm and dry and fed. Does she look unhealthy?'

'Arthur says she's growing already and he's taken to measuring her.'

Jack laughed.

'It's the scientist in him. He needs something to do.'

'Your instincts are usually right, Jack. So let's leave things as they are and hope Margaret stops worrying so much.'

'What about?'

'The law,' said Katherine. 'She's worried that one of her village friends will find out about Judith and start asking questions. Let's give it a few more days at least . . .'

She took Judith from him and put her to the breast.

'Ow! She bites. In fact . . .'

She pulled Judith gently from her nipple and felt her gums.

'She's got a tooth!'

'Impossible,' said Jack.

'Really. Look!'

Her nipple was bleeding.

'She's a vampire,' said Jack.

Gingerly Katherine put her back to the nipple.

'Ow!!'

She pulled her away again, whispered an affectionate 'No!' in her ear and then put her back.

Judith did not bite a third time.

'If she's a vampire she's learning fast not to be,' she said.

They went back to the house, their moment of sharing feeling like respite.

It was, but it didn't last long.

Half an hour later Judith began screaming again.

9

AWAKENING

Four hundred miles to the east, across the North Sea, far beneath the surface of the Earth, a mortal form lay cocooned in a nineteenth-century dentist's chair of rusting iron and mildewed leather.

Around him in the terrible dark were the chair's accoutrements: flexible tubes, drills on leads, an extending spittoon, a cast-iron footrest, a treadle to turn the wires that turn the wheels that turn the drills, and counterweights.

Leather straps with buckles hung loose from the chair by his hands and arms, ankles and legs, adjacent to his chest and up by his head. As if, sometime in the past, the chair had been a place of horrible restraint and might yet be again.

This antique assemblage was in the centre of a rock-bound Chamber so vast that it could have accommodated a human Gothic cathedral.

There was no light, none at all.

Only darkness palpable.

Had explorers found themselves on the threshold of this lost place and tried to penetrate the dark with the darting beams of their torches, the dreadful chair and its ghastly occupant would not have been immediately obvious.

They would first have been lulled by a sense of wonderment. For one thing, an endless drip, drip, drip of subterranean rain fell from the rocky shadows of the Chamber's roof. It created a swirling mistiness driven by strong draughts and sudden winds.

Then there were the strange unnerving objects that were scattered like ghosts across the vast, uneven floor.

The Chamber was human-made. It had been used as a sorting floor for grading coal and rock. The machinery for these operations had been left behind when the mine was abandoned, along with a host of wheels, derricks and chains, rail tracks, hawsers, giant tools and trolleys. Over time every single thing had been covered by thick layers of rock-hard lime deposited by the continuous 'rain'. These secretions had turned the objects into swollen versions of their former selves, some still identifiable, many not.

There were piles of pit props, massive spanners, a bucket, rectangular tanks, a table and three chairs and even a pit engine standing on its old track, complete with boiler, funnel and driver's cabin, all subsumed beneath deposits of lime.

Only when the explorers had passed through these unnerving relics, stumbling and slipping on the slimy floor, would they have found their lights fixed finally on the dentist's chair protected from the rain by a sloping canopy that kept it dry. Even then, they would have had to go very near to comprehend the appalling nature of the thing they had found.

It was a hydden, his wasted flesh mottled with decay; his muscles and sinews so twisted by disuse and shrinkage that his limbs and joints had contorted beyond any recognition of who and what he had once been; his teeth were discoloured and rotten, his hair, once sleek and blond, had thinned into transparency and was so matted with filth that it formed a cakey plaster on his scalp.

Yet he was not dead.

This ruination of a living thing lying helpless in a chair made for humans was Slaeke Sinistral I, Emperor of the Hyddenworld, most powerful hydden who ever lived, progenitor of the Empire and all its works, once a son, a spouse, a lover and a friend.

It was age that had struck him down, and that he was still alive at all seemed a miracle. The records clearly showed that he was over one hundred and sixty years old when he was incarcerated in the Chamber.

He had gone there voluntarily, not to die but to sleep. He had hoped and believed that when he finally woke certain prophecies would have come to pass and the means to his salvation, even his full recovery, would finally be at hand.

That was eighteen years ago.

How he had survived so long was not obvious, but there were small and large footprints in the slime about his chair, discarded rags which had been used to clean him up, and the tubes appeared to have been utilised to feed him water and nutrients. If so, he and his unseen helpers were running out of time. The Emperor's rate of decay was now such that keeping him alive in his state of sleep had become a losing battle, which was why he had sunk so far.

Now something had woken him to the nightmare of terminal decline to which time had delivered him . . . and down there in the dark, unseen, alone, he was struggling to let it be known that he was awake again.

A finger trembled, an eyelid struggled, lips stuck fast with filthy phlegm tried to part. But even had he opened them no meaningful sound would have issued forth. He was quite unable to call for help from hydden in the normal world above.

What had woken Slaeke Sinistral was a tremor of the Earth, the very same tremor that in those early hours of the first day of Summer had revealed the gem to Stort in Englalond.

Now Sinistral hoped his time had come again.

Life, so long lost to him, was going to return.

Power would be his once more.

Redeeming love, which did not quite elude him in all his long and dreadful years, might be enjoyed again.

He could not smile – his facial muscles were too wasted for that – so he smiled inside.

He could not speak, so the words he uttered were silent ones . . . and strange though this may seem, joyful.

His mouth finally opened into an attempted laugh. All that came forth into the darkness was the hiss of fetid breath and a dribble of gritty phlegm down his creased and straggle-bearded chin.

Yet still he strained to make his body work again.

A foot stirred, his left thigh twitched, his head began to move from side to side, faster and faster as if to hurl something from its brain.

An eyelid trembled once again, then the other too, the top and bottom eyelid struggling to pull apart lashes stuck fast with congealed, hardened, yellow tears, their hairs entangled. He wanted to open his once-beautiful eyes in the dark, to seek light, to see *anything*. To be trapped as he was by his own decay, able to hear but not to see, to think but not to speak, was a torture for the hydden who once ruled the world.

The part of his body he most needed to move was his right hand, with which, if only he could find a way, he could do a very simple thing: touch a finger to a button that would ring a bell and signal he was alive to someone from the upper hydden world who could help him. He tried to move his fingers and failed, utterly exhausted. He knew that though he was awake now he was also dying fast.

His head stilled and he ceased to struggle, controlling his panic with the same strong will that once created an empire. He decided to rest a little, to recoup, and try again.

His equilibrium returned. Slaeke Sinistral spoke silent words inside his head which, had they been able to break through his skull and be heard, might have sounded like the tolling of a warning bell right across the Hyddenworld.

My Summer has begun and I am coming home, he told himself.

10

RECOVERY

S tort remained in a bad way for several days after he was taken home and put into the care of Goodwife Cluckett.

She brought order and calm to his life, established the routine of a healthy diet, daily exercise, sleep and no visitors.

Try as they might, his friends Master Brief and Mister Pike could not get past the goodwife, who kept the door on a chain, eyed them beadily and claimed, 'My master is not yet ready to entertain!'

'Really, Madam!'

Cluckett invariably closed the door in the face of protest.

But after a week, when Stort was beginning to recover his old spirits and wished to see his friends, she relented a little.

'I have sent notice to Mister Barklice that he may attend you for tea today, sir,' she announced over breakfast.

It was a wise choice and a happy visit.

Barklice's friendship with Stort, built up over the years of their travels together, was of a gentler tenor than that which he enjoyed with Brief and Pike. The two had often talked late into the night by the campfire, usually of their deepest yearnings and most intimate desires. The mystery of love was their theme, along with the seeming impossibility of wanderers of the pilgrim road and independent spirits such as themselves ever finding an understanding mate.

Barklice was middle-aged and wiry. He was worn with the travel his job as a verderer, sorting out legal problems of land and property, made necessary. He was gentle by nature and liked harmony, perhaps one reason he had never been spoused.

'Mister Pike has a good marriage, of course, and Master Brief has no need of one since books are his bride,' he observed, their conversation turning to the old subject the moment Cluckett had brought them tea and left them.

'Indeed that is so,' said Stort, who was wrapped up in a fluffy dressing gown, with pink, quilted slippers on his feet and a tasselled hat upon his head, 'and I suppose the wonders of the Universe should be bride enough for me. But you know, Barklice, there are times when I wish to share those wonders with the beloved I seek but know I can never find, and there are times too . . .'

He fell into a ruminative silence.

'Times too . . . ?' prompted Barklice.

'When I have worries I would wish to share, doubts that rack me and burdens I . . . burdens that . . .'

'My dear fellow!' cried Barklice, seeing that Stort was becoming upset, 'is there something that burdens you now?'

It was clear he had something on his mind – perhaps that same thing that had troubled him so much when he had been found outside the city on May Day.

'No . . . no . . . I am happy and comfortable.'

He smiled wanly – and unconvincingly. The truth was that the gem of Spring, of which he had so far told no one and which he had successfully hidden in the very parlour where they sat, bore down upon him. With it went that concern and worry for the Shield Maiden who, he was quite sure from all the signs of Earth and stars, violent and otherwise, had most certainly been born the same night – perhaps at the same moment – he had found the gem.

'I am really very happy, Barklice . . . um . . . yes . . . really I am.'

'Well, if there's something . . . ?'

'There's nothing,' said Stort, 'so please have another cup of tea and a piece of this delicious cake.'

Though he could see Stort's continuing worry and unhappiness, Barklice did not press the matter.

'I must say that Goodwife Cluckett is looking after you very well. Your home is as clean and tidy as I have ever seen it . . . and you look . . . I mean you . . .'

Barklice eyed the fluffy dressing gown, slippers and nightcap.

'You look very ah . . . well . . .'

Stort looked mournful.

'I know what you are thinking and you are right. This garb she has dressed me in looks ridiculous. But if I removed it my life would be made miserable. To be happy when she is in my home I must be obedient.'

'But Stort, that is against everything your free and independent spirit stands for. Can you not defy her in such matters while accepting the good things she does for you?'

As often before, his friend had shown the way to go.

'You are right,' he cried impulsively, 'I will try to find a way!'

'When?' asked Barklice.

'Now!' replied Stort.

He stood up, kicked off his slippers, removed his hat and was in the act of taking off his dressing gown when the heavy tread of the goodwife was heard approaching down the corridor towards the parlour.

Blind panic overtook Stort at once and he cravenly returned the hat to his head and the slippers to his feet as Cluckett opened the door.

She stared about the room and then at them, her nostrils flaring as if she had smelt trouble. She spied at once that his dressing gown was loose and advanced upon him to pull it tight once more.

'I hope, sir, that your friend here is not putting wild ideas into your head about these warm clothes which I insist you must wear for a little time yet?'

He shook his head meekly, as did Barklice.

'Good. Actions have consequences, do not forget that fact,' she said warningly. 'Now. More tea, gentlemen?'

While she was absent making a new brew Barklice asked, 'Has she interfered with any aspect of your life other than your clothes?'

'She tidies anything she can lay her hands on, and I greatly fear that she threatens my laboratory with order! What am I to do, Barklice?'

'Stand up to her, Stort. Fight for your rights or you will be subsumed by her orderliness and put into a box whence it will be hard to get you out again except as a pale shade of your former self. Take heed, my friend!'

Stort did not sleep well after this visit, his rest disturbed by nightmare visions of boxes, padlocks and huge females with large hands and commanding voices.

He knew Barklice was right. Cluckett had many good qualities, but if she was to stay on as his housekeeper after he was better, as he sometimes felt was a good idea, he would need to assert himself. But that, he knew, might be no easy thing where a female of her mettle was concerned.

The crisis soon came and centred, as he had feared, upon his laboratory.

This untidy rambling space was at the far end of his home. Stort had cleverly subverted various nearby steam and gas pipes and live electrical supplies of human origin and used these as sources of power and light.

A day or two after Barklice's visit he ventured into it and was relieved to see that Cluckett had not yet touched anything.

What forgotten treasures of his past inquiries and research he found! He spied a mortar in which he had once ground up certain ingredients with a pestle that lay nearby. He had forgotten what it was and, dipping a moistened finger in, gave it a cautious taste.

'Ah! Aargh! Utterly vile!' he cried, stepping back. 'But now I remember! This was my last attempt to rediscover Lysurgian's lost recipe for that powder which he claimed in a footnote to his work was very efficacious in keeping dogs at bay!'

All wayfarers and pilgrims suffered from the problem of feral and rabid dogs abandoned by humans, which, unlike their former masters, could still see and scent hydden and enjoyed attacking them. He was sure that if he could rediscover that recipe his fortune would be made.

'Hmm,' he mused, spying some ingredients still waiting to be ground and mixed, 'how pleasant it is to be here once more, free to try such things out, at liberty to think my own thoughts and do as I please!'

He idly put more ingredients in the mortar, ground them, and put them in a lettered and numbered envelope that he might know which recipe it was. Such simple physical acts of experimentation, preparation and cataloguing always calmed Stort.

But he was disturbed in these actions by the clear, firm voice of Goodwife Cluckett from the doorway.

'I see you are up now, sir, *and* about! I am disappointed to see that you are engaged in some trivial pursuit rather than in tidying this messy place up! Let us do so now!'

She approached one of his untidy tables and swept its contents into a waste-paper bin.

Stort's heart beat faster.

Sweat broke out upon his brow.

'You shall not do that!' he said as firmly as he could.

She stilled and frowned ominously.

'My rule is,' she said, 'that if something remains untouched after three weeks it is probably best thrown out of the house. These items look as if they have not been touched in years! They should go!'

Stort grabbed a pencil and inscribed the number sixty-three upon the envelope he had just filled.

'Thus do I work!' he cried. 'Who can tell what will be needed?'

'Sixty-three,' she said, 'is that an important number? More important than sixty-two or four?'

He stared at her blankly.

'Well, of course it's important, Madam—'

'Cluckett, call me Cluckett.'

He stared at her again, his thoughts confused. What had he been saying, what was his drift? Why did she so bewilder him? He waved the envelope about.

'Sixty-three may be an important number, certainly it is an interesting one, but that is not quite—'

'If it's important, sir, would it not be better to look after that envelope more carefully?'

'That is not the point I am trying to make, Goodwife . . .'

'Cluckett is not a difficult name to remember, I would have thought, especially for a bookish kind of man like you.'

'Well then, sixty-three may or may not be important depending on what is contained within, which is a recipe for canine dispersal. My point is that it might be a great loss to science and to mortality were it to be "tidied away". I am ordering you to touch nothing.'

'Canine is dogs and I don't like 'em,' said Cluckett.

'Nor I,' said Stort, 'hence the vital, truly vital importance of this envelope and me being able to find it.'

'Well, sir, you cannot stop me tidying things, it is in my nature. You are not, I take it, intending to stop me?'

She stared at him boldly with challenge in her eyes and Stort knew the moment of truth had come. Back down now and all would be lost, his home tidied away to nothingness, the good work of many years destroyed, and he, as Barklice feared, tidied away as well.

She advanced upon him as an army to battle, keys clanking warningly on her belt.

'Madam, I . . . I . . .'

She came nearer still.

'Yes, Mister Stort, you have something to say?'

'I . . . yes . . . no . . .'

His chest felt constricted, his breath difficult, his throat so dry with trepidation that he could not speak. Nor finally could he stand up without the support of the nearest laboratory table, which he clutched, gasping for air.

This had a salutary effect on Cluckett, who rushed to a sink in the laboratory, filled an empty glass vessel with water, and proffered it to him. He took it gratefully and drank it at once, his stand against her beginning to weaken. The water tasted strange yet not unpleasant. It put a sudden fire to his throat and then his spirit too as it hit the lining of his stomach like a thunderbolt. Moments later his hair, as it felt, began to stand on end.

She stared at him in alarm as, while he still fought for words, his eyes turned a ferocious red.

Speechless still, he stared down at the retort in his hand and saw that what he had drunk was water mixed with the evaporated remains of a little experiment he had been working on a year before. The label on it read 'CURE FOR WARTS'.

His nostrils flared and his ears trembled as a dragon-like heat came out of them both.

Then he heard a voice deep and strong, which sounded only a little like his own. He felt himself advancing upon her in his turn. To his surprise she began to back away, fear in her eyes.

'Madam or Cluckett or whatever your name is,' he said, 'if you touch a single thing in this laboratory without my permission I will dismiss you instantly and without a reference!'

Her expression darkened, her cheeks and forehead turned red, she looked enraged.

'Sir, if you—'

'Cluckett,' he responded at once, 'if you continue like this I shall be forced to rid my home of you at once!'

'You would deal roughly with my person?'

He thought about this for a moment and finally said, 'I would and come to think of it – I shall!'

He loomed over her as if to carry through his threat.

Her response astonished him.

'Oh sir,' she said, backing off still further, her hands unclenching, a strange softness coming to her eyes and a flush to her cheeks, 'are you being masterful with me?'

Stort, who had never been masterful with another in his life, supposed he was but felt it best to say nothing. She filled the silence herself.

'Mister Cluckett was very masterful,' she said with unexpected compliance, 'and I do so miss that now he is gone!'

'Cluckett, stop talking,' said Stort, who felt suddenly tired, 'and please make a brew that we may discuss how best we are to continue together in this humble now that I am getting better.'

'I will, sir, at once! I like an employer who knows his own mind.'

'And I, Cluckett . . .'

He still felt queasy so she took his arm and helped him to a seat at the kitchen table. She made the brew and poured them both a cup.

'You were saying, sir?'

He looked around at the clean and tidy kitchen, the neat shelves, the breakfast things all ready.

'I am grateful for the care you have shown me and . . . and I like such a home as you have made for me in so short a time!'

'Oh sir!' she said, turning from him with emotion and dabbing at her eyes with the crisp, new-ironed kerchief she pulled from her sleeve.

From that moment on Stort became master of his house once more and both he and Cluckett respectful of their different domains.

He permitted her to tidy his books, and his parlour too, though he insisted that the dresser, filled as it was with a clutter of plates, cups, a teapot with a broken spout and other mementoes of his past, was left just as he liked it.

'As for my laboratory, if you place a waste bin by the door I shall endeavour to remember to put rubbish into it!'

'Thank you, sir, that is kind of you. And, sir . . .'

'Cluckett?'

'Wet towels. May I ask that you hang them up rather than leave them in a heap upon the floor?'

'You may and I shall do as you suggest.'

From that day Stort slept well again and his recovery was almost complete.

'Cluckett,' he said some days later, 'if Brief and the others call I shall wish to see them.'

She smiled happily.

'It is already arranged, sir. They are coming to tea tomorrow and it is not a social call.'

'It is not?'

She shook her head.

'Master Brief wishes to convene a summit conference in your parlour and I told him that I judged you well enough now for that. Does that have your approval, sir?'

'It does,' said Bedwyn Stort happily.

11

NIKLAS BLUT

It was several days before Emperor Slaeke Sinistral was ready once more to try to signal to the outer world that he was awake and needed rescuing. He had only to raise a finger and press a button to summon instant aid, but his reserves of energy were so low that each attempt robbed him of almost all he had left. He was also taking his time. He knew that the return to the real world was going to be painful, a rebirth, in body, mind and spirit.

Meanwhile the helpers who had tended him for eighteen years past, who were inhabitants of the vast complex of tunnels of which his Chamber was a small part, continued to do so. They came when he was asleep or nearly so and he knew neither their names nor faces. They did their best to slow down his foul decay, but since he had begun to wake and his mind and body grown more active the rate of his decline had speeded up and they could not keep up with it. It was not these creatures of the dark he needed now but the hydden of the day and light, and the stimulus and nourishment they could provide.

Yet though Sinistral knew well that when he woke from a period of deep sleep it was essential he returned to normal health and life as fast as possible, the Chamber held a continuing allure. This had to do with the beauty of its extraordinary acoustic as, from every crevice and crack, fault and fissure in the vast roof so high above, water dripped.

Drip . . . drip . . . drip . . .

The ever-changing pattern of sound was a function of the fact that each drip of the thousands that continually fell down did so after a different lapse of time from all the others and the sounds they made varied in their pitches and tones, themselves changing with subtle shifts in the Earth's own harmonies of tectonic movement, near and far; and the orographic patterns of rain on the surface above, the water filtering down in strengths and weaknesses that echoed the patterns of rainfall and surface flow, years, decades and sometimes centuries before.

A brief stay in the Chamber was not enough for the true nature of these sounds to be understood. They seemed chaotic until, after due time, their patterns emerged. Sinistral had come to understand that these patterns were recognized by him not only when awake but when asleep, perhaps even more so then.

In time, he believed, he had learned their language and that this communication was not one-way. He heard the sound, and it heard him and responded. It was a voice, an ancient and eternal one. The music of endless dripping made by the water was nothing less than the old voice of Earth and Universe. Like light from a star long dead that a mortal sees today, the Emperor heard all the ancient voices of the past through the echoes of this internal rain. In this he felt his times of extended sleep had given him something few mortals had ever had – direct communication with the divine.

He thought of what he heard as music – in fact he believed it to be that ethereal music which human and hydden philosophers alike described as *musica universalis* – the harmonic sound which rang out at frequencies beyond the mortal range, which was the energy which gave life and connection to all things.

He was sure, quite sure, that what had woken him after eighteen years was the Earth herself, speaking though tremors in her crust transmuted by the dripping into a *musica* that had told him that finally, after fifteen hundred years, the gem of Spring had been found.

Which mattered to him especially because, if he could find a way to possess it for himself, his youth and life would be extended even further. Spring was the genesis of life and he needed it.

So the days had drifted and now the time had come to call for help.

He knew that what he faced was nothing less than a pain beyond what most mortals ever know.

The pain of his whole body reclaiming life.

The pain of mortality itself.

The pain of being born: primal and terrible.

He listened to the *musica* a final time; he tried to hum, he tried to scream, and then, letting himself slip at last into mortal pain, he raised the cadaverous forefinger of his right hand in the dark from the decayed leather on which it rested. It quested blindly for the button, flexed what weak muscles it still had and held it down for those few seconds that were all his wasted strength allowed and then let go.

Nothing happened immediately yet he was satisfied it would soon enough. His rotted mouth exhaled another foul breath of long, vegetative sleep, through teeth not stronger nor more fragrant than the vilest cheese. Those eyelids, whose white, stubby lashes were caked with congealed rheum, still struggled to open into darkness and still failed.

A pale tongue flicked at thin dry lips.

Then Emperor Slaeke Sinistral's head, its hair greasy and thin, its ulcerous skin taut and weeping, turned slowly to one side, listening.

Still the eyes would not open.

The left side of the mouth bubbled and saliva broke forth, not quite clean, leaving a trail down the chin until it slipped, maggot-like, into his beard and nestled there.

Finally . . . a sound.

The turning of a well-oiled key, the metal on metal of one bolt and then another, a sliver of yellow light beneath an opening door, the moving shadows of feet and then, breaking the dark like a sharp and shining axe of gold cutting through the blackened hull of some great ship, a shaft of light raced right across the Chamber, right to where the Emperor lay, head turned towards it, eyes sensing light at last, eyelids straining to open.

Sinistral turned his head away lest he be blinded after so long in darkness. The door opened wider and more light flooded past him into the Chamber beyond. The door was quietly pulled to but not quite shut, so the light faded until all that was left was the thin line beneath the door. It was enough.

Lashes pulled apart and a single eye, dark and imperious, stared out. It slowly focused and finally saw the rain caught by the light from beneath the door. The Emperor saw a hundred thousand slowly falling golden pearls.

It was most beautiful.

The Emperor tried to speak but could not.

He heard the sound of footfalls coming across the Chamber towards his chair.

A hand touched his and a voice spoke.

It said, 'Welcome back my Lord. You have been much missed.'

The Emperor tried to smile but could not; again he tried to say something, but could not.

All he could do was utter a hiss of joy.

'I shall go now, Emperor, and summon your beloved. She will tend to you and see you safely back to health and life . . .'

The drumming of the rain instilled within the Emperor a calm that made him weep. He breathed, deep and slow.

His other eye was opening.

The subtle rain turned three-dimensional.

The Emperor's head turned and he said, 'Tell her . . .'

'Yes, Lord?'

'. . . that I . . .'

'Yes?'

'. . . have need of her.'

'I shall my Lord.'

The hydden who had responded to the Emperor's call, and for now the only person who knew he was awake, was an official named Niklas Blut.

His formal title was Commander of the Emperor's Office.

He was, de facto, the second most important person in the Hyddenworld, though nobody, including Blut himself, saw it that way. Even so, at only forty, Blut was still remarkably young for such responsibility.

But then he was a very remarkable hydden. As a sixteen-year-old he had scored the highest marks of any entrant in the Imperial triennial examinations in logic, mathematics, science and literature and gained a well-paid post as a civil servant. At age seventeen his enemies proved that he had made unlawful access to human literature and other resources. When he was eighteen he was found guilty of possessing a printed article entitled: *The truth about Emperor Slaeke Sinistral's strange longevity: its history, cause and likely outcomes.*

It had been sent unread, as such material always was, to the Emperor's Office. For to be found in possession of such an article was treasonable. To read it was a capital offence.

Blut's crime was much greater: he had written it.

He was put under sentence of death for which the Emperor's signature was needed.

Slaeke Sinistral, intrigued to learn that the ultimate sanction was being applied to so young a hydden, stayed the execution to give himself time to read the article.

He did so with an astonishment that was soon replaced with growing alarm. If anyone else discovered the truths Niklas Blut had exposed, the Emperor's position might be for ever undermined.

Niklas Blut's crime was to dare try to answer a question that had been on everybody's mind for decades: how did Slaeke Sinistral stay so young? Could he possibly hold the secret of eternal youth which had eluded the many who sought it in every age? If he did, what was it?

Blut began by stating the simple truth: the Emperor looked to be in his mid-thirties but the records very clearly showed that he had been alive for more than a century and a half and there was no one anywhere, however old, who remembered him as being anything other than the age he still appeared to be.

True, he grew tired and ill sometimes and disappeared from public view, but he always came back, revivified.

All sorts of rumours arose from this, including the possibility that it was not the same Sinistral who 'reappeared' as the one who had previously 'disappeared'.

What Blut had done was to look at the records going back a century and a half, plot Sinistral's periods of ill-health and his disappearances, and relate them to certain cosmic events and movements of the Earth. He had delved into the old historical records and found compelling evidence that certain individuals, human and hydden, appeared to have had powers beyond the ordinary and that some of these had lived to an extraordinarily old age.

Each had been secretive, each prone to periods of illness and retreat, and each had returned to their normal lives renewed, refreshed, and, in every respect, younger than their chronological age.

His conclusion was simple: since such powers and such cases of longevity had occurred only since the legendary creation of the gems of the seasons by Beornamund of Brum, they were probably directly related to the gems themselves. The fact that there were so many stories and rumours connecting particular gems with these individuals gave credence to Blut's ideas, if not proof positive.

As for the case of Slaeke Sinistral, Blut postulated that he had in his possession the gem of Summer, and it was to his occasional exposure to this gem that he owed his continuing youthfulness.

All perfectly true, but never stated so clearly by one of his subjects before. That was not all.

Blut had worked out something else, and it worried the Emperor that others might learn of it.

The use of the gem to delay physical ageing, Blut argued, came at a cost. Each time the Emperor submitted his body to the gem's fierce light, which he did strapped down in the dentist's chair, because the experience caused so much pain and violence to his internal organs, his period of rejuvenation afterwards was shorter and the subsequent period of recuperative sleep longer. That explained why the Emperor's absences grew ever more frequent and extended.

But Blut had even gone so far as to calculate the point at which the gem of Summer would become ineffective because the Emperor would enter a period of sleep so long that his physical body, even if carefully maintained, likely would not survive it. Even if it did, on waking his physical decay would be so rapid that, unless he had a system in place to get him back to health again, he would die before a new rejuvenation could take effect.

As the Emperor read this terrifyingly accurate assessment of his situation he knew he had to kill Blut to keep his secret, or employ him to help keep him alive.

There was much else in the young hydden's paper that the

Emperor wished to learn more about. Not least how it was that Blut had worked out the way in which the Emperor came to possess the gem. Again, his argument was spot on.

Everyone knew that one of the great hydden geniuses of the last two hundred years was the mysterious ã Faroün, lute player and architect, artist and mystic. Blut believed that he had been the possessor of the gem of Summer before Sinistral. Ã Faroün was Sinistral's teacher. On his passing, which occurred when Sinistral was in his mid-thirties, the Emperor-to-be had taken possession of the gem and the rest, quite literally, was history . . .

Having read the article Sinistral had thought about it for several days before deciding on the action he must take.

He had summoned his three most senior staff, who stood in obedient silence before him.

He was used to such silence. Tall, blond, well built, with intelligent eyes that could glitter with dark intent as easily as his face could wrinkle in mirth, the Emperor was intimidating.

'How many have read this document?' he asked the then Commander of his Office.

Sweat broke on the Commander's brow.

'Myself alone, Lord, but I felt I had to,' he said nervously. Sinistral looked around at his staff and nodded slightly and dismissed the other two.

Then he shrugged.

'A pity,' he said.

'Lord,' said the Commander desperately, 'Blut's paper is a fabrication, it is nonsense, and I have already forgotten what it said . . .'

'Unfortunately it is not nonsense and I cannot believe you have forgotten what it said. Nor can I live in the knowledge of that fact.'

Sinistral summoned his Fyrd guard. He knew the official could not be allowed to remain alive. The secret he knew gave him a power he must not have.

When the guards came the Emperor nodded towards the hapless Commander and said, 'Execute him.'

'Yes, Lord.'

'Here where I can see. I need to know he has not talked with anyone.'

'Yes, Lord,' said the senior guard, arming his crossbow. 'Now?'
'Now.'

The Emperor had stood up, turned his back, and stared at the view until he heard the click-bang of the crossbow bolt being fired.

'A pity,' he said again as the body was removed. 'He was an intelligent administrator and effective servant to the Empire. Give him an honourable funeral. Now . . . I shall have to find another to replace him.'

He had already decided to interview Blut, not simply to answer certain questions but to see if he might be groomed to administer his Office.

The Emperor commanded that he be brought to the Imperial headquarters in Bochum, north-east Germany. The interview was private.

'So . . . you're Niklas Blut?'
'Yes. One of them.'
'There are more?'
'My uncle. A butcher.'
'Do you know why you're here?'

Blut shrugged, the question did not interest him. The answer had to be surmise. He liked facts and calculation.

'No.'
'Can you guess?'
'Anyone can guess.'

The Emperor was not used to this kind of repartee. His officials treated him with a respect bordering on fear. Blut appeared fearless. Or perhaps he was simply ingenuous.

He stared at Blut who stared back at him.

The young civil servant was not much to look at. He was of average height, pallid, and the possessor of an annoying pair of spectacles which hooked so tightly round his ears that their oval glass pressed against his eyelashes. How he could see properly out of them Sinistral had no idea.

As the silence deepened Blut was moved to take off these gold-framed spectacles, wipe them with his kerchief and put them on again, pulling them tight once more to nose and eyes.

Sinistral found that he was looking into two mirrors simultaneously, whose facets diverged from each other and sent oval reflections dancing all around the room. These seemed an extension of Blut's bright, intelligent, blue-green eyes, sharp nose and firm mouth and added – rightly so – to the impression he gave close-to of extreme intelligence. Which Sinistral already saw was indeed the case.

His file showed him to be an able administrator and a brilliant researcher.

'You realize that researching the source of my youth is treasonable?'

'I do not think truth should ever be treasonable, my Lord.'

'You believe I possess the gem of Summer?'

'I can find no other explanation for the facts about your life that I have uncovered.'

'How do you imagine a mere bauble can give a hydden eternal youth?'

'I never said it was eternal. I think you are dying, my Lord, only at a rate slower than the rest of us.'

'How would you know that?'

'The records seem to indicate that no other hydden who has used a gem to prolong their life is still alive . . . and, well, close-to one can see signs of greater ageing.'

Sinistral had stood up, restless yet excited to be in the presence of this fearless and sharp mind. He made a decision.

'I have decided that you will work in my personal office, Blut. I ask only two things. First, that you never talk of the gem you rightly think I possess to anyone else.'

'Agreed, my Lord. And the second?'

'You will continue to speak the truth to me as directly and clearly as you just have. You understand?'

'I do, my Lord, and I will.'

The Emperor did not doubt it.

From that day Blut had begun his meteoric rise in the Emperor's employ.

Now he was greyer, had filled out a little and looked more comfortable in his plain grey uniform than he had when he first began to wear it two decades before. Now it bore, the Emperor noted, the simplest emblem that it could to mark his rank as Commander of the

Emperor's Office. He still wore the same style of spectacles except, in line with the natural asceticism of Blut's character, the frames were no longer gold but steel.

. . . And he had married during the Emperor's time of sleep.

'The marriage is a happy one?'

'Very, my Lord.'

'And regarding matters political things are broadly unchanged, you say?'

'The issues of daily life in Imperial Bochum are ever-changing in their detail but the factions and politics of administration, Fyrd and Court are broadly as you left them. There are no new faces in positions of power. I have prepared papers for when you are fully restored to health.'

It was now several days since the Emperor had woken.

'And the wider Empire?'

Blut hesitated. There was always much to say on that complex subject but it, too, should wait.

The Emperor seemed content to do no more than pass the time. Each hour, each day, he grew a little stronger in his mind, but, for his body, time was running out.

'And still my beloved does not come?'

'My Lady is on the way from Thuringia, Lord.'

'Did she say when?'

Blut shook his head.

'She never does,' said Sinistral indulgently.

'Just so, Lord Emperor.'

'Any other news?'

The Emperor was still in his dentist's chair, still in the Chamber, still a hideous sight. But he was eating food now and his mind was as active as ever it was.

'Of my Lady or the world at large?'

'Both. Give me a titbit from each, Blut, you are good at that.'

'My Lady had her second child, due, you will remember, just before you went into sleep . . .'

'Ah, yes . . . yes . . .'

He had forgotten.

'Male like the first, or female?'

'Er . . . male, my Lord.'

'You hesitate.'

'I had hoped to delay my briefing of you on that difficult subject.'

'Why?'

'He was no ordinary child . . .'

'He is dead?'

Blut shook his head.

'Oh no, not dead. Very much alive but . . . he . . . it was an unusual birth.'

The Emperor stilled.

'Really? Then I need to know—'

'My Lord,' said Blut firmly, 'you need to sleep. In Bochum all is well, what is happening beyond it will need your fullest attention, but not yet. The tremor that woke you was one of several and, if the predictions are right, others are on the way.'

The Emperor tried to sit up but it was too much, too soon. He fell back exhausted, breathing heavily.

'Were any of them in Brum?'

'I have heard one was.'

'A good augury if the gem of Spring is to be found, since that's where it was lost. All we need is evidence of a giant-born . . .'

He stilled again and then said quietly, 'You said her second child was an unusual birth.'

'Lord,' said Blut firmly, 'speculation is not what you now need. Rest is what's required.'

'Blut, you are holding something back.'

'Many things, but all can wait until my Lady comes and you have had opportunity to know the gem of Summer once again. Until then . . . we must not excite ourselves, my Lord. Sleep is needed now . . .'

The Emperor slept.

12
GROWING PAINS

Five days after Jack and Katherine made the decision to continue to keep Judith's existence a secret from the authorities for the time being, the speed of her growth became more obvious.

Jack had already described her as 'odd-looking', which had caused Katherine, still suffering post-natal mood swings, much grief. But the truth was, one moment her hands looked too big, the next it was her head: then her feet and her knees.

The relative positions of her facial features – nose, eyes, cheeks, ears and chin – kept shifting about as well. At times her oddness was almost gross, her sudden strength nearly demonic for one her age. But he was right: she was not, as yet, someone of whom it might be easily said, 'She's a pretty child'.

But it took Arthur's daily measurements, which he took every four hours, to confirm what they all suspected: she was growing at a rate of knots.

'The figures are so unexpected that I don't really trust them myself, but I'd say, according to normal child development, a day in Judith's life is the equivalent of a hundred days for a normal infant.'

'Goodness,' said Margaret, 'that sounds a lot!'

'It *is* a lot,' said Arthur. 'In fact it's astonishing.'

'So how old would that make her now?' asked Jack.

'Well, I'm reluctant to make that kind of assessment on such figures but . . .'

'But?'

'I would say that, physically speaking, after seven days of life, she's two years old.'

There was stunned silence.

'And . . .' pressed Jack. He could see that Arthur had a chart showing projections, which he had done a poor job of hiding.

'If she continues at that rate,' Arthur said heavily, 'she will be something like nine years old by the end of May and nearing sixteen by Midsummer . . .'

Their expressions moved from being stunned to being shocked.

'So . . .' began Katherine, her head reeling.

'By the end of July, your newborn child will be several years older than either of you are.'

'But . . .'

'But what if her mental and intellectual development does not keep pace with her physical changes?' continued Arthur. 'Well . . . I don't know . . .'

'It'll be a disaster,' said Margaret. 'Common sense tells you that. But then there's nothing commonsensical about any of this.'

'Yet it's happening,' said Jack, 'literally before our eyes.'

'If that's true,' said Katherine, 'if it's really true then she . . . she must be suffering terribly. Jack said this morning that he thought it might be growing pains, but this is something else again; she's got to cope with everything at once. Stuff that we took years to deal with – and haven't yet finished – she's having to deal with in a few days and months. And then . . . then . . .'

Katherine broke down as Jack went to her, put his arms around her.

'It's all right,' he said, realizing it was a provocative thing to say the moment he uttered it.

'It's not all right, it's all wrong. There's the future. At that rate . . .'

'Katherine!' said Arthur firmly. 'Stop it. Please. This is based on a few measurements and I'm an expert in none of this, I just know statistics. Maybe Judith'll stop growing next week . . . Maybe today . . . I don't know.'

The spectre of the future was among them. At the rate of Arthur's prediction Judith would be an old woman by the following Spring. That was too horrible to think about.

'Well,' said Arthur rather lamely, 'at least what I've done helps make sense of what's happening now.'

Jack turned to Margaret and said, 'You've gone silent.'

'I'm thinking. Even if Arthur's only right for a few more days we should make some plans. She'll be walking soon. Have you any idea . . . ?'

There was a crash from the direction of the study. Katherine and Jack went running and at first couldn't see what it had been.

Then they heard a crunching of glass and went round the far side of Margaret's desk.

The standard lamp had fallen over, the shade had bent and rolled away, the bulb and fitting were shattered, and a vase of flowers had been brought down and broken too. Judith, silent for once, was crawling on her hands and knees over wet broken glass and cut flowers, indifferent to the blood coming from her cuts, heading for the exposed electrical fitting.

Jack grabbed her and said, 'Not a brilliant idea, Judith.'

Katherine said, 'Naughty!' and then suddenly laughed.

'I never, ever thought I'd hear myself say that word,' she said. 'And anyway, it's not naughty, it's exploratory.'

'Humpphh,' said Jack, more shocked than Katherine, 'Margaret will not be pleased . . .'

They took Judith out of the study, closed the door, and went back to the kitchen and looks of enquiry from Arthur and Margaret.

'I think some serious talking needs to be done about how to make this house childproof,' said Katherine.

As they tended her cuts, which continued to provoke puzzled silence rather than tears, Arthur said very meekly, 'There's another thing that Jack and I found out.'

'If we take Judith to a doctor then they may well refer her case to a child protection officer if they think there's something unusual,' said Jack. 'Obviously there is and if she starts injuring herself like now there would have to be some kind of investigation.'

Arthur looked grim.

'Under the Child Welfare Protection Act officers acting for the agencies and courts have draconian powers,' he said. 'We could easily lose Judith into the system, and that would make it very hard to help her. You can imagine what officialdom would make of a child growing a hundred times faster than normal.'

Jack said, 'We're not only going to have to make the house childproof, we're going to have to find ways of stopping Judith getting out if and when she gets more mobile. It's already starting to happen . . .'

With Judith's hands cleaned, disinfected and in plasters, Katherine held her above the floor and slowly lowered her feet onto it.

'Go to Daddy,' she said.

Judith did, her arms reaching out to Jack's.

He laughed, so did they all. For once Judith was having a good, relatively quiet, hour.

She dropped back onto her hands and knees and crawled off again, straight for the open door.

Katherine closed it and Judith stopped before it, puzzled and frustrated.

She pulled herself upright and began screaming again and banging her head, very hard, against the door.

13

TREMOR

The night before the 'summit' conference Brief had convened at Stort's humble, Brum suffered new tremors.

Buildings trembled, beds shook and the Earth moaned so strangely that it sounded like a despairing wind blowing through a ruined city.

Stort did not sleep but listened to these intimations of disaster with a sinking heart. He tossed and turned wondering if he should maintain his silence about the gem, and if so how he was to do so. It was not in his nature to keep secrets, or dissemble with his friends, and Brief, Pike and Barklice knew him so well that he doubted he could keep his secret for long. If he tried they would get angry.

At breakfast he picked at his egg, sipped miserably at his tea, and declined more toast.

'Trouble, Mister Stort?' said Cluckett.

'Yes, I fear there may be.'

'If you're threatened during the meeting today, sir, bear in mind I have a rolling pin and know how to use it.'

Stort was grateful for the offer but shook his head.

'My friends will not be violent, though they may be disappointed in me . . .'

'Please know that I shall be at the ready, sir, lest you need rescuing.'

'Thank you,' said Stort and he meant it.

From the moment Brief arrived, his stave of office in hand and a businesslike look on his face, Stort knew his fears were justified.

He strode in, Pike and Barklice in his wake, and took over the parlour.

'We shall sit at your table, I at its head, and we shall proceed at once!'

'Well then—' began poor Stort.

'Sit down, sit down if you please! To order and to business!'

A silence fell as they all looked at Stort.

'Well, Stort? *Well?* What's been going on?'

'Nothing,' said Stort very unconvincingly.

'Ah! Nothing he says! We are not fools, Stort. We know you well. What are you hiding from us? Eh? Out with it!'

'I . . . I . . .'

'Come on, old fellow,' said Barklice, 'easier to spit it out!'

'But . . . there's nothing . . .'

Pike leaned forward, eyes narrowing, his lean face and grizzled grey hair the very picture of purposeful command.

'You return to Brum out of the wildest night in memory, you seem crazed, you refuse any examination of your person, you are covered in mud suggesting that you have been in water, your boots are thick with clay of a colour that all hereabout know comes from only one place . . .'

Stort looked involuntarily at his house-shoes, which were spotlessly clean, trying to remember the state of his boots when he arrived in Brum.

'What place is that?' he asked ingenuously.

'Waseley Hill,' said Pike. 'And you demand to see Brief, to whom, when you see him, you say nothing at all. Then when you arrive at your home you rush into this very room and lock the door. Doesn't add up to us. You're normally an open book and now you're a closed one. What are you hiding, Stort?'

Stort stared at them, eyes wide and unhappy.

Did he have no friends at all? Was he after all as alone as he had felt since he found the gem?

Barklice said, 'How long have I known you, Stort? How many the miles we've travelled together? Well, my dear friend who I would not see hurt for all the world, Master Brief and Mister Pike here may seem angry, even irritable, but they do not mean to be. They, well . . .

they'd not say so but – ' He reached a hand to Stort's arm ' – but they
are *concerned* for you, as I am. So what is it, dear friend, what's
wrong?'

Stort stared at him, mouth opening and closing, not knowing what
to say, caught between truth and responsibility, racked by the despair
that came with feeling that in the circumstance in which he found
himself one precluded the other but neither should be sacrificed.

'Stort,' began Brief more gently than before, yet still continuing the
assault, 'as so often in the past Barklice puts it in a better way than I,
irascible old fool that I am. Tell us what troubles you and we will
help if we can.'

'Aye,' said Pike gruffly, 'I say the same, for you know well, Stort,
since I've said it many times before, I've admired and respected you
since you were that gawky lad that saved my life the day I picked you
up in your home village of Wardine to bring you back to Brum and a
different life. I'd kill another if they so much as threatened you.'

Such was the intensity of the feelings expressed in that room that
not one of them, not even Brief who was facing the door, noticed that
it had been pushed open a little by Cluckett, who had a fresh tray of
tea in her hand. It was never her nature to pry, or listen at doors, but
she had not been able to help overhearing what was said and since
her hands were full she could not very easily stop the unexpected and
unwanted tears that began to course down her cheeks. She quietly
retreated again and returned to the kitchen, put down the tray and
dabbed at her eyes with a tea cloth.

'Oh Mister Stort,' she said aloud, 'you make my feelings turn and
turn about, you do!'

As she continued to wipe away her tears she did not immediately
notice that the wooden ladle in the large mixing bowl on the kitchen
table was trembling, shaking and beginning to move around the edge
of the bowl all of its own accord.

When she did a few moments later she stared at it in wonder.

Meanwhile Stort, faced by the unremitting but emotional appeals
of his friends, remained stupefied with indecision, wanting to talk
about the gem, wanting to show it to them, wanting to leap up and
cry, *My friends, you are right! I am withholding something from you!*

Something both wonderful and terrible! I cannot remain silent about it any longer.

He might very well have done so had not a thin, gritty trickle of plaster dust begun falling from the rafters above onto the table between them, among their cups and saucers. As they looked up to see what it was and from where it came, those same cups and saucers began to rattle, while other cups hanging from hooks on the dresser next to the table swung one way, then the other, then shook and jolted so violently that one of their handles broke and it crashed onto the shelf below and bits of it to the floor behind Pike.

No sooner had that happened than the parlour door, left a little open by Cluckett, slammed shut so violently that its latch rattled and the door jumped open again.

Pike leapt to his feet, the only one with the wits to react, and edged around the table to protect Brief. It was hard for him to do so because the floor beneath his feet was shaking and the table rocking and tilting this way and that, as if its legs had come alive and were trying to head off in different directions.

Then Barklice's chair tilted back and he nearly fell out of it, while Brief was forced to lean forward and cling to the table so that his own chair stayed where it was.

Time began to slow.

The fruit in a bowl on the table rose one by one and paused in the air without support, as it seemed, turning slowly in the light, their colour suddenly brighter, every detail showing, floating amidst them all so invitingly that it would have seemed a simple thing to reach out a hand to catch one or other of them.

But none of them did because they, like everything else, had slowed down too.

The arms of Pike's coat, which he had left draped over the back of his chair, rose up as if in search of him, while a cup slid languidly from one end of the table to the other as if in search of a saucer.

For a moment all fell silent and still but for rumblings far beneath their feet and the clattering of tiles on cobbles in the street outside. Then the shaking and rattling inside the humble began again. Crockery tumbled from the dresser and as they turned towards it, half rising in their chairs, it seemed possible that the dresser itself might tip over and fall headlong onto them.

Solid chunks of plaster fell among them, turning slowly through the air before their eyes, like the fruit which, meanwhile, had fallen back into its bowl where it whirled round and round.

But oddest of all these odd happenings was the way that the cracked teapot that was Stort's memento of his maternal grandfather began moving forward now from its dusty perch in the shadows on the highest shelf of the dresser.

They watched in fascination as it wobbled and slipped forward to the shelf's edge, where very slowly it tipped over, turned in slow motion through the air, and headed in free fall for the very centre of the table, accompanied as it seemed by a louder rumbling noise from the Earth far below, which grew louder and louder as the teapot neared the table top.

So that when it finally hit it, and broke asunder into many pieces, the subterranean noise of the Earth tremor reached a violent, crashing crescendo, like a succession of thunderclaps.

As the teapot broke, normal time resumed. Everything rushed to the end of its thousand different trajectories and dust fell on the head of all of them as something yet more extraordinary happened.

For as the teapot fell apart and the pieces scattered – the spout one way, the handle another, and the rest in decorated shards across the table and onto the floor – the leather pouch containing the gem which Stort had, as he thought, so cleverly hidden there, remained just where the pot had landed, as if a hand had placed it gently before them.

Then, as inevitably as a tide rolling in at sunset, the pouch fell to one side, opened, and from it rolled the pendant gem of Spring with its chain sliding after it.

Stort's friends stared at it in puzzlement, he in horror.

It began growing brighter, until finally there shone from it – and on all their astonished faces, lighting up their eyes, shining in their hair, glinting on their teeth – all the colours of the Spring. With that came the sights and the sounds and the scents of that season too.

Stort's parlour filled with sudden birdsong, as if they were in a wood; and the tinkling sound of streamlets; and with the whispering of a breeze through leaves not yet fully grown which carried on its breath the delicate scents of aconite and eyebright, snowdrops and the first bluebells.

Their astonishment and wonder were complete.

Stort said quietly, 'Master Brief, Mister Pike and you, Mister Barklice, I can stay silent no longer. I think . . . indeed I am quite certain . . . well . . . you can see with your own eyes that I have found the gem of Spring. It is this discovery and the responsibility that comes with it that I have been keeping from you.'

Brief eyed the gem in awe, taking his stave of office in his hand and holding it before him as if to protect himself from the gem's power. Its light played like liquid in the stave's ancient carvings, flowing in among them, twisting, turning, running back on itself.

Stort calmly reached forward, took the pendant, put it back in its pouch and slipped it in his pocket as if he was doing no more than putting away his purse after a trivial transaction with a trader.

The light of Spring fled the room at once and the Earth tremor came to an end.

Stort felt a great sense of relief that the secret was out and he saw in his friends' eyes not anger but sympathy. He was alone with his burden of secrecy no more.

'I think,' he said, 'that it is very plain what this discovery means.'

'Indeed,' said Brief. 'For one thing we may take it, for all the prophecies said it would be so, that the Shield Maiden has been born. When did you find it?'

'At the season's turn or soon after, on Waseley Hill . . .'

'You shall tell us that tale later. For now we must decide what to do. The coming of the Shield Maiden to the Earth presages difficult times ahead. Her sister Imbolc, the Peace-Weaver, whom we all knew, often said as much.'

'But if she's just a babe at the moment,' said Pike, 'those bad times are not likely to occur until she's full grown, so surely we have years to make preparations.'

Stort shook his head.

'My own researches, as Master Brief will confirm, show that a Shield Maiden lives life in a different time frame than a hydden or a human.'

'You mean more slowly, like an immortal?' said Barklice.

This time it was Brief's turn to look grave.

'We think it will be just the opposite. Even though she has had a mortal birth—'

Stort nodded and said, 'Katherine was near her time when I left her with Jack and they returned to the human world. I have no doubt the Shield Maiden is her child.

'But even though the child is born normally she will grow and age much faster than a human. A Shield Maiden's time is short on this Earth; her life filled with trouble and pain.'

'How short?' said Pike.

Brief and Stort looked at each other as if what they had to say was too incredible or too difficult to speak aloud.

'The great philosopher and lutenist ã Faroün,' said Brief finally, 'whose work I have studied carefully, was of the opinion that a Shield Maiden will live her whole life in the space of a mortal year. But be clear what this means, gentlemen. She has been alive in her mother's womb and we may take that as, in a way, her Spring, her time of new life. It may well be that even now her Spring is over and her Summer begun . . .'

'But . . .' said Barklice and Pike together.

'You may well say "but"!' said Brief. 'Stort – please explain.'

'Well . . . if ã Faroün was right then we must begin the search at once for the other gems, starting with that of Summer. The Shield Maiden will demand them, our Mother Earth will seek to yield them up wherever they may be . . . The tremors we are suffering are just the beginning of a time of trial of a kind no living mortal has ever known.'

Brief looked grave indeed.

'A time which there is every possibility mortal kind will not survive.'

Barklice, as gentle a hydden as ever was, looked horrified and said, 'What shall we do?'

'Well, it is plain enough that Stort must keep the gem for now, for he was the one chosen to find it. Meanwhile, nothing more of this need be said, gentlemen, until Mister Pike and I have informed Lord Festoon.'

They each reached a hand across the table and grasped the others' hands in silent acknowledgement that this was a secret they would keep.

'I think that Lord Festoon will say that a Privy Council meeting is called for so that plans may be properly made! Therefore let us wait for his decision.'

'Agreed,' said Pike and Barklice.

'Stort, do you agree as well?' said Brief.

'Agreed,' murmured Stort, though not entirely happily. As he had feared from the beginning, once it was known that the gem of Spring had been found the rest of the world immediately wanted to get involved.

'Then all is well,' said Brief, 'and this meeting is over.'

But as they left Stort felt all was not well, not well at all.

14

IMPERIAL CITY

The capital of the Hyddenworld occupied a vast complex of abandoned mine shafts and tunnels beneath the human city of Bochum, in North Germany.

It centred on an area of waste land to the west and south of the city. Most people lived at Level 1. The business of the Court and much else took place at Level 2, in and around the Great Hall. This was one of hydden Bochum's glories. Inside it was tall and spacious, with sunny windows set at the highest level.

It was located in the middle of a vast human rubbish tip, where feral dogs roamed and over which carrion birds wheeled and scrapped. Humans rarely penetrated to the central point. It was there that the Hall had been built downwards, cleverly using the ruined footings of a human-waste water cleansing plant which stood no more than a few feet high at its roof. It was filthy with the excreta of birds and rats and stank of human waste. The hydden had dug below, connected with old mining tunnels and arranged for more fragrant ventilation to be pumped in from woodland areas to the far south.

Few hydden would have guessed, as the sun streamed in, at the horrors above. No human could have imagined the courtly delights below.

In the lower levels of Bochum the Administration had its offices, the Fyrd had their operation rooms and the utilities that made the capital function so well were established and maintained.

It was deep down, at Level 18, that the Emperor had his Chamber of Sleep, entrance forbidden, out of harm's way, secret and unknown.

Down there he dared keep the gem of Summer and use it to restore himself to health when he needed to, in the knowledge that accidents of history and his own wyrd had provided him with a place where his secret might be safe.

The region was rich in coal and iron ore and successive generations of its human inhabitants had hollowed out the Earth as maggots eat cheese. They covered her surface with their spoil, polluted her rivers, desecrated her forests and destroyed her natural drainage.

Whenever the coal ran out or their technologies improved, the human miners moved on to new and deeper seams, leaving behind a network of subterranean ruins beneath their settlements on the surface above. By the end of the nineteenth century the area, called the Ruhr after one of the rivers flowing through it, had become one of the greatest human industrial conurbations on Earth, its countless tall chimneys casting a pall of smoke so thick that the sun was often blotted out, even on the brightest of days, for miles about. In the twentieth century the area became a world centre for the manufacture of armaments and all the products and services needed for them.

Meanwhile, over the centuries of the Ruhr's development, successive generations of hydden moved into the lost and abandoned tunnels beneath it. They had extended their hydden settlements over hundreds of square miles and down many levels.

Over these long centuries too, dozens of hydden tribes and communities, with many different languages and dialects, traditions and beliefs, came into existence. Local empires rose and fell. Whole literatures flourished, schools of music rose up and died, artists, architects and philosophers thrived or were persecuted.

No single region of the Hyddenworld knew a subterranean history quite like it.

And yet . . .

During the late nineteenth century there came to the tunnels of the Ruhr something rotten and dark. Probably it was caused by the leaching of poisons and gases from the filthy industrial waste and spoil tips on the surface above.

Life in the tunnels, once so flourishing, began to wither and slowly die. The old communities went, the arts and crafts became corrupted;

a place of general order became one of nearly universal chaos and anarchy.

Except that here and there, keeping themselves to themselves, their members pallid and wan from chronic illness, a few of the old underground settlements and cultures remained intact. Their stronger, more perverse enemies roamed the wastelands above using dogs as their instruments of power – the big, aggressive dogs that some humans admire and breed – so that the gentler survivors grew to fear the surface and its good sun and the verdant surface of the Earth, preferring isolation, secrecy, and the perpetual darkness of the deep tunnels below the city. The human city of Bochum lay above the very centre of this unseen world, unknown to its human inhabitants.

It happened that one of those gentler abandoned hydden communities had lost the powers of sight. They began to communicate by touch and vibration as well as speech, and kept alive their ancient language and preserved their heritage even if they could no longer see the wondrous art their ancestors made, or play so readily the astonishing and complex music their musicians had composed.

This community was not fecund.

The poisons that had through the generations deprived them of sight had made the seed of their males nearly sterile, the eggs of the females nearly useless.

But not quite.

Babies were born once in a while: tiny, pale, struggling scraps of hydden life which the entire community worked to nourish and bring up, teaching them what knowledge they had preserved of their histories.

They taught that in past times their ancestors were more beautiful than they were now – taller, stronger and more agile. They taught that there had been a thing called light, stolen from them by the evil forces all about and on the surface of the Earth. One day, they said, a Great One would bring it back, and with it life anew, such that they would see again. They taught that peace was good, war ill; that every life was precious, even an evil one; that kindness bred kindness, hurt bred hurt; that for all their decline through the centuries they had one great blessing.

It came in the form of vibration, which to them was sound.

It echoed in the dripping, falling, flowing of the waters.

It was the sound of the Universe itself.

It was the *musica*.

Every newborn child of this gentle people was ritually named in the falling waters of the Earth in what the Emperor of the Hydden-world, coming so much later, called his Chamber of Sleep.

That had become the centre of the community's belief and faith. Indeed, it was their eye, through sound, into the Universe.

It was for this reason that these people secretly called themselves, in their silent language of vibration and touch, the Remnant. Yet they were not exclusive. They admitted to their community others of different ethnic origin, including bilgesnipe, whose strength and good nature served them well.

While others, their enemies outside, who could not get past the barriers of dissonance with which they protected themselves, began to fear the Remnants.

Remnants, that is, of all that had once been good and glorious. Remnants of something that surely could never be revived.

Such was that strange world beneath Bochum until 1942, when all changed on the human surface above and so in the Remnants' world below.

Armaments invite war, in humans as in hydden.

The great world conflict among humans that started in 1939 brought a hail of destruction from England on the human cities of the Ruhr, Bochum included. The bombs fell, the houses and factories burned, firestorms raged and the Remnants suffered.

Tunnels collapsed, floods invaded, poison gas spread, the barriers of dissonance broke down and incursions from the evil hydden thereabout increased.

The Remnants retreated lower, reduced their tunnels to the minimum and centred their life on their great Chamber.

Births ceased, fear reigned, hope began to die, the young ones began to leave and all seemed lost.

Then, in 1945, when the war above stopped, a miracle happened.

The Great One whose coming had for so long been prophesied came among them as they believed. The hydden who had stumbled upon the Chamber was Slaeke Sinistral himself. He was looking for a place to keep the gem of Summer in safety. What he found was far more than that.

Not that he knew they were there, for they did not show themselves.

He came noisily as others had, yet not in enmity and nor in numbers.

He was alone and courageous.

They heard him many days before he reached the Chamber. They were fearful at first but began to feel new hope.

He came alone, quietly, taking his time. They sensed his darkness straightaway, but also something he could not himself: that beyond the Sinistral the wider world knew and feared was a being of great intelligence and sensitivity.

Feeling his way, slipping here and falling there, he came on and down, level by level, his vibrations subtle and filled with the light of Summer whose source they could not know nor even guess. It seemed to them that he put into the *musica* they heard the light of their forgotten Springs, the warmth of their lost Summers, the haunting poetry of Autumns remembered only through their old art and the bleak, clean cold of Winter fled. The stranger had about him as he came all the seasons that their history remembered but they themselves had never known.

Until at last he approached the Chamber.

After much debate they decided not to make the dissonance, which so close would surely have killed him.

'He may be the Great One,' one of the old ones said. 'Give him his chance. We can feel he means us no harm.'

'He doesn't know we're here!'

'What's he doing?'

'Listening.'

'What does he look like?'

'Beautiful, like we once looked. Tall, strong, agile, like a god. Can you not see him?'

Of course they could, for the Remnants see through sound, and when the stranger stood in the Chamber and took off his clothes and let the dripping water fall upon him, as if he wished to cleanse his soul, they heard his shape in the changes in the sound, in the flow of water over his body, in the way he raised his arms and, crying out his pain and fear, called to the Universe.

But that was neither the miracle nor the evidence of who he truly was. No, that came hours later.

He moved from the centre of the Chamber to a dry approach tunnel where he stowed his clothes. He dressed, he slept, he ate, he thought.

Then, after much hesitation, he opened the bag they could hear he carried.

He took a boxlike shape out.

He opened it.

He hesitated more.

Then, taking something from it, he doffed his clothes again and advanced naked to the centre of the Chamber, his light a lantern they could hear but naturally not see, which he covered.

Then the true miracle.

He took the object, which was in a pouch whose softness was a delight to them, and placed it on a rise on the Chamber's floor.

Nothing could have prepared them or anyone for what happened next, glorious and light, potent and powerful, the *musica* turned to something nearly unimaginable in its glory and praise of the Earth and Universe. For the first time in many, many generations the Remnants knew the beauty of all life.

They could not see it, yet glimmerings they caught from the rays of sound of what seemed a sun that shone myriad ways, shot through with the drips of falling water.

Warmth, laziness, a slowing of time, the sounds of earthly life and heavenly delight, all came to the Remnants there.

As for the stranger, he stood before the object for a time before reaching forward and touching it as its power and light came forth and suffused his body outside and within.

Then, weakening, screaming, hurt, frightened, he covered the object up, returned to the edge of the Chamber, and slept.

It was then that the bravest of the brave among the Remnants dared venture near, looking at him through touch and sound rather than mere sound.

He was indeed most beautiful.

'He is the Great One and he has brought us light.'

Slaeke Sinistral, who brought with him the gem of Summer, had searched all Germany for a place like the Chamber below Bochum.

Until 1943 he had lived in the tunnels beneath Hamburg, a hundred miles to the east on the northern coast. Then the bombers came and a firestorm like no other seen before, and the Konzern, which was his business empire, was destroyed.

He and a few survivors set off on an odyssey across a landscape riven by war. In 1945 they came to the Ruhr, heard tales of the Remnants, and Sinistral went to explore the tunnels thereabout.

After human war he found hydden peace.

Gifted with a musician's ear and a mathematician's mind he recognized at once the gentle harmonies as something greater than any music he had ever heard.

Ill, seeking peace, seeking recovery, wondering where he might dare expose himself to the gem of Summer's light, he found the Chamber.

The Remnants he neither heard nor saw, but he sensed they were there and not a hydden folk to be afraid of. Just the opposite.

After, he stood in the subterranean rain.

He let it fall upon his flesh.

He touched the gem to let it do its work before raising his arms in gratitude to feel the healing it had given, which was its potent rejuvenation of himself.

Slaeke Sinistral felt, as well, the Universe.

He had found his true home.

Later, he slept.

When he woke he knew they had been.

There was food, there were warm clothes, there was pure water and much else.

He did not recognize them then as offerings.

No matter, there was harmony and trust between them and he knew, as surely they did too, that he would come again and bring with him the gem whose rays would begin their healing, their return to light, as it healed him too.

Soon after, Sinistral brought his people to Bochum and rebuilt his Empire there, but this time as a community, not just as a business.

The Remnants were left in peace.

The tunnels beyond Bochum, by which the evil hydden of the Ruhr brought destruction, were sealed off and guarded by the Fyrd.

Beneath Bochum an Imperial City came to be.

There the Empire was born.

And now the Emperor was ready to return and rule again.

'Blut! *Blut!?*'

Blut came running.

'What news?'

The Emperor was getting more restive by the day. He was also showing more and more signs of final breakdown. He could sit up now, but his skin was opening into raw red fissures beyond Blut's skill to tend. He could talk and laugh, but sometimes he began a cough that was hard to stop. He could think clearly, even acutely, but his mind drifted to notions of the Universe that seemed to make no sense.

'When you are well, my Lord, and return to the court, you will find you have a new Master of Shadows. You will not be displeased.'

'His name?'

Blut had been saving this item up for just such a moment.

'Witold Slew.'

'Well, now there's a thing!'

'There is a thing indeed, Lord.'

The Master of Shadows was the Emperor's Champion, the wielder of his stave. On formal occasions in the Great Hall, up on Level 2, the Master took a position in front of the Emperor, his guardian and protector. When occasion demanded it he was sent forth, as Champion, to defend the Emperor's rights in single combat or to act as his agent, secretly or otherwise.

The position was not just honorary, but won in combat against the existing Master. Only the greatest masters of the stave ever won the position, and their skill lay in knowing how to shadow-fight.

'Slew! My beloved's firstborn!'

'Yes, Lord, your hopes have been fulfilled. He defeated Otta Kreche before all the Court, fairly.'

'It *would* be fair,' murmured Sinistral.

Kreche had been Master for ten years and seen off many challenges. He and the Emperor were close.

'He has sworn his loyalty to Slew and his fealty to yourself. He enjoys his retirement.'

'Kreche would.'

'He does the practice daily, nurturing the young.'

'That too I would expect. I am well pleased in this and I will see both as soon as I am recovered. Now, about my Lady . . .'

Blut sighed and said apologetically, 'She has been delayed. The Earth, as we now know, is angry. There have been tremors and travelling is difficult.'

'But *she* is safe?'

'I sent Kreche to fetch her; since he is no longer Master of Shadows he had time.'

'Her son Witold Slew was surely more suitable?'

'Mother and son they may be, Lord, but they do not get on.'

'Kreche knows her, likes her, and will see she gets here safe and sound.'

'Just so.'

The Emperor laughed and then coughed painfully.

'She . . . she . . . she was always late,' he said eventually, then added, 'Let us hope she gets here in time to help me.'

'I told her exactly that; I said, "My Lady, this will not do, your"—'

The Emperor held up his hand. 'You scolded her?'

'I did.'

'Never did any good, but thank you all the same. She'll arrive as death takes me and haul me back from its grasp. I knew that from the first.'

'Even so, Lord . . .'

'Even so.'

15

DECISION

Three days after his friends so dramatically discovered he had found the gem of Spring, Stort was summoned to Lord Festoon's Official Residence opposite the Main Library. Brief, Pike and Barklice were already there and others arriving.

Festoon greeted Stort warmly. He was pink-cheeked and well groomed, his dark hair silvering, and he wore a flowing silk robe of grey, with a chain of office in a semicircle across his chest.

Also present was General Meyor Feld, middle-aged, grey-haired and the second in command of the military in Brum, and Captain Backhaus, the young aide-de-camp of Marshal Igor Brunte, leader of the coup against the Fyrd two years before.

The last to arrive had been Igor Brunte himself. He was in his early thirties and had a stocky, well-muscled body. Though his manner was friendly and his expression genial there was menacing glitter in his dark eyes and power and confidence to his movements.

He had been trained as a Fyrd and came originally from Poland, with the stolid stance, strong chin and resolute gaze that Stort associated with hydden from Eastern Europe.

Festoon indicated that they should take their places in easy chairs in his large and elegant salon with refreshments to be served and left available on a sideboard.

'There are many issues to discuss,' he said, 'so I have brought together all those who, I think, may have something useful to contribute. We shall not be disturbed, nor will minutes be taken. Feel free to say, do and eat what you like!'

He turned to Stort.

'Perhaps you can start with an account of the finding of the gem?'

They all leaned forward expectantly.

Stort never did like such meetings and he certainly didn't like this one. To be asked to speak of the gem so publicly felt like a betrayal of something private. In fact his first instinct was to get up and leave, but he realized that this might not be wise. Instead he kept his account of the discovery brief and unemotional, describing what had happened on Waseley Hill in the early hours of the first of May and afterward.

'If I behaved strangely it was because the gem has great power and perhaps I should not have actually touched it, but in the circumstances I had to. I would not recommend anyone else to do so. It is for the Shield Maiden to wear one day and meanwhile we should hide it away out of sight.'

'Excellent, Mister Stort, thank you! Perhaps we could see the gem. I assume you have it with you?'

To Stort such a request seemed too much too soon and he murmured, 'Perhaps later, High Ealdor . . .'

He did his best to pay attention to the discussion that followed, which ranged widely, but he could not get out of his head the notion that their main purpose was to see the gem and handle it, which was the last thing he wanted. Again and again each of them asked to see it; each was refused.

It was when, for the umpteenth time, Stort found himself saying, 'It's for the Shield Maiden to take it from me, gentlemen, her alone,' that Igor Brunte intervened. He reached a hand towards Stort and said, 'Show me the gem, Mister Stort, or I shall have to conclude that you do not have it, never found it and you are wasting my time. That is not something I take lightly or can let go unpunished.'

Stort stared at the hand, which was scarred. It had a mean, grasping look about it.

Stort suddenly closed his eyes, put his hands to his ears, sat humming for a few moments until at last, his decision apparently made, he stood up.

'You all want to see it, that's obvious enough,' he cried, 'and I am reluctant to show it, that's obvious too, which is as much a surprise to me as it is to you. Have I got it? Of course I have!'

With that he dug into his jerkin, felt about, pulled out the leather pouch in which he kept the gem and tossed it on the sideboard.

'You want it, take it! Examine it. Peer at it, caress it, poke it, polish it . . . Discuss its security, value, and Mirror knows what else but . . . but . . . *but* . . . remember that the gem is not mine or yours and least of all is it a committee's.

'The gem of Spring is our heritage. It is a thing of power. It is beauty. It is the fire of life. What it is not is an object to be gawped at and pawed by ex-Fyrd, by Ealdors, by scriveners and stavermen . . . or even by a Marshal, especially one who threatens me! We of Brum, foolish though we must seem to others, do not like to be browbeaten into doing things our instincts tell us we should not.'

He stuffed the pouch back in his jerkin and said, 'I shall now go and hide the gem somewhere safe and I . . . I'll not stay here a moment more!'

With that he headed for the doors.

He had almost reached them when he heard someone say, '*Mister Stort!*'

The voice was so sharp, so strong, so full of command, that it would have stopped a herd of charging elephants. It certainly stopped Stort.

It was Marshal Brunte again.

He was smiling.

'Mister Stort,' he said, very gently now, 'may I ask a question?'

'You may,' said Bedwyn Stort.

'It's a simple question but one which, before you answer it, I wish you to confirm that you will answer truthfully.'

'I must do so I suppose,' said Stort, who perhaps sensed what the question was going to be.

He came back and stood by his seat once more.

'Do you, or do you not, have the gem?' asked Brunte.

'I do.'

'And do you, or do you not, have the gem in that pouch?'

For answer Stort came to the edge of the table, loosened the cords and turned the pouch upside down.

A small nut tumbled onto the table, bounced about and then lay still.

Everyone but Brunte looked utterly astonished.

'Whatever is that?' asked Barklice.

'A cobnut,' said Stort. 'The truth is I have already hidden the gem where no one is likely to find it.'

Everybody looked shocked but for Brunte, who beamed.

He alone had guessed the truth.

'Gentlemen,' he said, 'I think what we have just been witness to is rather more than the spirit of freedom and liberty, and quirky bloody-mindedness, for which Brum is rightly famed throughout the Hydden-world. We have seen demonstrated why the gem of Spring, which certainly would appear to have a mind of its own, has chosen Bedwyn Stort as its guardian. He is clearly a hydden of very remarkable tenacity, cleverness and courage.

'First, he was sensible enough not to bring it with him today. Second, he has been canny enough to resist all attempts to reveal it here. Finally, when his options were all gone, and we had as good as put a knife to his throat, he bluffed us! It seems to me that the time has come for this meeting to stop telling Mister Stort what to do and ask him what he wants *us* to do!'

The Marshal stood up, reached a hand across the table, and shook Stort's vigorously, and rather less painfully, than the first time.

'Now,' continued Brunte after a short recess, 'before Mister Stort addresses us again may I briefly say something more?'

They all sat down again.

'I have heard from various sources that Slaeke Sinistral, Emperor of the Hyddenworld, has in the last week or two woken from his sleep of eighteen years.'

Festoon nodded, Pike too, for he had also been informed.

'It may well be, as Master Brief told me privately only yesterday, that there is a direct connection between the re-emergence of the Emperor into daily life and the discovery by Mister Stort of the gem of Spring. That bodes ill for Brum. I know the Fyrd, I know the Empire and I know the Emperor. They will attack, take the gem and then destroy us. So while Stort here must decide what he is to do about the gem, we who love Brum must plan its defence against the Empire.

'Now, I am neither scholar nor historian, but if I remember the legends about Beornamund's gems right, is it not true that once Spring has made its way into mortal hands it becomes an imperative that the gems of Summer, Autumn and Winter are found as well? Am I right?'

Brief thought for a moment and said, 'It was no accident that Stort found Spring on the first day of Summer. One season leads to another, so do the gems lead on to each other. The Summer gem is surely next in line to be found, and of course the rumours from Bochum, about the Emperor's waking and that he possesses Summer, are well known and I believe well substantiated.'

'The gem's discovery by Stort brings grave danger to this city,' said Brunte. 'There seems little doubt that Sinistral owes his continuing youth to the gem of Summer. But his prolonged rests suggest its power for good is waning with him while its bad effects are increasing. Sinistral will want to gain possession of the gem of Spring to compensate. I suspect he will send the Fyrd to get it. But more than that, if he gets it, then, trust me, in combination with the gem of Summer he will be invincible and in time will gain for himself the gems of Autumn and Winter, wherever they may be.'

'But they could be anywhere,' said Barklice.

'That is true,' said Brief. 'The Peace-Weaver travelled the world in her long life and the gems will not be easy to find. However, now that Spring has been found the other gems will wish to join it. Beornamund made them to be together, not apart. He did so in the knowledge that the day would come when the Universe would have need of the fires they carry within.

'Those fires are for the general good, not to keep a privileged hydden young. Had Spring wished to be found by such a hydden I am sure it would have done so! But it did not. It chose – and I do not use the word lightly – Bedwyn Stort, and I can think of no better choice.'

There was a murmur of agreement.

'So,' said Festoon, leaning back in his chair and looking round the table, 'if we are all content to put our trust in Stort I think we had best ask him what he thinks he should now do. Stort?'

'When Imbolc entrusted me with the gem on Waseley Hill, she did so with the request that it was for her sister the Shield Maiden that I should be its guardian . . . which is all very well, except that I'm not sure I know what a Shield Maiden is! In fact no one does. Which makes it a bit difficult to know exactly what we're meant to do with the gem of Spring while we wait for her to grow up!'

'Is that really true, Master Brief?'

'Oh, yes, Stort's right. The historical record for the Peace-Weaver is huge, for her sister virtually non-existent. There are really three things to think about regarding Shield Maidens, all theoretical, since no one living has ever met one. First, are they a help or hindrance to mortal kind? Second, how long do they live? Third, what do they do?'

He stood up and reached for his stave.

What light glinted in its carvings then, what bright intelligence in his eyes, what compassion in his whole being? In such a mood, with such a flow of words, Brief could be magnificent.

'With respect to the first question, whether or not the Shield Maiden can help us, I believe that she will only be benign so long as we give her what she needs and craves, which is what the gems, and the fires within them, provide. That is why Stort is right to protect the gem against all who seek to divert its power to any end other than that which serves the Shield Maiden.'

He paused and drank some water.

'Next, to the matter of her longevity, a subject much discussed in the literature. If she is to live for fifteen hundred years, as the Peace-Weaver has, then we have a very long period of Earth anger before us, to the end of which none of us in this room will live and about which we can make no useful prediction. On the other hand, if her life is shorter than her sister's, perhaps very much shorter, then it may be that what *we* decide, because of its impact on her for good or ill, will determine the safety or otherwise of mortal kind for all future time. I cannot know how long she will live but I do believe that *we* must act as if the future of all things and perhaps the Universe itself lies in our hands, or more particularly in Bedwyn Stort's.'

He gazed for a few moments on Stort as upon a son who has come of age and must go out into the world. The trust between the two was plain to see.

'Finally,' continued Brief, 'what does she actually *do*, this Shield Maiden of whom we know so little? We know only that in some way she mirrors one aspect of the Earth's existence, as her sister mirrored the other. They are two sides of the same coin, that coin being the Earth. We might refer to war on one hand, peace on the other. Or to disharmony and harmony. Or to imbalance and balance.

'Some thinkers on this subject, including myself, prefer to think of it in terms of *musica universalis*, that exquisite and beauteous universal music that runs through all things, sentient or not. The history of mortal kind and the history of the Earth, which are intertwined, as well as that of the Universe, shows that sometimes even the *musica* loses its way. Its harmony is lost so that for a time all things great and small grow dissonant, harsh, hurtful and most terrible. It is well known that dissonance is quite capable of breaking a glass. Well, gentlemen, imagine it on a universal scale. All would be lost, all things would cease to be, the Mirror-of-All in whose reflection we live our lives would crack and we would be no more.

'My friends, we cannot know the truth of these things but it is in our power to act on our beliefs. Often, for all the logic and reason that scholars like me offer up to the world, it is our inner instincts that matter most. Mine says that from the moment Stort took up the gem he took up a challenge on behalf of all mortal kind. Dissonance is upon us, the Earth's recent violence, which I predict will rapidly get worse, is a symptom. The Shield Maiden must be treated as a friend, but a fearsome and terrible one. We have the gem, she will need it, and frail though we are – and none more willing to admit it than Bedwyn Stort, who has my utmost confidence – we must help him find a way to get it to her in the right way. Are we therefore to wait until she grows to maturity, or give it while still a babe? I do not know. But my instinct is that time is running out and Stort has been chosen by the gem as its finder before all others because it trusts in him.'

With that Brief sat down, took a drink of water and muttered beneath a furrowed brow, 'Mirror help us!'

A long silence followed, broken at last by Stort.

'Every instinct tells me that I should go now to Woolstone to verify that my friend Katherine has, as I think, given birth to a child who is the Shield Maiden. But that is not the only reason for going on that journey. My mission has another purpose.

'It's obvious from all that's been said here that we . . . that is those of us who have the safety of the gem and the life of the Shield Maiden uppermost in our minds . . . have need of leadership. All of you know well enough that that is not and never was my calling.

'I believe, however, that it is Jack's wyrd to be leader in this matter, something you said yourself Master Brief a long time ago. If I'm right in my belief that the Shield Maiden has been born to them, then he is her father. He is also a giant-born, a bold mover between worlds and a warrior. Who better to lead us?

'In the dangerous times ahead for the gem, for his child, for Brum and for the Hyddenworld, we need him. If a way can be found to persuade him to return to us then I must try and find it, which will surely be easier in Woolstone than here . . .'

Pike and Brunte immediately offered to send stavermen and guards with him.

But Stort shook his head.

'This is not a military operation but a personal and delicate one in which we will be dealing not just with Jack but his daughter too,' he said, 'As Master Brief has explained, the Shield Maiden ages differently and more rapidly than mortals, and I expect her to be a good deal older in body and mind than her chronological age would be were she an ordinary mortal.'

'You mean she might not be a babe in arms any more?' asked Pike.

'Exactly. In such circumstances a military presence will seem too fearsome. I need only have Mister Barklice at my side, for he knows what to do when I lose my way or my common sense. Also, he is not intimidating to children, in the way Mister Pike and a few stavermen might be.'

'Oh,' said Barklice faintly, unsure whether to feel flattered or not.

Stort's eyes were gleaming and he looked and sounded better than at any time since he had brought the gem of Spring to Brum.

'We leave for Woolstone tomorrow!' he cried, the decision made.

16
BELOVED

'**M**y Lord Emperor . . . ?'

'Blut?' he said softly, drifting back to wakefulness and a gentle, scented, calm. Candles had been placed about his chair. Pine needles smouldered in a bowl, their forest scent a reminder of his youth. Water in a glass as clear as a mountain stream stood ready for him to drink. He felt much loved.

Blut was there. He said, 'She is in Bochum, Lord.'

'She has been *here* I think,' he said, gesturing with pleasure towards the candles and water.

'She came and went, not wishing to wake you. She will be back quite soon.'

'Did she look well?'

'My Lady looked as she always does, quite beautiful.'

Slaeke Sinistral nodded and smiled.

'She has always seemed to me most beautiful, from the first time I ever saw her . . .'

In 1966, two decades after Sinistral brought his people to Bochum from Hamburg and turned his business into an empire, an odd incident occurred in the Great Hall on Level 2, where the daily business of Empire was conducted.

A citizen of the Empire, a woman from distant Thuringia very near her time with child, had bravely come to Bochum, alone, to petition the Emperor himself on Midsummer's Day, when such individuals were permitted to take such action.

Normally the occasion was a festive one for courtiers, the claimants being carefully picked, their petitions easily granted. How the woman got past officials no one knew, but there she was, before the Emperor's throne, speaking clearly and well and justly bringing attention to an abuse by the Fyrd, which was rarely heard.

Unfortunately the stress of her long journey, the tussle she had with courtiers and officials to be heard, and perhaps finding herself in the presence of the Emperor himself, brought her suddenly into labour, right there, right then.

The Court officials did not know what to do, the courtiers were horrified, and the then Master of Shadows took up the Imperial Stave as if the Emperor was being attacked.

Meanwhile the woman screamed her labour through, sun streamed in upon the strange, unexpected scene, and the Hall suddenly echoed with a baby's cries.

All might have been well and the incident laughed off, but that shortly afterwards, her loss of blood too great, the mother died. No petition for help and continuing support could ever have been more articulate than that.

The child, a girl, was made a ward of Court at once, a wet nurse was found, and enquiries put in hand to establish what family and kin she had in Thuringia. They took time and produced no satisfactory result. The child was, effectively, an orphan without even extended family.

Meanwhile the Emperor took a personal interest in the case, perhaps because in all his long years he had never been able to father a child nor been witness to birth itself.

'What's her name?' he had asked a few days after she was born.

'She has none, my Lord, and who now is there to give it but yourself?'

He did not pick her up, but looked down at the bright thing, too young yet to even squirm, or smile. She could stare, and did so, and open up a finger or two. The dancing, the singing, the laughter that came later, the maddening play and sudden disappearances; the silences and the reappearances, returning with eyes wide as if to say she never went away – and the dangerous curiosity in things that were never her business – these were yet to come.

Before all that wondrous journey into life had begun he looked at her again and said impulsively, 'Why not call her . . . '

Names flashed through his mind: his mother's? Vile! His sister's? No! Anybody? No one offered theirs and he was not good at names. He turned to Slolte Kreche, a Fyrd he trusted.

'Give me a name,' he said.

'Anna.'

'Dull.'

'Lizbet.'

'No.'

Kreche frowned. He was running out of names.

'What's your grandmother's name?'

'Um . . . er . . . Margretta, I think. She came from the south.'

'Margret then,' said the Emperor. 'Call her that!'

They did, but it never suited her and she never liked it.

Whatever else she was, she was not a Margret.

One day, aged eleven, by then the Emperor's adoptive child and a free spirit in the Court and corridors of Bochum, running with the boys but weeping and wailing and already putting it on when it suited her, she stood up at her birthday feast and announced, 'From now on everybody, my name is . . . '

She paused because people were talking and she wished them to hear. She stood in silence, staring down the noisy ones, looking serious until silence reigned.

She had the power to do that, even then. Fair, well made, cheerful, smiling, blue-eyed and challenging.

'My new name, which everyone will use because if you don't I will never talk to you again and if you use Margret I will kill you very slowly with my hairpins, my name is . . . '

She looked about the Hall, up into the shadows of the roof, down along the shafts of afternoon light, at the dancing flames of the candles on her cake, at the smiling people all about, because already she was loved.

'My name is . . . '

The Court and its Emperor waited with bated breath.

She shook her head with irritation, caught out and unready by her own impulse and realizing whatever name she chose would stick, so it had better be good.

She sighed, dramatically, looked at the shafts of sunlight once again and moved from her place next to Sinistral and went to stand in their warmth. The light caught in her fair hair, shone on her party frock, played among the ribbons she loved.

'My name is Leetha,' Leetha said.

My Lord Sinistral rose up, a golden goblet in his hand, and proposed a toast: 'To Leetha who, her mother gone, her father unknown, has finally named herself. Any who calls her by any other name will have me to answer to!'

He was laughing too, but when he sat down his expression darkened, his eyes glanced to his hands, whose skin was breaking up again, his nails already thickening and ugly.

He hid his hands and said to no one but himself, 'Why Leetha? Why that name? What's in her wyrd that I don't know?'

She danced back to her place.

'Do you like my name?' she asked.

'Yes, I do.'

'Call me it.'

'Yes, I do, er . . . Leetha.'

'Do you like *him*?'

She pointed at a courtier's son who was mouthing words at her.

'What's he saying?' asked Sinistral.

'Margret, Margret, Margret, but I won't kill him because I love him.'

'I won't either then,' he whispered.

'Why have you hidden your hands, my Lord?' she asked.

'I think I may have to leave you for a time . . .'

'Does it hurt, being old?'

'Yes.'

'A lot?'

'Sometimes.'

'Is it getting worse again?'

No one else spoke to him like that, no one ever had.

'I'm afraid it is.'

'Everyone wants to know your cure. They say you hide away and drink an elixir made by ancient gods. Then you wait a bit until it works and emerge again looking young.'

'Do they?'

She stared at him quizzically, saying nothing. He wondered where she got her looks, her joy. It was something he once had, which he had lost.

'*So*, is it an elixir?'

'Something like that, I suppose.'

'Will you tell me what it is one day?'

It was a moment of truth.

He had wondered if he ever would tell her, or tell anybody. Now, at that moment, he finally knew he would. If he was going to die, someone should know. Leetha was . . .

Leetha was . . .

He was astonished her new name had embedded itself in his mind so fast, but then, he had to agree with her, Margret was not the best of names and its choosing had been offhand and disrespectful of her newborn life.

Leetha as a name was as good as any other and better than most. Now it was her name. It had just been waiting for its owner to discover it.

'Do you know what it means?' he asked her.

She shook her head.

'You chose well. It's a word from Englalond, the country of my birth, used long ago in Beornamund's time.'

'So, what does it mean?'

'Midsummer,' he said, 'which is the day you were born.'

Leetha came to him in the Chamber at last, her hand to his.

'My Lord,' she began.

'Leetha . . .' he continued.

Their conversations never seemed to cease, continuing seamlessly where they left off, the first time in his long life that Slaeke Sinistral knew what it felt like to be loved simply for himself, his real self, whoever that might be.

'You look worse than I have ever seen you,' she said. 'Disgusting really. I got here just in time.'

'You did. Tomorrow, I think I must submit to the gem's power once more . . .'

'Tomorrow, definitely. I have told Blut that. I've even told the Remnants, not that I needed to. They know. They're terrified you're going to die. But happy they will know the gem's light once more.'

'I'm the one who should be terrified.'

'We'll be here, the two who love you, Blut and me. We'll see you through it.'

They sat in companionable silence.

'Blut says that your son Witold Slew has become Master of Shadows,' said Lord Sinistral.

'He can become whatever he likes. I do not like him and he does not like me.'

'Well, I like him . . . and I wish to see him.'

'Now, Lord, before your trial?'

'I might die. He *is* your son. I wish to see him . . . *Blut!*'

Not long after, Witold Slew was ushered in.

He was tall, taller even than the Emperor in his prime. His black Fyrd uniform, of leather in parts and of the highest quality and cut, contrasted with the near-white-blond of his neat, greased hair. He had pale skin, black eyes and the glittering cold beauty of a cut diamond.

Court gossip was scurrilous but mistaken regarding the connection between Slew and the Emperor – their similarity of height and hair was chance.

The chair had been swung round.

Light flooded over the Emperor's hideous form.

Blut whispered to Slew, 'He does not see as well as he once did. You will be a blur to him.'

'I wish,' said Slaeke Sinistral, his voice a little slurred, his eyes weeping yellow pus, 'that I could see you better. But I cannot. So I must rely on words and on the *musica*. Look on me, Witold Slew, look on me hard and long . . .'

Slew, who towered over Blut as well, examined the Emperor coldly, dispassionately, without expression.

The music of the rain played around them.

Among the skeins of mist shapes wound and unwound.

The air grew cold.

'What do you see?' asked the Emperor.

'Decay,' said Slew.

'Who do you see?'

'He who was Emperor but, for now, is only so in name. I hope—'

'I am not interested in your hopes,' said Sinistral sharply, 'but in your education. Who taught you to fight so well?'

Slew named his teacher.

'The best,' said the Emperor. 'Did he tell you that I taught him?'

The first flicker of an expression in Slew's eyes: surprise, then respect.

'Who else do you see, apart from an Emperor?'

Slew hesitated.

'As I am Master of Shadows, so I see my Lord to whom I owe life and loyalty before all.'

'Good. And as Master you shall follow the command I now give you which, whatever may happen to me on the morrow, you will see through to the end. Understood?'

Slew nodded.

'So . . . my orders are simple enough. They are to be acted on at once. I want you out of Bochum and heading for the coast within the hour . . . time is precious. Blut here will give you the details.

'I command you to journey to Englalond and bring back the one thing it has which I need. Blut will tell you what that is. Be speedy, be resolute, if you must kill to get that object, then kill, but do so sparingly.'

Slew nodded.

The interview seemed over.

The Emperor's eyes were closing.

But as Blut led Slew out Sinistral called out, 'Witold, you should know that I am pleased with you but . . . why is it your mother is . . . wary of you?'

'She dislikes me, Lord.'

'Why?'

He shrugged indifferently.

'She told me once but I did not know what she meant.'

'What did she say?'

'That I have no compassion.'

'She's right. I can feel it like a cold breeze. You will need to find it one day.'

'Why, my Lord Emperor?'

'You'll know why, just as I did, only in the moment that you find it; for your sake, I hope it will not be too late. You accept the command of your Emperor?'

'I do. What is this thing that I must bring back to you?'

'Nothing much, just a little stone, that is all. Blut will explain. He knows about such things. He has studied them . . . Trust him, as I do.'

As he left, Leetha came from where she had been eavesdropping.

'I like him, my love.'

'I do not.'

'You will. Now, your other son, Leetha, the one due as I went into my latest sleep. How is he?'

'Didn't Blut tell you? I gave him up for his own good. He's gone. You would not have liked him.'

'Why not?'

'You like perfection and he was a giant-born. The Fyrd chased us because you were not there to protect me and Blut had not then found his feet in power. They would have killed him.'

'What's his name?'

'I don't know.'

'My love . . . what is it?'

She buried her head in his weak chest. His hand went slowly to her head and caressed her hair. He could bear his pain much better than he could hers.

'What is it?'

She wept.

'My beloved, whatever is it?'

'I miss him, he was so beautiful. I gave up the thing I treasured most because I loved him too well.'

He sighed, weak from the effort of responding to her tears.

'Witold knew it, hence his anger. But . . . what's a mother to do? Be thankful you have only me to worry about, my Lord!'

'Leetha, go away . . . If I am to hold the gem tomorrow I must sleep again today.'

'Don't be afraid,' she said before, looking down at him with love, she kissed him on his ruined head.

But he did not sleep and nor did she go away.

Leetha was so worried by the Emperor's state of mind that she dozed on a palliasse in the cold, damp quarters of the office Blut had made his own, adjacent to the Chamber of Sleep. Blut himself slept in his own room nearby, the doors all open. That way they could hear the Emperor's mutterings in the dark, his cries through the broken rain, his sobs, his pain.

'Blut!'

She roused him from sleep.

'My . . . my Lady?'

'He wants something we cannot give him.'

She had been up and sat with him and he talked to her, asking for something.

Together they hurried to his side.

'I am afraid I may have too little strength left to survive the gem's scorching power, Blut, and I am afraid I will never see the world again. I have been too long in this dark in which there is not night or day.'

'My Lord,' Leetha whispered, 'there are but a few hours to go until we can begin. The Remnants take things slowly, they will be ready then.'

He reached for her hand, he shook his head, he wept.

'Is it night up there in the real world?'

'It is, but—'

'I want to see the stars.'

'We cannot take you there, my Lord, it will kill you,' said Blut.

'If I cannot even see the stars when I wish to, what is it that I am the Emperor of? Eh? *Eh!?*'

The Emperor of the Hyddenworld moaned in his agony.

'I . . . want . . . to . . .'

Leetha made a decision.

'Fetch Kreche, Blut,' said Leetha. '*Now!*'

'Lord . . . my Lady!'

'Help me, Blut. Tomorrow I may die, tonight . . . I . . . want . . .'

'My beloved,' said Leetha, stroking his gaunt cheek and wiping his dribbling mouth and eyes, 'it is all right, we'll take you where you need to go. It will give you strength for the morrow.'

Otta Kreche, once the Emperor's Master of Shadows, still his friend, was brought into the Chamber by Blut.

He was a huge hydden, old now but strong, with arms and hands like the branches of an oak.

He had seen his Lord sick and ill many times, but never as he was now. He looked at him and wept.

'My friend, I want to see the stars,' said Sinistral.

Kreche, who was a father and grandfather and knew how to be gentle, bent down and eased his hands and arms under the skin and bones that were all his Lord Emperor was.

He picked him up like a sick child and cradled him.

Leetha put a blanket over him, Blut another.

They covered his head with a corner of the soft material.

Blut went ahead to the old lift shaft that was the only way to the surface from Level 18. The space was narrow but they all squeezed inside. As the lift jerked its way up, the Emperor's head resting against Kreche's chest, the movement was painful, his moans very pitiful.

But up they went, level by slow level, clanketing their way to the surface of the Earth, up into the cold night air.

'Do not drop me, Kreche, do not let me fall . . .'

'No, Lord.'

They moved outside.

The night sky, all stars and moon, stretched away for ever and for ever. My Lord Emperor reached a hand to touch it, laughing with joy, crying with pain.

'It is so beautiful,' he said. 'Listen!'

'What can you hear?' asked Kreche.

'The *musica*, my friend, I hear the *musica*, it is the starshine in my eyes, it is the cold air on my face, it is the strength of your arms and the touch of my beloved. And Blut . . . ?'

'My Lord?'

'The *musica* is you as well. Can you not hear it?'

They stood listening to the night beneath the stars of Bochum.

'It is everything and everywhere,' he said.

'It is you as well,' said Leetha.

They listened more until, at last, a shiver of cold ran among them.

'I am ready to sleep now,' he said. 'Tomorrow . . .'

'Tomorrow is already come,' said Blut.

17

DANGEROUS MILESTONE

'At three,' shouted Arthur above the noise of the tantrum that Judith was having on the kitchen floor, 'he or she, as they put it, is capable of holding a crayon and drawing a face, putting on a coat and taking it off again, using a spoon without spilling – very funny – and . . . *of having a tantrum.*'

Katherine picked Judith up with some difficulty as she continued to kick and scream loud enough that their eardrums felt the strain, and handed her back to Jack.

'She can do all those things,' she said. 'She can also walk, talk, have imaginary friends and pedal the tricycle . . .'

'And steer it . . . *can't you?*'

Jack grinned up at Judith suspended in the air and she, red-faced, stared back furiously and tried to kick him.

Her appearance had improved. She still looked odd but now acceptably so. Her hair was dark like Jack's. Her eyes were brown, her mouth quite full, her nose snubby, her skin darker than light, her chin firm and her face capable of all kinds of expressions including a smile, though that was a very rare event.

Her face also showed her suffering.

For she was still in constant pain, which was worse at night. So she did not sleep well and looked tired.

Her teeth, briefly uncomfortable for Katherine, were strong and white. She still breast-fed, which to Margaret seemed strange in so large a child, even distasteful, but so it was. Great big gurgling sucks, her legs kicking with pleasure as she took them, her strong hands pulling at Katherine's nursing bra, heaving her blouses out of shape.

For her part, and they were a symbiotic pair when it came to feeding, Katherine ate like a horse: anything and everything, without discrimination. Shopping – which Margaret and Arthur had always done in a slow, bumbly sort of way, arguing over every item, toying with things organic, hesitating over cola, which Margaret liked, and pondering the lettuces since Margaret grew them better – shopping had become a nightmare.

At first she had bought too little.

Then she bought too little of what the rest of them wanted, because Katherine ate it.

Now – and this was in the space of less than a fortnight – they piled the junk food in that Katherine demanded, racing round the supermarket to get back home and help.

As Katherine wolfed things down it sometimes felt, as Judith reached out her hands for a hoist up and eagerly latched on, that she was sucking it right back out there and then. The two were inseparable in bed, Jack ousted to the nursery as once was, but not put out by the fact. He slept on the floor, a habit he had gained when he was in the Hyddenworld and to which he now happily returned.

Beds – 'human' beds as he thought of them – were too soft for him. For him, too, the Hyddenworld was still a place just over there, almost reachable. Not so for Katherine. She had returned home, had a child, and all that past seemed a distant thing, like an unimportant memory.

It was not that coming back through the broken henge at the Devil's Quoits had wiped her mind clean of the Hyddenworld so much that it had shifted her perspective and priority. It no longer mattered. It was over and done. Had she been asked – which Jack was careful not to do – she would have said she had no wish to go back because she had no need to. She might have worried that she was even asked the question, thinking that Jack did want to go back.

Naturally he didn't. His priority was Judith now, and Katherine, his family. But . . .

But sometimes he stared out of their bedroom window, down towards the henge, and felt the call of that place where he had been born, a world that felt richer to him and more real than the human one, even after what had now happened.

He knew where he needed and wanted to be, but the draw to return was there and the henge as well . . . a door of a kind that had been in his unconscious all his life but was only made real by journeying through it. The door remained open and he knew it would always be so, but it was impossible to imagine any circumstance that would make him want to return.

Jack placed Judith carefully back on the kitchen floor and said, 'So, she's effectively something more than three years old and we're going to have to make some plans for her own safety . . .'

The demands Judith's existence made on them were endless.

'Do we assume she's mentally three as well?'

'Dada,' said Judith, smashing her fists into his shins and thighs, 'garden.'

Arthur looked at the sheet of information he had printed from the internet.

'Let me see . . . "takes joy in family mealtimes" . . . hmmm . . . "takes joy in assisting you when tidying up" – *what!?* . . . "heads for friends when sees them" . . . she hasn't got any . . . wait a minute, that's under social development. "Can name three shapes", yes; "can count up to ten", sort of . . . yes, Jack, I think we can take it that Judith is developing mentally as well.'

'Garden!' said Judith, kicking him again, but harder.

'And that she can communicate.'

'Seriously, Arthur. She's going to start roaming and we could lose her. In the house that's manageable, outside it could be a disaster. She might get hurt.'

'I'll make a list of prevention and containment measures,' said Katherine, who though still existing on very little sleep was already beginning to recover her strength and spirits.

It was agreed.

'Come on!' Jack said to Judith, 'you can get to the garden yourself, but once you're there we don't want you getting lost.'

Judith followed Jack out, reverting to half crawling, half walking and banging and shouting, to show she wanted to be carried.

But Jack had said no and she was learning that his 'no' was final. Then they were gone, leaving the kitchen in peace for a time.

18

SUMMER

It was time and the Emperor lay waiting in his chair as still as death.

The Remnants had set up candlelights, which hung like soft moons in the misty rain. They themselves were nowhere to be seen.

The forms of the lime-ridden engine and winding gear and the other shapes and voids in the Chamber were hard to make out, looming up here, falling away there, and adding to the feeling of uncertainty and fear in the air.

Blut saw that near to the chair, beyond the canopy, was a lime-covered mound about three feet high. It was not so obscured that its detail was entirely lost. It was mortal-made, a stand to hold something on, with three thick legs, also covered in lime. At its base, clean and shiny, lay some mining tools: two large hammers, a pickaxe, an axe and a huge pair of cast-iron tongs of the kind used in steel making to hold containers of red-hot boiling metal.

'You can't see the Remnants but they're here,' whispered Leetha, her hand on Blut's shoulder to give reassurance.

'My Lady, are you sure I—'

'You should be here, he wants you to be. He trusts you as he trusts the Remnants and myself. The journey he is about to make is more painful even than the one he made when waking back to our world. He needs to know he has support.'

She went to the Emperor's side and called to Blut at once.

'Bring that candle, yes, no more light than that! Hurry.'

They could see that Sinistral was finally dying.

His eyes were closed, his head had fallen to one side, his mouth sagged horribly open and from his throat and nasal passages came the beginnings of a stentorian rattle, the last few breaths.

'My Lord,' she said, taking his right hand, 'stay with us for a few moments longer . . . Stay . . .'

He stirred, the rattling slowed, the breathing stopped, he jerked awake, the candlelight flickering in eyes that overnight had turned white and blind.

'My Lord, can you hear me?'

Blut took the other hand.

'*My Lord* . . .' Her voice was a sob.

The Emperor's hand squeezed Blut's, who nodded at Leetha.

The Emperor stirred and said in a whisper, 'Do not leave me, I do not want to be alone. I am afraid of ã Faroün, that he will come and punish me, I am afraid.'

'We will not leave you, my beloved, and he will not come,' she said.

'I fear him . . .'

'He is dead, Lord, long-since dead . . .'

To Blut this seemed a strange diversion at such a moment. The name they spoke had been the Emperor's mentor when a boy. From him he had gained the gem. Why would he be frightened of his return? Such questions Blut always asked, for information was power and fear was a tool.

Leetha grasped his arm.

'Listen and listen well, Niklas Blut,' she said. 'You must stay and you shall watch but try not to look too long into the gem's light. Fortunately its greatest power for good and ill is transmitted only through touch, but even so, be cautious. It can change objects and artefacts but will only affect you if you touch it.'

'Lady . . .' he began again, doubtfully, not wanting to stay.

'No, it is right that you bear witness to what he must suffer if he is to return to us.'

'I have seen already, my Lady.'

'You have not seen this.'

'My Lady, why is he so fearful of ã Faroün?'

'It is nothing, an old fancy, ignore it and forget it, do you hear? There are more important things than that!'

Her irritation made him more curious still. Blut's mind was a filing cabinet. He would not forget.

She turned back to Sinistral and whispered, 'Ready yourself for what must be, for the time is now and we who love you are close by your chair. When the gem is given to you, grasp it in one hand and then grasp that hand with the other. In that I will help you. You must not let it go.'

Together they turned his chair and raised it so that he was more upright, facing out into the Chamber and its glimmering moons. Blut guessed that the stand by which the implements lay, and which was no more than a few yards away, was what the gem would be placed upon.

'Move the lantern ... yes, to there,' she said, pointing to the hammers by the lime-clad mound.

He went and did so.

'Good. Now, help me bind him to the chair.'

'My Lady—'

'Do it, there is little time. It will be necessary.'

Blut pulled the leather straps over the Emperor's arms and legs.

'Tighter!' she said.

He buckled them tight, though the Emperor protested with slight movements and terrible, tortured whines.

'And this over his forehead. Help me!'

This too Blut did.

Sinistral cried.

'Now,' she said softly, 'make sure his hands and arms can move, so he can hold the gem. So ... it is done ... Stay here, hold fast whatever may happen, keep the chair in place and facing this way.'

'It has a lock,' he said, 'at the base, which I think will—'

'*Do it*. There is no more time . . .'

She left him then, going round the chair, beyond the mound and hammers, out into the Chamber. The rain had stopped, or simply turned into the finest of mists.

Light caught the flow of her dress, it played at its ribbons, as if they were mirrors, reflecting bright red and green, blue and yellow, great flashes of colour time after time, briefly illuminating the murk.

She danced a slow dance, she sang a song of greeting and encouragement.

What Blut then saw he was not sure.

Shapes certainly, movement possibly, pale hydden, thin as wraiths, now here, now there, timid as deer in a forest.

He heard her laugh.

He heard the echo of her laugh.

And then he heard the tramp, tramp, tramp of feet.

She retreated and stood with her hand on the back of the chair with Blut.

'Now is the time!' she said, leaning forward to whisper in the Emperor's ear. 'Now you will live again.'

The answer the Emperor gave was a half scream, his eyes wild and pleading. 'Naaahhhh!' he said.

The tramp of feet grew louder, the Remnants having been summoned by Leetha's dance and song. Blut saw them come out of the darker recesses of the Chamber, four great brutes of things, giants compared to the creatures he saw before; bilgesnipe stock by the look of them.

Their eyes white, opaque orbs, shot through with the colours that Leetha wore which were, Blut realized, all the colours of a bright summer's day. Blind though they were they knew exactly where to come, heading straight for the stand and each taking up one or other of the tools.

'It is time, my love, time . . .' she said, 'and I am here. Blut is here . . .'

The white skin of the Emperor's face was taut, his eyes now terrified, his breathing very fast and nervous.

The giant Remnants began circling the stand, tools in hand, their booted feet heavy on the ground. The two with hammers suddenly stepped nearer, ranged themselves close to the stand, raised their hammers up and suddenly, massively, began to bring them down . . . bang! bang! bang! bang!

One after the other they struck, rhythmically.

Blut's ears began to ring with the sound, which was that of metal on the hardest rock, the ringing a reverberation that grew ever more powerful, insistent, gaining a life and rhythm of its own.

The Emperor suddenly jerked, his mouth opening with a terrible shout.

'Nah! Naaaahh!'

Then the chair begin to shake and move as he tried to lever himself out of it and get away.

'NaaaaaaaaaaaaaaaaaAAAAAAAAAhhhhh!'

The hammering continued, though the heavy blows appeared to have no effect on the surface of the lime. The ringing sound became a horrible pulse as the Emperor's screams grew louder still before they changed to soft pleadings, 'Oh . . . naaah . . . naaah . . . naaaah!'

The hammering stopped and the Remnant giants stood in silence before the lime for a few moments before they all moved even nearer to it, hulking around it, touching it, one even bending down to put his ear to it.

Silence reigned but for, somewhere, the moaning of a tunnel wind and of the Emperor.

The Remnants pulled back and stared at the mound again, waiting, until one of them pointed at it, another bent closer, a third turned to the Chamber as if to an audience and shouted a word, a warning perhaps.

The one with the pickaxe came forward, raised it, and brought it down hard.

Crack!

He had trouble getting it back out, the point having penetrated the hard surface. Another Remnant moved to help him and together they worked the pickaxe clear.

It was brought down hard again.

The rock split, its crack like thunder across the sky. Bits fell away to reveal that what was beneath was a box-like metal casing standing on three massive legs that went deep into the ground. Two more blows took off the rest of the lime.

The casing was made of strips of woven, riveted steel, the box was hexagonal, its top coming to a shallow point formed by six sides, linked with a loop of steel through which, holding them together, was threaded a massive padlock.

Some of the encrustation was still attached to this strange object and one of the Remnants took his hammer and tapped it gently off until the container, on its legs, stood free.

The Emperor was still and silent now, head to one side listening, blind eyes and face filled with fear.

'Na . . . aaaahhh,' he whispered.

Blut guessed that the worst was yet to come.

The giants examined the padlock with their hands, feeling it, trying it, sniffing it, licking it, shaking their heads and muttering gruffly to each other about it.

The Emperor arched his back, contorted his hands, tried to turn his head and stare at Blut.

'Naa . . .' he rasped.

It seemed he preferred death to the pain of life to come.

One of the Remnants took a cord from his neck to which was attached an enormous key. He tried it in the lock but shook his head.

It had rusted, and was impossible to open.

They consulted, their bodies melding into one, their great arms and legs and hands around the handles of the hammers. Eventually, agreement was reached.

Again they all stood back but for the one who had the axe.

One of the others left the group and went across the Chamber to where a great triangle of metal had been hung.

He looked back, waited for a call from the others, and when it came began banging the triangle urgently with his hammer. The sound was louder by far than the earlier singing of the hammers on the rock. Blut had to shield his ears, Leetha too.

The Emperor struggled and screamed most pitifully.

Blut guessed that this was a signal of some kind to the ordinary Remnants, wherever they were, perhaps to tell them what was about to happen. Whatever it was, the Remnant striking the triangle seemed suddenly sure he had done his job, because he stopped and the ringing sound, pulsing still, slowly died away.

When it was gone Blut had never known such a silence as remained. It pressed into his ears, right inside his head, until what he heard, as he thought, were a hundred thousand sounds he had forgotten that he had heard before: his mother's call, his sister's song, the scurry of a creature in the grass, a curlew's call he heard but once, and the running of rain in a gutter in Hamburg when he took up his post as clerk.

These began to fade and he felt their loss even as he remembered in a rush of fragmented memory all the other sounds they reminded him of, and the memories of those.

They had a common theme: he had heard them all in Summer and the last was a skylark's trill and the soft rill of the river he knew as a boy, right to that Summer's end, after which he never heard them more.

Then all he could hear, if sound it was, was the fall of the axe the Remnant wielded as he brought it down to break the padlock that held the casing of what it was the Emperor feared, yet had wanted so much to know again . . .

Bang!

The padlock broke apart and the six sides of the casing it had held together fell open like the petals of a Summer flower.

There, so long in the dark within the dark, was a small gem. It was pale yellow, faceted but seemingly dull and lying by itself on a rusted metal surface.

The thin mist in the air swirled about it, condensing on its surface before it appeared to carry on inside, round and round, turning to a lurid internal fire that began to flare and spark. This fire, or light, though not yet bright, shone out upon the faces and blind eyes of the Remnants, who stared at it as if they could see it, their eyes taking on its pale yellows and life as they had taken to themselves the colours of Leetha's ribbons earlier.

But just as Blut was thinking it a gentle thing, soft in its colours, slow in its ways, the stone shot forth a beam of light like no other he had ever seen. Its speed was lightning, its width no greater than a hydden's head, its colour white and dancing yellow shifting into green and blue.

It was intense and purposeful.

This beam of light went straight at the Emperor's face, and when it reached it another shot forth and hit him in the chest. Then a third, bigger than the first two, hit his whole body and his chair like a great fist's blow.

The chair shot back, the Emperor cried out, Blut felt the beam or beams of light smash into his face and push him sideways, spinning him away so hard that, had his grip on the Emperor's chair not been strong, he would have lost hold of it altogether. Only with Leetha's help did he regain his position as beam after beam of light pulsed out from the gem until there were too many to count.

'Now!' he heard Leetha cry. 'Now you must hold firm and keep the chair as it is.'

Then: 'My Lord,' she cried, 'be ready to take up the gem!'

How the Emperor was going to do this despite the fact he was strapped down to the chair became suddenly clear.

One of the Remnants picked up the long-handled tongs by the stand, and with the help of another, raised them over the gem. Though they were thick, clumsy things the Remnants moved them with delicacy and skill, picking up the gem with no more difficulty than if they were plucking a berry from a bush.

Then, the tongs suddenly heavier it seemed, they moved as one towards the Emperor, the gem's rays myriad lights that came and went over everything, and proffered it to him.

Blind though he was he seemed to see it.

'Naaaah!' he cried again, trying to pull back.

Leetha reached a hand to his arm.

'Take it, my love, grasp it, dare to live again!'

He did so and she helped him put his other hand on the first so that the gem was his to hold in both hands.

'Now!' she cried.

The Remnants fell back, the tongs tumbled to the ground and the Emperor became the centre of a storm of light, cool at first but soon quite warm, changing colour as it went, roaring as it soared to the highest, furthest, deepest corners of the Chamber of Sleep.

Then, right before Blut's eyes, all changed.

What was dark was light.

What had been wet now steamed.

What was dull began to shine.

The encrustations of lime upon the objects about them withered and fell to dust and what lay beneath, whether of metal or wood, its rust or rot very plain to see, was suddenly renewed as if it were fresh cast or made.

In the midst of this rapid, overwhelming change in things, not blinding so much as enlightening, the Emperor too began to change. Blut could scarcely believe what he saw.

The nearest part of the Emperor to Blut was his hair, which, though Leetha had washed and cleaned it, had been thin and grey, barely able to cling on to his scaly scalp. The hair thickened and grew glossy and blond before his eyes while the Emperor's arms struggled at their straps, his withered body gaining strength, his cries deepening as he regained his youthful voice, his skin filling, his lines smoothing.

Blut might have continued to watch this transformation had not something else entirely taken his attention, or rather overtaken his mind. He could not tell if it was real or not, though it certainly seemed so.

The Chamber was suddenly filled with what looked like elongated shards of glass or mirror, passing at speed before his eyes in rows, or groups of rows, but turning slowly, spiralling together and away and then returning to cross through other such groups of shards. Their centre was the gem, their pattern complex, their intermingling of form and colour extremely beautiful and the sound they made so exquisite that he could scarcely breathe.

Musica, he told himself, *universalis*.

It was not just sound he heard but, as it seemed, the shards at front and back as well, as they turned separately and together, paper-thin.

One after another they flowed, in their hundreds, their thousands perhaps; the reflections that each held were a glimpse of moments of Blut's past Summers, like the memories he had earlier, now made more intense and real. Wherever he looked he saw an old memory, whatever he heard seemed like the music of his life for good and for ill.

The flight of a bee when he was a child, late blossom scattered in early Summer winds, blood flowing from a cut, the sunshine bright in the blood, his sister again, falling, falling into a clear stream on a Summer's day. With these moments of memory came the feelings that went with them, most happy, some sad, some exciting, a few dull.

He stared at this fragmented world of his own Summers, never seeing himself but once, in a mirror, dark-eyed, a hand rising into green leaves and the cooing of a dove in the wood in which he roamed.

'Niklas! Niklas!' he heard her call, that Summer, when he was thirteen, wondering . . . before he turned to her and touched her hand.

This stream of a thousand fragments turned and swooped like a flock of starlings across the Bochum sky, each one real, each there before him now as it had been then.

Until, the vision darkening, he was astonished to see another stream of mirror shards, reflections, of summers not his own: the Emperor's? Leetha's? He had no idea. He reached towards them and they drove through his hand, swept through his mind, caught him up until he tried to hold the Emperor's chair but no longer could and he felt himself flattening, turning, his body reflecting what it saw, which was the Emperor in his chair, threshing, struggling, strong now, laughing, the chair turning into the light, the shards, and Blut himself a shard, becoming a thousand shards, each different from the other, each a memory of that chair, some dark, some with no light at all, the Emperor's time of sleep. Then the old Emperor was gone and his young self returned, his trial over, back to the Summer of his life again.

'Blut?'

He opened his eyes out of images of sunlight to the dark of the Chamber once more.

'*Niklas!*'

He struggled to stand and looked up into eyes dark and beautiful. He smelt her smell, which was the good scent of Summer.

She smiled on him.

'Thank you,' she said, 'the Emperor is himself again.'

The Chamber was in darkness, the moon lights gone, the straps of the chair broken, the air warm and filled with the throb of life and abundant scents of summer.

The Emperor took his hand and looked at him with eyes as beautiful as they had always been, his hair thick and wild, a field of wheat blown by a June-time breeze.

'Blut, my friend, you have done well.'

The eyes smiled, the mouth was firm, the cheek bronzed, the body strong, the hands as hands should be of a hydden in his prime.

'But now you have work to do.'

Blut tried to focus, to work out where he was.

He tried to make sense of the vision that stood before him, which was no vision at all, but real.

'Go and tell them, Blut, that their Emperor has returned.'

'My Lord . . . Lady . . .' he said breathlessly.

They stood before him, shining with health.

'Is it . . . have you . . . are we . . . ?'

'Yes,' said Slaeke Sinistral I, Emperor of the Hyddenworld, 'my trial is over, your job here is done, I have returned. Go now, tell my people their good news!'

'I will, my Lord, I will . . .'

Yet up on Level 2, approaching the Great Hall through an excited throng which already sensed that their Emperor was well again, Blut felt strangely sad.

He remembered the sick old Emperor he had got to know through the strange weeks past: impatient, quick, courageous, pained, funny, as real as real can be. Blut wondered where exactly he had gone and why he missed him.

He remembered too the flight through the vast space of the Chamber of all his Summer times, fragments that lightened a dark place, moments gone.

He entered the Great Hall, strode its length as the courtiers fell silent and turned, smiling at them.

'Your Emperor . . .' he began.

As he spoke these words and they began to cheer, and trumpets sounded the Emperor's arrival, his beloved on his arm, Blut heard words again inside spoken by their mother that Summer when his sister died and he suffered the first hard tears of life: *Enjoy things while you can, my love, for Summers never last.*

19
BROTHER SLEW

Witold Slew sailed for Englalond in a black-hulled cutter out of Emden, North Germany, at twilight.

The crew were Frisians, toughest and most skilled sailors in the Fyrd fleet, well used to making fast North Sea crossings in that night's kind of rough harsh weather.

A strong northerly wind with no moon or stars offers ideal conditions to get across fast and make a secret landfall on the flat Essex coast for those who know what they are doing.

Who are not many.

Too far north and the landfalls are bad. Drift south and it's not so hard to never get landward at all and run afoul of the Goodwins, which can break a ship's back in a moment. So Slew had sought out the best of skippers, whose ancestors had been making the crossing in worse weather than that going back fifteen hundred years.

'Borkum Riff?'

'Who's asking?'

Slew, in his shadow cloak, armed, emerged from a darkness that was not there before and proffered the Emperor's seal.

'No name is necessary I think.'

Riff had taken many Fyrd across before, but never one like Slew.

He examined the seal with calloused hands and without expression and said, 'We sail now. Don't want to know your name or business. Stay below. It's a rising northerly so don't expect to sleep and you'll puke.'

'Will I?' said Slew.

'When you do,' said Riff, 'you clear up the mess yourself before we let you onshore. That's the rule. It would apply to the Emperor himself if he ever deigned to make this short voyage.'

'He will one day no doubt. He was born in Brum. All hydden like to return home once in their life.'

Riff, unused to conversation of that kind, said, 'Understood?'

Slew smiled, went straight below, slept and didn't puke.

When he woke, dawn was showing behind their craft and straight ahead the coast of Essex was a flat, black sliver against a dark grey sky. Human lights showed. The bells of buoys tolled. A lightship's beam arced across the sky.

'Morning!' he said.

The crew were silent but respectful. They liked passengers who caused no trouble and didn't complain when they emerged. They liked them still more when they didn't leave a smell behind.

Borkum Riff, bearded and barrel-chested, nodded an acknowledgement.

'Water?' said Slew.

A crew member gave him a tin bowl of it.

'Fresh?'

'As a daisy.'

Slew swilled it round his mouth, spat it overboard, doused his face and neck, and asked, 'How long?'

Riff replied at length, for him: 'You can't tell it from here but straight ahead's the Isle of Maldon. It's connected to the mainland by a causeway that'll be exposed in half an hour's time when the tide's halfway out. Sunrise is in an hour.'

The rest of the voyage they did in darkness, side by side, which normally Riff would not have liked.

But Slew was something else.

The first who had never puked or felt ill or said something unsailorly.

'How do you like to be called?' asked Slew as they came in on the seaward side of the Isle.

'Riff will do. And you?'

'I thought you needed no names.'

'It is in the wyrd of things that you and I will meet again. The sea tells me so. The waves hold it in their rise and fall. The likes of you and the likes of me are rare. We will meet again and you'll have need of me and I of you. So . . . what's your name?'

'Witold Slew,' said Slew.

They shook hands.

'I need three weeks, and I want you to pick me up, Riff, no one else.'

'A pleasure. We'll wait three days after twenty-one, which is a full moon. After that, you'll have to take passage with whoever comes along. On this stage they're only Fyrd.'

'Understood.'

Slew was over the side and on the wooden landing stage as fast as a shadow disappears when light is no more.

A crew member threw down his portersac.

Riff held his stave.

'Can't see you,' he said to the shadows before the cutter's side.

'Throw it and it will find my right hand,' said Slew.

The stave arced through the night, from boat to shore, from the right hand of one dark hydden to that of another.

The cutter eased away, the wind riffling her briefly slack sails before, with a *thwump*! they were full again and the prow was slicing through the waves.

Borkum Riff looked back.

Light had come, Slew was gone.

'That's a hell of a one,' said a member of the crew.

'That's the future of the Hyddenworld,' said Riff.

Slew headed east, his objective Chelmsford, one of the meeting points for pilgrims on their way to Brum from Harwich and smaller ports along the east coast. From there the pilgrims preferred to travel in caravans or groups for safety. The next leg of their journey, which was St Albans, required that they negotiate the dangerous damplands of Hertfordshire, with their obscure valleys, confusing green roads, and thickets and winding hedgerows that lured even the most experienced traveller to ambush and death.

Slew packed his dark cloak and donned rough fustian, the pilgrim pendant of Beornamund embroidered boldly on his jerkin, sign of a past completed pilgrimage. He also dyed his hair black.

He kept to himself, affecting a spiritual quiet and answering any enquiry briefly, saying – which was true – that he came from the Thuringer Wald of Germany. He carried himself and his stave firmly enough not to be troubled by the many that preyed on others along the route.

He watched and he listened, seeking out not the group-inclined pilgrims aiming directly for Brum, but the solitaries whose objectives were more spiritual, who wished to test their courage and faith by travelling alone.

'Whither bound, pilgrim?' he would be asked.

'Brum.'

'Alone?'

'So it seems.'

'Rumours fly, my friend.'

'They do for good and ill. Let us share them over mead . . .'

This meeting and others like them informed Slew of all manner of things, including naturally the one rumour more important than all others, that the gem of Spring had been found.

'It's true then?' Slew asked one solitary, a monk in brown from the Netherlands.

'I had it directly from one returning from Brum only yesterday. It was found on Waseley Hill.'

'It would be. Who by?'

The solitary traveller shrugged. 'Someone who got lucky, or was blessed by the Mirror.'

'We shall see it I should hope,' said Slew.

'You before me, brother, for I'm making a diversion to worship at the holy well in . . .'

So Slew found out things, learnt about the different groups, pretended he was resting before the big trek to Brum. Until, two days later, he found what he wanted: a group of four religious, not celibates because two had their plump daughters with them, making six travellers in all.

Slew avoided contact but at night, on the periphery of the campfire, he listened in. They were a perfect cover and offered appealing opportunities as well. The next day he struck camp at first light, ahead of the solitary he had talked with on the first day and from whom he found out his route. Slew found a lonely spot along it and lay in wait.

A pleasant time for Slew.

Englalond's Summer was moister, gentler, more beautiful than any he had known in his own land. He meditated. He ate a little and drank water from a stream and then he caught and killed two rabbits from snares set when he first arrived in that dell.

One he skinned, cleaned, washed and readied for a stew. The other he left as it was, for the moment.

Then he waited until he saw his acquaintance of the previous day coming up the valley. He stood astride his path, his stave hand relaxed.

'Whither bound, pilgrim?' he said, ironically raising his stave, musing whether or not to make a fight of it. He decided against, for he had nothing to prove, and before the pilgrim, who had shared food with him, could even greet him in return or understand the threat, he struck him straight between the eyes as if he had unleashed a bolt from a crossbow and then, as he fell, he delivered a second blow into his throat.

Dying but not yet dead, the pilgrim could not stop Slew stripping him of his brown robe, removing two of the pilgrim seals from his stave and putting them on his own. Both were from popular and well-visited sites and their combination was not unusual. The others he left on the monk's stave.

He hauled him by the collar of his shirt up among the trees to one, an oak, whose bole was split and the inside rotten. He stuffed the body in and stuck his knife in hard, twisted it and spilled the guts. Then he took the rabbit he had left nearby, placed it in the bole against the body and sliced its chest and belly open so the stomach and guts spewed out as the hydden's had done, masking by sight and smell the horror within the tree.

There he left them together in death, their stench an attraction to predators. Foxes, badgers, rats, it didn't matter. They would come and anyone drawn by the stench would see rabbit fur before mortal skin and, not wanting to go closer, would infer the wrong thing. Slew had never done that before but he had heard of it and took pleasure in such tricks as those.

But he had his superstitions: he took the monk's stave and broke it because he didn't want to be followed by a well-armed ghost. His habit, however, he put on.

Then, newly disguised and ready for the onward journey, he made the trek back to the route to St Albans. He met some other travellers, enquired after the party of six he had an eye on, satisfied himself they had not passed and, finding a thick piece of woodland, crept into its shadows.

The place was crawling with villainy and smelt of highway robbery and murder. He scouted about and found two groups of robbers: one a group of three thieves of no great consequence, the second a group of six, a gang, that looked worthy of the name.

The group of three appeared first, and no doubt to harmless travellers would look intimidating. They did not to Slew. They took a vantage point not far from his, lurking as stupid incompetents do, lumpishly. The gang, which he doubted had anything to do with them, stayed out of his line of sight, though they could see the three.

The day began on the pilgrim way below and the first groups of pilgrims came along from Chelmsford, loud and full of false cheer as they hurried through the dank woods, palms sweating on staves, imagining dangers, loud in their fearfulness.

The three robbers spotted a group coming, not part of the one Slew was after, and ambled down to it, as they thought looking carefree and innocent. They were, in fact, as conspicuous as a lump of shit on a maiden's shoe.

The would-be assailants greeted their intended victims but saw they were well-armed, no-nonsense folk from France. Slew had seen them himself the day before.

The robbers backed off and returned to their temporary lair to wait for easier prey and pickings.

Not long after, Slew saw the pilgrim party he was interested in striding along, the young wyfkin, rested now, bright of eye and cheek, well-coiffed, attractive. Foolish to so display themselves in those parts where females have value beyond their domestic skills.

The three robbers were as good as licking their lips and sucking their rotten teeth when a bolt from a crossbow went straight through the head of the largest of them and another into the side of the next as he turned.

The last was knifed in the throat as he stood up, open-mouthed, and the gang came at him, like rats swarming over living prey.

Slew was content to have the trio out of the way.

The numbers were perfect for his purpose: two would linger where they were, four would go down and take the group below, with crossbows first to kill and disable, then with ironclads, for fun. The females would be kept alive, hauled back into the woods and wishing as time went by – days and weeks, even a month or two, as they were traded and degraded and their value steadily fell – that they were dead.

Slew's plan was to be their saviour.

It happened as he predicted. The moment the four went on down, leaving the two behind, Slew eased over to them and killed this pair in silence, one knifed, the other garotted.

Then he watched the scene on the path below unfold, creeping nearer, weighing the odds of four against four, the females discounted.

When the assault began he waited until one of the pilgrims was disabled and another bleeding badly and the females uncertain, white-faced.

Then he appeared, shot one of the gang from behind and clubbed down a second.

The odds had shifted but the other two fought harder still, expecting their friends to come down from their hiding place. Slew did not want a death among the pilgrims. It would change things, and his desire was to be accepted as one of them, not to be one of a party of mourners.

He interposed himself between the fighters, doing what he did with such easy grace and skill it looked a little lucky. Cries, screams, moans, the villains turning and fleeing, Slew in pursuit, rough and ready and monkish and foolishly brave. Or so he hoped it seemed.

It did.

The wounded pilgrims were patched up.

The unscathed ones badly shaken and eternally grateful.

Slew, who introduced himself as Brother Slew, was modesty itself. He explained he had foolishly pulled off the track to relieve himself. He saw the gang descend, disposed of two of them who had no idea he was in the bushes – 'One does not dance and sing when one is relieving oneself under cover of brambles,' he said – and the rest they knew.

They had all been lucky.

'Would you travel on with us, Brother Slew?'

He said that it would be a pleasure but he had a confession to make – he was not a real religious like the other noble solitaries along the way. No, no, he was a trained Fyrd who had earned his leave and wished to make a pilgrimage to Brum to ease a soul troubled by things he had done.

'A worthy aim, friend. We'll call you brother all the same . . . and the stave, the other seals of pilgrimage?'

'Folk are good,' he said, 'and a pilgrimage produces good things. I promised a dying pilgrim in Harwich, whose ambition had been to add the seal of Brum to these two for reasons of his own, to carry his stave as penance to that fabled city and leave it as an offering on Waseley Hill. This I shall do.'

'In our company, if you'll honour us with yours.'

Their daughters' eyes lit up when they shook his hand. Dark eyes, strong grip, modesty – a hero.

By the time they had reached the East Gate of Brum, in fine fettle and health, Brother Slew was as close to them as a real brother might be. As for the females, he had had his hand up the skirts of one and bedded the other.

In short, he had a good time of it.

But time was running out.

He did not have long to find the gem, steal it, and get back for his rendezvous with Borkum Riff.

'Good Brother Slew,' they cried, 'you can take lodgings with us!'

'If you insist, I will!'

20
WILD CHILD

Judith woke and stared at the ceiling, her Mum big and heavy at her side.

She could hear birds, see the skein of a cobweb hanging from the cracked plaster, floating back and forth in a draught, and Mum's shape.

Impulsively she rolled over and out of bed, clad in her nightie which was her Dad's T-shirt, which came to her ankles, and stood staring at the black tuft of hair that was all she could see of Mum. Not awake. Her breathing was a slow, soft rhythm in the room and the birds were loud outside.

She turned to the open door, padded across to the room where Dad slept on the floor and went in, standing, her calves cold.

Something was wrong, the world had changed.

It took her a few seconds to work it out and then she did: she felt no pain.

Nothing.

That was what was wrong.

There was cold air on her ankles and legs but that wasn't pain.

Mum was a tuft of black hair among the folds of their duvet, Dad was a hairy leg and boxer shorts.

Mum was a milky, soapy smell.

Dad was something stubbly and shaverly and warmerly, like a great hairy scarf round her face and head.

Both were big and this morning her knees didn't hurt or her ankles or her back and her arms or her wrists or the big bones in her legs or anything.

She went down the corridor to where Arthur and Margaret slept, but the door was closed.

She stood outside listening, and hearing nothing reached up and touched a white plastic light switch, then pulled loose wallpaper below it looser still and, feeling the rough carpet beneath her feet, itched her right foot against it, rub rub.

She wanted the wee that woke her and headed for the toilet, but through the banisters she saw the sun slanting across the floor in the hall below. She turned and went down the stairs, feeling the bounce of her fingers against the rails as she went and the way they sprang back to position; bounce spring: bounce spring: bounce spring.

The sun had come through the door, which was ajar, that led into the conservatory.

Judith pushed it open with a little shove, the way she had before. It swung with a creak and as sun covered her body all over with its warmth the door stilled and swung back as it liked to do.

She did it again and stepped forward into the light, the door swinging back behind her.

Birdsong filled the conservatory and its greenery with trills and squeaks and clicks and shrill repetitions. She closed her eyes and whirled around in the birdsong sound, her toes wiggling towards the blue sky above the glass.

Opening her eyes again Judith stepped onto a rug, the tessellated floor being cold, from where she contemplated the doors outside. The key hung on a nail to one side, out of her reach without a chair.

There was a wicker one, and for the first time since she woke she minded that others might wake as well. She struggled to lift the chair off the floor and eventually pulled and shoved it to the door, climbed up and got the key.

It was easy turning it, hard to stop the door swinging and banging but, carefully, she managed it.

Then going out into the cool morning air, the song and sounds of nature, lit by sun, like a glistening road before her, she stepped outside, walked across the broken patio and onto the dewy grass beyond.

Her toes wiggled again, in the wet this time, deliciously.

Judith saw a snail, thin, tentacly ear-things questing, moving slowly along. Its shell was a spiral of black and pale yellow. There was another near it.

She stilled, suddenly alert, hearing a sound; no, feeling the sound; no, seeing it.

Life moved somewhere across the lawn.

Judith crouched down and, reaching for the snail, stopped that and stayed absolutely still, brought her gaze up, the sun warm on the tops of her feet and nice on her nose, and sensed the fox.

She stood up and looked at it a hundred yards away and it looked at her. She began walking towards it, grass and dew between them, mistress of her domain, staring it down, eyes alight to see it.

It turned and slunk but did not disappear, as if not allowed.

You stay there Mister Fox until I say you can go!

The fox, uneasy but not frightened, dithered uncertainly, paws here and there, eyes on Judith.

You stay!

The fox retreated between two of the trees of the henge.

The chimes sounded to Judith's right.

The trees shimmered with light and sound high above her head and she slowed, feeling the life of the Earth above and below, to all sides.

She wanted to wee herself into the ground, the grass and the Earth, so she did, by the rhododendrons, listening to the chimes and the birds skittering in the undergrowth and above her head as she squatted.

Relieved, she stood up, let her nightie fall back down her legs and knew what she wanted.

She went and stood at the entrance to the henge, her two favourite trees towering protectively above her, and stared between them to contemplate the White Horse on the hill. It seemed to her never to stop moving.

'Mister Fox,' she whispered, not taking her eyes off the Horse, 'you're there.'

Mister Squirrel was also, and ants on her feet among the pine needles where the grass ended, and the collared dove and its cooing

in the trees like an echo in a high room, and the Horse, from which
she did not take her eyes for a moment, all were there.

But it was the Horse that held her as the ants walked off her feet
again and the dove flapped off among the branches of the henge.

Judith smiled.

No pain, just standing in the world.

She wanted to run and dance and turn a somersault, each foot,
head, hand and her long dark hair touching the Earth and sky and
trees and leaves and the coat of Mister Fox, but she couldn't.

She was missing something she never missed before.

Something different than Dad and Mum and Margaret and Arthur.

She felt no pain but she felt an ache for what she was missing.

She didn't know its name or even if it existed.

She had no word for it.

The word was 'friend'.

Jack woke, stretched and got up like he usually did, no messing.

Wake and up and out of bed, that was Jack, on with his trainers
and the day.

He had a pee and went downstairs and saw, across the hall, wet
footprints, small, coming his way. He frowned, not comprehending.

He looked at the carpet of the stairs and saw they came on up and
past him and headed past his door. He felt a draught from downstairs
and knew a door was open.

He turned, went back upstairs and pushed Katherine's door gently
open.

The usual tuft of her hair at the top end of the bed, deep breathing,
and over her back Judith's arm. He stared and saw projecting from
beneath the duvet over the side of the bed two small feet, grassy and
dotted with pine needles.

He looked at them and their pink soft roundness and the way grass
and needles had accumulated in the arch, and between the toes and
wondered if he had ever in his life felt such love for another as he did
for Judith then. A surge of love so powerful it took his breath away.
He wanted to reach out and touch her feet but didn't do so. She slept
so deeply, she lay so free and wild and he loved her so much.

Jack went to the window and looked out.

He could see her trail through the grass, a triangle of tracks.

From the patio to the rhododendrons, then to the two conifers, then back to the house again.

He retreated quietly, went down to the conservatory, saw the chair, worked things out, shook his head and smiled and went outside as she had, kicking off his trainers and walking barefoot through the grass.

He went straight to the two trees, stood where she had, smelt the fox and saw the White Horse. He contemplated the Horse, as she had done, imagining it to be moving as she had, as he often had before.

He could put up more barbed wire, build fences, lock doors, close the gate out onto the road, watch and worry and fret, but she had started her exploration of the world and no way was he going to be able to stop her and nor would he ever want to. Time was running out for all of them, very fast. People were born into the world to run and dance, not to be restrained.

Over breakfast, in the midst of the usual chaos and cacophony, he said, 'We'll go for a walk, Katherine, like we used to, up to the White Horse; it's time. With Judith.'

'Judith?'

'Every moment's precious,' said Jack.

'It is,' she replied.

21

ON THE ROAD

Stort's journey from Brum to Woolstone with Barklice to assess the situation with the Shield Maiden and perhaps make contact with Jack and Katherine should have been straightforward.

They had made the journey before and Barklice was a master of the minutiae of such travel over distance and under pressure of time. The quickest method of transport also involved the most dangerous for hydden – undermost human trains. It involved waiting for a train at a junction near the West Gate, where they always stopped briefly, and using wooden boards to form a platform beneath the train on which a hydden could easily lie.

It needed deft hands and a bold approach. Barklice had long since trained Stort in the method and he was now reliable, but once on, with the train rattling along, the track just beneath the boards, there were two problems. One was keeping staves and portersacs from falling off and the other was knowing when to get off.

Unscheduled stops confused the issue, as did rerouting. This was where Barklice's experience came in, provided the stop where they needed to get off was a long enough one and not likely to involve running into humans.

Having reached a stopping point near Didcot and disembarked, the hydden traveller faced an easy hike up the Thames Valley by green road and open field. The last few miles, across meadow lands, were often flooded but the dramatic sight of White Horse Hill, which loomed over Woolstone, gave a hiker the energizing sense that the end was in sight.

Unfortunately the tremors and earthquakes of the past three weeks had disrupted human transport systems, especially the trains, which were delayed, rerouted or plain chaotic.

The two-day journey turned into a five-day one, and that was just to get them to the green road on the north side of the Thames but a great deal further to the east than they wished to be, making for a much longer walk.

The hydden road they were on was normally little used, for there were no hydden settlements along that stretch of it for many miles. Yet, though overgrown, it was obvious even to Stort, untrained in detailed route finding, that others had been that way recently.

'Judging from the direction of their footprints in the mud,' said Stort, 'there's a good few of them and they're going in our direction.'

To his surprise Barklice gave no reply better than a grunt, as if he was put out to see that other hydden were about. Normally some company did not go amiss, but Stort supposed that the importance of their mission and Barklice's assumed role of getting him there and back safely made him mislike interruptions.

'Let's not dally,' said Barklice shortly. 'We need to get along a fair way before we set up camp if we're not to have too long a day of it on the morrow.'

But a short while later he noticed Barklice look rather intently into some branches to their left, then look sharply away, veer to the right and speed up a bit.

What Stort spotted was some coloured ribbon woven betwixt two gnarled twigs, set in amongst the branches a little above head height. It was the kind of sign used by bilgesnipe, that mysterious but benign group of wayfarers so commonly found, as now, in the vicinity of a river. He had often seen them on routes to and from sites where the bilgesnipe indulged in communal rituals involving splendid fires and nocturnal feasting. No doubt, he told himself, such a moot was happening that week in the area they had come to.

He hurried to catch Barklice up to share these thoughts, but the verderer had set such a pace that by the time he had done so the point was lost. Except that a little later, twilight falling, he saw a similar sign in the branches again, right above their heads.

'Do you imagine that might be a sign that—?' he began, not completing his question before Barklice cut him short.

'What might be?' said the verderer indifferently.

'Those twigs with ribbon, like the one before . . .'

'I saw no such thing,' said Barklice, 'now or then.'

'But look, it's right above your head!'

Barklice affected to look up and then said, 'There is nothing there but branches and the darkening sky,' before hurrying on.

'Is it possible,' said Stort, not to be denied when it came to reasonable enquiry, 'that there is a moot afoot? I have read somewhere that it is generally in the third week of May that the bilgesnipe . . .'

Barklice came to an abrupt halt.

'Mister Stort, you go too far. You call me a liar to my face, saying I see what I do not see, and you parade your shallow scholarship regarding moots falsely and to my annoyance.'

'But I only—'

'There are no moots, never were, never will be.'

'But my dear chap,' said Stort, stung by his friend's gratuitous charge of 'shallow' scholarship and remembering only too well the day Master Brief had introduced him to that marvellous work: Brother Moreton's *Folklore, Tradition and Rituals of the Northern Hyddenworld*, 'certain moots are very famous indeed, their existence well attested.'

Barklice stared at him with unabashed alarm, but Stort was not one to be put off when truth was on the rack.

'Like for example Paley's Creek, the origin and location of which no one has ever satisfactorily found, though there are plenty of records of hydden attending it, their memories after being somewhat, well, befuddled.'

Barklice's expression changed from alarm to anger.

'If you continue like this,' he snapped, 'I shall be . . . *annoyed*. You talk too much nonsense, Stort. Everybody who does more than simply read books knows that there never was and never will be such a place as Paley's Creek! Now, darkness is falling and this is wet ground to make camp on. We need to find somewhere drier!'

Even after this unexpected exchange Stort might have forgotten the incident, as Barklice soon appeared to, had they not caught up with a family of bilgesnipe a short while later. They were making a brew and in fine fettle and form, the women dressed as ever in their coloured silks, the men in gay fustian, the children singing their strange, exotic roundels as they played games, as such children did.

'How be and a felon's eve!' cried one of the males when he saw them.

'Don't talk to them, don't even *answer* them!' hissed Barklice, hurrying on past as if there was no one there. 'Given half a chance they'll put a knife through your ribs.'

'But . . .' began Stort, amazed at his friend's unaccustomed rudeness and distressed to see the bilgesnipes' smiles begin to fade.

'Good evening,' he said, 'never mind my friend, he's . . . well . . . and where are you off to?'

The answer was astounding.

'To the Creek o' course!' one of them cried. 'For a chubbly time. Allers welcome, all matters and mind of mortality, yourself included!'

'The Creek?' repeated Stort softly. 'You mean Paley's Creek?'

'Old Paley's dead so, in a manner o'speaking, it bain't his name no more but you'm right another way, for it don't have no other name but his, Mirror rest his wicked soul.'

'It's a long way from here I daresay?' said Stort.

'Nary that, sir, 'tis nattle Woolstone way, 'neath that great hoary beast, down t'river and along fro' meadow and mead for we'm northerly now and southerly to waterside.'

'Um . . .' began Stort, thinking that if these were directions they were very welcome but not quite clear and he would like some.

'Don't fuddle up yerseln my sir, just wait on t'night o' Maytime moon . . .'

'The full moon?' said Stort.

'Aye, as full as it gets an' more, where the light spills over into wonderland and aller's that be murky be made plain, and aller's plain be forgot for that nonce. But wanderin' sir, you'll hear, you'll hear. Listen, that's all you ever have to do. Listen and follow and you'll be there in Paley's Creek.'

They all fell silent, inclining their cheerful, chubby faces as if to listen to the wind.

Then Stort heard it, or imagined he did, music of a kind, singing of another kind, alluring, siren-like.

'Is that from Paley's Creek?'

'That *is* Paley's Creek in the formin' by folks that's gone ahead o' us and you,' said one of them. 'If you be wending your ways fronterly but come backerly in time we'll be there. Ask for the Nance family and a brew'll be yours for the asking and remedies aplenty.'

'For what?'

'Ills, that's what, and what ails. If Old Ma Nance can't do it 'nother will.'

'Nance?' repeated Stort.

'That'll be it, and yourn?'

'Our names? Stort, Bedwyn Stort, and Mister Barklice, both of Brum.'

'Familiar,' one of them said. 'Barklice you say?'

He turned and said the name again and someone said, 'Ah, there you go, he'm come to his sense that feller has, ha! Comes to 'em all in time.'

'You know Mister Barklice then?'

They laughed in a knowing but not unpleasant way and one of them said, 'There's not a bilgesnipe in Englalond doesn't know that old name and hopes it'll do right not wrong. So, now, brew's up and we got to eat. Follow the signs and you'll not get lost; wyrd's the way to Paley's Creek and there's no avoiding it!'

They went one way and Stort the other, hurrying to catch Barklice up once more, eager to share what he had discovered, if only he could work out exactly what that was.

'I was right, Barklice, the Creek's just—'

'It isn't.'

'But they were going—'

'They weren't.'

The wind strengthened and brought the sound of strange music.

'But I can hear music . . .'

'You can't!'

Barklice marched on faster still, refusing to talk or to stop, on and on, long after darkness had fallen.

'Barklice, I'm stopping. I don't know what's got into you but—'

'Nothing's got into me but your foolishness.'

'But—'

'Now, help me find a dry spot off the road . . .'

It was their habit, after eating supper, to sit and watch the stars if there were any, enjoy a warm brew and talk.

Many of Stort's happiest times had been with Mister Barklice, talking in that way, for though their callings were different their lives were similar: both were wanderers, both more or less alone in the world, both innocent of many worldly things, both kindly to others, generous with their time; and both sometimes lonely.

So it was that often, sitting talking like that, their thoughts turned to the one mystery which, to them, was as unfathomable as the Universe whose stars and planets, suns and moons, gave them such comfort: love.

Each craved it, neither had known it.

Not love of the adult kind.

Not love given freely as a female might; nor, therefore, of wyfkin and childer. Stort had no hope of it, much though he craved a family. As for Barklice, he could only shake his head and wonder why it had passed him by.

'But you are older than me and have had time enough,' Stort would say, 'so have you never . . . ?'

'Never,' said Barklice. 'Too shy I suppose, wouldn't know what to say or do . . . and no one ever showed me.'

'And would you have liked childer?' Stort had once asked.

To which, in the darkness of that distant remembered night, their fire dying, their mead all done, their beds calling, Barklice had finally replied, 'I would, I would.'

But love as a topic of conversation was not on the agenda that night when they camped near Paley's Creek – or didn't – as the case might be.

Nothing was on the agenda, because Barklice's strange ill temper continued. A fire they had, hot mead too, but of conversation little or none.

Yet Barklice did not retire and seemed glad, so far as Stort could tell, when he recharged his cup with mead. He wanted to talk, to say something, but nothing came. When the wind freshened and brought to them the haunting sound of bilgesnipe music, it seemed to Stort that his friend stared into the fire with real loss in his eyes.

'I believe,' he said quietly, thinking to provoke his friend into confiding what so obviously hung heavy on him, 'or I have heard it said, that Paley's Creek is not so much a place as an idea . . . Perhaps this is what you meant, and I apologize if I put it badly, when you said—'

Barklice got up saying, 'Leave it there, Stort, let it go at that, there's a good fellow.'

Stort watched as his friend walked a little way from the fire to stand by himself, listening to the music, staring at the stars.

'Barklice, I . . . You . . .' he essayed.

'I'm turning in,' said Barklice, and Stort thought he had never heard him sound so defeated, nor so sad.

The next day dawned bright and the green road, which had been so damp and difficult for a time, became firm underfoot and easier.

They met no more travellers, though they saw more bilgesnipe in the distance, wending offaways, and Barklice's mood lifted and seemed gone on the Summer breeze.

A few miles to their left, across fields interwoven with hedges and dykes and already showing the fresh shoots of wheat and corn, the chalk downlands rose.

'Uffington Hill,' said Barklice happily, 'will soon be in sight. There's a dozen easy ways from here to the foot of it where Woolstone lies and we'll wend whichever hydden ways appeal.'

Church bells rang from one village, dogs barked in another and a tractor, its yellow trailer bouncing along a wider track than theirs, headed towards another.

'The humans are up and about with the Summer,' said Stort. 'Less troubled here by tremors and the like than folks in Brum.'

Soon they saw Jack and Katherine's village in the distance, finally approaching the tree henge in the great garden of Woolstone House from the south, through the same copse of trees where Brief, Stort and Pike had brought Jack to safety after his failed attempt to rescue Katherine from the icy shadows of the Fyrd.

Stort remembered Jack's account of it, Barklice recalled Brief's.

'How things change, Stort,' said his friend. 'Less than two years ago General Meyor Feld, as he now is, abducted Katherine from Woolstone on Brunte's behalf and tried to kill Jack in the process, and now here we are as envoys to parley with them and persuade Jack to return to Brum and leave Katherine behind. A tall order I think!'

'It's a topsy-turvy world,' said Stort. 'You were better off not being involved in that incident, though I confess it was a fine sight watching Jack wield Brief's stave of office so formidably. I was glad not to get in his way . . . How far off that incident now seems! How much has happened since!'

They ducked under the wire fence that formed the only boundary to the garden and, in a few steps more, found themselves in the henge Stort remembered so well.

'Well, I've got you here in one piece, Stort. What now? Making contact with humans is your domain I think. For myself I think it dangerous work and will leave it to you to find the best approach.'

While Barklice set up camp nearby and made a brew Stort explored the far side of the henge, from where he had a view of the main part of the garden and the house.

He saw that the conservatory doors were open but no sign of people. He lingered longer than he should, enjoying the afternoon and, like the last time he was here, the chimes. The like of them he had seen nowhere else in the Hyddenworld, nor in the literature. Their purpose seemed something more than to make pleasant music, and when he had examined them before they seemed, though frail, quite old.

Jack's explanation had been unsatisfactory, telling him merely that no one in the house remembered a time when they were not there, which made them older than half a century. Also that Katherine's mother believed they offered protection of some kind and had to do with little people . . .

'Which is to say ourselves,' Stort said to himself as, cautiously wandering over to where they hung, he watched them turn and swing in the breeze, never still, always making a sound of one kind and another.

'Tomatoes!' he said suddenly, for there was a haphazard row of them nearby which he did not recall before.

He liked the scent of their leaves and, had they been ripe, might have been tempted to take a few for breakfast.

He heard a call from Barklice from the edge of the henge to say their brew was ready and waiting and time moving on; supper was served.

He turned back at once and the two went back to the camp and sat talking like the friends they truly were.

Darkness fell, the stars showed, and as with the previous evening they heard the alluring sound of bilgesnipe music carried on the breeze.

'Paley's Creek,' murmured Stort, and this time Barklice did not object, for it is given to true friends to say the right things in the right way at the right time. So Stort then.

Barklice said nothing, but Stort heard his friend blowing his nose and wiping his eyes and he guessed that the deep emotions provoked the day before and expressed as anger had surfaced again and turned into quiet tears. For what, Stort had no idea and he did not feel it his business to ask.

While Barklice pondered his thoughts, Stort pondered his own. On the morrow, he hoped, he would see the Shield Maiden for the first time. She would be young and small no doubt . . . but he didn't really know.

'Have you ever looked into the eyes of a child, Barklice?'

Stort knew the moment he asked it that he had inadvertently reached into his friend's heart's core.

Barklice was a long time replying.

When he did he simply said, rather softly, 'Yes.'

'And may I ask, what did you feel?'

'Love,' said Barklice, more quietly still, 'I felt love I think. Yes, love.'

'Oh!' murmured Stort at this very unexpected reply. 'Love? That is a strong emotion. Whose child were you looking at?'

Barklice's head sank a little and his brew almost spilled, so forgetful of holding it did he become.

'I would rather you had not asked that question, Stort.'

'Then I un-ask it at once! Think of it no more!'

Barklice shook his head.

'That cannot be, my dear friend. Such a question as that, once asked, cannot be denied. To do so is to turn my back on a truth I have run from too long. Certain things of late have forcibly reminded me of my cowardice, which explains my rudeness last evening, for which I apologize.'

'What truth?' asked Stort.

'The truth is that I am a fraud, Stort,' said Barklice brokenly, 'and have been for many years. All my talk of not having loved, of not having known the joys of which we have so often spoken, was . . . a lie.'

'But Barklice,' began Stort, dumbfounded, 'you—'

'I lied. I have known love, both carnal and spiritual, and I cannot deny it more. You asked who the child was into whose eyes I looked with love.'

'Yes, I did,' said Stort.

'He was my own, Stort, he was my own and I turned my back on him!'

'Oh Barklice,' said Stort very quietly, 'oh my dear friend!'

And there by the henge, with the tinkle of the chimes to one side of them, and the mysterious music of Paley's Creek to the other, Barklice wept and whispered, 'He was mine, Stort, but I denied him and gave up the most precious thing I ever had! Yes, I looked once into the eyes of a child but knew not the wonder of what I saw!'

22

WANDERING SCHOLAR

B y the time Slew arrived in Brum, the group into whose trust
and affections he had murderously insinuated himself treated
him like a brother, and also as the Brother he affected to be.
They fell in different ways under his spell. Their leader Gerolt,
who had been wounded in the attack from which Slew saved him, felt
physically and mentally undermined. Ansel was sick in body and heart
from the attack and was happy to let Slew take the lead. Bente,
Gerolt's brother, gave way to him; Diederick, their uncle, could make
no objection to him, though Slew was too smooth, too sophisticated,
to be likeable to him.

Of the females, Evelien, who was Diederick's daughter, had yielded
quickest to Slew's demands. She did so for two reasons, each as
potent as the other. One was lust, which came the moment she saw
him killing their assailants and in command, powerful, bloodied on
their behalf. She felt raw, visceral, naked desire.

She lay sleepless in the night for him, and was his long before his
first, demanding, expectant touch; yielding before his first kiss; his for
ever and a day before their first, strong, silent, almost brutal moment
of union.

The second reason was more base, more common.

She knew her cousin felt the same and wished to make her jealous.
In taking Slew to herself she took him from her uncle's daughter,
Machtild. The younger woman, though only by a few years, triumph-
ing over the older.

But not the weaker, not the less passionate, not the less powerful.

When Slew, in the night, in secret from the males who slept and snored in their heavy way, grew bored with Evelien, he slipped away to Machtild's bed.

Of the two, that is Slew and Machtild, who toyed with whom would be hard to say, but, probably, she with him. She let him go only so far before she said in his ear, 'You are Evelien's, Mirror help you, not mine. Go back to her.'

Which Slew liked.

It roused him to be rejected by one who wanted him.

It amused him, so he laughed.

'I will,' he said, removing his hands but not quite his body and turning on his back, 'I will go back to her. But tell me something, sweet Machtild.'

She was in fact, anything but sweet. Beautiful, yes; intelligent, yes; amusing, certainly; courageous, definitely. But sweet? As salt.

'Yes?'

They talked then into the night, not touching like lovers but flank to flank, familiar, comfortable, like horses in a field. Touching in a way he had never touched a female before, her body good, her full breasts sometimes brushing his chest; her hands sometimes caressing him in passing by, but nothing more.

His body was the same with her.

So they talked until the dawn and the time came to return briefly to Evelien's bed for courtesy's sake.

The males were routine-bound and as they slept so they woke, almost by rote, always at the same time. Slew might have been making love with Evelien until five minutes before their due time to wake arrived and still he could continue a minute or two more, knowing they would stir but not quite wake. It pleased him to make fools of them.

Machtild sensed that in Slew she had found her destiny.

Whatever he was, she knew he was no ordinary hydden, nor ordinary Fyrd. His body was a god's. His touch divine. His intelligence an excitement and incitement to her own. His humour, dark and treacherous, was like her own.

'You are not so bad yourself,' he said, parrying her compliments. 'Not what I would have expected from loins as doltish as this family's!'

'You are acute, Slew,' she said, 'very. He is not, I think, my father.'

'Then . . . ?'

'Go back to Evelien. Dawn approaches, she will have need of you, and that done you will have need of sleep. Her opportunities to enjoy you get less and less.'

'Why, am I leaving?'

'I think you may be, sooner than you say.'

'It's you, not I, who's acute, Machtild!'

Brum was awash with rumours of the gem of Spring when they arrived. The one thing that was agreed was that the well-known scholar Bedwyn Stort had found it up on Waseley Hill, as had been so long predicted.

The second thing that seemed certain was that the City Elders could not long resist the growing public demand for it to be put on display, however briefly.

One thing that was clear, to Slew at least, as he listened to the talk, was that Stort was not just then in residence. He had gone off on some mission or other to do with the gem.

The question then was had he taken the gem with him or not? It seemed unlikely and that pleased Slew.

The city was so full of pilgrims that Summer that there were not enough lodgings to go round.

Pilgrims, even elderly ones, were forced to camp out in the city squares, or in the open spaces by its walls, taking their chances on rain and flood and the rats.

This was not Slew's style, and while the others were willing to accept the situation, he was not. In any case, his purpose in coming to Brum was not served by being austere and uncomfortable, nor were his different needs with respect to Evelien and Machtild.

'Leave it to me,' he said.

He had established early on that the hostelry where Stort, when in town, liked to eat was the Muggy Duck in Digbeth. It was run by one

Ma'Shuqa, a bilgesnipe. She, it soon emerged, was a good friend of
the scholar and occasionally his protector. Slew did not ask questions
directly, not wishing to give his game away. He preferred to come
and go unnoticed, though someone of his obvious strength and
confidence, and striking, saturnine good looks, was not easily missed.

Slew did not normally drink but he did not wish to draw attention
to himself, so he drank modestly and not so little as to seem mean; he
ate well and he tipped generously.

He made friends among the locals, all of whom claimed close
acquaintance with the famous Stort, but none of whom, it seemed,
actually had it. Finally it was a staverman who told Slew what it was
he wanted to hear: where Stort lived.

That much achieved, and careful to leave it to another day,
meaning a second day of discomfort on the edge of the town ditch,
sleeping on rough ground with his new friends, within reach but no
longer touch of the two females, who lay in the dark as frustrated as
he, Slew paid a visit to the narrow street where Stort lived.

His ruse was to knock on doors asking for lodgings, saying a friend
of his had been injured en route to Brum and needed something
more in the way of a bed than cobbles and earth.

The humbles were small, the chance of accommodation slight and,
anyway, others had tried the same thing before him.

But he was Slew and he was not Master of Shadows for nothing.
Men and women found their minds confused under the power of his
gaze; they might want to say 'No' but they found themselves saying
'Yes'.

But information was his real intent; rooms would be a bonus.

Only when he had learned what he could from Stort's neighbours
further down the street did he approach his humble, well aware by
then who would answer the door.

'Yes?'

'Goodwife Cluckett, I believe.'

He smiled and something even in her large and formidable bosom
yielded.

'If it's Mister Stort you want . . . ?'

He shook his head.

'No, I . . . we . . . would not disturb your great master's peace, not at all.'

Flattered by association, a little more of Cluckett became Slew's.

'We are but pilgrims visiting Brum to make the trek—'

'We?' said Cluckett. 'I see no "we", just you.'

'Injured,' he explained, 'nearly killed, my fellow brothers were cruelly ambushed on the way to Brum. No, we were looking for bed and board and I can think of no other way than to knock on doors and hope against hope that some gentle heart will take pity on us and . . .'

Cluckett eyed him and liked him.

Dark, strong, modest, possibly masterful.

'Do you know someone here who might help?' he said, looming closer, bold with his gaze upon her.

'Well I . . . not here of course . . .'

He looked past her into Stort's humble. Neat as two pins, even the books far down the corridor ranged like a platoon of Fyrd on parade.

'I am sorry, I could not help being impressed . . .'

That was a step too far yet not a mistake.

She narrowed the door only slightly, intrigued by what he said.

'Impressed by what?'

'The books, their order. I like order, many do not.'

'Ah,' said Cluckett softly, not quite knowing why, 'well I am thinking, sir . . .'

'Brother,' he purred. 'What were you thinking, Goodwife?'

'Cluckett will do nicely, sir, no need for the Goodwife. I was thinking that my neighbour next door, who lives alone and is elderly, might be willing . . . perhaps . . . if . . . how many of you are there?'

'Too many I fear. Six in all. Four males, including myself and two females.'

'Willing to share?'

'Of course.'

'I could, I suppose, talk with her . . . her home used to be a workshop and it is bigger than it seems from the outside. She has taken groups of pilgrims before and could do with the money.'

'We shall be generous, and no trouble,' he said, large and solid before her.

Her bosom heaved.

'Come back later,' she said.

'I will, Goodwife Cluckett, and thank you.'

So it was that Slew inveigled his way into the humble next to Stort's, the group of which he was now de facto leader, moving in with all the courtesy and tact they could, money in advance. Stort's neighbour was both flustered and thrilled and Cluckett inclined to pop in and out to see how things were progressing and if there was anything she could do.

Only two evenings later, by way of thanks, the women in the group, at Slew's prompting, laid on a celebration feast at their own expense and to say thanks for their safe journey, more or less, to Brum; to Cluckett and the hostess; to Slew and to life in general. They had made the trek, seen where Beornamund's forge had been from beneath which Mister Stort was said to have extracted the gem. All was well and the mead flowed.

Slew sat next to Cluckett, serving her food, pouring her drink, impressed by her discretion where Stort was concerned. Even so, Slew found out enough for his dark purpose.

He learned that after Stort got back to Brum he had made but one visit before an important meeting with the High Ealdor and others and after that single visit 'his mind seemed easier'.

'And where was that visit to?'

'The Library,' she answered, 'just as you would expect. Then soon after that he was gone again on his travels.'

'Where to this time?' said Slew jocularly.

'He didn't say,' she replied, but Slew didn't care.

He now had, he believed, what he needed most of all, a clue to the whereabouts of the gem. Not a good one, but a possibility. Stort would not arrive in Brum with the gem, cause a great deal of fuss and bother, have it nearly taken off him by the city hierarchy (as the rumours probably correctly had it) and then leave again carrying it in his pocket.

No, Stort might be an innocent, as by all accounts he was, but he was no fool. He would have hidden the gem somewhere in the city while he went away, and all Slew needed to do was work out where in Brum a *scholar* would hide a gem.

Not difficult.

That much sorted out, Slew enjoyed the rest of the celebration, and having as usual avoided all intoxicating liquor because of his supposed vows but in fact because he needed no such stimulus, retired to bed, alone.

In the morning he abluted and dressed carefully, donning the robe he had stolen from the monk he murdered, now cleaned and ironed to his satisfaction, and touching up his dyed hair.

Machtild had commented on the fact.

Evelien had not dared.

'What are you trying to hide?' Machtild had asked.

She was indeed the clever one.

Neat, tidy, cleansed, and without his stave, looking intelligent and scholarly and suitably modest and in awe of the establishment, he presented himself at Brum's Great Library.

A lie is all the better for being very near the truth, and the question that had preoccupied Slew was which truth would make it easiest for him to get past Master Brief without suspicion.

Brief was, perhaps, the greatest scholar in the Hyddenworld, certainly the most famous. It was well known that in recent years he had travelled only reluctantly, his journeying now being done, he said, inside his mind with the help of his books. But – and for Slew it was a dangerous 'but' – his range of scholarly contacts was vast and unknowable to any but himself.

Therefore, a scholar presenting himself at the Library was likely, very likely, to have worked for or with someone Brief already knew; or in an institution whose reputation and personnel were familiar to the great scrivener.

'Ah! Master Monk! Slew, I believe.'

Slew fell to his knees before Brief, which he hoped would embarrass him. He attempted to kiss his red velvet robe which, to his relief, Brief pulled away. Close-to it was grubby and ragged and Slew was particular about such things.

'Please, Brother Slew, there's no need for any of this . . . I am but a scholar like any other . . .'

'But a great one, Master, indeed a very great one.'

'Well, well . . .' said Brief, 'and what may we do for you?'

'I come, Master Brief, in all humility while I am on pilgrimage in Brum to pursue a small, private study of my own . . . nothing much, a field I am sure, many have visited before . . .'

'The subject being?' said Brief, a mite impatiently.

Slew's garb was clean, that was certain. His sandals, too. But he looked all brushed up for the occasion, too much so, not like a serious scholar from one of the great Continental Schools or Libraries.

'The Seasons,' said Slew.

Brief sighed, it was just the kind of vague subject scholars like this would pursue.

'Fine, excellent, a worthy study!' said Brief rather tetchily. 'And your Library . . . I mean the one where you normally study or to which you are in some way attached?'

Slew sighed and shrugged and said in a heavy kind of way, with a hint of despair and hopefulness, 'I am a wandering scholar, Master Brief, in search wherever I may find it of truth, of insight, of a greater understanding of the meaning of things and, naturally, but you would understand this, I feel that—'

Brief sighed inwardly still more.

A *wandering* scholar, the very worst kind: unattached because no one wants them, pursuing dubious theses and wild propositions that cannot be tested, incapable of studying a subject in any depth because hard work might be involved.

'Splendid,' said Brief, cutting him short, 'we welcome you to Brum and to this Library and look forward to the contribution which, I am quite sure, in time, you will make to the world of scholarship on the subject of . . . of . . . what did you say you were studying?'

'The Seasons,' said Slew.

Brief snapped his fingers.

An assistant came running.

'Any particular one, or all of them?' asked Brief, a touch acidly.

'Spring and Summer,' said Slew.

'Show Brother Slew to the stacks in the lower reading room,' Brief commanded his assistant, 'and ask Librarian Thwart to give him what help and guidance he might need.'

Slew looked eager and ingenuous.

'Are the books in the lower reading room younger or older?' he asked.

'Older,' said Brief shortly.

'Ah, to sit where other scholars greater than myself have sat, perhaps even that wonder of our age Master Stort!'

'*Wonder?*' repeated Brief doubtfully. 'Whether he is that or not I may tell you he never sits, he is nearly incapable of doing so. But I must . . .'

He left Slew to it, glad to have no need at his time of life to listen to the blathering of a third-rate wandering scholar.

Slew watched him go, pretended awe in his eyes, dislike in his heart.

In fact the awe was not so hard to masquerade, because the moment Brief was gone and Slew knew he was accepted, the great, ancient, dusty, murky, many-cornered sense of history of the place bore in on him.

He arrived at the lower level and found himself faced with a long high room whose walls were of dressed stone. To one side was a desk at which a wan, thin librarian sat, his spectacles propped on his forehead as he examined a document.

On the room's other side was a series of arches leading into corridors and chambers of various kinds in which books and manuscripts were stored on shelves. Some of the arches were open, others closed with barred gates, heavily padlocked.

'Yers?'

'Librarian Thwart?'

'Yers.'

'Master Brief sent me.'

'Yers?'

'He said you would show me the way things work down here.'

'Subject?'

'The Seasons.'

'Be specific.'

'Summer.'

'Be more specific.'

'Well—'

'Days? Dates? Fauna? Flora? History ancient, history modern? Climatological records? Meaning of?'

'History, ancient.'

'English or Estrange?'

'Estrange?'

'Old hydden or foreign.'

'English and perhaps Estrange. I have some titles . . .'

'I am listening.'

Throughout this terse exchange Librarian Thwart continued to read his document. He now stopped and eyed Slew.

'You are monkish,' he said.

'I am. A pilgrim, a modest wandering scholar.'

'Ah, yes, taking the high road and the low in search of truth and wisdom. Which titles?'

Slew decided to be clear-cut. 'I need to look at Pluvar's *Phases* of course, and Hindrick's *Lencten* and *The Boke of the Abundant Sumor* . . .'

'Well sir – '

Slew rattled off a few more titles kenned in the Bochum Library on the basis of the research Stort was known to have done. He was aware that some were a good deal rarer than others.

The assistant was at once impressed and stressed, trying to stop Slew's expert flow, to explain that . . . well, access was . . . and the fact that Master Brief had . . . yes . . . it didn't mean . . . no . . . but . . . well . . . he supposed . . .

'I'll start with The Meister's *Monologue on the Earthly Seasons*,' he began firmly.

'We have copies,' suggested Thwart.

'The original has notes in the margins by Skurt.'

'But—'

'You have gloves I take it?'

'Yes indeed we have.'

They descended a spiral medieval stone staircase, past bolted gates, on down to an open vault where, in a cool, dry, perfect temperature, the greatest collection in the Hyddenworld of material on the four seasons sat on shelves, hid itself away in boxes, or curled in ancient script-rolls, all in arched corridors, also gated and padlocked and very secure.

'These are the open shelves of what might be called the main collection. There is always an assistant hereabout to help.'

'You . . . ?'

'I'm one of them.'

'And these special collections?' said Slew.

'Depends. Best to ask what you want.'

'How do I ask for what I don't know you have?'

'That's scholarship I suppose!'

'I suppose it is,' laughed Slew icily.

No matter, he was here and here was where, somewhere, Stort would probably have hidden the gem.

'I would rather not sit where Master Scrivener Stort works, out of respect.'

'He generally stands,' said Thwart, 'but that's his desk. He prefers it not to be disturbed.'

He pointed to an untidy desk which, to Slew, looked like a treasure trove of clues as to where the gem might be.

'Thank you,' said Slew, 'I'll be careful not to sit where that great scholar stands!'

Thwart smiled appreciatively. 'Let me show you how things work around here,' he said.

23

ON THE HILL

Three days after Judith's early morning exploration of the garden, which Jack had not felt it necessary to mention to anyone else, he and Katherine, with Arthur too, took her up White Horse Hill.

She had been alive for just three weeks but by Arthur's calculations, based on his continuing measurements, she was now physically and mentally six years old. Until then she had dressed haphazardly, everything having been bought in a rush, it being nearly impossible to keep up with her. Katherine got her new trainers for the outing, a new T-shirt and trousers. Also, a child's backpack into which she put some snacks.

The walk had special significance for Katherine.

When she first came to Woolstone her mother Clare could still walk, though with difficulty. Arthur had led them both through the garden, through the henge and onto the path across the meadow and so up the Hill. In those days she knew nothing about the Hydden-world and had no idea that the path crossed the old pilgrim way by which, so many years later, she and Jack would return to Woolstone from their venture among the hydden. It had been a happy day, but never repeated once Clare became bed-ridden.

This memory came back as she went the same way with Judith. From the start strange things happened. Judith stopped still in the henge, looking about with wary curiosity, sniffing at the air and peering among the trees.

'What is it?' said Katherine.

'Nobody,' was her odd reply but one to which they did not attach significance.

They stopped to point out where she had been born and Jack took her arms and swung her round and round saying, 'Look at the sky, watch the trees being a carousel.'

'What's a carousel?' she asked later, having thought about it for a while.

'Like a roundabout only golden and with horses and music,' said Arthur.

Judith's development had been so rapid that it had dawned on them only slowly that she needed feeding with ideas and experience as well as food. The food had been easy, the rest was more difficult. But both the Foales had their childhood books and Katherine had hers as well, so there was no shortage of reading material. Added to which theirs was not a house lacking in conversation and ideas.

Toys were a different matter, and that was left to Jack to work out with the assistance of shops he went to in Wantage and Oxford.

Judith learnt very fast, though her reading was slow, perhaps like that of a four-year-old. But she absorbed everything around her like a sponge, one thing after another, so that they were constantly surprised by her growing vocabulary and the things she knew.

'Her speech is keeping pace at least,' said Arthur.

'And she can say "Anglo-Saxon",' said Margaret, 'because I taught her.'

'Much good may that do her, my dear,' growled Arthur.

They had no television that worked. But there was the internet and all of them but Margaret sat with her and showed her things on screen.

Margaret's role was different and more hands-on.

'You can help me plant some lettuces, Judith . . . They're called scones, my dear, do you want to make some . . . ? Come and help me pick some daffodils, Arthur likes to have them on his desk and your mum puts them in her room . . .'

One way or another Judith learnt things and learnt them fast.

What she lacked was friends. Arthur, now the expert on child development, said warningly, 'She needs friends if she is to learn to socialize, otherwise she could become a criminal.'

'Yes, well,' muttered Katherine, 'even if the law ever caught up with her, which I doubt, I'm not sure under whose jurisdiction a Shield Maiden falls . . .'

The walk up White Horse Hill was a landmark event in Judith's short life which Margaret was sorry to miss, but she got more tired these days, she explained, and it would be nice to have the house to herself for a little while.

'She gets more than tired,' said Arthur, 'she gets pains in her arms and legs. Her days for walking are long over and she's on pills for blood pressure which she won't take unless I force-feed her, which I do!'

They climbed the Hill quite slowly, letting Judith take her time. It was not the climb itself that slowed her but the sights and the sounds of other people as they climbed. When they reached the top Judith hid behind Jack's legs, staring, especially at children of her own size.

Later she took his hand and ventured forth a little.

'She wants to make contact but doesn't know how,' whispered Katherine.

'Shall I . . . ?' began Jack, always one to push things forward.

'Let her do it her way.'

Arthur sat down on the grass, huffing and puffing as he produced an old-fashioned vacuum flask of tea.

Judith sat with him.

'The Horse,' he said, 'is just there, over the brow of the hill. We passed it coming up but it's not exactly obvious.'

'Where?' she said.

'Show her,' said Arthur, not wishing to heave himself up.

'No, you,' said Judith.

'Well . . .'

But he didn't mind, she had been easier and less in pain for the last day or two.

With Judith and Arthur exploring the Horse, Jack and Katherine put their arms around each other and had a moment to themselves.

'Our special place,' she said.

They had often walked up from the house two years before in the Summer when they renewed their brief childhood friendship and fell in love. He turned her round to look across the other side of the Hill towards the Ridgeway, the old prehistoric way that ran from Avebury twenty miles to the west; and to the east along the downs to the Chilterns and from there up into East Anglia, where it became another path, but still part of the ancient system.

'We promised each other that one day we'd go that way right to the end,' she said.

'We will,' he murmured, 'somehow we will, I can feel it . . .'

He could too, in his bones, in his spirit, he and Katherine and Judith, one day . . . somehow . . . they might . . . they must. Some journeys feel written in the stars.

'We will,' he said again.

They turned their attention back to Judith, who was arguing with Arthur.

'It isn't a horse, it's white lines. Like a picture.'

'A picture of a horse,' said Arthur.

'Where?' she persisted.

He peered about, helplessly, because she was quite right, it was too big, too abstract, to make sense of from the ground.

'There's a picture of it from the air here on the public noticeboard,' said Jack.

Judith came to him and he picked her up to have a look.

'It's a picture of a horse,' he said. 'This horse,' he added.

'Where?' she said a third time, unable to make the conceptual leap of imagination needed to turn the diverging, ancient lines into something as concrete as the legs, head and body of a horse.

Jack took her hand and placed one of her fingers on the eye of the Horse. It had a special significance for him because he had climbed up here on the day Clare, Katherine's mother, had died, and he had met Imbolc the Peace-Weaver, legendary sister of the Shield Maiden.

'That's the Horse's eye,' he said. 'We're not meant to but let's stand on it.'

He helped her down the steep sward and they stood together on the eye.

'This is how the Horse sees,' he said.

'Here?' she said, dropping to her knees and looking straight into the eye, which was just a white circle of bare chalk. 'Here! I can see the Horse and the Horse can see me!'

There was sudden wonder in her voice.

She stood up, stared at the complex lines of the head, then at the legs and back and she said, 'I can dance the Horse alive.'

She raised her arms, stepped from the eye and walked to one of the lines and began hopping and skipping along the lines, as if she was in a maze finding the way in.

'Look, Daddy, look!'

She danced the lines all by herself, over the rise, off down the slope, back and back down, leg by leg, along the body, back to the head and eye.

'I danced the Horse and he's gloppolling over the grass towards the sky, look!'

She was happy and in touch with something beyond herself. All might have been well had not a primary school group come along and seen her and stared.

Judith, not street-aware, misread the signals and, wanting friends, danced over to them, perhaps a little scarily. Someone or something among them had caught her eye. They backed off and one of them said, 'She looks weird.'

Judith, stubborn, went towards them again and grabbed at a girl her own size.

Before Jack or Katherine could intervene there was a scream, a push, a shove and Judith was on the sloping ground, rolling a couple of rolls down the grass to where it steepened towards the Horse and then carried on down and down into the great deep combe below, so far that people above looked down on the birds flying there.

The girl was on the ground, messed up and crying. A bigger boy looked belligerent. A teacher, purposeful, headed towards Jack, who also purposeful, but angry and protective too, headed towards him.

But for Judith there might have been a war.

She got up, slowly raised her hands, and said, 'Look! I'll glallop with the Horse!'

With that she went to the edge of the grass escarpment, cartwheeled over it down to the Horse, came upright with her feet plumb centre of the eye and before anyone could say or do a thing, tumbled on, bouncing, jumping, dancing the sward and earth, cartwheeling the clouds, laughing the breeze, flying the knapweed and the scabious until she disappeared from view halfway down the slope.

A car was coming up a road, another going down, they disappeared where she had gone and wow! Like a bird she shot from off the road she had landed on and carried on free-running down the terracettes, on and on through a flock of sheep, Jack and Katherine and Arthur open-mouthed, the teacher standing still alarmed, the kids staring wide-eyed, as on Judith went until with a cartwheel and slow turn in the air she landed upright on a green swathe of horizontal ground, the perfect stage for her finale, which was to look back up, apparently all right, and raise a hand.

Stumbling, tripping, grumbling, Jack and Katherine, with Arthur taking the long way round, made their way down to her. It had been magnificently terrifying and when they got up close they thought at first she was all right: hair a mess, clothes grass- and earth-stained, face scratched, hands and nails torn, but all right.

'Let's go home,' said Jack heavily, not knowing what else to say.

He didn't look back upslope to where some in the crowd still stared.

Judith said, 'I want a dress like that girl, I want to be pretty. I don't want to be me.'

Jack replied, 'But *you* danced the Horse.'

'Yes,' she whispered, taking his hand and then Katherine's too, 'and he danced me.'

The strain of what happened, the climb and the tumbling down, proved too much for her. Next day she was in pain again and tired, and all that consoled her was to be left alone by the chimes, rocking back and forth and staring in between the trees of the henge.

Jack found her in the sun, pretending to sleep among Arthur's tomato plants, bees buzzing, ants crawling, Judith's dark hair mingling with the earth, whose colour was the same.

He had heard her say, 'Dad's coming, you must go away.'

'Who must?' he asked.

'My friend.'

'Aah!' said Jack non-committally, looking around and seeing nobody. He had heard of imaginary friends.

24

FRIENDS

Judith hovered on the edge of the lives of Stort and Barklice for several days after their arrival in Woolstone, venturing into the henge, looking about, sitting over by the tomato plants and talking as if to something or somebody she knew was there.

They made no attempt to communicate with her or to attract her attention, preferring to watch cautiously from a distance and move away from her direct line of vision.

Despite taking these precautions while they thought about whether or not to make themselves known, their bigger concern being how and when to contact Jack, with each day that passed she came closer. Whether she heard or saw them, or even scented them, they did not know. She would appear nearby, better at hyddening than themselves. Once or twice she mischievously stood in their way and they were forced to retreat. However she did it, it was evident she knew they were there and, too, that she was not afraid.

Barklice was surprised that she even sensed their presence.

'In my experience humans never seem to,' said Barklice, 'because they've long since forgotten how. But there's no denying she's aware we're here.'

It was this fact more than any other that convinced Stort that she was the Shield Maiden and had Jack's blood in her.

In the first two or three days they had retreated the moment adult humans had appeared, sensing their approach by the heaviness of their steps, their scent, their noise.

From the first she was different, treading more lightly, her scent benign. Gradually they dared sit in open shadow when the humans came and Stort was in no doubt that the larger of the two was Jack, the other Katherine.

It was not as simple as looking at them and seeing a larger version of the friends he knew so well. The hydden rarely look at humans close-to, nor even from the middle distance, not directly. They know they're there, they see their shape in their peripheral vision and they disappear from view.

In short, hydden have got out of the habit of looking closely at humans and see them rather as they might the blur of a vehicle rushing by on a fast road, unclearly.

Added to which Stort had no wish to see Jack writ large.

That version was not the Jack he knew, the same with Katherine.

So when they appeared in the garden with the Shield Maiden, Stort mentally blocked them out of sight, registering their presence and not much more.

Their daughter was different.

From the first she was there and she was real and she unabashedly invaded their hydden space, peering at the shadows where they hid, chattering away as if they could hear.

Which was another thing.

To the hydden, human voices are as blurry as their visual aspect, deep and broken, hard to make out but by intonation. So distorted is the sound that words can seem like a foreign language.

Not so the Shield Maiden; her talk was clear to them.

Or rather, it was to Stort.

Barklice, still nervous, never got near enough to hear.

'What is it she says?' he asked.

'At the moment she is much concerned about tomatoes which, she tells her friend, who appears to be me, turn red in the sun and can be fried in butter and taste good on toast.'

'How does she describe the taste?'

'The word she uses sounds like "yummy".'

'Hmm,' said Barklice, 'that's a word worth borrowing.'

She seemed to them very large for a child, since she was the same size as themselves, taller than Barklice, shorter than Stort but more solid.

'I wouldn't want to get in a fight with her,' whispered Barklice one day when she appeared as if from nowhere and began running at trees and leaping up to catch the lowest branches.

'Nor I,' agreed Stort, in whose mind a way of contacting Jack was forming.

Judith began running round in and out of the henge, tumbling and falling for fun, always agile and acrobatic.

'We should put a stop to that,' said Stort, 'she's going sinister and that's not good in a henge.'

Sinister meant leftward and that way weakened someone in a henge if the pattern of it was left incomplete. Dexter would have been better.

'Over to you, Barklice . . .'

The verderer moved into the shadows ahead of Judith, slid between trees, led her by shadows outward, then by shadows back until, interweaving her path the other way, she entered the henge from the opposite direction. It was a dance, mathematical in its precision.

He came back breathless and said, 'She's got power, Stort. Runs like a creature of the wild. A dog couldn't keep up with her . . . She'd look beautiful if she didn't dress so oddly. It isn't my preference to see a female in trews and a vest.'

Her sudden appearance disturbed them.

It seemed that she was learning the art of hyddening by instinct, realizing that if she was to get to see the person she talked to, namely Stort, she was going to have to learn to take him unawares. At first, light though her tread was, they were aware of her presence almost as soon as she left the house. Soon she appeared as they did, from dappled shade, from round a bush, out of bright, blinding sunlight.

'In no time,' said Barklice, 'she'll find us out.'

'Which will be a good thing, for I do not wish to scare her away.'

It was the early morning after this conversation, when the two hydden were having a pleasant breakfast some way from the henge, and Stort was pouring himself a third cannikin of scented tea, that Barklice stilled and his face went white.

'Er . . . Stort,' he said in a voice of barely concealed panic, 'I don't want to alarm you and nor should you overreact lest it causes trouble but . . . we have a visitor.'

Stort's mouth went dry, aware from the direction in which Barklice was looking that the visitor stood somewhere behind him.

'You mean . . . ?'

'Yes, Stort, that's just what I mean.'

Stort straightened up, turned round and stood up.

He found himself looking straight into the Shield Maiden's eyes. She was standing ten feet away, stock-still, wary yet not afraid.

Stort gulped.

Judith half smiled.

'Hello,' she said.

'Hello,' he replied.

The sounds of the world fell away from Stort's ears, but the light was there, the sunshine, which fell on her as it did on him. A moment of Summer.

Hello, and the word hovered between them, like a dragonfly shot through with gold and green and iridescent blue, over the banks of a clear stream, and then another, still in the air before darting away, one after the other, before pausing again.

So then as Stort stared at her and she at him, there were no barriers of any kind between them.

She raised one hand and reached it towards him, opening her palm.

The sun caught that too and what it was she offered him.

'You can have it,' she said.

It was a cherry tomato, orangey-red, and her voice as clear and bright as a hydden's.

He stepped forward and took it.

'You can eat it,' she said. 'Look!'

She raised the other hand to her mouth and popped another tomato in.

'Eat it,' she said again, her eyes dreamy, 'and make it burst!'

Stort did so and it did burst, a wonderful explosion of colourful taste in his mouth as he stared at her and she at him.

'Yummy,' she said and, as he began to laugh, she ran and danced away shouting, 'Yummy!' again.

He stood dumbfounded and was still standing when she rushed back, stopping nearer to him, not breathless at all.

'I'm Judith,' she said.

Stort smiled, which wasn't hard because the laughter of a moment before had not left his face.

'I'm Bedwyn Stort.'

She whispered the name carefully and then mouthed it in silence.

'Judith,' he said and she smiled to hear her name spoken by a friend. With that she was gone, answering a shout from the house, grinning and dancing as she went.

'I don't think,' said Barklice in the vast silence that her absence left behind, 'that she noticed me.'

She came back that afternoon and she and Stort talked of this and that, inconsequentially, out by the chimes.

'I can't reach them,' she said, standing on tiptoe and losing her balance as she tried to touch the nearest.

'*I* can,' he said, which he could.

'Look!'

They studied the ants blundering up and down the hairy tomato stems.

They lay and listened to the Earth.

'You can hear the worms,' he said, 'crawling.'

'Where?'

'Down there, crawling along, *that* sound.'

'That one?'

'Mmm . . . and you know where they're crawling?'

'Uh uh,' she said, shaking her head, curious.

'Towards your ears.'

For a moment she believed him, then she didn't and she got up laughing, running, being chased, but had to pause to let him catch her up.

'You're slow.'

'You're fast, but then you would be.'

They stopped, sat in long grass, watched the insects buzz by over their heads and the light, white clouds of summer floating by.

'I ache sometimes. Like my knees and shins and everything. It hurts a lot.'

'Growing pains,' said Stort, 'I had them. Tall people do. Ache ache ache all day long.'

'What's your friend's name?'

'Barklice.'

'He looks unhappy, not like us.'

'He is unhappy. He's got a worry.'

'Oh.'

Over their fire, stewing tomatoes, breaking brot together, she asked Barklice, 'What's your worry?'

He glanced at Stort, who affected innocence with a shrug.

'Something I left undone.'

'What?'

'Something.'

'Tell me.'

'No,' said Barklice.

She giggled and, for the first time in days, so did he.

She came and went, that day and the next.

The one after, following much pain through the night, she was pale and miserable, but later in the afternoon, having been back to the house for a sleep, she came out and said, 'Let's look at the chimes again!'

This time she reached higher than Stort could and nearly tugged one off a branch.

'No!' he said with alarm. 'They're not ours to take.'

She looked dismayed and shook her head.

'They are,' she said, but did not take one, 'they are!'

She turned away and wandered to the tomatoes and was happy again.

She picked one and gave it him and with a smile as light and happy as ever he had seen.

'Thank you,' he said.

The chimes shimmered close by, shifting, changing as they did, never the same.

Before he could stop her she pulled one off. It was tied by a golden thread so long it hung from her hand to the ground.

She looked at it and he looked at her, the picture of concentration, filled with life and energy.

She made a loop of the thread and reached up and hung the chime around his neck.

'You're my friend,' she said, 'for ever and ever.'

'I think I am,' said Stort, tucking the chime inside his jerkin, knowing he would never let it go.

Then, laughing, she fled to the house.

The day was warm, the afternoon clear and long, twilight gentle, and she came outside again, searching him out.

Nothing was said, why should it be?

'Judith . . .' he began a little later, because she was growing and their time was running out and he had to find a way to talk with Jack, 'I . . .' but he didn't finish.

'What?'

He shook his head.

When evening came and she'd been back to tea and then came out, she heard music on the wind.

'What's that?'

'Paley's Creek,' said Barklice.

'Can we go to it?' she asked.

'No,' said Barklice.

'Yes,' said Stort, regretting it at once, 'sometime.'

'Judith, come and help!'

It was Margaret's voice.

They were having drinks on the patio, or Arthur and Margaret were. Old times, memories of when Clare was alive. Katherine had water, Jack a cola, and when Judith came running, her clothes looking too small for her all of a sudden, she had a cola too.

'We'll have another try at buying something more suitable,' said Katherine rather properly. She had never been one for skirts and dresses, but since the walk on the Hill Judith had wanted one or the other or both.

'Another tremor,' Arthur murmured, looking up from the paper he was reading.

'Where?' someone said. 'When?'

He peered over his spectacles at the date of the paper. It was two days old. Woolstone House time was slower than the rest of the world, except where Judith was concerned.

'Redditch, three days ago, more to come. Weird.'

'Not so weird,' said Jack, 'the Shield Maiden's been born. Remember?'

They all did, they all knew the story of Beornamund and the lost gem of Spring, waiting to be found. They knew and believed, even Margaret. They had been too busy to talk about it, or think about it . . . or they had done both and hoped its implications would go away.

Judith got up.

'It's nearly bedtime,' Arthur said.

'I'll say goodnight to my friends.'

'Oh!' said Arthur. 'Their number has increased!'

They let her go down the garden into the twilight and heard music on the wind, haunting and alluring. Jack looked suddenly restive and alarmed, sitting forward on his chair, watching after Judith.

'If she's playing with her imaginary friends she'll come to no harm,' said Katherine.

The evening was warm, the music came and went, almost inaudibly, and just as Jack was going to get up and go in search of her, the worry on his face remaining, she wandered back, trailing ivy in both hands like a train to her dress.

'We've been listening to the chimes,' she said.

'Who has?' asked Arthur.

'Me and my friends,' she said.

'What are their names, my dear?' he asked.

'Barklice,' she replied, 'and Bedwyn Stort.'

25

REUNION

'Stort?'

Stort!?

The moment they heard Judith utter that familiar name Jack and Katherine felt a mix of shock and delight, but they said nothing for fear of worrying her.

Arthur, as surprised as they were, saw at once that the two needed to talk. He and Margaret found an excuse to get Judith back inside the house and left them to get on with it.

'Stort's *here!?*' exclaimed Jack. 'Here in Woolstone?'

'Sounds like it,' said Katherine.

Her first thought was that he had come to find out what had happened with the birth and to congratulate them.

Jack was more circumspect.

Stort had left them at the Devil's Quoits barely a month before when he headed off for Brum. He had been eager to get there, to share his news (and their good news) and reacquaint himself with his many friends. He would not have wanted to leave again so soon and make such a long trek simply to give his congratulations. No, he had come for a reason, and if he had come with Barklice the reason was in some way official.

'If I know Festoon,' said Jack, 'he sent Barklice because he wanted to make sure Stort actually got here, probably quickly. It's something urgent and maybe because something's wrong.'

Katherine looked worried.

'They surely can't think that you'd go rushing off to Brum at a moment's notice when we've just had a baby . . . would they?'

She needed reassurance.

'They could think that, they probably do, because children don't figure highly in anyone's mind in Brum among the people we know, but Pike's . . .'

He put his arms around her and then kissed her.

It felt like a while since he had done that, like that. He did it again. They talked again later, outside after dark.

'But I'm not going to go back to Brum, I'm staying here with you and Judith. There can be nothing more important than that, especially when she's growing as she is. She's changing all the time and I'm beginning to realize how precious this time is . . . but . . .'

He looked towards the henge, dark and secret in the night. But the moon was showing through the clouds, large and nearly full.

'Imagine, Stort's in there and . . .'

She held him close. 'You want to go and see him don't you?'

'Yes, of course I do. He's our best friend. There's things to talk to him about apart from what he might want. And I bet you do too.'

'No,' she whispered, 'not as much as you. My needs are different now, but you . . . Jack, we haven't talked seriously for weeks, maybe months. Babies take up time and mental space and since Judith was born it's been non-stop.'

'No, we haven't talked.'

Arthur came to the patio door, Judith getting ready for bed upstairs with Margaret. He saw them holding each other in the night and stepped back and closed the door. Beyond them in the sky the moon loomed.

'Full tomorrow,' he murmured, and turning went off to his study to think what Stort's coming meant.

Margaret appeared.

'She's gone down just like that but I expect she'll wake later and in pain. Arthur, are you thinking what I'm thinking?'

'About Stort's appearance here? Probably.'

'I think it can mean only one thing, don't you?'

'Beornamund's lost gem of Spring?'

'It's been found, my love, the legend was true. I never thought when I started studying Anglo-Saxon literature that the day would come when something that seemed purely mythical would be proved true.'

'Let's wait and see . . . They're outside, talking. Leave them be, Margaret.'

'I was going to say the same to you, Professor Arthur Foale.'

'Come here!'

Laughing, she did and embraced him among the books.

'Go on,' said Katherine, 'go to him in the henge. If you don't come back within the hour I'll divorce you.'

'But we aren't married.'

'Aren't we, Jack? If the church and the state didn't marry us, the Hyddenworld did. Give Stort my love.'

He looked suddenly nervous, which was unusual for him.

'Are you worried about whether or not you can use the henge like you did before?'

'Yes.'

'You said once that going betwixt the worlds, once you know how to do it, is like riding a bike – you can do it but you don't quite know how.'

'Exactly.'

'Do you want me to come as far as the conifers?'

'Yes, I do.'

They walked across the lawn, the moon racing against the clouds over the conifers, hand in hand.

'Do you remember when . . .?'

'I remember everything,' said Jack. 'You are my life, Katherine.'

'Go on . . . go on . . .'

He passed between the conifers and crossed the threshold into the henge, their hands parting as he did so.

He let his mind be free, his body too, turning dexter, sliding into the shadows, reaching sinister, feeling his body thin and stretch, reach up one way and down the other, as thin as a shard, reflecting both worlds, spinning, turning and dancing through the shadows of the henge and looking back to the conifers, taller now, vast as the shadow that was Katherine turned towards the house and the lit windows there and was gone.

Jack stood listening, breathing heavily, stilling himself until, catching the scent of a brew, he smiled, mischievous, content. He'd teach Stort to come calling sneakily.

He eased himself backwards from the henge, away from the scent, working out where they were and circling round the unexpected way. Stort was hopeless at detecting intruders, but Barklice was a more difficult challenge.

He moved back into the orbit of the scent of their brew, heard their voices, came to where they were sitting tree by tree, and finally stood listening to their talk.

Of love, of course, that was always their theme.

He moved closer, finally saw them, Stort tall and thin, Barklice wiry, by the slightest of fires whose smoke, no more than a grey winding thread up into the skies, was lit by moonlight now.

And what he heard took him by surprise.

'That's what I am, Stort, and that's the simple truth!' cried Barklice standing up to quite literally beat his breast in self-disgust.

'You are not, Barklice, well, not exactly. It would not be the word I would use.'

But it was no use, Barklice was filled with such remorse and shame about his son that he was not listening.

'A fraud and a cheat, to my friends and . . . and . . . to those others. You don't understand, Stort, that I am terrified . . . One cannot recover the past. It's gone for ever.'

'And yet, Barklice, it would seem that Paley's Creek is somewhere nearby. Day by day we see folk wending their way there by the old paths hereabout. Night by night we hear the music carried on the wind. It comes from northerly I think, and that's the way folk are going. Towards the River, that's where it is, isn't it?'

'Paley's Creek,' said Barklice very nervously.

'You were there before, weren't you? Something happened, didn't it?'

'Yes, it did,' said Barklice miserably.

'And you've been avoiding it ever since, haven't you?'

'Yes, I have.'

'Well, one thing's certain, if Jack were here he'd grab your collar and haul you there whether you liked it or not. Failing that I think I'll do it anyway and make you face what you have been avoiding so long.'

'They'll kill me probably, then boil me and eat me. It's the kind of thing they do at Paley's Creek.'

'They've mainly been bilgesnipe we've seen on their way there and none of them look like cannibals to me!'

'Maybe not, but the simple fact is it's too late. Paley's Creek happens around a full moon, or the main part of it does. At moonset it's over and that's tomorrow night.'

'Time enough to get there.'

He shook his head, not without a certain sense of relief. There is nothing more comforting than a good excuse for not doing something difficult.

'We have to stay here and see if we can find a way of attracting Jack's attention.'

'Humpphh!' said Stort, 'I suppose you're right.'

'Yes, I am right,' said Barklice happily, 'it's obvious we can't possibly go. The full moon will rise, it will journey the sky, Paley's Creek will be and then it will be gone – sad, but true. I cannot be there. I did the best I could. Have another brew.'

'I think I will,' said Jack quietly from the shadows.

Barklice grabbed his stave.

Stort almost choked on his brew.

'*Jack!?*'

'Hello,' said Jack, stepping into the moonlight where he could be seen.

He hugged them both, big, strong, bearlike.

'Jack,' said Stort.

'Stort,' he replied.

'She . . . ?'

'She did.'

'And she is the Shield Maiden?'

'She is. And there's so much to tell you.'

They let Jack talk, telling them about the birth and what had happened since.

'Such pain, Stort, it made me weep not to be able to help. Even now . . . well, you've seen her.'

'She is certainly in pain – Barklice and I agree on that. She needs a healing beyond anything we can give . . . but if Brief was here, he'd know what to do.'

They talked some more but could see no solution.

The conversation moved back to Barklice.

'So why exactly is tomorrow night the last chance you've got to do whatever it is you haven't done?' said Jack.

'Tomorrow's the twelfth anniversary of my shame, and after that they give me no more chances. That's just how it is.'

Jack looked baffled.

'I've come into this halfway through, but it's obvious you're avoiding something, so tell me right here and right now what exactly you're talking about.'

Barklice paced about a bit and then said, 'I suppose that it is still possible – if I can find the courage, with your help, to get along to Paley's Creek. Come! Let's go now! If I falter bang me over the head with your stave, Jack.'

'I haven't got my stave and we're not going tonight. I have a family. Katherine's threatening to divorce me.'

'When did you get spoused?' asked Stort. 'Quick work, Jack. A month ago you were saying you never would, talking about being free spirits, that sort of thing.'

'No, I'm not spoused, but having a child changes everything, especially one like Judith . . . We'll have to see. Meanwhile, tell us what it's all about, Barklice, you know I like a good story.'

They charged their cannikins, stoked the fire, put some sweetmeats in easy reach and let Barklice talk. Like many hydden he had always heard of Paley's Creek as a place difficult to find, but which the bilgesnipe knew about, where strange things happened but to which ordinary folk ventured at their peril.

A place where things were not as they seemed, where time was not quite itself, where a circumstance started out as one thing but changed magically to another, like a melody in one key that changes to a tune in quite another and yet . . . yet, when all is done, is still the same.

Barklice's natural curiosity had caused him to ask many people where it might be, and many were the different answers that he got. The only certainty was not where it was, but when it was: early Summer, towards the end of May. It was, then, a kind of festival, a moot, a happening . . . but where was the Creek itself?

Barklice had never quite found out and so could never find it until, one year, making a journey across the misty landscape of Wychwood, Oxfordshire, thinking of other things, he fell in with a company of bilgesnipe full of good cheer, songs and merriment, as bilgesnipe often are.

'Where are you going?' they asked.

'Business for Brum,' was his reply.

'Leave off it a while, enjoy these last days of May, come with us to Paley's Creek.'

The mission he was on was not urgent and the offer they made seemed too good to refuse.

He joined them, camping separately of course, but sharing their fire and their food and giving some of his own.

Their songs were strange, their music deep, their way with words once the food was done and the mead flowing, all sinewy and mysterious, alluring.

'Baccy?' they said, offering him an aromatic weed.

'No . . . well, yes,' he'd said, taking some, partaking of it, and wondering which way they had come the day before and where they were going now as he found himself enjoined with them upon a journey like no other he had ever known.

'Paley's Creek, of course.' They laughed, their laughter seeming to travel on ahead, the mist rising at the dawn, other folk joining their trek, tales told of mysteries past, a candle in his hand, females such as he had never seen, hands in his such as he had never touched, darkness sublime, and firelight, and a river, the Thames he thought, maybe that . . . the river drifting by, lighted ships upon its flow which – he thought but wasn't sure – were huge, like galleons, vast in the night from where he lay in what seemed a bower or perfumed bed.

'When will we get there?' he asked many times.

'Where?' they replied, puzzled he should ask.

'Why . . . Paley's Creek,' he said. 'You said . . .'

'You've been here for days, Mister Barklice of Brum. Careful now or you'll never escape.'

'But where . . . ?'

Their laughter was his own, like the tinkling of chimes or the flight of a vast flock of the starlings of memory above his head. And then she came, the female.

'Where am I?' he said in the overwhelming flow of darkness.

'With me, Barklice, with me,' she said. 'If you will, if you want, if you must, with me . . .'

'But . . . I was only trying to . . . to get to . . . to see . . . I wanted . . .'

'Hush,' she said, 'hush . . . for many things are Paley's Creek . . .'

Barklice looked at Jack and Stort, his account apparently over.

'At this point,' he said, 'modesty and common decency suggest I stop. All I will say is that I discovered the truth oft uttered by my mother in relation to her brother, my uncle, namely, "A moment of pleasure leads to a lifetime of regret!" You see my point, Stort?'

'I'm not quite sure I do,' replied Stort ingenuously, not understanding that the reference to his meeting with an alluring female at Paley's Creek had to do with matters carnal. 'We have listened to you for the past hour or so but I am still not quite sure what exactly Paley's Creek is, or even where it is—'

'I would have thought I had made that very clear,' said Barklice tartly, 'without my having to be quite specific. Would you agree, Jack?'

'I think I get the gist,' said Jack cautiously.

'There we are, Stort, the problem is yours not ours.'

'Let me be clear about this,' he replied. 'Somehow or other you were responsible for the conception of a child?'

'A boy.'

'Somehow or other you left him behind with a female?'

'His mother.'

'And somehow or other you have avoided returning to this place which may not exactly be a place, more a sort of shifting sands, for twelve years more or less?'

'Twelve years tomorrow, to be precise.'

'After which time you can no longer claim him?'

'Midnight tomorrow is the witching hour, and up till then they will be there waiting for me to claim my boy.'

'I, or Jack and I, shall get you there! What is your boy's name?'

'I have no idea,' said Barklice testily.

'What's he look like?'

'Now? I have no idea. What happened on the night of his conception occurred in a passing sort of manner . . . when I was rather the worse for wear. I saw him later but only as a tiny infant.'

Stort looked astonished. 'You mean to say you were drunk when . . . when you . . . when . . .?'

'No, I was not.'

'You were sober?'

'My mind was adrift, floating gently across a sea of tranquillity, my body was entwined, enveloped even . . .'

'By what?'

'Ask not by what but by whom.'

'By whom then?'

'By a vast floribunda, scented and glorious, whose silks were loose, whose hands were free, who—'

'Ah! This female, this mother person, is or was a bilgesnipe girl?'

'Your questions are too scientific, Stort. All I know is that nine months after this sojourn in a drifting nocturnal paradise a child was born. He—'

'How do you even know he's a he?'

'Because they told me.'

'*Who* did?'

Barklice came closer, peering to right and left as he did so lest some lurking stranger in the dark might overhear.

'Bilgesnipe. I meet them all the time of course but the first was four years after this unfortunate event. Two females nudged each other, grinned at me and said, "You been and had a good time then Mister Barklice . . . four year'n ago!"

'They laughed themselves silly at my expense and said the ominous words, before they left, "But nary you fear, the lad's doing well."

'"What lad!?" I cried after them in horror, but they were gone.

'So it has been ever since, at odd moments, always unexpected, when a bilgesnipe will say, "He's a-growing fast Mister Barklice, a sprightly kind of boy who'll be your'n to nurture forrard in no time at all!"

'"Who is?" I would ask and, "Where is he?"

'But they are elusive are the bilgesnipe, their words lingering after they have gone, but leading nowhere as if they were never there at all. Try as I might I could discover nothing more about him but that he existed and he lived somewhere, or other. As for Paley's Creek, until we heard its music on our way to Woolstone, I was never able to find it again.'

'And this was twelve years ago less a night?' said Jack.

'It was.'

Stort turned to Jack and said, 'I feel we are finally making progress and getting this matter clear. Now . . .' He turned back to Barklice. 'When exactly does the moot that is Paley's Creek come to an end?'

'On the cusps and the turns of the moons of May, which is to say towards the end of the month, depending.'

'It's nearly the end of the month,' said Jack. 'Barklice is right – we haven't got long and tomorrow may be his last chance.'

Stort glanced at the sky. The moon had just turned to the wane.

'The simple fact is, my friends, if I do not go tomorrow I never can again, for my failure to take responsibility for the boy is deemed proof that I am incapable of being his father . . . and the boy will stay for ever with his mother and I will be as anathema among the bilgesnipe and deemed to be one who has shirked his responsibilities.'

Jack got up.

'I must go,' he said.

'But I haven't said what it is I came all this way to say,' cried Stort.

'Leave it till tomorrow evening when, I would suggest, whether Barklice agrees or not, that we all go to Paley's Creek. Sounds like a good party to me.'

'All of us?' said Barklice unhappily.

'Yes,' said Jack. 'You, me, Stort here, Judith, Katherine . . . every-body. Let's make a family outing of it.'

'But . . .?' spluttered Barklice. 'This is a very sensitive matter and needs delicate handling.'

'That's right,' said Jack, 'the more the merrier. We've had a hard few weeks of it and everyone, especially Katherine, needs a break. See you at twilight tomorrow.'

'But—'

'Sleep well, Mister Barklice. Stort, it's very good to see you again.'

The two friends walked back to the edge of the henge.

'So . . . what *did* you come to tell me? Tell me in brief so I can think about it between now and tomorrow.'

'The gem's been found, Jack. I found it myself . . . and from that much else flows. You are needed in Brum and urgently.'

'I am needed here,' said Jack, 'and here I stay.'

'But Jack, let me try to explain—'

'No point. I'm not going back to Brum or even the Hyddenworld permanently and nothing will persuade me to. How can I? Let's not spoil our reunion. As for tomorrow we'll go to Paley's Creek and have a good time.'

'Humph!' muttered Stort, as Jack went off into the shadows of the henge and turned back into the human world. 'It's in your wyrd to come to Brum and help us, Jack. You know that as well as I!'

26

SHADOW

As the days had gone by in Brum and the demand from citizens and pilgrims alike grew on the city council to show the gem of Spring publicly, it became ever clearer to Witold Slew that no one knew where it was. They were waiting for the return of Bedwyn Stort. Slew was confident that having found it, Stort had done the sensible thing before going away and hidden it where no one else could find it.

He would not have taken it with him on the journey he was making, nor would he have hidden it somewhere impossible for someone else to find. If he had, and something happened to him while he was away, the gem might remain undiscovered for another fifteen hundred years and Stort would surely not want that.

While Slew went into the library daily, his disguise as a wandering scholar having fooled everybody, he took the opportunity of the light, summery evenings to explore Brum, drinking in its taverns and finding out more about Stort.

Whilst he was confident that the scrivener would have hidden the gem in the Library, he was hoping that more knowledge of the hydden might narrow down the actual hiding place.

His earlier assumption that he was a hydden who had stumbled upon the gem by chance he soon dismissed. Everything he heard about the scrivener affirmed that he was a remarkable hydden: intelligent, learned and, surprisingly, courageous in an unusual kind of way. Slew had little doubt that such a hydden could not handle a stave and would not know what to do in a fight.

It was a pity he was not in Brum. If he was, Slew would have found him and forced him to say where the gem was. There were ways and means with shadow skills which would wrest that information from the hydden without him knowing what was happening.

That option would have existed too had anyone remaining in Brum known where the stone was.

Failing that, Slew was content to sit in the Library during the day and pretend to study one thing while studying quite another – the procedures by which the Library was run and, more difficult, where it was most likely that the gem was hidden.

On this point Slew trusted his first instincts.

There was something about the energy of things in the lower reading room where Stort worked which was insistent and unusual. In such matters Slew was an adept.

Shadow skills were of the mind and spirit and involved the exercise of will over material objects and natural phenomena. He had only to still himself a little to sense at once that something was down there among the books and that it was powerful, dangerous even, but desirable.

Given a free run of the place he had no doubt that like a dog sniffing out a trembling rabbit he would have been able to work his way ever nearer to Stort's hiding place. It was simply a matter of letting the gem's life force reach him and him taking it.

Thwart, the librarian in charge of the section where Stort worked most, had become both unwitting ally and inconvenience. He could not have been more helpful, dropping whatever he was doing to run bookish errands for the fraudulent scholar and answering queries in a state of eager panic, as if Slew's needs were so pressing that they must be satisfied at once.

The errands to bring certain books and the queries about certain references were all false. Or rather, Slew was clever enough to make them real and with a consistent end, namely the study of Summer, though he had no real interest in the results.

His aim was to gain the librarian's confidence and lull him into such a state of false security that if the timing was right he might open doors into stack rooms he should not, or leave keys lying around that should remain on his person.

But Thwart had a romantic bent, which irritated Slew.

'It must be a fine life, Brother Slew, to set forth upon the green road of learning, literally and metaphorically, if I may put it that way!'

'That's a good way to express it,' said Slew.

'I'm glad you say that because others have said I have a way with words. Of course, Brother, you need that if you're to turn your studies into something others will enjoy, like an original commentary or compilation or a series of lectures at one of the colleges great or small along the way, of which, I have heard, there are a good number extant still in Germany.'

'Really?' growled Slew.

'Indeed it is so. I trust I am not talking too much but I feel it is important to say this ... mind you, the ultimate purpose of scholarship is the same as those who follow a more strictly spiritual path and spend their days praying and meditating. Wouldn't you agree?'

'Er ... ah ... um ... yes I would,' Slew would reply at such moments, 'but I must study now.'

During the season of pilgrimage the Library was open every day. This meant that on Sundays, when Master Brief and some other librarians had a day off, the Library was understaffed and librarians like Thwart overworked.

In this Slew saw an opportunity.

One of Thwart's jobs was to take books that had been returned back to their proper places on the shelves. Occasionally that entailed opening the barred doors into the more obscure stack rooms where rarer or larger volumes were kept. Sometimes he did this with a volume in his hand so large and cumbersome that he needed the help of another librarian, which was not always to be had.

When he had more than one volume to carry this procedure was even more difficult. He might put the books down on a nearby table while he got his key and unlocked the door. Or he might go and deal with the door before going to retrieve the books and take them in.

Either way, the door or the books were left briefly unattended, and Thwart allowed himself to get into a fret and a worry at such moments.

Slew also noticed that the busiest times in the Library were when it was raining outside. On such days pilgrims with a scholarly turn of mind, who might otherwise be tempted to carouse with their friends al fresco, or make the trek up Waseley Hill, wandered in to get out of the rain and browse a little.

The librarians dreaded such days, for these occasional readers took up much more of their time than the regular ones. Indeed, at such times a certain 'us and them' mood took over. Slew saw that this too offered opportunities.

While he studied these procedures under the guise of scholarship this daily chore of simply being there bore fruit. He rapidly became a fixture in the place, his passage to and from his lair downstairs being greeted by familiar nods, even from Master Brief himself.

On more than one occasion, too, people said, 'Going well is it? Finding what you need?'

'Indeed, indeed,' murmured Slew, 'a scholar's work is never done, even on a sunny day like this!'

It was true enough; the Summer was a good one and the rainy days too few and far between for Slew's taste. What he needed was a period of prolonged rain and for the Library to get busy and Master Brief and his more senior colleagues to be preoccupied with other things or away.

Meanwhile his extra-curricular activities in Brum continued. His quarters next to Bedwyn Stort's house were comfortable and provided him with ample nightly respite from scholarship in the arms of Evelien and her cousin Machtild.

The truth was he was beginning to grow weary of the demands of the younger wyf, a fact that caused Machtild much amusement. For her part she resisted Slew's demands, or rather kept it to sensual nocturnal conversation of a kind for which Slew had met his match: playful, intelligent, suggestive and witty but nothing more.

The male members of the family, their protectors as Slew presumed them to be, remained astonishingly ignorant of these routine goings-on. They liked their mead, in which habit Slew encouraged them, as did his two consorts, and so they were either out drinking or abed sleeping it off.

On his first arrival in Brum, Slew had been noticeable for his height and obvious strength. Some days into their sojourn there a large group of pilgrims from Norseland, some as tall as himself, arrived. They were the kind to pick a fight.

It was they who first approached him, in the Muggy Duck, asking if he or his forebears came from their country. He immediately saw advantage in associating with them. They looked like they enjoyed a fight and he had not been able to give time of late to stave practice in the way he normally did. The Norseners to a hydden carried staves, and big ones too.

Ma'Shuqa did not allow staves in the Muggy Duck because their presence led to fighting when the mead was flowing, so the group left theirs on the wharf outside, placed upright and together as a visual declaration of their combined might and a message to others that to mess with one of them was to risk having to deal with the whole lot.

But Slew knew the type, there were plenty such in Thuringia, always ready to test the mettle of those they met and, if they could, humiliate them. So when they asked publicly and insultingly about his bloodline he lied and said he had heard it was true: he had Norse blood in him.

'But you are a monk!' one of them said, 'and we Norseners do not make good monks!'

'Come to think of it,' said another, 'we don't *like* monks.'

Slew looked at them dismissively.

Ma'Shuqa, who had an ear for trouble and a fight, said, 'You gennelmen can steam down a little if you please. He's a solitary monk and he's of the Mirror, you're twelve and you're stewed.'

'Pickled I'd say,' said Slew, 'like a dozen filleted fish all in a row. Eh?'

He raised his mead in mock salute.

'Now then . . .' said Ma'Shuqa warningly.

One of the Norse stood up, furious. The Duck's clientele fell quiet. They liked a good fight once in a while, and were glad when strangers such as these ignored Ma'Shuqa.

'If you weren't in a habit, my friend,' he said, 'I'd throw you over the wharf outside.'

Slew reached across the table with such speed and strength that no one knew what had happened before it did. He grasped the Norse-man's jerkin in such a way that he began to choke.

'Shall I throw him out?' he asked Ma'Shuqa, 'or shall I just throw him?'

He did not wait for an answer.

He stood up, still holding the enormous troublemaker with one hand, hauled him effortlessly across the table and cried out, 'Open the door!' which one of the regulars did, and he heaved his would-be foe outside.

'Now close it,' said Slew, 'so the smell doesn't creep back in!'

It was all done so swiftly that the other Norseners were barely able to move before Slew sat down opposite them once again, smiling.

None of them, nor any of the regulars, had ever seen the like. As for Ma'Shuqa, she was speechless for once.

'Well then,' she said eventually, 'if you want to fight each other do it outside.'

'We will,' said Slew, his eyes narrowing, gazing darkly at the other Norseners one by one, 'won't we?'

It was, by any standards, one of the best stave fights the clientele of the Muggy Duck were ever witness to.

Ma'Shuqa might discourage fighting in-house, but right outside it was good business. If she could see a fight was on the way she had trellis tables of mead set up, deputed a couple of her sturdier wenches to serve, and ordered that the flares along the wharf be lit.

Slew took his time, appearing to drink mead to gain courage but in fact barely touching a drop.

Eventually he said loudly, as if the worse for wear, 'My stave if you will, landlady, for I'm off. I have business outside with some folk who claim their whore's blood is purer than mine!'

As insults went it was a poor one but it was enough.

The Norseners piled out after him, along with everyone else; mead was served aplenty, and a book started on how long the monk would last and the number he would put down before he himself was felled.

It was never Slew's intention to win the fight, which for a Master of Shadows would not have been very hard. His real aim was to win some friends and gain some sparring partners. Such hydden as those were not to be dismissed just because they drank too much. Get them sober, train them to be as disciplined as he was, and he would have a fighting force which in time might be useful for one whose youth precluded him from being accepted by some senior members of the Fyrd, even though he was Master of Shadows.

He felled five with seemingly increasing difficulty before he let himself be buffeted to the ground, laughing, making a jest of it, turning anger to japery and jollity with his charm and strength.

'Drinks on the house!' called out Ma'Shuqa, bringing to a halt further unpleasantness, 'and a flagon of mead to the fair winner of a round robin of bouts!'

This was an invitation for an instant competition whose rules of time and handicap all knew and which, the evening being young and the weather warm and thirsty-making, would increase her business still more and extend it.

It was this latter turn of events that brought Brum's stavermen hurrying, in case the peace needed to be kept. With them came Mister Pike, who had been having an enjoyable supper with Master Brief, who came too for the exercise.

When he saw that Slew was of that rough, carousing company, Brief pulled back into the shadows, not wishing to be seen.

He'd had his doubts about Brother Slew from the beginning, but there had been nothing to put a finger on and instinct was not proof. Slew's credentials were not in doubt, nor his intelligence, nor his knowledge of the scholarship of the Seasons and Summer.

'I cannot very well stop him studying, Mister Pike, but I don't like him!' Brief had said not an hour before to his friend. Now there he was, mixing it with a rowdy group of stave fighters from the North and, from what they soon learnt, the cause of all the trouble.

So Brief kept out of sight while Pike, intrigued, went forward to listen and learn what he could.

It didn't take him long to learn something very remarkable, not by word but by a brief deed.

It happened that the bouts of the competition had reached such a point that it was impossible for everyone there not to be more or less involved, especially the monk, as he was generally referred to, and the Norseners, now his friends.

Folk called for them to take on a fair bout as well, one by one of course, and Slew could not get out of fighting one either.

Alerted by Brief, Pike watched that particular bout with care. Slew's opponent was the Norsener he had originally thrown out. He had a sore head and wanted to recover respect. Pike knew a good fighter when he saw one, and from the moment the Norsener took the ring he could see from the way he held his stave he was very good.

The monk on the other hand looked curiously incompetent for one who, Pike had learned, had earlier done so well.

'It be the booze,' said a regular he knew, 'and this be a needle match for all it's meant to be friendly. You might have to step in and stop it, Mister Pike, if the monk goes down.'

It was obvious from the first that the monk was going to lose, but it needed an expert staverman like Pike to see what was really going on. Losing a fight can sometimes require more skill than winning it, if the 'loser' is not to get seriously hurt. It was obvious to all that the Norsener wanted his revenge and that given half a chance he was going to take it.

So Pike watched carefully and readied a couple of his colleagues to go in fast if real hurt was going to be done.

The fight started, the monk took a few blows, weakened, briefly came back strong again, his movements rather more fluid to Pike's eyes than they should have been for one meant to be the worse for wear. He weakened again, fell back, his attacker saw his chance, closed in and made an expert feint, the kind that it is hard for the other not to respond to if they are feigning tiredness and defeat. So Slew responded, opening himself to a swift and brutal end to the bout. Perhaps he knew that the staverman would step in, perhaps not, however it was one of the other Norseners who stuck out his foot to make Slew's fall all the worse, his brief humiliation greater. It was the way of things, of fighters: honours even, honour satisfied, all friends together on the morrow, cuts and bruises and broken ribs and all.

It didn't happen like that.

Pike did not see the foot stuck out, nor his friends, and nor apparently did Slew. Had he shown he had done so he might have given his game away.

So already disadvantaged he stumbled on the foot and began to fall in such a way that it was surely irrecoverable. He was going to get hurt.

It was an old Norseners' trick.

It always worked.

Teach a foe a lesson, gain respect, no harm done.

Except that the Norsener wielding his heavy stave wanted to cause harm and on Slew, now lying in shadow on the edge of the wharf, that was not going to be hard.

Only Pike saw what happened, and he had never seen the like in his life. One moment Slew was in the shadow and the next, for the briefest of moments, he *was* shadow and the Norsener's stave thumped not into his ribs, to break a few, but into the cobbles of the wharf, putting him off balance and jarring his arms.

Even as that happened the shadow that had been Slew manifested back into something solid but elsewhere by a few inches. His hand shot up, it grasped the stave and held it, and with a strength and skill Pike had never witnessed, slowly toppled the Norsener to the ground.

It was better even than that.

He might easily, Pike saw, have had his foe into the water, but that he did not do. He brought him down upon himself, let himself be winded yet held on to the other's stave throughout.

Then, he rose, yielding the bout, laughing and gasping for breath at the same time.

Honours even.

No harm done.

Brief saw it too and saw something else.

Something dark and dangerous.

A shadow that put a chill deep into him.

'He's not what he claims to be,' said Pike later, 'and he's dangerous.'

'I don't doubt that, Mister Pike, but the question is, what is it he's doing in my Library?'

The question was rhetorical and in any case Pike never quite heard it. For as Brief spoke the heavens opened with a crackling crash of thunder and lightning and the muggy evening became one of torrential rain.

The trellis tables were hauled inside, the imbibers followed them, along with the wenches, the Norseners and the rest of the company.

But for one, who lingered outside, his monk's habit turning dark as it grew wet, and shiny. He stood staring at the lights inside and the flares dying in the rain and he watched two figures who hurried away: Mister Pike and Master Brief.

He followed them, he studied them, he assessed their likely strengths and weaknesses, and that done, and well satisfied, he made his way to his lodgings and, for once, slept in his own bed all the night through.

27

PALEY'S CREEK

'No,' said Katherine, 'I just don't think it's a good idea, that's all. It's too risky and we might lose her in the dark and anyway you don't even know where Paley's Creek is, do you?'

Jack knew she was quite right – and also absolutely wrong.

Twilight was already falling on the day after his reunion with Stort, and Jack had tried every way he could think of to persuade her. A break from everything was what was needed, a night out, a chance to see the world from outside themselves.

'It's just an hour or two . . . into the henge, back into the Hyddenworld . . . a way for us to show Judith how—'

'No, Jack, I won't agree to it.'

He knew that if she didn't he couldn't take Judith. It was both or none.

He had even tried the threat of saying he would go without them.

'That's probably for the best anyway,' she had said, which wasn't what he wanted.

He had tried to tell her that Paley's Creek, as he understood it, was a carnival – liberty, freedom from normal restraint, *fun*.

And there was what he couldn't say, had never said: that Katherine was too serious, too old in the head, too fuddy-duddy in the way she thought, the way she was, even dressed, even did her hair, too lacking in the joy in life he felt so much.

He looked at her with love and couldn't say it.

Your father died, your mother was ill, and you lost your childhood when you became the primary carer ... that's what happened and you've forgotten how to let go, assuming you ever could ...

'Please,' he said, 'trust me.'

'Not over this,' she said stiffly. 'We'll get an early night.'

'But Arthur's coming and maybe Margaret.'

'No,' she said. 'Come on, Judith, we have things to do.'

As they were leaving a short while later, Judith appeared.

'Are you going out?'

'We are.'

'Can I come?'

'Mummy would prefer if you didn't.'

'Why?'

'Because she feels it's unsafe for you.'

She looked him in the eyes.

'Where are you going?'

He hesitated.

Judith said, 'You're going to Paley's Creek and I want to come.'

Damn Stort and Barklice, they talk too much!

'I know, my love, but—'

'Why doesn't Mummy want to come? Is she scared?'

Again he hesitated.

'I am too,' she said with a bright smile, 'and I can't go anyway, even if Mummy wanted.'

'Why not?'

'We never got me any nice clothes.'

They left at twilight with a sense of carnival in the air.

Margaret decided to come because, she said, 'There'll never be another chance. Arthur had all the fun with the Hyddenworld, I had none. So for once ...'

'I'm not sure I can remember how to use the henge,' said Arthur.

'Hold my hand, Margaret, and Arthur you hold her other one ... It doesn't hurt.'

They went between the conifers, made dexter and then sinister and all the deasil ways of the shadows that were there, the moon turning a circle above their heads as, so easily, they slid betwixt and then between and they were there, the trees vast above them and Stort waiting.

'This is Barklice,' said Stort, introducing him to Margaret. 'Don't let him out of your sight. And Judith, Katherine . . . ?'

'Not coming,' said Jack shortly.

'Is it far, dear?' wondered Margaret.

'No distance at all and it's on the flat. Follow Jack.'

'That's right,' said Jack, 'and I'm following Stort.'

'Who, I believe,' said Stort dreamily as they wended their way forth from the henge towards the sound of distant music, 'is following Mister Barklice here who ought to know because he's been there before.'

'Yes,' muttered Barklice, 'I ought to and I do, which is why I'm following our leader, who is Jack, because that's the right way to Paley's Creek, the blind leading the blind and all following the moon . . .'

So they went and soon they had left Woolstone behind them and were walking in the dark with others near, going the same way, chattering and laughing and enjoying themselves in anticipation of more to come when they got to where they hoped they were going.

'Not far, my dear,' said Arthur.

'I feel I could walk as far as the stars tonight,' Margaret replied, taking his arm as she had done the first day they began courting.

'Remember?' she whispered as they went.

'I do.'

It was not long before the path, clear now in the moonlight and marked by lights, veered away from the green road, turning away downslope towards the river.

The air grew cooler and more moist, but not unpleasantly so.

The music grew ever more noticeable, now loud, now soft, but rising with the wind and ever more insistent.

'It is certainly seductive,' said Stort, who found himself starting to hum along with it and his two hands dancing about as if conducting an orchestra and chorus comprising large, perfumed silken female bilgesnipe, each one with a song of welcome on her lips.

'Be warned, Stort,' said Barklice, 'and you too Jack, especially as you're spoken for. Before you know it you'll have lost your soul to them.'

'Never!' cried Stort happily and unconvincingly.

'Never,' said Jack.

The music grew louder and more seductive still, lights danced among the trees, figures, some diaphanous, flitted before them and behind them until, quite suddenly, they found themselves upon the river bank with lights drifting past them on bark and slivers of wood, candles perhaps, oil lamps maybe ... drifting by, some fast some slow, some across and others towards, entwining, entangling.

'Be careful, Stort,' warned Barklice again, 'we'll be there in a trice and then ... then what?'

'Then ... then ...' whispered Stort, for anything louder than a whisper seemed a kind of sacrilege, 'then ...'

'Welcome.'

A voice. Laughter.

'Welcome one and all.'

Stort looked around but could not see anyone near, not even Barklice.

'But where—?'

The verderer ran straight into him, panting, 'I thought I'd lost you, I couldn't see you, you seemed to drift in and out of the trees and I ... I ...'

They saw a great fire ahead, sparks rising with its smoke into the night.

They heard song.

They were offered mead, which they took, and food, which they ate.

'Welcome, Mister Barklice.'

They turned, but in the shadows of the people, and the barges on the river, and the tented humbles all about, it was hard to say who was quite where, and who might have spoken.

'So she bain't here then natterway, Mister Jack?' said a voice out of the gloom.

'Who?'

He turned, unsure who had spoken, shapes of people all about.

'That girl o' your'n who be a maid worth seein' this night I'd say, i' the cups o' the moon, wouldn't you?'

'You mean Judith, I'm afraid she—'

'Welcome, Bedwyn Stort . . .'

Stort stopped still and grabbed Barklice's arm and Jack's.

'We have work to do, an appointment to keep and my task is to see you keep it. Now let us explore this . . . this Paley's Creek and find your son!'

'How?' said Barklice, not unreasonably, since whichever way they looked a pathway went, picked out by stars, turning through firelight, and faces hard to see.

'Where are Arthur and Margaret?'

Stort shrugged, as did Barklice, with other things on their minds. Jack shook his head and followed on, or thought he did, until he realized they were following him.

'I thought we'd lost you,' he said when he saw Arthur.

'You did, you have, but that's what must happen in Paley's Creek and Margaret's having the time of her life. Where's Stort?'

Jack turned in the flickering dark but Stort was not there, and when he turned back to Arthur he had gone too.

So he stood still and let himself be right where he was as present, past and future whirled around in his mind and the music entered his head and he began to smile.

'I wish,' he said, 'I'd found the words to persuade Katherine to come here and then Judith would have had to and we'd be here together like everyone else.'

'You did, Jack, you did find the words; you did, my dear . . .'

Her voice was old, old as darkness itself, and he could feel the touch of her hand on his arm.

'Did I?'

'I know you did,' the crone said, taking his arm.

'Mum? *Mum!?*'

They were in bed and Katherine was asleep.

She woke instantly.

'What's wrong?'

'Nothing. Listen!'

They could hear the music of the night.

Judith got out of bed, grabbed Katherine's leg and pulled.

Katherine's body actually moved to the edge of the bed.

'Judith, stop it.'

'No. I want to go to Paley's Creek.'

'No.'

'It's maybe scary but Bedwyn Stort said they'd cure my pain.'

'Who would?'

'Doctory women with balms and erm . . . erm . . .'

'Embrocations.'

'Yes.'

'No.'

'Dad wanted you to. He was sad that you didn't. He thinks it would do you good.'

'What did he say?'

'That you've lost it.'

Katherine smiled.

'Lost what?'

'Joy, whatever that is.'

'When did he say that? And who to?'

'Let's go.'

'Don't be ridiculous, Judith, we can't now.'

'I can take you there.'

'How?'

'Let me show you. You might enjoy it. Dad would be pleased. Everyone else has gone.'

'It's too late.'

She looked at the time but the time seemed strange and not quite itself.

Judith grabbed her leg and pulled again.

Katherine half fell out of the bed.

'Judith!'

'Come on, Mum, you're not that old. Margaret went.'

'I thought you didn't want to go because you have no clothes.'

'I don't, but Dad was sad and you are too. Have you any ribbons?'

'Yes.'

'Get them.'

'Please.'

'Please get them, Mum, there's no time to lose.'

Katherine turned on the light, went and found her mother's old sewing box.

'These were your grandmother's, she bought them for me, but we never had time for that sort of thing . . .'

'You can wear anything at Paley's Creek, but if you're a girl you need ribbons.'

'We're not going, we can't go; we won't even try to go.'

'Hold still, Mum, I want to tie ribbons in your hair.' And Judith did, sitting on the bed. 'And you can tie some in mine. Red, green, really nice.'

Their eyes concentrated on each other's hair, their arms intertwined as they tied the ribbons.

'Mum, you look pretty.'

'Judith, you look beautiful.'

They looked at each other with happiness.

'Mum . . . let's go . . . I'll show you the way.'

'But—'

'Paley's Creek is special. *Please* . . .'

'We'll have to hurry.'

'Come on!'

They dressed and Judith led Katherine downstairs and out into the garden.

'We'll have to lock up . . .'

'It's all right tonight.'

'Where do we go?'

'We dance,' said Judith, showing Katherine how, because no one ever had.

'Where?'

'Over here,' she called, 'this way, dancing to the music you can hear when you listen to the flow of time.'

'Who told you that?' called out Katherine, as the ribbons in her hair began to stream behind her in the wind and she tried to keep up with her daughter the Shield Maiden.

'Bedwyn Stort. *Come on!*'

✳

It turned out, then, that Paley's Creek was by no means what it at first seemed. There was not one fire, but many; not one river, but several.

The site was large and confusing and linked by planks and small bridges that seemed never to go in quite the same direction. One way and another it was girthed by water on all sides, interspersed with coppices, making it impossible to get any general sense of things.

As for the fires, they were the focus of different groups. Around some were singers, others attracted players of bulpipes and the tuble, while still more food was being prepared: brots of many kinds, pasties, graddles and broad scones, and the many-seeded baggot, shot through with moist peppers and pimento.

Then there were the stews, steaming in great cast-iron cauldrons and fish chops of the pike and the mullion.

They feasted as they went, unwilling to stop folk offering them food, quite unable to decline.

Having feasted, they sat on cushions beneath awnings flickering with fire fore and aft.

Having sat they rose, tottered about, lost their way, joined the dance and began to forget why they had come.

'I am sure,' said Stort, 'there was a good reason, but I confess my mind tonight seems a little awry.'

'Yes,' replied Barklice, 'we did come for a purpose, an important one which . . . if only you would try, I might remember!'

Until, the moon beginning to wane, the crowds to thin, it dawned on them that the night was drawing to a close and whatever it was they had come for was slipping away.

'Good to see you here, Mister Barklice, goodly and grand!'

The voice was male, deep, bilgesnipe, warm.

'Who . . . where . . . ?'

They turned and saw a great bilgesnipe disappearing over a footbridge.

'Sir! Please don't go!'

The bilgesnipe turned, fire on his cheerful face, smiling and raising a hand in acknowledgement.

'Please . . .' said Barklice, suddenly sober, suddenly scared, suddenly remembering why he had come . . . '*please* . . .'

'You'm ready now then, Master Verderer, you'm ready to reap what you did sow?'

It was another voice, a female, closer-to, ancient, a voice from out of time.

'I don't know what to do,' said Barklice, 'and I'm sorry I ever . . . I didn't know . . . I don't know . . . but, yes, I'm ready.'

'You are and you'll be and you'll *learn*,' she said gently. 'Now, on you go, Mister Barklice, take up what you're due . . .'

He turned, wild-eyed.

'Stort . . . come with me . . . I . . .'

But the crone took Stort's arm and he shook his head.

'I got you here,' said Stort, 'and now I think it's you must do the rest . . . but I'll not be far behind.'

Barklice took a path into darkness, which led towards the river and the craft clinking at their moorings there.

As for Stort he went straight on, across the grass, among the people, towards one of the larger fires, one of the last to still be roaring and young.

But such were the flickering shadows of the night, and the state of his befuddled mind, that though he looked at the one who held his arm, needing his support perhaps, walking slow with head bent saying no more nor who she was, he knew only that she was old, very old.

'I must help Barklice,' he said, trying to break away.

'Let Mister Barklice make his own discoveries and mistakes, but watch and learn, Bedwyn Stort, for what you'll see here this night is what Paley's Creek was always meant to be, which some might call magic, others . . . well . . . you're the one with words, not me.'

Her voice, like her eyes, was distantly familiar, as if he had met her briefly a very long time before. Her hand tightened on his arm and she looked ahead, though with difficulty, for her body was troubled with stiffness.

'Watch,' she whispered, 'watch your friend, my dear.'

They had passed the great fire on their left-hand side and were walking out of its light towards a long landing stage they had seen twice before. First it had been crowded with craft arriving and letting people off but taking few away. Later more folk, mainly young ones as he recalled, had been standing there, boats coming for them one by one.

Now only one remained, a boy, standing alone at the end of the staging, staring across the water, on which the orange lights floated. There were a few people on the landward side of the stage, huddled together as a family might be, old and young, male and female, quiet, subdued, whispering.

They were discreetly watching the boy from a distance, their mood sombre. They were watching the water too, for signs of a boat.

'He'll not move until the sun rises,' Stort heard one of them say, 'though middenacht be the witching hour.'

'He'll never believe and he never did but that his pa would come for him for certain this night, but . . .'tis hard, there's always one left at Paley's Creek, one to wish for what never was . . .'

Stort turned to the crone and whispered, 'Who are they talking about?'

'The boy.'

'What's he waiting for?'

'You'll see and you'll know.'

'But I do know,' said Stort, 'of course I know because once I stood on a stage like that and waited like he is now. Right through a night and then another and then another until he—'

Her hand grew tighter on his arm. 'You did,' she said.

'But he . . .'

Stort could not bear to tell that truth, as he could not bear to watch the waiting boy, alone on the stage watching the rise of the mist, hoping that out of it, against all odds, despite all fears, out of it . . .

'He never came for me,' said Stort.

Her hand was tighter still.

'And that's why you're Barklice's true friend,' she said, 'and brought him here because you know what's right and what's wrong and what blights a little life . . . now . . . now . . .'

Stort dared look again.

Still nobody came.

Still the lurid mist drifted by, the boy sturdy and solid against it, refusing to give up, his new-packed portersac on the stage at his feet, ready to embark on a craft that hadn't arrived, with a father who had never come back, leaving him to be the last and the left. There he stood, refusing to believe a truth that would break his heart.

The talking among the gathered group ceased; it seemed they *had* given up. Stort noticed one in particular, no longer quite young, rather plain, but graceful, gentle in the way she stood, the firelight catching the back of her head as she stared at the boy, her hair touched with grey, the fire turning it red. She turned to one of the others, taking her eyes off the boy for a moment, and Stort saw her face. Even she, it seemed, now had her doubts, and there was a measure of sadness in her eyes.

Well, she seemed to say, *well then . . . I suppose . . .*

An older woman went to her, and a man, bilgesnipe both, large, warm, hands ready to reach out to any who needed comforting.

So they didn't see that out on the landing stage the boy had suddenly stiffened and taken a step forward.

Stort, his old hurt memory gone, stiffened too.

Then he saw a light wavering in the mist, a lantern held aloft, and a voice very familiar to Bedwyn Stort which called out, 'You be a warnin' me where that blessed stage may be, my chumly Mister Barklice, for Arnold cannot see a thing! Not even his own nose!'

It was Arnold Mallarkhi, grandson of Old Mallarkhi of the Muggy Duck, bringing a craft out of the mist, across the current.

'What do you see, Mister Barklice?'

The light showed first and then an arm and then, as the arm came through the mist, the prow of the craft on which stood, precariously, his hand shaking, holding the lantern with one hand and a lanyard with another for support, the Master Verderer of Brum.

'I see a . . . I think . . . it is . . .'

'Call it plain, Mister Barklice, call it good,' cried Arnold, 'be it near or be it far?'

'Near.'

'What's near, chumly, a river bank, a rocky obstruction, a landing stage?'

The boy stepped forward eagerly, Barklice let go the lanyard and stood up straight.

'It's my boy,' he said simply.

The boy turned suddenly landward, for the briefest of moments, and never in his life had Stort ever seen such joy and pride on a face.

'It's my pa!' he called out and then, very simply, 'Ma allers said he'd come for me, down all those years she said he'd come and here he be!'

Of the next few moments Stort never remembered much.

Barklice forgot to tell Arnold how close they were.

For once that bilgeyboy missed a trick and hit a landing stage.

The boat smacked hard, Barklice staggered off, the boy held him fast, his ma came running, her ma and pa came running too, and then the whole lot were clattering down the landing stage . . .

'Hold fast, lubbers!' yelled Arnold with a laugh, 'else the stage and its planks and all you folk'll collapse in the water.'

Together, all as one, as a family they held fast to the boy and his pa and led them safe to shore, clacketing down the planks back to shore with happiness.

'This be him,' said the boy, and Stort watched as Barklice shook so many hands he lost count, 'this be my pa!'

'Be it true you'm the Master Verderer of Brum?' cried out one.

'Well, I suppose, if you put it that way, I do bear that title but—'

'And you know all sorts of folk, low and high, high and low?'

'Quite a few, yes, but I don't know . . .'

'Like Lord Festive?'

'Festoon,' said Barklice, 'yes, I certainly know him in more than a passing way but . . . I would like . . . I mean . . . I ought . . .'

The boy had hold of Barklice's hand and pulled him towards the woman Stort had noticed before.

'Be it true, Mister Barklice sir, that Brum is as big as a city ought to be?' called another.

'That's true but really . . . I can answer your questions later . . . but you see I'd very much like to know . . . my . . . my son's name.'

The boy reached the woman and pulled Barklice towards her.

'Pa, meet Ma,' he said.

And the woman, bilgylike, warm as toast, good as a plate of stewed tomatoes on a misty morn, laughing, put her arms around Barklice and whispered, 'Ask him yourself!'

So Barklice looked at the boy and knelt down so they were one and the same and said, 'Tell me your name.'

'Bratfire,' said the boy, 'and I've learnt hyddening better than most but they say you'll teach me a trick or two.'

'I will.'

'And is it true, Ma says it is but no one else thinks it so, that . . . that . . .'

'What?'

'That you know the most famous hydden of them all?'

'Well, I'm not sure who—'

'That you've talked to him, like we are now . . .'

'I may well have done but . . . who . . . ah! You mean Master Brief. Well, of course . . .'

Bratfire shook his head rather impatiently.

'Pa,' he asked rather severely, 'tell us one and all, here and now, if it be true or not that my pa actually knows and has talked to, maybe even shaken the hand of, the famous Mister Stort?'

Barklice looked astonished. Then a slow smile came over his face, the firelight dancing in his eyes.

'You mean the famous Mister *Bedwyn* Stort?'

'Yes.'

'The one who rescued Lord Festoon?'

'That's the one.'

'The one who speaks so many languages that sometimes he forgets to speak his own clearly?'

'He'm the one we've heard of.'

'The inventor of . . . of all sorts of things?'

'Well, do you or no?'

Barklice laughed, really laughed, for the first time in days, perhaps in a certain way for the first time in years, if ever.

'If your mother says I do then of course I do, because she's always right and never tells a lie!' he said, tempted suddenly to tell a slight one himself.

But not a bad one.

In such circumstances a certain massaging of the truth seemed permissible.

'I am a little late,' he said, 'because it took a great deal of persuading to get Master Scrivener Stort to agree to come to Paley's Creek tonight to—'

'He's *here!?*' said Bratfire in delighted astonishment. 'Like . . . *here?*'

Bratfire looked round to see if his mother had heard, which she had. Indeed, she was looking as amazed – and as impressed – as their son.

Barklice stood up and looked around indifferently, as if it was the most natural thing in the world that one of Englalond's greatest scholars should be wandering about Paley's Creek with him for no good reason other than to be there.

For Bratfire the night was turning magical.

'Yes, he's certainly here somewhere or other . . . now let me see if I can spot him . . . Ah, there he is!'

Bratfire looked in the same direction but all he spotted was someone he had noticed before and dismissed – a tall, rather distracted-looking hydden, whose arms and legs seemed too long for his body.

'That's him,' said Barklice, 'that's Mister Stort of Brum, the best friend a hydden ever had.'

'*Him!?* And who be that standing akin to him? Stocky feller, fierce eyes?'

'He,' said Barklice sternly, 'is not to be dismissed as a mere "him" in that tone of voice. And that other gentleman is not a mere "that".

'In fact, the fine upstanding hydden next to Mister Stort is a very great and important hydden indeed, namely Jack . . .'

Bratfire looked suddenly terrified.

'Jack? Not he who . . . ?'

'The same. Stort and Jack, friends indeed. But of course, if you don't want to meet them just because one looks fierce and the other odd, then . . .'

'I do want to meet them,' said Bratfire, 'and I think Ma does too.'

'Well then,' said Barklice, 'now's the time!'

He put his hand on Bratfire's shoulder as naturally as if he had done it a thousand times before and led him over to Stort and Jack.

'Mister Stort!' cried out Barklice rather grandly, 'here's someone who would like to meet you, and you too, Jack!'

They looked down at the young hydden, saw at once how much like Barklice he was, smiled benignly and shook his hand.

Bratfire was tongue-tied.

'You can introduce them to your mother,' said Barklice in a fatherly way, 'and then get us a hot brew, one with a bit of kick to it if you please!'

'Yes, sir!' said Bratfire. 'And something to eat. That's the thing tonight, isn't it?'

'I think it may be,' said Barklice, 'eh, gentlemen?'

'I think it may very well be!' they replied.

That was a Paley's Creek to remember . . .

And it didn't end there.

Bratfire's family was not going to let their lad go without a long hello, a good bit of storytelling and a long goodbye. The visitors were given seats of honour by the fire where they couldn't so much as raise a hand without some new sweetmeat, delicacy, brew or pottage being thrust into it.

Full was not in it.

They were filled to bursting.

Then, something more amazing to round things off, but it wasn't food, it was unexpected guests.

'Look!' said Jack.

They came through the crowd of people with ribbons in their hair and folk knew what and who they were, for they fell back amazed. Katherine looked afire with life, Judith with excitement.

'Be that or be that not 'oo I think it be and honerring us with their presence?'

'Aye, it be the Shield Maiden in making, Mirror bless 'er old soul.'

The females went to them, reached their hands to them and made a dance around the fire, the most elusive of dances, for the bilge-snipes' silks and ribbons seemed to slowly adorn Katherine and Judith with each flare and flame of the fire until, when the circle stopped and brought them in front of Jack, they were the most beautiful, the prettiest, of the night.

'Welcome to 'ee mother, welcome daughter, go and sit by your spouse'll friend and your'n father too. Bratfire, show 'em food! This was Paley's way to be and we'm honrin' his memory and more.'

'Sound the tuble, beat the skirmish drum, hammer the rhythm of the night and tell time to stand still a while longer, for we in this family bain't done yet!'

Eating, dancing, making merry, making love and making friends.

'What's your name?'

'Bratfire and your'n?'

'Judith. Can you dance?'

'Wind-like and across the field, I will one day, but nary yet,' said Judith, using wild words from out of a wild night.'

'Hmmm, come on, I'll show you. If Mum can, you can . . .'

All the while Barklice's new family extended itself around them, other bilgesnipe and hydden strolling over and introducing themselves as cousins, aunts, great nieces, uncles, great uncles, mothers-of and brothers-to and 'old friends who were one of the family'.

Barklice, Stort and Bratfire, with Arnold at the helm, did not make passage from Paley's Creek for Brum until dawn, by when they were well fed, well watered and nearly asleep. Jack was staying behind, unconvinced he could be of use in Brum, certain his duty lay with Katherine and Judith.

The entire assembly came to say goodbye, gathering on the river bank, weeping, wailing, hugging and kissing them all before finally allowing them aboard.

Yet that was not quite Stort's final memory.

The dawn mist was shot through with rising Summer sun, and as the last of Bratfire's family was lost to sight behind them, and he sat down next to Barklice looking tired and nervous at the prospect ahead, Stort saw a bent figure on the far side.

She was very old, older than he remembered from the night before. The Modor, the wise hydden, watching as he went. Was that who had asked for his arm?

He felt a pang of sadness and loss so deep that he had to stand up in the craft and raise a hand in farewell as if that movement and gesture might alleviate the unexpected grief he felt.

She did not raise a hand, perhaps she was too weak to do so, but she nodded towards him and perhaps she smiled.

Jack saw it too from the bank, Katherine as well, but Judith most of all.

'Who is she?' she asked.

'A wise woman who's seen much and learnt more,' said Jack.

'Why's she sad and bent?'

'Loneliness,' said Katherine, 'that's why. For wisdom's the hardest and most lonely path of all to find and stick with to the end.'

'Hasn't she got a friend?'

'Too old,' said Katherine.

'Too hard to find again once they're lost,' said Jack, taking Katherine's hand and holding it tight, 'so don't go and lose your friends if you can help it.'

'No,' said Judith, 'no . . .'

Then, though none could swear it, they thought they saw loom out of the mist behind the Modor wise and old, the white flank of a horse, and puffs of what seemed steam from great nostrils, which filled with light from the sun and swirled with the swish of the horse's tail.

Then she and the horse were gone.

When the mist lifted and the morning emerged in its full Summer glory along the river bank, there was nothing left to see but the sun in the dew.

'Pa?' said Bratfire later, when he had slept, 'how long will it be afore we get to Brum?'

'A bit of time,' said Barklice happily.

Stort and he raised their hands to wave goodbye to Jack and the others.

'He didn't come,' said Barklice.

'I didn't ask him to,' replied Stort. 'He'll have to do that for himself but it's already stirring in the wind . . . it's on its way . . . and Jack will know he's needed.'

'What is?'

'Trouble,' said Stort.

28

THIEF

The Great Library of Brum opened its doors on a Sunday at nine, when, in a time of pilgrimage, most folk were still asleep, or just getting up.

But every library had its Sad Readers, their lives bound to the hours of opening and closing of their alma mater, they having so little else in their lives that to avoid the reality of its emptiness they must escape into filing cards, bibliographies, the comfort of a solitary desk, the pursuit of reference, the rediscovery of something forgotten which was not worth remembering, attachment to things so obscure that the only other hydden who know what they are talking about are Sad Readers in other libraries somewhere across the Hyddenworld. Their only respite from the dusty hours inside being the daily small pleasure of the miserable munched brotkin of a lunch alone outside watching the real world go by. Then back to work and the long walk to the scholar's grave.

Pity them, for they know no other life than that, slinking back and forth from board, bed and guttering hearth, their minds filled with scholarship of a desperate kind and strange thoughts that are best suppressed. Like: is the most exciting thing that ever happened to this tome, which only two or three folk have looked at in eight hundred years, that it was half eaten by bookworms and half burnt by fire?

'What is it you do?' their acquaintances ask uneasily.

'I . . . well, I . . .' But the explanation falters before the incomprehension of their interlocutor and they never say much that makes sense.

For such as these, late opening or shorter Winter hours or, something worse by far, no opening at all, are trials to be borne with the seasons and the years as their hair grows grey, their skin ever more pale, their muscles flaccid, their minds unused except in parts, their emotions flat.

Until something happens and their world briefly turns to something different and new.

A flood perhaps – that's news.

A commotion in a reading room – that's exciting.

A retirement of a librarian loved, so far as love creeps about the stacks, wan and unexpressed as it must be – that's sad.

Then back to normal, and another year or two or three rolls on until something else, so exciting that it's news, happens and their year is made.

Or, once in a rarer while, ten years perhaps, part of the library roof falls in. That's a year to remember.

Or, through mismanagement and a confluence of unfortunate events, every fifty years or so, a fire happens, or a Reader goes insane.

That's good news as well.

Only once a century, or even once in five centuries, does something truly terrible happen, so terrible that it is too much for such Readers as those to bear. They deny it ever did. They return the following day as if all is normal and well.

They deny that sometimes life itself is changed for ever and their world, perhaps the whole of the Hyddenworld, will never be the same again.

That morning, at a few minutes before nine, last night's rain still falling and setting in under a low-clouded sky, the Sad Readers of Brum huddled in the shelter of the doors of the Great Library, not talking to each other as they waited to be let in.

Inside, it being Sunday, and there being Summer colds about, which had left two junior librarians with a fever in bed, Librarian Thwart and those other few who had come in to work were trying to prepare the Library for the coming day: opening doors, turning on lights, clearing things that should have been cleared the evening before, airing rooms, checking that paper was available, pencils too, and the boxes into which cards had to be put were in place.

So much to do and too little time, for the doors must be opened on the stroke of nine, even if it meant things being left undone, or half done. The Sad Readers must be let in for, strangely, it was their existence that gave the librarians their reason for being.

It was Thwart's task that day to open the great doors. This meant more than just turning a key. There were bolts on both sides, above and below, and in wet weather they stuck. There was a foot mat to put out which was large and heavy; there was a rack for coats, another for portersacs, a third for hats.

These things done and with the clock in the Library striking nine, Thwart pulled the doors open and welcomed the Sad Readers in. He knew them all by sight, some by name.

This done he might have rushed back to do the next job and catch up with himself except that he saw a striking figure advancing across the Square, striding as if indifferent to the rain, his robes flowing out behind him, his stave as tall as he was, his hair sleeked back and streaming wet.

It took Thwart a few moments to realize that it was Brother Slew, who he had only ever seen in the interior of the Library, modest, obliging and approachable. The figure he saw now was anything but. He was formidable, he was purposeful and Thwart's strange instinct was to close the great doors again, shoot the bolts, seal the windows and gather his fellow librarians into an army, puny and feeble though it might be, and protect the books and documents it was their lifetime's work to conserve and preserve from destruction.

Why this strange fancy should so suddenly come to him he had no idea, and of course he did not act on it.

Instead he retreated inside, as he always did, but this time with a thumping heart and sense of great unease. He passed the Sad Readers taking their familiar seats, and the Master Scrivener's empty office, and saw his colleagues busy at their tasks, but most of all as he hurried between the stacks of books from one room to another and thence to the stairs down to the basement where he worked, he felt as someone does who has lost something but is not sure what.

'A wet morning, Librarian Thwart!' said Slew, coming down the stairs a short while later. 'I have left my robes by the door but forgive me if I bring my stave. I value it and there have, I have heard, been thieves about.'

The stave, like Slew's hair, was wet.

It looked out of place in the basement, leaning against a wall, the rain from it dripping to the old flagged floor like a flow of tears.

'Well, I . . .'

Slew approached, looming over Thwart.

'It is food and drink I think that is banned, not staves! Eh!?'

He laughed.

Thwart felt ever more uneasy.

The more so because the garb that Brother Slew wore beneath his robes, which he had not seen before, was of leather and black, high-quality and of a fabrication that gave it a strange and disconcerting shimmer or sheen. It was hard to quite make it out and made Slew seem in some way intimidating, so much so that Thwart did not want to stay near him.

'No . . . I think . . . provided that the wet from your stave . . . I mean . . .'

'I will not get it on our books,' said Slew, all charm, taking off the leather jacket and revealing an ordinary jerkin. 'That's better. It's hot down here.'

It was better.

Brother Slew seemed suddenly his normal self.

'Well, I must get on,' said Thwart, less eager for conversation than usual, 'I imagine you have work to do. I daresay your time in Brum is drawing to a close?'

Where that question came from he had no idea and nor did Slew.

It alerted Slew to the fact that Thwart was not as happy to see him there as he normally was. Well, he could be as unhappy as he liked. Slew had no intention of lingering for much longer.

'Yes, I shall soon be gone – the green road calls!'

'If you need help, Brother Slew . . .'

'Thank you, I shall ask. I may say the same, Thwart, for today will be a busy one I think . . . the rain . . . and Master Brief being absent, eh!?'

Slew was good but not perfect. Even the Master of Shadows had things to learn. He should not have made his comment about Brief interrogative. Thwart might be feeble but he was not stupid.

Slew watched after him as he went about his duties, stood up, and sniffed the air, glowering.

The gem was hereabout, he could feel it, even if he could not quite smell it.

He went over to Stort's familiar place, at which he had never sat, and sat down.

'Where have you hidden it, scholar?' he murmured, eyeing the untidy papers and pigeonholes above Stort's desk. 'Where is it? Not in one of those, that's sure. It's behind bars, it's in a book, though none that I have had out. Nor one in any way connected with Summer, I think. Too obvious. But it's here. It's down *here* . . .'

He got up and paced about, eyes narrowed, looking at the metal gates, old and rusted, that barred access to the several short corridors, really no more than cellars, where the old tomes were kept. If he had met Stort he might have been better able to read his mind, to know how his thinking would have worked.

To hide a gem . . . There was always logic behind a choice, however unlikely that logic was.

He sat again in Stort's chair, which was worn and frayed, and wondered which other scholars had used it down the decades, apart from Brief himself when he was young.

Brief, Stort's mentor.

Brief. Now there was a thought.

'Tell me, Thwart,' he said a little later, 'has Master Brief himself ever scrivened tomes which are held in the Library? I would like to handle one before I leave.'

The moment he said it, it felt good.

'Several, Brother Slew.'

'I often think that if I ever finally wrote a tome myself,' said Slew, 'then I would do nothing all day long but look at it!'

'Not Master Brief! That's certain. He once said to me that the last thing a scholar wants to look at is his own work once it's done. Reminds him too much of the toil of writing it I daresay, and when you think of it . . .'

Thwart was happier now, his old talkative self.

Slew gave him a lulling, encouraging smile.

'. . . When you think of it, once the tome's done what more is there to do but write another?'

'Quite so,' said Slew. 'So, tell me what he's scrivened and I'll request that you fetch me one!'

'Well now . . . let's see . . .'

Thwart consulted his cards for a minute or two, then: 'Five in all, Brother Slew, all upstairs on the open shelves . . . no . . . four upstairs, one down here. Hmmm . . . oh yes, it is a guide . . . a catalogue of the works of ã Faroün.'

Slew looked puzzled.

'The lute player,' said Thwart.

'The architect,' replied Slew.

Thwart nodded. 'The same. The Library has a great collection of ã Faroün's works, original manuscripts and the like. It was Master Brief's task, started when he was a junior, completed only when he was Master, to catalogue them. Ã Faroün worked in Brum for one of Lord Festoon's forebears, who contributed the material.'

'It would be an honour to examine the catalogue, I am not familiar with ã Faroün or what he did, beyond his name of course.'

'Nor I,' said Thwart. 'I'll retrieve it here and now!'

He did so, unlocking one of the gates, locking it behind him, and going in amongst the gloomy stacks.

He came back only minutes later, a slim, new-looking volume in his hand.

'Not much to show for a lifetime's work!'

He came back into the main room and offered the volume to Slew who, feigning a general rather than particular interest, as if all he wanted to do was hold it for a little and flick through it for a short time, sat down at his table.

'Hmmm, it's a listing of . . . goodness . . . this scholar had a wide variety of interests . . . music seems a main one, mathematics . . . architecture . . .'

His voice trailed off as his eye was caught by a subheading under a subheading.

The main head was Architecture, the subhead Brum, and the subhead beneath sang out to him: The Chamber of Seasons.

'Something of interest?' said the ever-inquisitive Thwart.

It took an effort for Slew to stay sounding calm and disinterested.

'Not really,' he lied, his mind racing. 'No, just a realization . . . I have not visited the Chamber of Seasons since I came to Brum.'

'Oh, you can't do that, it's in Lord Festoon's residence.'

In fact, though his heart had leapt for a moment, Slew had already dismissed the possibility that the gem was there.

It's here, within yards of where I'm sitting.

He turned the page of the catalogue and was surprised to see a great many documents and other material listed under the heading Chamber of Seasons.

'I can see why it might have taken Master Brief so long . . .'

Again he paused, for the subhead had yet another, the last of which read 'Extraneous Matter and Drawings'.

Slew knew he was near now, and getting nearer still.

'I suppose,' he said, 'that if one cannot get to see the Chamber with one's own eyes then the next best thing is to look at a drawing of it? Eh?'

He proffered the catalogue to Thwart, who took one look and said, 'Those items can only be viewed in the presence of the Master himself and with gloves on.'

Slew laughed.

'Well, we have gloves but no Master, so who's to know?'

'I wish I . . . I wish . . .'

Slew had stood up.

He put on his black leather jacket again.

He ran his hands through his mane of hair, streaked and curled by rain.

He eyed Thwart in a way he had not before.

Thwart retreated slightly.

'Who's to know, my dear friend? Who's ever to know we looked at what we should not, for a moment, seeing what others may not, journeying into the shadows of the stack, a world . . .?'

As he spoke his voice seemed to slide apart from himself and into Thwart's mind, confusing it.

Slew gently took up his stave.

'Who's to accuse who did not do a thing...?' he asked, reaching out a hand. 'Give me your keys and then it cannot be said that you—'

'I cannot, I must not.'

'Give me your keys,' commanded Slew.

'I ... Brother Slew, please – '

The shadows circled Thwart's mind, and they were cold, so cold, and Slew's eyes were dark and glittered everywhere.

He gave Slew the keys.

'Which gate, my friend?'

Thwart pointed.

Slew opened the gate, ushered the librarian in, closed and locked it behind them so no one would know they were there.

'Where now?'

'I ... please – '

It was the last vestigial resistance Thwart showed.

He was cold, very cold, and what Slew commanded he had to do.

'*Show me!*'

Show him he did, leading him into the inner sanctum, that should have been accessible to no one, where the greatest collection of ā Faroün's manuscripts and material was kept.

'Now,' said Slew, 'let us finally begin.'

'Faster!' ordered Slew much later as Thwart pulled down one file after another marked 'Chamber of Seasons' and then began on a series of boxes marked the same.

There was a table in the barred stack, and as quickly as each file or box came down Slew opened it. Most of the items were loose papers or sketch books and he riffled through these in the hope that he might find the gem, or a clue to its hiding place, among them.

But thus far there had been nothing.

The larger boxes were more promising, containing smaller boxes with notes in them, scrolls and other items that could not be stacked or filed like books and papers.

But still nothing.

'What's that one – up there?'

Thwart could not reach it, it was too high and it had been pushed too far back on the shelf.

Slew took his stave to it and levered it forward.

The librarian in Thwart was not yet quite dead.

'Out of order,' he muttered, seeing the number, 'it's in the wrong place. Lucky to find it or otherwise . . .'

Slew relaxed.

He knew he was close now.

It would be the clever thing to do, to hide the gem in a box in a part of the Library inaccessible to all but a few, and then deliberately put the box in the wrong place so that it was almost impossible to find unless you knew . . . which meant that only Stort and Brief would be likely ever to find it. Thwart, shivering with cold and distress, began to snivel and weep.

'Please,' he said, 'you mustn't—'

'Be quiet,' snarled Slew, 'and give me the box.'

The box was large, its lid tied to the main part with twine through a loop of wire. The box was also tied with ribbon, running round it two ways.

He undid the ribbon and then the string and lifted off the lid.

He was surprised at what was inside.

It looked like a woven blanket or perhaps a thin rug.

'You mustn't . . .' said Thwart again, 'and you could still get out and no one would know because I wouldn't . . .'

Slew looked at Thwart and his long patience finally snapped.

He curled his hand into a hard fist and smashed the defenceless librarian so hard that he fell back, blood streaming from his face.

'You . . . I . . . please don't hurt anything . . .'

Even now, weak though he was, and in the power of a hydden more powerful than most, Thwart tried to defend those things it was his job to defend.

Slew hit him again, harder now, and kicked him for good measure.

'Be quiet now,' he said softly, blood seeping from the fallen librarian's right ear, 'say no more.'

Thwart shivered briefly and stilled, his face pale in the semi-dark, his life dangerously near its end, his world broken about him, his mind unable to comprehend why he felt so cold and why . . .

'Be still,' commanded Slew, kicking him hard again, and Thwart was still.

Slew saw that what he now held in his hands was a very large cloth, enough to cover a table or more, heavily worked with embroidery, appliqué and lustrous sequins and stones. Even in the ill-lit stacks its colours were vibrant, beautiful. But close-to it was impossible to make out the overall pattern.

He swept the files and boxes off the table, sending ā Faroün's precious documents flying in all directions.

He laid the embroidered cloth on the table, opened it out as fully as he could and stepped back. His heart nearly stopped when a small leather pouch, caught in its folds, tumbled to the floor. It was empty. Had it held the gem? Was it placed there to be deliberately misleading? He had no idea.

He saw at once that the cloth was exquisite, but still could not quite work out what it was. He looked at it more until it suddenly dawned on him what he was looking at.

It was a succession of scenes, first of Spring and then of Summer and so on through Autumn to Winter, which was dark and brooding. The colours were astonishing, the images of trees and birds, mountains and rivers, sky and earth, very beautiful, so much so that Slew found that he was drawn into it, as if the embroidery held within its stitches the magic of each of the four seasons it depicted.

'My Lord would like to possess this, I think,' murmured Slew. 'But I have not yet found what I came for . . . Now let us examine Spring . . .'

He was guessing that Stort had in some way tucked the gem under the stitching, or within an appliquéd piece of cloth, but the whole thing was large and complex, full of bumps and hollows any one of which might hold a small gem, or be a place to hide it. The cloth's many colours served as camouflage as well, for no one colour stood out and a gem of any colour might easily be hidden within. He looked, he ran his fingers over it, and he looked again.

No sign of it.

He looked at Summer, thinking that Stort had chosen not to do the obvious thing. Then at Autumn and Winter. Running his fingers over the beautiful thing, examining each part, holding it up to the light from the main room in the hope that the gem, assuming it was there, would glint or in some way show itself.

Nothing.

But he could feel it was there somewhere, entangled with the seasons, hidden by them, protected from him by them.

'Where are you?' he whispered. '*Talk* to me . . .'

Then he began looking more closely still.

Mister Pike had had a bad night and a worse morning.

He had slept hardly at all, the stave fight on the quay by the Muggy Duck between the monk and the Norsener nagging at him into the small hours. He could not work out how it was that an ordinary monk should be able to fight like that unless he was an extraordinary one; and if he was, which Pike suspected, then what was he doing in Brum?

Master Brief had been able to identify him as a Brother Slew, a wandering scholar of no great interest who, like many pilgrims who came to Brum in the Summer, liked to spend time in the Library.

'They do no harm and they have as much right as anyone else to consult our books. Scholars can be rather too protective and precious about their own world and all its works. It's there to share with others, not covet for oneself!'

This was a worthy sentiment but Pike smelt trouble and danger.

He had not asked the obvious further question concerning Slew, which was what he was studying in the Library, because it had not seemed of such importance as what he might be doing outside it. His enquiries very soon established the pattern of Slew's day, from which no conclusion could be drawn out of the ordinary except that his visits to the Library were regular and extended.

Not wishing yet to disturb Brief, whose day off it was, on the basis of nothing more than his usual worry and fretting about matters of security in Brum, he paid a call on another of the senior librarians, who had also taken the Sunday off.

'I know the fellow, earnest and dull and not a great scholar by any means but worthy enough I'm sure.'

'What's his area of interest?'

'The seasons, especially the Spring. Unsurprising really, considering Bedwyn Stort's great discovery. Everyone has an interest in that subject at the moment, though few show quite the persistence of our Brother Slew. Incidentally, when are we going to get to actually see the gem Stort found?'

Pike did not dally.

First he ascertained that Slew was even at that moment in the Library, next he visited his lodgings and talked with his fellow travellers. He realized that news of his enquiries would be known to Slew the moment he returned to his lodging and the advantage of surprise, if surprise was needed, would be completely lost.

He had decided that he must talk again with Brief, and it was as he was on his way to see him that the awful truth suddenly dawned. He himself had spoken with Stort about the gem's safety before he left Brum and decided that the safest thing of all was to leave it up to him where it was hidden during his absence. After that he might be persuaded to give it up to the safe keeping of the city itself, but before, he had certainly been unwilling to part with it.

Stort had at least been persuaded not to carry the gem about with him and said, suddenly, that he knew where it might be placed in complete and utter safety. No one could get to it but himself and one other – and that other (Stort did not name him) would never give the game away.

'So you're going to tell this other, this him or her, are you?'

Stort had said there was no need. If anything happened to him he, or she, would be sure to be able to work it out.

It was Stort's mischievous mention of a 'she' that had fooled Pike. Of course there was no she. Stort had nothing to do with females, except Cluckett, and she was certainly too recent an acquaintance to be entrusted with a secret of that magnitude.

It was quite obvious now who that other was – Master Brief, Stort's former mentor.

Obvious, therefore, where the gem was hidden: in the Library and most probably in a part of it that Stort knew best.

Brief's residence was adjacent to the Library and Pike hurried through the rain towards it, his hand tightening on his stave as he did so. Nothing felt right about any of this any more: everything felt wrong.

Brief was not in, he had taken it into his head to go to the Library.

'On a Sunday?'

'First time he's ever done so in my memory,' said Brief's house-keeper, 'but he said it was urgent. He took his stave of office with him. That's unusual too!'

Pike cursed himself and ran down to the Library.

'Where's Master Brief?' he asked a startled librarian.

'He went down to the basement, Mister Pike, and he was hurrying like you are. What's afoot?'

All eyes were on Pike, from those of the librarians down to the most withdrawn of the Sad Readers.

'Nothing,' said Pike, but obviously it was.

Slew, having failed to find the gem in the cloth the second time, stepped back once more and tried to look at it anew.

He had seen the scenes of nature in the imagery but the figures in the landscape had seemed less important.

Now he wondered if that was the point – they were less noticeable and so less obvious.

A girl, a youth, a wedding . . . an older couple among them, Slew thought their parents . . . all in Spring.

Lovers and their parents?

A spousal certainly, the beginnings of the making of new life.

And in Summer they were older, children born, life rich and good, the Summer of their lives . . . whose lives? Slew stared and tried to make the story of them out and ask himself to which of these figures Stort might attach himself, or his imagination, seeking out a place to hide the gem whose magic and resonance would make it all the harder to see . . .

Slew pulled himself away, for the imagery was reaching into him, or drawing him into it, like some play, not of shadows but of colour and life.

He took up the pouch again to check once more that the gem was not in it. It was not.

But was that itself a clue?

He returned to the embroidery and moved on to Autumn.

A river flowed, the leaves along its bank had turned, the lovers in Spring, who became parents in Summer, now seemed distraught.

Something, someone, had died. Autumn was when the whole world began to die.

Slew remembered the magical Autumns of his youth in Thuringia, his mother, her preoccupations, her concerns for others than himself, he felt that loss as a falling of leaves, a blowing through of unwelcome winds.

He felt old sadness which even his training with the shadows could not ease.

Clever.

Stort had been so clever.

He had hidden the gem in a place to which most people might find it hard to go.

Courage, he had that; and resourcefulness. Now . . . cunning.

Stort was no ordinary opponent.

So, where might a person not want to go with the passing of the years, the seasons of their life? Where would they not want to look?

At their Winter and their death, obviously.

Slew found he had to support himself, shadows of his own chilling him now, reaching into him, trying to stop him . . . clever Bedwyn Stort, stopping him . . .

He pulled back yet again, found the pouch still in his hand, shoved it in his pocket before returning to Spring to see if somewhere there among the figures was one who carried such a pouch. So many, when he looked, more it seemed than the first time he looked, crowding at the wedding, laughing, young and old.

Then he saw her.

A girl, hidden by her father, and her mother too, watching the wedding as if from behind the bars and barriers of their legs and arms. In her belt a pouch like the one he had now in his hand.

He reached to touch the embroidery, his finger feeling it for something inside, as if it was real, there in the most magical embroidery he had ever seen.

He touched it and felt nothing but stitches and a sadness greater than before. Did the girl see him? It felt as if she did; did he imagine her eyes on him then? He did, he did, and he looked away, distressed.

He knew now where the gem was going to be, but to get there he would have to go through the seasons of her life, which he did not want to do, not then, not ever.

In Summer, she was there all right. Nearly lost to sight again, behind a thicket of brambles whose berries were blood-red and black, she looking out, parentless, alone, angry. As for the pouch, it was there in her belt which, when he touched it, pricked him like a thorn, which it should not do, being only cloth. But it did.

Slew felt tired and lost, as she did, and weary, as she was; and alone and lonely.

He could barely stand now, nor did he want to go on. He wanted to leave the gem where Stort had so wisely put it; it was not his but hers, it was not for mortal touch, not for him.

When he reached Autumn he thought he saw Sinistral's eyes in the crowd urging him on, and he obeyed, searching for the girl, then woman, now something older still: unfulfilled, ageing, so angry and so lost, so sad, so very sad.

That pouch she had was empty of all life, empty of hope, empty of its gem and Slew was unable to go on.

'Open this door!'

It was Master Brief, only a few yards behind him, on the far side of the barred gate. 'What are you doing? What have you done?'

Brief had seen Thwart on the ground, blood pooled by his head, eyes open but now sightless.

'What have you done!'

The shouting brought Slew back to himself, though the sadness was still there.

He put Brief out of his mind and returned to his task and turned finally to the embroidery of Winter.

It was not hard to find her, alone at Winter's end, all people gone, all life absent, just she herself wandering through a bleak mountain pass, the tops above covered in blizzard snow. He reached to touch her where she walked, but it was hard, so hard, to enter into such wretched loneliness as that.

Her pouch was where it always was, there on her belt, but it was old and tattered now, the stitches worn and broken. She too was broken by her life's terrible journey, angry from first to last, her eyes bereft, her body bent, an old woman in pain of body and heart, unloved in the high passes of the mountains, chilled by the bleak winds, frozen by the ice and snow.

So clever was the imagery, so powerful the presentation, that it seemed to him that what he saw was real and the old woman was right there before him, pitiful and alone.

Which, being so, it felt as if he were stealing from her personally, not simply finding a cleverly hidden gem. Even more than that was the sense that the cloth put into him a dark reality, a future history, a place he had not wished to go.

For all these reasons his every instinct told him not to go closer, as it felt, to try to find the gem. But then he glimpsed it. Not on or in her woven pouch but secreted away in her hand, a glimmer of something catching the dull light. He reached forward, tugged at it and found he had grasped the first link of a chain. It unravelled itself free from where Stort had cleverly hidden it, behind her hand, behind the woven pouch; the chain to which a pendant was attached, empty of all stones it seemed but one, and that, at first, non-descript. He pulled it clear and took her last hope away.

Then, awed, empty, desolate, he looked at it and it seemed nothing much at all. Just a little grey stone in a battered old pendant. Had he journeyed so far for this? Further than across the sea with Borkum Riff.

Further than a lifetime.

For this stone?

Then suddenly it glimmered, it shot through briefly with light, the pendant turned and twisted in his hand, it began to have a life of its own and it shone forth so brightly he was blinded.

He struggled, fell back, fell down, the gem in its setting rolled from him, its green, exquisite dangerous rays across Thwart's deadened eyes, its rays in Slew's, its light entering a thousand books, bouncing about, beginning to be uncontrollable.

He reached and grasped it, and with an enormous effort of will closed his great hand about it, cutting off the rays one by one until none were felt and he was able to thrust it into the pouch he held. At once all grew dark again.

Moments later the gate into the cell crashed open, Brief having sought and found another key.

He stood there; bold in his robes, angry and wary, his stave of office in his hand. Its ancient carvings still held something of the fires of Spring just seen.

But Slew had the advantage of youth.

He took his dark stave and watched as Brief's swung at him through the air.

He moved and it missed him.

He moved a second time and it missed again.

Brief had fought the shadows once and won, more or less.

But this was something different.

Slew, too, was a Master, and to his strength was added that of the gem he carried.

Perhaps if Brief had been able to strike Slew then, while he was still saddened and bewildered by his journey in the embroidered cloth to retrieve the gem, he might have been able to defeat him.

Perhaps if Pike had been able to reach the Library sooner, then, well, the wyrd of things would have been different.

The one who came closest to stopping Slew was Thwart.

The light of Spring had shone into his dying eyes, it had reached to his spirit, fleeing as it had been from life, and whispered it back home again. Thwart awoke to life terrified.

He saw his Master trying his best to fight.

He saw a darker Master raising his stave with one hand, holding the embroidery with another. Of the gem he knew nothing at all.

Thwart might have stayed as he was, he might have feigned death and not risked his life again.

But he saw chaos where only order should be and he saw the greatest and most loved scholar of his age bravely fighting a younger, stronger hydden than himself.

So Thwart stood up and, weak though he was, and frightened too, he found his courage to challenge the Master of Shadows.

Slew turned, saw him, was amazed and moved to kill him where he stood.

No one knew then or after, least of all Thwart himself, why he did not do so. Perhaps in passing from Spring to Winter and feeling the sadness of she who had the gem, he had no will to hurt Thwart more. Maybe in himself he saw, somewhere deep in his dark, hurt heart, the better thing.

Maybe it was Brief who saved his life when he roared out, 'Take me but do not hurt him, he has a whole life left to live, take me.'

Slew turned back to Brief, saw he was in his way, needed to escape the terrors of that place and his own self, raised his dark stave and moved as shadows do, one way and another. His thrust at Brief then was deep and powerful; there was no defence against such a thing.

His second thrust was something worse, a killing blow to Brief's old head.

His third and last was into the Master Scrivener's chest, into his heart.

As Brief fell amongst the tomes he loved, Slew stepped over him, passed through to the stairs, took them like the shadow of a hydden he truly was, and passed right through the Library and out of its doors.

Pike did not see him.

No one saw him.

He was gone down the lanes and ginnels of fabled Brum, his robes left behind, his dark stave going before.

Thwart survived.

Pike found him in the shadows the murderer left behind, cradling his dying Master's broken head and body.

Pike did the same, distraught to know that he had not been there to protect the hydden he respected and loved most in all the world.

'He saved my life,' said Thwart.

Brief stirred and with his last breath said, 'No, no . . . you saved your own and found the true direction in which your wyrd will lead you. Trust and follow it as I did mine. Live your life, Thwart, make every second count, it is the only way.'

'I will try, Master Brief.'

'I know you will . . .'

Then he turned to Pike and said, 'Old friend, I saw the gem of Spring, think of it, I saw it with my own eyes . . .'

They say that as Brief died there was a roar of anguish from the Library that he cherished all his life.

They say that it rocked and shook with grief . . .

Such that its doors would not properly close, so that his great spirit, free for ever now, could come and go just as it pleased.

All, in a way, quite true.

For as Brief died, the earthquake presaged by the tremors of the weeks before, ever since Stort had found the gem, finally hit Brum hard. Many buildings seemed to roar and rock and shake. Many collapsed and in their awful ruins humans and hydden died alike.

As for the Library doors of Brum, they never did hang true again.

29

QUAKE

The earthquake that devastated Brum in the dark hour of Brief's passing was one of many felt across Englalond and all Europe then and in the days following.

Taken together these events left no doubt in any hydden mind that Mother Earth was angry and taking revenge for mortal kind's disrespect towards her nature and being. What anyone could do about it no one knew, and long-held feelings among Brum's citizenry of impotent foreboding for their city and the world deepened still more.

That Brief himself had such worries was well known to many who had known him.

'I was there myself, Lord Festoon,' Pike told the High Ealdor in the days after, and before the funeral, when folk like to recount their memories of one who has died and who they loved, 'when Imbolc the Peace-Weaver told him, not for the first time, that the world was coming to an end and the bad weather we'd been having was a foretaste of worse things to come. She said something to the effect that the world was not a larder to raid or a well to let run dry and that we need to tend it and honour it.

'If we did not, she said, Mother Earth would wreak havoc upon us.

'Of course Brief wasn't going to agree outright to that, for he took a more positive view of things, but I know for a fact that since the gem was found and we began to experience tremors he had begun to fear the worst.

'"Pike," he said to me not a week ago, "the Earth's building Herself up to something very nasty, very nasty indeed!"

'Of course,' continued Pike, 'I don't say the Earth's directly responsible for his death, but whoever said wyrd worked directly?! Not Brief, that's certain. He taught me that all things are connected and when one bit goes wrong, another goes awry. Who's to say there's not a link, however strange this may seem, between an angry word spoken at one end of Deritend and a slap in the face by someone completely different in Digbeth? Well, maybe the wider world's like that too. Spill the Earth's guts by mining for gold in Cornwall and a blizzard wipes out a hydden village in the Pennines! Brief's thoughts not mine, may the Mirror guard his spirit!

'No, there's not a hydden in Brum doesn't think that his death and the quakes we're having are connected. But Mirror knows that neither he nor I ever thought it would come to this!'

Lord Festoon considered this and said, 'There are certainly connections there, though whether it's with us mortals that the Earth is angry, or with the fact that a great one like Brief has been killed, or that the gem's discovery is upsetting Her, I haven't yet made up my mind. Then there's the humans and what they do which, by comparison with the hydden, is monstrous and terrible.

'Perhaps once Bedwyn Stort comes back and my friend Igor Brunte, who is now in the North with Feld establishing what support Brum might hope for up there in the event of us being attacked by the Fyrd, we may together and separately see these things in a better perspective. Then, too, we must have Brief's funeral and a proper period of mourning. But for now, Pike, I'm more worried for Brum than I ever have been since I became its High Ealdor. Never in my lifetime have we needed more than we do now the vigour and energy of thought and deed for which Brum has always been famed throughout the Hydddenworld.'

Pike nodded.

'Stort's no leader, that's for sure, but Mirror knows there's never been a hydden in whom the future has shone so bright. Brief himself believed that.'

Lord Festoon rose up and went to the window of his parlour, where the two were talking, and looked out on ruined buildings nearby.

'I trust that his mission to persuade Jack to return to Brum is successful, but I have my doubts it will be. If it be true that he and

Katherine have had a babe, what is there in the world could possibly persuade Jack to leave them and return to us, especially if she is the Shield Maiden? That said, I always thought the lad had destiny written in his bold face! But in which world? Ours or his?'

After some thought Pike replied, 'That's the crux of it, High Ealdor: which world does he belong to? That's his decision to make. A giant-born does not cross our path every day and I trust he'll come back. You should have seen him fight the shadows of the Fyrd as I did in the henge in Woolstone. No more than a lad he was then, with no weapon to hand until Brief threw him his stave, and yet he held them off.'

Festoon nodded and said, 'He did the same in the Chamber of Seasons in that dark hour when Brunte tried to arraign me. How that has turned about! See how the young like Stort and Jack have it in their power to do what we so often failed to do. Yes, we need those two and we need them soon if Brunte's right and the Empire is soon to take its revenge on us in Brum.'

'Bad times,' murmured Pike.

'Times in which I'd feel a lot happier if I knew that Stort had got through these days of quakes and tremors and was on his way home to us.'

Pike laughed.

'Forces of nature do not perturb Stort as they do the rest of us. Trust me, if anyone can survive the Earth's anger it's Bedwyn Stort. Unwittingly of course . . .'

'Be that as it may, Pike, I'd like to see him get back in time for the funeral of Brief, for he'll be upset indeed if he returns too late for it.'

Even as Pike and Lord Festoon in Brum were talking of future dangers, Stort and his friends were dealing with a present one.

Arnold Mallarkhi had taken Stort's urgent desire to get back to Brum, for fear that something horrible had happened there, to heart. He was helming them at speed up the Thames, using sail to cut through the river's flow. It was against them but fortunately, it being Summer, the flow was slight.

They had not too far to go before they reached Oxenford, which Barklice judged to be the best point of disembarkation for the onward journey by foot to Brum. The possibility of returning undermost a train they had given up, the recent tremors having disrupted the human world – and worse.

'Aye, it be bad indeed, my goodlies,' the normally cheerful Arnold had been forced to concede in the last few hours.

Human bodies had floated past them down the river, swollen and discoloured.

'There be male and female and childer and all sorts,' Arnold said, shaking his head. 'Mayhap it be best your lad see none o' this, Mister Barklice.'

But Barklice took a different view.

'If he's going to learn about the Earth, and he must, he'd better see Her as she is. I denied too much too long and I'll not ever let him do the same. Eh, Bratfire?'

'No, Pa, 'tis best. Look!'

It was a human village near the river, burning.

'Look!'

A human church had collapsed.

'Look!'

A car had rolled off the edge of an embankment where the bridge went over the river. No one had come for the dead.

Arnold noted other things.

The Summer birds among the riverbank, the swans, the mallard and the coot, ought to have been tired from the rearing of their near-fledged young and content to take things easy.

But time and again they were restive, strange, some flying about nervously, not tending their young as they should.

'It's like they want to be done with Summer and those that must be off on their migration to their Winter roosting grounds early,' said Arnold.

'The fish ain't no better,' added Bratfire, whose bilgesnipe blood and upbringing had made him something of an expert in matters of rivercraft and nature. 'They're easier to catch than I've ever known, like their noddles have been frazzled.'

Yet, for all this, their journey had its good points. Arnold's energy never seemed to flag and Bratfire was a willing and excellent pupil at the stern, as he was on all other fronts. His turn of phrase might be bilgesnipe but his mind was sharp and his skills great.

Barklice was especially gratified that his hyddening skills were so well honed, his own being legendary.

'I think, one and all,' observed Stort cheerfully, at about that same moment when his friends Pike and Festoon in Brum were telling each other that they were hoping for his safe return – which to be precise was at twenty-seven minutes past midday by the clock on the tower of Northmoor church – 'that now we're almost within sight of Oxenford, about which if you wish it I shall be glad to give you a lecture, so to say . . . no?'

No one said 'Yes!'

'Not quite now?' he continued judiciously. 'Well then . . . I think I can at least say that the journey . . . has been . . . a . . . well . . . I was going to say a safe one . . . but I think . . . I shall now . . . revise that a little . . . and – gentlemen, what is *that*!?'

They turned as one to look in the direction in which he was pointing, which was upstream of the wide, meandering river, across some fields where they could see, at a bend in the river, a dark and brooding wall of water bearing down.

'It's a . . .' began Barklice, his voice trembling.

'It's a . . .' continued Stort.

'That,' declared Arnold, his eyes popping out of his head, 'that be a . . .'

'It's a wave, a big one,' said Bratfire.

A dark wall of water tore at the river bank, uprooting shrubs and holding in its curling maw two dead swans and their young, a wrecked boat, various spars and a whole tree whose branches threshed white in the water.

Arnold stood at the prow of their craft, dwarfed by what he saw. He had seen big waves in his time but had never known or heard of a wave like this one. It could freeze the mind.

But not his.

He stood easy, the oar in one hand, bringing down their mizzen sail with the other.

'Hold tight in the gunnels, lads, and Bratfire, hold fast to your Pa's leather belt! Mister Stort, hold this, and hold it good for my life's at the end of it!'

He had dared to lay down his oar for a moment and had taken up a coiled rope that he kept nearby in case of emergencies, though never one such as this.

He looped it round his middle, knotted it loosely, and threw the ends to Stort.

'Hold me well, Mister Stort, hold me good, but swear on the Mirror's holy self you'll let me go afore you're dragged o'er the side as well! Swear it!'

Stort murmured that he would have to think about it.

'You be no good to nowt, Mister Stort, if you be dead!' cried Arnold. 'So swear.'

'I swear to do the best I can, Arnold,' said Stort.

'You be a stubborn wonder, that's what you be!' said Arnold as the wave came down upon them.

'Swear it!' called out Arnold as the craft struggled to rise through the spray.

'No,' shouted Stort, wrapping the rope around his arm, 'I won't!'

Then the main part of the wave hit them and the craft juddered as if it had hit a huge baulk of timber.

They saw Arnold lean into the wall of water that was already crashing over them, holding his oar firm against the flow, bracing his body against forces he on his own could not stand.

Stort saw nothing more after that as the rope grew tight and the water swept over Arnold. He felt his arm half pulled from its socket, and his body beginning to slide down to hit the cross-seats one by one, which splintered and broke as he went . . .

Until he felt himself being pulled over the side such that the only thing that held him fast aboard was his foot, hooked to a rib of the craft.

But he did not let go.

When the wave was past and all that was left was swell after swell that lifted the boat up and down, he saw the arm of his jerkin had been ripped right off and his flesh was red-raw and bleeding where it had been.

But the rope was still tight and Arnold, whether dead or alive he had no idea, at the end of it.

'Help me, Barklice!'

They all helped him heave Arnold back up to the surface of the troubled water from where he pulled himself back on-board.

'That were a wave and a half, Mister Stort,' he said nonchalantly, as water streamed off him, 'and I thank 'ee for holding on, otherwise I'd be on my way to Davy's locker and maybe a good way beyond.'

'Look!'

It was Bratfire, as if nothing had happened, pointing ashore at the copse of trees. Every one of them was down and the land and fields thereabout looking all torn and sundered, as sorry for themselves as a great fighter fallen, or a creature with a broken back.

This sad sight provoked in Bedwyn Stort new and different thoughts, ones that made him genuinely afraid.

'You don't look quite your normal self,' said Barklice, once they had dried themselves out and tidied the craft and got their journey under way again.

'I am not. My mind is elsewhere and worrying.'

'What about?' asked Barklice, who was used to Stort's sometimes startling jumps of thought.

'Tell me, Barklice, if you had to make a guess, where would you imagine I would hide something precious?'

'The Library,' replied Barklice at once. 'You mean the gem, I take it?'

'I do. Is it that obvious?'

'We hide things in places we know. Everyone knows you know the Library better than anyone. So my guess would be you'd hide the gem there.'

'I'm very much afraid,' said Stort after some reflection, 'that I have done something stupid. I may as a result have put the lives of my colleagues and friends at risk, which may be why, when we began this journey, I felt something was wrong. Arnold, make more haste if you can. We *must* get home, though it may already be too late!'

Marshal Brunte's decision to travel to the North with General Meyor Feld to ascertain the level of support for Brum's insurrection and its strength in terms of numbers and skill paid dividends. He and Feld thought that if an attack by the Fyrd on Brum came they needed to know and to secure the city's lines of retreat.

'No good getting killed today if we can retreat and come back and fight them tomorrow,' he told Pike, who in their absence was put in charge of Brum's defences.

They had taken Captain Backhaus north with him as well, to keep a record, and they journeyed to all the major hydden centres north of Brum. The tremors had not seriously affected that end of Englalond, the roads and railways were working, and Brunte, like Barklice, knew how to use them the hydden way.

They got as far as the human general Hadrian's Wall, a structure that stretched right across Englalond, beyond which few civilized hydden had ever ventured. There were settlements there, they were told, but the living was sparse and the conditions harsh and the area was ruled by the infamous Reivers who, it was said, rode fierce dogs.

The two main hydden settlements on the Wall, Carlisle and Chesters, cooperated in its control and defence against occasional incursions from the Reivers.

'Usually it's only in a bad Winter, when they're after food, that we see the Reivers. If they can they'll snatch a wyfkin or two, but we know their tricks and these days we see little of them, though we hear them a-howling sometimes.'

'How so?' asked Brunte.

'We leave food for them in bad weather beyond the Wall, marking it with flares. Call it tribute if you like. We see them racing round the food on their dogs, hurling spears and shooting arrows and the like. To intimidate us perhaps or to show their skills to each other. You'll find no support for Brum's cause there, but if it comes to it we'll do what we can.'

'And the howling?'

'It's wolf-like. A way of saying they're well fed and keeping in touch with other Reivers across their bleak land.'

Brunte and his colleagues learned much, gained friends, and ascertained the best northward lines of retreat and where to make their stands. The direction would make it harder for the Fyrd to catch up with them without dangerously extending their lines of communication.

Up there, on the great rises of the wild Pennines, Brunte felt the clean air clear his head and lungs. He talked to Feld as he never had.

Feld knew that Brunte was a Pole and an urban one, raised in hydden Warszawa, and that after the Fyrd killed his family he swore to get revenge on them when he could. He had judged that the best way to do that was to join the force he hated and learn what he could about them. So he became a Fyrd himself and began wreaking his revenge by secretly killing them and disrupting their systems when he could.

Feld noticed that he always carried an iron bar with him wherever he went. A dirk and a stiletto were his favourite weapons, but the bar?

'I keep it by me for the Fyrd who killed my family, should his wyrd and mine conspire to bring us together.'

'It's heavy to carry round as you do,' said Feld.

'All the better to remind me of my duty of revenge.'

Yet for all this kind of talk, up there in the mountain air, drinking the clean, cold waters of wild streams and eating the simple fare of the hydden they met, Brunte mellowed a little. Perhaps the insurrection he had led was all the revenge he needed. Perhaps the good nature of Brum's citizens had a softening effect.

Or was it the years passing and the sights and sounds of wild country-side that put in him a liking for the Earth he hardly knew, and with that a realization there was more to life than soldiering?

They travelled south again, meeting more communities and exploring on the way the gentler uplands of the Yorkshire Dales and the sturdy hydden communities there.

They came to Darnbrookdale, beneath whose spoil tips, left by human quarrymen, they found hydden living in the shadow of the human past, making good use of what the humans had abandoned.

The hydden children had never met people like Brunte and Feld, well armed, strangely spoken, with glittering eyes that took things in. But they weren't afraid and in the shadow of the tips they showed the Brummies what they knew, their piping little voices counting numbers and reciting the alphabet while the breeze ruffled their hair.

They asked questions about Brum. To them it seemed a wonderland.

Feld said, 'It's good to see, sir, worth knowing what we're defending. This is liberty.'

But Brunte had a different thought.

'Yet, Feld, I'm afraid even these good places will one day be lost to us mortals whether Fyrd or not, hydden or human. Look what humans have done, on which we hydden have thrived too long!'

He pointed to the spoil tips looming above, the shadows of Summer clouds drifting across their steep sides.

'But it's mostly overgrown,' said Feld, 'and no one would know.'

'The scars remain,' replied Brunte, 'and the tunnels underground. Do you think that Mother Earth does not feel them?'

'These are but pinpricks to her,' said Backhaus indifferently. 'Now, sir, we need to—'

'Bare your arm,' said Brunte, producing one of the two dirks he always carried in his belt.

'Sir—'

'Bare it,' barked Brunte. 'Now, tell me if a pinprick hurts!'

He stabbed Backhaus's arm. He gasped with pain.

'Did that hurt, Captain?'

'It did, sir.'

'Never again tell me Mother Earth does not hurt. She feels the pain we inflict on her. I am just a practical hydden, a simple soldier, but I'd bet my own mother's life on the fact that the Earth feels pain. Mirror help us if she ever chooses to use her full strength against us!'

That night, the earthquakes which so far had not touched the North of Englalond hit the Dales. The three hydden, encamped on the fells above with their guards, woke to a violent shaking of the ground. Not once but three times did it happen. They heard screaming and hurried downslope to the settlement whose kinder had welcomed them so happily in the daylight hours before.

That settlement was no more.

In the dawning light they saw that the tip had slumped and twenty feet of shattered stone, raw as a deep wound, had buried all of them. Not a single member of that community survived but for the male who had guided them up to the fells and, talking late, stayed with them for the night.

He had lost everything.

No one that he knew in all the world remained alive.

His grief cast him into silence.

'Mother Earth,' said Brunte grimly, 'is angry. Feld, Backhaus . . . The pinpricks hurt, remember that. And, too, that it may be the Earth Herself and not the Fyrd who is our greatest enemy.'

30
TO THE GREEN ROAD

The first thing that Jack and Katherine did when another tremor caused a mini-tsunami to travel down the River Thames and cause havoc to farms and kill livestock was to get a television. They wanted to see live pictures for themselves of places which, as hydden travellers, they had passed through.

'There's Birmingham as well. It's had tremors over the last weeks and there might be more. We just want to know . . .'

'And if Brum's hit, which it will be if central Birmingham is affected, what do you propose doing about it?' asked Arthur.

Jack hesitated, torn between the instinct to stay and his natural desire to help his friends, especially having just seen them again.

'I stay here,' he said, repeating what he had said to Katherine. 'This is where my family is.'

It did not take long for the nightmare to come true.

Three days later Birmingham was hit and they watched footage of flooded streets in the old quarter of the city.

'Which means Brum,' he said. 'I feel I ought to be there . . . but I know it would be wrong.'

Katherine said nothing, understanding his worry, feeling his pain.

'How would I ever know if something happened to Stort, or Barklice or any of them? How would I know?'

He took it out on the house, suddenly taking it into his head to decorate a room, clear the loft, dig the garden, anything.

He took it out on them, even on Judith, at whom, for the first time, he shouted.

He was watching a report on a tremor in Oxford and she turned the set off without explaining why.

'For God's sake, Judith, just go away – I'm trying to ... I'm ... sorry.'

Her face had fallen. She had wanted to talk to him.

He cuddled her and the moment passed but the guilt remained.

They all began following the news, for there was rarely a day when a seismic event didn't happen in a country where it had previously been almost unheard of.

'And it's happening on the Continent too,' said Katherine. 'The world's falling apart.'

'The Earth's angry more like.'

The experts quoted in the paper and on television said the tremors were freak seismic occurrences but in the normal range of historical probabilities.

Arthur said little but kept a record of everything. Astral Cosmology was his subject and he knew the records as well as anyone. In medieval times, in various places in England, buildings had collapsed and church steeples had fallen; coastal dune lands were submerged for ever beneath the North Sea.

'There's no doubt either that such events as these occurred during Beornamund's life. Of course it has to do with Judith's birth, or the other way round. It's chicken and egg and I believe far, far worse is going to come.'

For the commentators there had to be a scientific explanation – but they couldn't find one in the terms of conventional science. The media wheeled out every expert and crackpot opinion they could find, but soon grew tired of it.

After the big tremors came the smaller ones that got only a line or two in the inside pages. Like a tremor in Darnbrookdale where the spoil tips of an old limestone quarry collapsed with no one hurt. No one had lived near the place for years.

'Humans, that is,' said Jack.

Like Arthur, he was beginning to wonder what the real toll was in the Hyddenworld.

He began to look haunted, conflicted between his desire to go back to what he thought of as his hydden people, and the need and duty to stay with his human family. He was a doer by nature and doing nothing was torture.

When the quakes began occurring on the Continent Arthur got a new scrapbook and started keeping his own records all over again.

'There seems no way that science alone can provide an explanation for these kind of seismic events,' said Arthur, 'but I think we all know what a hydden would say.'

'You don't need to be a hydden to work it out,' said Katherine. 'Being pagan will do. What my mother would have said is that the Earth is angry, but so am I . . . so am I when I think what we've done to the Earth over the centuries.'

'Join the club,' said Margaret. 'It's an old one. This was being said fifty years ago.'

In the end it was Katherine who made the decision for Jack to leave, a rather more local earthquake being the cause. It shook Woolstone House hard enough for glass to fall out of three of the conservatory windows and a crack to appear in a ceiling upstairs. It was more omen than warning, but it was also decision made.

'Right,' she said, 'you're going to Brum, Jack, I'm worried about our friends there too. You could go up quickly by the pilgrim road we travelled down on and try to get Stort and some others out of there. They can come here . . .'

Jack shook his head.

'I thought that's what you wanted?' she said.

'I do and I will. But I was thinking of something else. Do you remember when your mother died we thought it would be good to go north and spend time in Arthur's cottage in the border country?'

'Y . . . es,' she said hesitatingly.

'I think you should take Judith there. She needs more and more space to roam and maybe it would be safer; there have been no tremors that far north . . . What do you think, Arthur?'

'Good idea, horrible cottage, I believe. It's years since we went.'

'Horrible place,' said Margaret, 'but plenty of trees and moorland and mist for Judith to lose herself in and at this time of year it shouldn't be so bad. I think it's a good idea.'

It was agreed. Jack to Brum, the rest up north and Woolstone House closed for a while.

'You can join us up there when you've finished in Brum.'

He dallied two or three days longer, getting Judith used to the idea. Other fathers left for a while, mothers too, it couldn't hurt for a week or two.

'I'd prefer you being absent for a while and content to be back than restless all the while, Jack. You understand?' Katherine said. 'In my heart I never thought we'd keep you from the Hyddenworld for ever, so a visit once in a while seems like a good idea.'

Those last days and hours they were a family, close and warm. It was a happy time, a time to cherish, but at last he had to leave, which he did with the rising sun.

'Got to go,' said Jack finally to Judith, kneeling down to give her a hug. She was too big to pick up easily any more. 'Excited about your holiday?'

She nodded and hugged him, her hands tight on the rough scars on his neck.

'Look after each other,' he said. 'Judith, keep an eye on your Mum. Katherine, watch out for Margaret. Arthur, don't take any nonsense from them . . .'

He walked down to the entrance to the henge, telling them to wave from the house. Some hope. Judith ran down to say her own final goodbye by the henge.

The chimes said their own farewell, and in the shimmer and shift of their sound it seemed to his family, watching him leave, that the great tall conifers bowed and bent away into the distance towards White Horse Hill and formed the green road down which he journeyed away until they could see him no more.

'Will Dad come back?' asked Judith.

'Soon,' whispered Katherine. 'Soon.'

31
GOOD FUNERAL

The funeral of Master Brief took place a week after his tragic death.

It had been his wish that he be conveyed by boat to the place of burning. Because of the enormous love felt for him, and the anger and grief at the nature of his passing, everyone wanted to see his coffin pass by.

Lord Festoon decided that his cortege should be taken westward by canal and road, before being laid upon a craft moored on the River Rea in Northfield where Brief was born, for its final journey through the city. The route was packed with mourners who threw lilies on his passing coffin, which brightened the sad scene and cloudy day.

Bedwyn Stort and his party had arrived back from Woolstone only two days before. Stort's shock was deep and his dreadful guilt very real, for he felt sure that Brief would still be alive if he had not hidden the gem where he had. His friends tried to reassure him that it was not his fault, but Stort was not consoled.

He journeyed wanly by the coffin all the way to its embarkation point and then sat sadly beside it, ignoring everyone and everything. Barklice and Pike sat nearby too, silent and grim.

Brunte, who had himself only recently returned to Brum, sat with Feld and Backhaus and some Councillors in a second craft behind the first.

A great pyre of faggots had been raised on the wide, open marshy ground at the confluence of the Rea and the River Trent, Brum's traditional place of farewell to its great ones.

It was mid-afternoon, the day was still murky and the short way from boat to pyre marked by flares, whose flames leapt upwards, sending down sparks like fiery tears.

In all the sadness and commotion surrounding the appalling event, only Librarian Thwart had thought to bring Brief's carved stave to the funeral, but he held it uneasily, no one else willing to. It was associated with Brief alone and its deep, strange carvings, so powerful and potent when he'd carried the stave, glowing angrily, their depths all reds and blacks, made the stave look far too big and impressive for one such as Thwart.

But there it was, and what else he was meant to do with it he did not know. Yet by virtue of the fact he held it he found himself thrust next to the coffin as it was carried to the pyre, and then to one side once it had been placed in position, as if he was a solitary and reluctant guard of honour.

'Mister Pike,' said Thwart, 'I really don't think it should be me . . .'

Pike shook his head.

'Mister Stort, you were so close to Master Brief, surely you—'

'I could not and I cannot hold his stave, Thwart, I am not worthy for that, and anyway I do not think it in the wyrd of things that I do!'

'Well,' whispered poor Thwart, this not being a conversation fitted for public consumption, 'it's certainly not in *my* wyrd but . . . ah, Lord Festoon . . . perhaps you would . . . ?'

Festoon gazed down at the hapless librarian.

'You're doing a fine job, my dear fellow, a fine job!'

So there Thwart stood, very unhappily, holding the great stave and waiting for the ritual, a long one, to get under way.

To heighten the sadness and the grief of the occasion there was dismay as well, and not a little concern, its undercurrents spreading in whispers, as the day wore on.

At the heart of this was a very real sense that no one, from Lord Festoon down, knew what was going to happen when the funeral was over. In short, what to do about recovering the stolen gem.

The true identity of Slew, as Master of Shadows, was by then well known, though what the true meaning of that title meant, and the likely near-invincibility of he who held it, was known only to a few.

To wrest the gem back from him, which meant taking it from the protection of the Emperor himself, was an attractive dream but a dangerous cause. One, Brunte and Festoon understood very well, that would inevitably bring forward the Empire's attack on their city.

The truth was too that possession of the gem would have been a bargaining chip in any coming negotiations between the city and Bochum. Now that advantage was gone and they lay open to Imperial might.

These were thorny problems that needed clear thinking and leadership, both of which now seemed to be lacking between Brunte and Festoon, for neither knew quite what to do next. They could not very well attack Bochum. Nor did they want to just sit and wait to be destroyed.

'When the funeral's over we'll work something out,' Festoon had said to those close to him, like Pike.

'Until I've had time to think about it properly I cannot see a clear way forward,' Brunte declared to Feld and the others.

All that the citizens of Brum wanted was their gem back, and Brief's death avenged.

It was no surprise therefore that there was unease and unrest at the funeral, even as the rituals began.

The pyre funeral rituals of Brum were simple ones. They began with an invocation to the Mirror-of-All to accept the deceased back into her eternal, reflective depths.

This was spoken by Festoon.

There were silence and prayers, some mournful tunes and a valedictory address from Brunte on one hand and Mister Pike on the other, both commendable but neither catching quite the mood or the deep communal need of the occasion.

Sometimes fine words are not enough. This was an occasion when only an open expression of real feeling could make something of the moment that was memorable and true.

So it was that when the call went out to begin the burning the crowd muttered that they would like first to hear a few words from Mister Stort, for he had been Brief's greatest pupil, and all there knew that the Master Scrivener had regarded him as the nearest thing he'd ever had to a son.

Of course Festoon and Pike had already asked Stort to speak, but he had refused. He was never one for public speaking anyway, but how could he, who had as good as caused Brief's death himself, possibly add anything of value or importance?

'I cannot, I just cannot,' he had said.

But now the pyre waited, and the hands of those who would light it had been stayed, and, whatever Stort might feel, all eyes were upon him and expectant.

It so happened that at this very moment, unseen by the crowd, for it was lost behind them a little way up the river, a bilgesnipe craft approached.

At the helm, looking utterly exhausted and yet very pleased with himself, was Old Mallarkhi.

'I be damned if they war goin' stop me a-being witness to the Master's funereal! And if you'll only . . . oops, I nearly went scatterways into the water.'

The strong arms of his passenger kept him upright and lifted him onto firm ground.

He was, it must be said, a little worse for wear in the alcoholic sense. Not much, but enough. The sight of the cortege passing by earlier had started it, and his desire to drown his very real sorrows when it disappeared from sight continued it. But what had provoked it still more, and made him prop a bottle of Muggy Mead in the bilges lest he need it en route, was a request from a late mourner to be conveyed to the funeral.

'Can't do it,' he had said. 'I'm at death's door.'

'You've been at death's door for years and you can do it.'

'Can I?'

'It's the least Brief would have expected.'

'You sure?'

'I'm sure. And how else am I to get there myself?'

'I mustn't; Ma'Shuqa forbade it.'

'Are you your daughter's father or her scullywench?'

'Dang me,' said Old Mallarkhi, 'I'll do it for 'ee and for me both!'

And he had.

Now he had arrived at the rear of the crowd with his passenger just at the moment when Stort found himself being thrust to his feet before a crowd that needed desperately to hear words that expressed

their loss and their fears at Brief's unhappy passing and their forlorn
hopes that out of it some good might yet be found.

'Well, one and all—' began Stort.

'Can't hear you! Speak up, Mister Stort!'

'Oh . . . well . . . I was . . .'

'Still can't!'

'I was going to say, I want to say that . . . well, Master Brief, he . . .
was . . . I mean, without him . . . without . . .'

There is no shame in tears, especially heartfelt ones, and there was
not one person in the crowd who did not sympathize with Stort or
was not glad that he shed them.

'He was the hydden who gave me most in all the world,' he said
when he had recovered a little, 'the hydden who stood for what was
right and what was wrong even if, sometimes . . . well, often . . . he
could be and in fact was . . .'

He wept again.

'Say it lad when you're ready, don't give up!'

'He was, I would say, grumpy. Sort of. And when I was young and
he thought I wasn't working as I should he . . . I didn't mind this,
really I didn't . . . but he was inclined to . . . it didn't hurt exactly . . .
but . . .'

More tears.

More patience from his audience.

There was a growing sense among them that having started poorly
Brief's funeral was turning into something that might be memorable.

'If I fell asleep at my books, he was inclined to rap my knuckles
with his stave, that one just there in fact, and say, "Bedwyn, are you
paying proper attention?"'

'And there was something else . . .'

In this faltering way Stort managed to say enough to begin to bring
alive again the hydden now gone from Brum for good.

Then suddenly, when he faltered once too often and seemed at last
to be heading down a cul de sac, there was a cry from the back of the
crowd and to everyone's horror someone shouted, 'Master Brief 'ad a
guilty secret and it be time it were out!'

The crowd parted and Old Mallarkhi advanced upon Stort, carrying
his half-consumed bottle of Muggy Mead.

'Master Stort 'ere won't mind I daresay if Brief's old friend and drinking partner says a word or two . . .'

'Pa, you should be home abed not tottering about the countryside!' cried Ma'Shuqa, appalled to see her father bringing shame upon the family.

'A pox on that, daughter!' he retorted. 'Brief would have done the same fer me!'

This brought a cheer, and Stort, glad of diversion and support, actually clapped, which others did as well.

'All Old Mallarkhi was agoin' to reveal, and it ain't been told afore, is this.'

He stopped and swigged at his bottle of mead and took his time doing so.

The crowd waited until he was ready.

When he had finished he held the bottle up and pointed at it.

'This 'ere brew was never to my recipe, no it never war. It war Master Brief who come up and out with it, from a ancient tome on the subject of toping the yeast and the hop, "it" being a receipt, as he said they said in them gone days, for a mead offering a quick way to salvation invented by the knavish monks of Lichfield, where once there be'd a monasterium as bookish folks say it. So here, now and ever more this mead wot you all know of and some of you drink is being renamed The Master's Mead, or Masters for short. In his memory. And that's allus Old Mallarkhi's got to say on that subject! Now you can carry on, Master Stort!'

With that Old Mallarkhi collapsed sideways into his daughter's arms, who revived him with a daughterly embrace and the words, 'Pa, you are a one, you are!'

Somehow the mood changed.

It was suddenly more serious and the undercurrent of concern for the future that ran among the fold there was still not expressed, nor tamed nor harnessed.

Stort sensed it.

'I wanted to say another thing,' he said, beginning again, 'but I'm not the one to know how such things *are* said, and I don't think that any of us who loved Master Brief can say what he would have said so well. For the gem has been stolen, and with it something of Brum's great heart, and we want it back . . . we want it back. But I don't know what words he would have used to lead us forward, or how he would have spoken them, because you see . . . you should know, that he thought this moment would come one day when we'd have to stand up for what's right in the Hyddenworld and oppose what's wrong. But it wasn't me he wanted to say this because he knew I wouldn't get it right. Anyway . . . anyway . . . it's my fault that . . . I mean if I hadn't done what I did he wouldn't have died and we would, I mean I wouldn't be here now and be feeling, well . . . so . . . I'm sorry . . . so *ashamed*.'

Poor Stort, how he began to weep before them all, the funeral pyre behind him, Brief's body laid out upon it, and no one knowing what to say next or what to do.

Or nearly no one.

Because Old Mallarkhi's passenger, taller than most of them, stronger-looking too, finally showed himself.

He came calmly, gravely, and only slowly did folk see him, and those few that knew him by sight whispered his name to others there, so that by the time he came to the front all knew who he was.

He reached a hand to the forlorn Thwart, bowed down by grief like Stort, and by that burden no one else would carry.

'Give me the Master's stave,' he said.

Did Stort hear that familiar voice? Did he think he dreamt it?

Certainly, his head still bowed, he murmured, sniffing at his tears, 'The thing is, you see, Brief read the future better than anyone and he knew it wasn't me who would . . . would . . . lead you . . . no, not me . . .'

A strong hand touched his shoulder and Stort dared finally to look up and see who he had hoped he would see back in the Hyddenworld and Brum.

'. . . but Jack!'

There was a cheer for both of them as Jack gave him a hug and Stort wiped his tears.

They turned to the silent crowd, who stood awed and wondering at Jack's resurrection among them, Brief's stave in his hand.

'There is nothing that Mister Bedwyn Stort has, or ever had, or ever will have to be ashamed of,' said Jack. 'Nothing! And if there's a hydden here who says there is let them say so now to me!'

No one spoke and certainly no one came forward.

'It was the greatest wish of Master Brief's great life that the gem of Spring should be found and that he should see it before he died. Well, it was found and I'm told he did see it.

'No one would have been prouder and yet less surprised than he that it was his greatest pupil Stort who did the finding!

'That Brief died trying to protect the gem, and also the life of Librarian Thwart here, as I was told only a short while ago, was typical of a hydden who battled all his life for the cause of truth and what he once described to me as the right way.

'Not a bad legacy! Not a bad end to a great life! And yet he was modest, and if he was only remembered as the librarian who rediscovered a recipe for the wickedest mead in the Hyddenworld then that would have been enough for him.

'But Stort's right, as he so often is. Master Brief would not stand idle in this hour of Brum's loss and danger.

'I believe he would have held up his great stave, as I do now, and he would have said, "Citizens of Brum, we must and shall get that gem back!" '

The mourners began cheering.

Jack raised his voice, the stave now almost alive in his hand, as if Brief himself was back among them. 'And then he would have said, "If no one else is going to do it I'll have to do it myself!" '

The cheering grew louder still.

'But he is not here to say that, *we* are. Most of all Bedwyn Stort is! He found the gem and he will find it again and bring it back to Brum!'

Stort looked startled at this prospect but managed a smile of sorts, helped by Thwart, who patted him vigorously on the back as if to say that the gem was already as good as delivered back home.

'Light the flames on Master Brief's pyre,' cried out Jack, 'and let them leap up into the sky as does the spirit of this great city! Let them be a warning to the Empire that when our preparations are made we shall journey to its very heart in Bochum and demand that which has been taken shall be returned to us!'

The flames did not light easily. Perhaps the wood was damp. Perhaps reluctant to burn so great a hydden.

However that might be, it was Old Mallarkhi who once again saved the moment and the day.

'Daughter, heave me upright. Thwart, give me the Master's Mead, and you bright and bonny hydden making a hash of lighting a fire, 'ow do you suppose we at the Duck do it day by day? With this, that's how!'

Once more he held up the bottle and then, tottering by himself to where they wanted to start the flames, he poured the remaining contents of the bottle on the wood.

'There, me hearties, she be set and ready and Master Brief can go back to the Mirror with the help of his own fiery mead!'

A lucifer was lit, and when it was applied the flames went up with a whoosh! and the pyre roared to life and the body of Master Brief was consumed in its fire.

As night fell and the fire died the crowd began to disperse. Jack was able to give way to the fatigue of his hurried journey from Brum and confess to his reluctance to have left Katherine and their daughter behind and the sadness he felt now he had.

'I would not have come but that she understood why I must and even encouraged it,' he said. 'But this is my adoptive city and if the call comes to any citizen they must answer it! As for a mission to Bochum, it'll need thought and planning and we should not raise hopes of undertaking it for a long time yet.'

Which Stort thought was an odd thing to say, especially as it was accompanied by a wink.

As the last embers of the pyre smouldered, Jack, Festoon and the others gathered together.

'That was well said, Jack,' said Pike, shaking his hand.

'It was,' agreed Brunte.

'It certainly did seem to strike a chord with many,' observed Barklice, his son wide-eyed and tired at his side, astonished at the amazing and exciting things that seemed to happen wherever his father went.

'Certainly,' said Stort, 'when the dust has settled on this horrible affair and some weeks have gone by, we must discuss the possibility that in time to come, a month or two or twelve, we shall find a way to recover the gem that my foolishness has . . .'

Jack shook his head.

'I have no intention of waiting twelve months,' he said, 'nor even two. But I hope I implied that we were in no hurry . . . Do you think a great crowd like that would not have among it spies for the Empire? Eh? Marshal Brunte?'

He nodded gravely.

'There were spies here, that's certain.'

'And what message will they pass to the Empire?'

'That in a few weeks we'll send a deputation of worthy citizens to Bochum, led by Stort, which will politely ask for the gem back, assuming they have it.'

'Exactly what I hoped you'd say. I wanted to lull them into a false sense of security.'

'You mean we might go a little sooner?' said Stort.

'I mean, Stort, that you and I, and one or two others we shall decide about here and now, will go at once.'

Stort looked unhappy.

'You mean, I take it, in a week or two.'

'I mean tonight,' said Jack. 'General Brunte, have you someone who can make the arrangements fast?'

'Backhaus.'

'Lord Festoon, can you make available the supplies and equipment we'll need?'

'Of course.'

'But Jack . . .' spluttered Stort.

'Let's get on with it,' said Jack, 'we've lost enough time as it is. And anyway I need to get back; I have a daughter to think about and . . . nearly . . . a wife! Katherine would not want me back until the gem is in Brum's safe-keeping once more.'

'You think this will take so little time?'

'I think that the longer we take doing it the harder it will become.'

32

ENSHADOWED

Slew's escape from Brum back to the coast and his rendezvous with Borkum Riff did not go as fast, or as smoothly, as Jack and the others assumed.

Pike had taken swift action to send out alerts along the routes Slew was likely to take, and this slowed down his escape from Englalond by many days.

Even his departure from Brum was not made without difficulty, and had he reached the East Gate only an hour or two later he might easily have been apprehended before he left the city boundary.

Things would have been easier had it been possible for him to maintain the shadow power that he had exercised in the Library against Brief, but even the Master of Shadows may be subject to a loss of the special energy and strength of will needed for that kind of combat.

But the gem's sudden light, a salvation for Thwart, was debilitating to Slew. Then there was the effect that Brief had on him, or rather Brief and his stave. It surprised him that an elderly hydden should summon such power that it took all Slew's skill and strength to control and quell it.

But so it had been, and he had shadow strength enough only to escape the Library and cross the main square into the alleys beyond before he was forced to pause in a doorway, catch his breath and recover a little.

Even so, when he heard the sound of pursuit he was not overly concerned. Slew was a hydden who liked to cover all eventualities.

He had foreseen that difficulties of some kind might arise during his escape, though a loss of shadow power was never one he thought of. But he had already decided that back-up of some kind might be needed and he had arranged it.

Harald and Bjarne, two of the Norseners he had fought at the Muggy Duck, had been impressed by his superior fighting skills. They were brothers and their original journey to Brum had been less in the cause of pilgrimage than from the desire to find a new direction.

Slew decided they would make valuable travelling companions. His talk of opportunities in Bochum, his natural charisma, and his declared intention to leave Brum soon – he did not say why, or how soon – persuaded them to offer their services.

They arranged to meet in a low tavern in Digbeth that same morning, the Norseners having Slew's portersac with them, lest it arouse suspicions of his imminent departure at the Library. The moment he arrived, no questions were asked as to what he had been doing, and they left.

When they reached the East Gate its keeper, the fearsome bilge-snipe Tirrikh, did ask questions. It was his job to do so.

Why were the two leaving without the friends they had arrived with? And why were they now travelling with so unlikely a companion as a hydden of the cloth?

He was unimpressed by their explanations, but three against one is no good basis on which to hold such tough-looking hydden against their will, and he let them go. Immediately they were out of sight, however, he sent a description to Pike, as he normally did in such circumstances.

Too late. By the time Pike got back to him two hours later with news of the theft of the gem the three were long gone and the chance to stop them missed.

Slew had guessed what Tirrikh's questions might lead to, and rightly fearing that pursuit would continue he discarded his monk's habit and took a longer and less obvious route to Maldon, where Borkum Riff had promised to give him passage back across the North Sea.

Harald and Bjarne were odd twins. The first was tall, broad and fair-haired; the other short, stocky and dark. But they were devoted to each other.

'We were cast adrift by the murder and mayhem inflicted on our home port by the ill-starred folk of Bergen and have been looking after each other ever since,' explained Bjarne, the more talkative of the two.

'And wondering what to do next,' added Harald.

'You've been wondering all these years?' asked Slew. 'You've never found a cause or person to follow?'

'Never found someone could beat us in combat like you did, Brother.'

Slew liked the title Brother. There was comfort in it, and community, and that was something he had felt in need of from the moment he stole the gem.

It sat heavily in its pouch in his inside pocket, but Slew didn't say so. It disturbed his mind and baffled clear thinking. It washed emotions through him he didn't like. It put doubts in his head.

So Harald and Bjarne were rather more welcome as companions than he could have expected.

'The plural of Brother is Brethren,' he said. 'Let us see where this first venture of ours together may take us, and if the title Brethren might in time offer an advantage to us all.'

They reached Maldon in those same night hours that saw the conclusion of Brief's funeral. The tide was coming in fast and the only way of crossing from the mainland was on a causeway already covered by the sea and swept by its strong current.

This was meat and drink to the Norseners, who crossed without complaint, each strong enough to hold his heavy portersac over his head all the way.

To Slew as well such difficulties seemed trivial.

When they reached the far side a brisk, cool wind whipped across the dunes and marram grass, though it was Summer.

'A hot brew would do us good,' said Slew, 'but I want to cross the island and be ready at the quay for the high tide. The moon's already on the wane and I doubt that our craft will wait beyond tonight.'

When they reached the quay where Slew had first arrived there was no sign of a boat at all. Nor any light, or sign of one.

'Listen!' said Bjarne.

It was the clink clink clink of a hawser on a mast somewhere out on the dark waters.

They made a small fire, shielded it such that its flames would only be visible from the sea, a sign that they were there.

'There's a swell, a current and a veering wind,' said Harald. 'Not easy conditions. Are you sure you'll be picked up?'

'My captain's not the kind to let folk down.'

'His name?'

Thus far Slew had given nothing away about the boat or its skipper.

'Would a name mean anything to you?'

'Some would, yes,' said Harald. 'We know the captains for the ports to the north which serve our own, but thisaway there's only three names worth mentioning.'

Slew waited.

'Sneek Larsson, Beda Hoorne and . . . well . . . you know the other I daresay?'

'I daresay I do,' said Slew.

'Well, provided it isn't him we'll be all right, Harald,' growled Bjarne.

'"Him" being?'

'That bastard Borkum Riff.'

'What have you against him? He's the best North Sea sailor alive.'

'Humph!' said Bjarne. 'That's what folks say, but in a storm and provided she's had a jar or two I'd put my money on Beda Hoorne. As for Riff . . .'

Bjarne spat his opinion at their feet.

'He left us stranded once on the forsaken shore of Ferkingstad. We only asked for a bit of tribute for him making passage that way. Said we were no better than pirates and if we had a wyrd at all it would protect us. Freezing it was. We swore . . . what did we swear, Harald?'

'To gut and skin the bugger like a codfish and leave him hanging out to dry in the Winter winds.'

The two laughed. Slew, however, did not. He had seen the shadow of a cloaked hydden looming out of the darkness behind them, storm lantern in hand.

'And that's still your intention is it,' a gruff voice asked, 'to gut and skin me?'

'By the Mirror, it's Riff himself,' cried Harald, grabbing his stave.

Indeed it was, dressed dark and heavy against the night wind and opening his lantern's shutter to show his face. It was impossible to say if he was half smiling or simply screwing his eyes up against the wind. His beard was as black as night.

Slew stayed Harald's hand and Bjarne's too.

'These are friends of mine,' he said, 'so I suggest we shake hands before we leave. Let whatever happened pass. We've better things to do now than have an argument before we've even set sail.'

'I never thought these two would fetch up on this shore,' said Riff, 'but provided they don't ask for tribute here as well I'm content to let bygones be bygones and offer you a fish stew that'll clear us all of lingering ill-feeling and warm your innards true.'

'Offer accepted!' said Harald, and there in the dark they shook a good hand.

'What are you doing onshore?' asked Slew. 'We thought we heard your craft lying to out on the water.'

Riff smiled.

'I thought you might return in company. I like to take a good look at passengers that want my skills afore they embark.'

He sent out a piping call like an oyster catcher roosting on the shore and got an answering one back. Soon after the craft appeared, hove to temporarily by the quay and was off almost before the last of them had boarded.

'Get her homeward bound, lads, homeward bound!'

The crew sang in low voices as they went round on the wind and rough hands passed up bowls of stew for them all from the galley below.

'You know the rules on this cutter, boys,' said Riff as the boat began to take the swell up and down, up and down. 'Spew it up and you clean it up!'

'We know,' said the Norseners in unison.

Slew said nothing.

The food was good, he had never been sick on or off a craft in all his life, but the gem sat heavy with him and darkened his mood, enshadowed his mind, filled him with doubt.

The craft sped on; he stayed outside with the sea wind and spray hard in his face.

'Witold Slew, what ails you?' asked Borkum Riff.

'The days and weeks ahead of this strange Summer,' muttered Slew, 'and the seasons after that.'

'Rough times,' said Riff. 'Out here we see the waves large and small, and the driving weather like that ahead of us which you can't see but which I can hear and feel to my craft's core. There's been tremors and quakes across the land and underneath the sea, and one of these days they'll have a go at me as well, and you.'

Slew felt sick.

He hunched against the wind. Three things he knew.

That the gem had not been his to take.

That Master Brief had seen through him like sunlight through glass.

That Thwart had courage and did not deserve to die, so the gem had favoured him.

Slew hunched into his unaccustomed doubts, wanting to cast off his garb and the gem and everything, as if to be clean again, his head filled with sick pain, his eyes throbbing, his dark stave just a piece of stick, his life a straw on wind.

'Go below,' commanded Riff. 'We're about to hit troubled waters.'

Slew gripped the gunnels and spewed over the side.

A member of the crew laughed, the others began to sing their strength and skill into the weather.

Someone else rasped in a low voice to another, 'Skipper says he's our future? Maybe, but he vomits just the same as everyone else!'

'Come below,' said Riff softly, 'and try to sleep. Things will look different back on the home shore.'

33
TITLES AND PLANS

J ack's return to Brum, and his speech at Brief's funeral, changed everything.

The city, which had lain so long under the threat of Fyrd retaliation, and been demoralized by earthquakes, was filled with new hope and purpose and the belief that it could withstand the Fyrd and even recover the gem.

In Festoon and Brunte they had civic and military leaders they could trust and who, having settled their differences, seemed able to work in harmony.

In the loss of the gem of Spring and their determination to get it back, they had a righteous cause against their sworn enemy.

In Jack and Bedwyn Stort they had a new generation they could get behind. The first spoke for every Brummie's fighting spirit; the second personified their characteristic individuality, love of freedom and occasional absurdity. For these things Stort was loved just as Brief had been.

Jack's impulsive suggestion that they leave at once for Bochum to win back the gem was tempered straight away by the sage counsels of Festoon and Brunte. But only slightly.

After an impromptu war council beside the embers of Brief's funeral pyre, which continued to the dawn, Jack finally agreed to defer their departure until the following evening. This was to give time for the equipment for the mission to be assembled, along with certain intelligence regarding Bochum, its tunnels and its inhabitants.

'When you get there you're going to need all the help you can get,' said Brunte. 'Only three of us, myself, Feld and Backhaus, know the hydden city of Bochum. I must stay here and Backhaus too. Feld has agreed to go with you.'

Jack eyed him, surprised.

'You are willing to accept the command of someone untrained, younger and less experienced?'

'I am.'

'You do it willingly? I'd rather have no one than someone reluctant.'

'I do,' said Feld.

What Jack could not see were the changes wrought in him over the past year and the recent weeks following the Shield Maiden's birth. He looked older and wiser.

Nor was it obvious to him, as it was to the others including Stort, what had happened when he had taken up Brief's great stave. Perhaps it was the flickering embers of the pyre, or the deep reflections of ancient wisdom that came from the carvings on the stave, but his face assumed an authority beyond his years and seeming experience.

'I accept your authority,' said Feld, 'but . . . as a soldier it would be easier for me if you had a title rather than a personal name. Forgive me, but I am made that way.'

Jack grinned.

'A title? Like a rank?'

Brunte said, 'A good point, I think,' and glanced at Pike. 'Mister Pike, yours is a civilian office though it involves military matters. The same goes for Jack. Any suggestions as to an appropriate title?'

Pike rubbed his stubbled chin and nodded slowly.

'Master Brief was not just a scrivener and a librarian. It is not generally known that though he had a stave of office, the "office" or position it referred to was not that of Master Scrivener, but something else. But . . . well . . .'

'Speak plainly, Pike,' said Lord Festoon.

'The office it refers to is one that I only ever saw Brief exercise twice in his life. Both times, as it happens, Jack was there and so were you, General Feld.

'The first was in the henge at Woolstone. The second in the Chamber of Seasons. On both occasions Jack ended up wielding Brief's great stave.'

'You did so too effectively for my taste!' murmured Feld ruefully.

'Exactly,' said Pike. 'Now, this is not something I should be doing, but rather Brief himself. In his absence I'll do my best. If you'll permit me, gentlemen, we can confer this office on Jack right now, but there is a certain ritual involving all of us . . . Stand up, Jack. Take up Brief's stave.'

He did so and at once looked all the more fearsome for holding it straight and true in his right hand.

'Each one of us should attempt to strike Jack a blow with his own stave.'

'But I haven't got mine,' said Stort, 'and anyway I can't and won't.'

'Stort,' said Pike sternly, 'I ask you just this once to keep nice and quiet. Words do not need saying. The Captain can begin. Lord Festoon, you should be the last. A single blow at Jack. I ask you to give it your best!'

One by one they tried, the strongest blows coming from Feld, a seasoned fighter, and Pike himself.

Jack wielded Brief's stave as to the manner born and parried both with ease.

Brunte stood up and said, 'I use knives not staves. Are you sure?'

'I am sure,' said Pike.

Brunte carried two stabbing weapons in his belt, a dirk and a stiletto. He seemed to understand that the point of the ritual was not to pretend but to attack Jack for real. He did so suddenly and brutally, but Jack simply dealt double swingeing blows to his hands and wrists and the weapons spun away, reflecting fire in the dark.

Next it was Stort's turn. Pike gave him his stave.

He stood staring at Jack but not moving.

'Can't do it,' he said finally. 'He's my friend.'

Jack laughed and stood easy.

'Try!'

'Won't,' said Stort.

'Well then,' said Pike gently, 'better not try.'

He took the stave back and Stort sat down gratefully.

'Lord Festoon?'

Festoon stood up, taller and broader than any of them. 'I haven't struck a blow of any kind for many years,' he said, 'but if I must I will. Give me your stave, General Feld.'

He took it, made a brave attempt at taking up a bold stance, and said, 'Well, Jack, I'm ready.'

Jack laughed and immediately laid down Brief's stave at Festoon's feet and knelt down himself.

'I'm not striking a single blow against the High Ealdor of Brum,' he said, 'even if it costs me this mysterious title. If it was just Lord Festoon it would be my pleasure, but his office is sacrosanct and I owe it my fealty.'

Pike smiled with relief for Jack had said and done the right thing.

'There,' he said, 'it's done, though a bit rough and ready. Stay where you are, Jack, for the title now needs to be conferred on you.'

He whispered in Festoon's ear.

'Well, well, well,' said the High Ealdor, 'I learn something new in this position every day. I often wondered about that title, which I believe goes back to medieval times, does it not, Mister Pike?'

'I believe that Beornamund himself was the first to hold it,' said Pike. 'We have seen the three qualities Jack needs in his new role. First authority, which his skill against Marshal Brunte, General Feld and myself demonstrated. Second to be loved, which our friend Stort showed in his unwillingness to fight his friend. Finally obedience to his Lord, which he has shown to the High Ealdor. He has passed the tests.'

Silence fell and the embers at their feet shone for a moment with new light.

Festoon bent down, picked up Brief's stave, and tapped Jack lightly on each shoulder twice.

'Here and now, in the presence of witnesses before whom you have shown the three qualities you need for this great and ancient office of our city, which is held on behalf of all hydden in our great land, you shall assume the title of Stavemeister of Brum and of Englalond. Rise, Stavemeister, and do your duties true, and the grace and plenty of the Mirror be with you!'

Jack received back what was now his own stave of office, and from his stance and gaze they could see at once that it was a title well conferred.

'Gentlemen,' said Festoon quietly, 'there is another matter that needs attention, and I can think of no better moment than here and now. Librarian Thwart. I believe . . . ah – there you are . . . hiding in the shadows!'

'Well, I wasn't sure if I should stay or leave but—'

'Staying was the best option, trust me,' said Festoon. 'Now, I will not beat about the bush, for time presses. We have lost in Brief a very great Master Scrivener, and I think, Thwart, you would agree that there are very few hydden in Brum, or without it in libraries in Englalond or on the Continent, capable of filling his shoes?'

'That is true, Lord Festoon, so very true. But if it is my advice you seek . . . ?'

'It is,' said Festoon.

'There is no one in Brum or Englalond who could disagree with me when I say that it must surely be upon Mister Stort here that Brief's title is conferred.'

'Me?' said Stort. 'I couldn't possibly . . . and anyway I'm always travelling about the place. No, I am not suitable.'

Festoon held up his hand.

'In this, Stort, I will not be gainsaid!'

'Gainsaid! An excellent usage. You mean you will not be opposed,' said Stort, 'objected to, argued with, that kind of thing in this matter?'

'Exactly. Nor will I agree with Librarian Thwart's estimate of your character and qualifications, which I regard as too generous by far and, in fact, mistaken. You play a subtle game, Thwart!'

Thwart looked dumbfounded. If ever there was a hydden less capable of a subtle game it was he.

Festoon laughed. 'Gentlemen, I doubt that a truer, more straightforward and honest scholar could be found in Englalond than Librarian Thwart, and I therefore here and now let it be known that your High Ealdor confers the title of Master Scrivener of Brum, and Master Librarian, upon Ephraim Thwart.'

'Me!?' he said faintly. 'Follow in Brief's shoes?'

'You,' said Festoon, 'as of now.'

'Excellent choice,' said Stort with relief. 'Capital! He has my vote!'

'This is not a voting matter, fortunately,' said Festoon. 'The post is in my gift and I've now given it.'

'Well—' began Thwart.

'Well done!' growled Brunte. 'As for subtlety, you'll soon learn, trust me!'

'Ah!' murmured Thwart, which might have meant anything.

These things achieved, dawn now showing and the detailed planning of their mission put in the experienced hands of Feld and Backhaus, it remained only for Marshal Brunte to outline the general approach.

'The objective is to get back the gem of Spring, simple as that. The team, as I now understand it, will consist of Stort, Barklice and Feld, led by the new Stavemeister, Jack.'

Bratfire, who had been asleep and forgotten about, woke up.

'What about me?' he said ruefully.

'You stay behind in Brum and make yourself useful,' said Barklice, who was finding it easier than he had expected to adopt a father's role.

'Good, that's agreed,' said Brunte, 'four in all. I need hardly say that secrecy is paramount and speed of the very essence. I want you back here within ten days or else the moment will be lost. Eh, Festoon?'

'Quite so,' said the High Ealdor. 'Ten days to recover the city's pride and ready ourselves for war! They won't know what hit them. Meanwhile, Stavemeister, be content that the more detailed elements of your mission are in capable and experienced hands and go and sleep.'

Jack did not move.

'There is one matter that remains uncertain. My daughter Judith.'

'The Shield Maiden?' said Brunte. It was a question, a doubt.

'I think you may take it that that is exactly what she is,' said Jack. He told them about her abnormal growth and behaviour and her affinity with the chimes.

'We've heard something of this from Messrs Stort and Barklice,' said Brunte. 'Will she be safe in Woolstone?'

Jack shook his head.

'I asked – well, I ordered really – Katherine to take her north to Northumberland. The Foales have a cottage there, and if I remember my hydden geography that area is beyond easy hydden reach.'

'It is, but it's under the control of the Reivers, who though hydden are not what you'd call hyddenish,' said Feld. 'They ride dogs, they take no prisoners, they hold the locals to ransom . . . But humans will be untouched and there's no reason why your friends or the Shield Maiden should ever be disturbed by them.'

'Mister Stort, you look unhappy,' said Festoon.

'I am. I should never have let the gem fall into the Empire's hands. Judith – the Shield Maiden – will have need of it someday, but I confess, in the brief and happy days when I saw her at Woolstone, gems were the last thing on her mind.'

Jack laughed.

'You're right, but she'll be Shield Maiden one day. She's already got a toughness and spirit about her like no one I've ever known.'

'She will,' said Stort quietly, 'but an immortal is mortal too, that's what people don't understand . . .'

Jack said, 'Agreed. Is it possible to send some stavermen up there to watch over her? Is the place accessible?'

Brunte shook his head.

'Not easily. Northumberland lies beyond the Wall of Emperor Hadrian which, though a human artefact, marks the northern limit of our boundary and jurisdiction. I suppose . . .'

'Leave it with us, Jack,' said Pike. 'There may be ways and means to keep an eye on her.'

Jack nodded.

'Stort, Barklice, General Feld . . .' he said, taking up his stave of office, 'we need rest, food and sleep before we leave.'

34

QUEEN OF THE REIVERS

The Foales' cottage was in the tiny hamlet of Byrness in Redesdale, Northumberland. It is one of those wild, bleak dales that lie in the border country of Englalond and Scotland. The property had come to Arthur through the Scottish branch of his family, who had used it once in a while, for this and that, but finally left it in a state of neglect.

Rough-stoned, grey-slated, mean-windowed and with a peat fire that guttered and smoked if the wind blew, which it did incessantly, it lay deep in the narrow valley of the River Rede. Forestry Commission plantings, dark, unyielding and unnatural, hemmed the village in to north and south. Eastward and downslope the trees came to the roadside and gave any traveller the feeling that if they dallied too long they'd not get out again.

Westward, upslope, the dark, malign waters of the Catcleugh Reservoir reflected the black, dank trees and a white-grey sky. The dam that held the water presented a massive and unwelcoming wall to those trying to escape that way.

'Now I remember why none of the family wanted it,' said Arthur, the first evening he got there with Katherine and Judith, 'and why I never much liked coming here. It does not lift the spirits.'

'Children like it, and their dogs,' said Judith unexpectedly. 'You can see their footprints in the mud outside.'

She loved it from the first moment they got there. Her speech had come on apace, her physical development too. Her fatigue had left

her and the growing pains, though she felt them all the time, were
more under control.

Come the first morning she was up and out into the dark woods
before anyone could stop her.

'Judith, you've come here to be safe, not . . .' Katherine called after
her, but already she was gone.

Katherine smiled and relaxed. The reason she had decided with
Jack to bring her here was to give her space. In the early days of her
strange life it had been about physical growth. Now it was a mental
growth, probably a spiritual one, and Katherine, with the Foales'
support, believed that in that respect she could give Judith the help
she needed in a way the more impulsive and, yes, less spiritual Jack
could not do.

The 'help' consisted of simply letting her be, that she might
understand things which Katherine's life had taught her: that there is
a difference between the learning found in solitude and the withering
suffered in loneliness.

Growth was painful whatever form it took. It had been for Katherine, and still was; it most certainly would be for the Shield Maiden.
All Katherine needed to do was simply be there.

Byrness had nothing to it. Folk kept to themselves, and when
they met each other there were no welcomes given, no questions
asked.

'I'm glad we brought books,' said Margaret, 'because otherwise I'd
die of boredom and despair within a month. But I suppose Jack was
right . . . it's not exactly hydden country is it?'

'No,' said Arthur, 'it's not. It's Reiver country and that's a very
different thing. It's as well we're humans and there's nowhere hereabout in the way of henges and circles, not that I've heard of. So
there'll be no crossing over even if we wanted to – '

'Have a cup of tea, my love.'

' – which we don't.'

They had come equipped for country walks, but Judith, ever contrary
and still careless of her appearance despite an occasional flirtation
with more feminine clothes, used the gear already there, left by

Arthur's aunts and uncles or their children over the years: studded army boots; rough thick trousers of worsted; a heavy lumber jacket; leather leggings; a shapeless hat into which she pushed her wild, dark hair.

. . . And a stick, maybe a man's; worn, cracked, carved in a sinewy kind of way which reflected such light as it could and baffled Arthur, who found it impossible to draw or photograph it.

'Judith!'

But she was off again, stick in hand like an alpenstock, up through the close-planted trees that bore down upon the cottage and made them feel oppressed.

'I've got my lunch. See you at twilight.'

She felt freer than she had in Woolstone, even up on the Hill. Too many walls, too many people. Freer now of the excruciating pains that came with her rapid growth. Everything had ached, no one had understood. She had been born into that pain, she journeyed through that pain, which wasn't just her limbs but her hands, her hips, her jaw, her very head.

Her Dad kind of understood, and kind of didn't.

She liked to think that he and Mum didn't understand but . . . well . . . her Mum was deep. Her Mum annoyed her. Her Mum was something else again.

'Mum?'

'Mmm, Judith?'

'You weren't here when I got back.'

'I am now. I'm always near, more or less.'

That was her Mum: annoying.

Margaret was old, and if she understood she didn't let on. She just made tea and read journals about the Anglo-Saxons.

Arthur was all right.

All of them had been as confused and frightened as she had been when she screamed and screamed her pain, but now that was past, especially since the day she met Bedwyn Stort. *He* understood, staring at her without fear, his eyes on the same level as her own.

Then the hours and days of discovery following. She had stood and he had, near by the entrance to the henge in the garden in Woolstone House, near the chimes, in the scent and shifting shadows of eglantine.

'Judith,' he said once, 'did your Mum tell you I met you before you were born? She put my hand on her belly and I felt you move.'

Judith felt Stort knew her better than anyone.

He was the one person she missed and ached to see again, because being with him was like coming home.

But that was something she could not say to anyone, because it would spoil it, like picking a wildflower that then begins to die.

Whoever Stort was, and she wasn't sure, he drew her pain away and bore some of it himself. Already she had worked out that it worked both ways: she carried some of his. Pain is better borne when it is shared.

Now, in Byrness, she was free to journey as she never had been down south. There she was confined to the garden in case anyone saw her oddity. Here she had a whole world, as it felt, and if sometimes the pains still came she could and did scream them into the forgiving, understanding trees whose sterile darkness in the secret of the forest felt something like her own. They too felt pain, planted where they never wished to be, row on row, year on year, standing for ever in fear of being cut down.

Or she thought that was their fear.

'Hello,' she began to say to them in the days after she arrived, 'hello, trees. I'm Judith and I'm the Shield Maiden and I don't know what that means or where to find out what it means. Hello . . . I can feel your fear and I know you feel mine like Stort did.'

She stood there in the rain, looking very odd, like one of the giantesses she had read about in Margaret's childhood books: big, cumbersome, ugly.

She was days old, or at most weeks, but then she wasn't human.

She was fourteen, maybe fifteen, no one knew, certainly pubescent, in pain, wild and angry, and she wasn't a hydden.

'I don't know who or what I am but here I *am*, and every moment that passes I'm still here but different.'

She stood to attention with the Forestry Commission trees in their endless close-packed sterile rows, battery-chicken trees, very dark, almost black, their lower branches dead of life, brittle, dry, dusty even in the wet because rain did not penetrate the canopy above.

'Sorry we did this to you, trees.'

One day, a week after she arrived, she knew she was being watched.

'Come out and show yourself,' she said, utterly unafraid. Pain robs the spirit of its fear and replaces it with compassion.

Whoever was watching was in pain as well.

She turned in the small clearing she was in and found herself staring at a foul-looking dog. She stared at it and it growled. She stared at it more and she turned and ran and ran and ran, listening to its feet padding across the sterile forest floor as it growled and panted after her.

Still she felt no fear and nor did she know how she knew where to run to and that it was a sanctuary.

Then she was up and out on the moor, and what had been morning was now dusk, and around her as she ran and jumped and leapt over the rough waterlogged ground others gave chase, and not just dogs.

Sitting on them, holding reins to the dogs' gasping mouths and jagged teeth, were twisted, unkempt hydden of a kind. Males maybe, females perhaps. Their garb gave nothing away.

The first dog was still panting behind her fit to bust.

They circled her on their dogs, pathetic, like oversized dwarves, distorted, foul, vile things.

One of them spoke, his voice a rasp.

'She can't see us.'

Judith stared at him.

He carried a crossbow, a beautiful thing. The others had stones on strings, knives, a bow and arrow, spears. In the twilight these things shone and glinted as they circled her, getting nearer.

'Shall I shoot her, just for fun? She's human. She'll think she hit a sharp branch when she ran.'

He was downslope, his dog was snarling, the others were too. They all wanted to get at her, every single one.

Their pain, she could feel it.

In the trees, in the Earth beneath her feet, in the gathering darkness, in all of them.

She turned downslope and ran straight at one of them on his dog. She ran hard, to thump into him, to shake him.

Before he and his dog reared up and out of the way she saw the whites of his eyes and laughed, not pleasantly.

'Want to shoot me, hurt me? Then catch me!'

And she ran and ran and ran, leaving them behind until, angry now, filled with bloodlust, guessing the human girl was playing a game and mocking them, they gave chase and began gaining on her.

She felt herself, she felt her strength, felt all the strong sinews of her being, through her limbs, sliding and pulling through her mind, her whole being running, wonderful.

Ahead a stone, two stones and then three. As tall as she was, four and five, more and more.

She closed her eyes in bliss, ran among them, circling sinister, her hands to the stones, playing the music of them, loving each as if it was a dream she wanted, letting her body meld with all of them.

'I am Judith,' she cried out, 'I feel your pain, I am the Shield Maiden and I don't know anything!'

Then, laughing, this time pleasantly, she stopped, opened her eyes, stared past the stones of the henge and saw them out there, malevolent, huge, menacing, the men and women on the dogs, staring at her, aggressive but afraid.

'Send Morten in,' said the woman on a dog next to the male with the crossbow. She looked a bitch, the woman that is.

Judith knew the word but not where it came from. It was not one her parents used but it lingered at the back of her mind unpleasantly.

'Bitch!'

'Whistle that bloody dog in to rip her and tear her and hurt her.'

Someone whistled into the dark of the wood.

Out of the darkness behind them all he came, very fast and unafraid, teeth bared, hackles raised, as big as Judith now felt herself to be. The stones, no bigger than she had been, now towered over her. She was back without even trying, in the Hyddenworld.

The dog came fast and the female laughed.

'Bitch,' she said, 'Morten will bite you and bite you so it hurts.'

Judith pulled off her hat and let her hair stream in the night wind.

She unbuttoned her jacket, the better to be able to kick.

She licked her lips, the better to enjoy herself.

Then, as the dog came twixt one stone and another she ran at it so hard and fast that turf and grass and peat shot up behind her, as it might from a galloping horse's hoofs.

'Bastard,' she said, and she didn't know where that word came from either, and she kicked the dog in the mouth and nose, then again, then a third time, driving it from her henge, and then kicked it for good measure in its chest.

It fell back, yelping, and the other dogs fell back too, despite what their riders wanted.

'Dog,' she said, kneeling down, reaching a hand to its bleeding mouth and sharp, dangerous teeth, 'I feel your pain because it is my own.'

It bent its head, blood dripping in the dark, and it whined and she commanded it, 'Don't do that! Roar, scream, shout, bark or whatever it is you do, but never whine.'

The dog stood up, moved to her left side, and howled.

'Yes,' she said, her hand resting on its neck, drawing out its pain, 'that'll do . . .'

They stared, amazed.

'Who are you, girl?' their leader said.

'No, who are *you*?' she asked.

'We are the Reivers and you're not afraid of us or our dogs.'

'Why should I be? I am the Shield Maiden and this is how I am, unafraid, in pain, feeling yours, wondering who I am.'

'You are our queen,' they said.

'Yes,' whispered Judith in the dark, the stones all about her, tall as humans. 'Yes, I am but I don't want to be. I want . . . I want . . .'

She turned from them, back into the henge, circling again, dexter now, knowing better what to do, closing her eyes into bliss, learning what she was, wishing she wasn't, dreaming of eyes that once looked into hers, which smiled a little before he said, 'Hello, Judith, I met you before you were born.'

'Who is Stort?' she asked herself as she circled a final time and came back to her other self once more, 'and what is he to me?'

She said this not as an expression of indifference but from genuine curiosity.

'He's my friend,' she told herself. It was comforting.

She wanted to go home and she was already so adept at the Shield Maiden's art that that wish alone was sufficient for her to slip betwixt the worlds again and return to the human world, and home. It was like waking up.

The Reivers were gone, Judith was human again and Katherine said, 'Where have you been? It's dark. We were—'

'Worried. I know, I know . . .'

She turned to Arthur and said, 'There's a stone circle here after all. Bottom of the village, up among the trees, four hundred yards north-east of Tod Laws, that's the name of the hill up there. It's covered with trees.'

'You learn fast, Judith,' said Arthur.

'I need to; my time is running out faster than yours. If you go up there, go with me, you'll need protection. Now—'

'Judith, you need food,' said Margaret.

'I need sleep,' she said.

For once she smiled, her face blooming with the fresh air and the exercise.

'She's beautiful,' said Margaret after she had gone upstairs.

'Jack would be proud of her,' replied Katherine.

'Protection?' said Arthur. 'What did she mean?'

Upstairs in that creaking, sad old cottage, Judith the Shield Maiden opened her curtains and left a candle in a jar at the window, as Jack sometimes had when she was young and screaming, thinking she was afraid of the dark.

She climbed into bed, turned the light off, stared at the candle's flickering, and wept for the pain she felt in the world, and for loneliness.

35

IN SICKNESS AND
IN HEALTH

S lew did not recover from his unaccustomed sickness on Riff's boat once he was on dry land. He felt ill and there were things that troubled him.

Carrying the gem for one – that was no pleasure for him.

Feeling sick for no good reason – that was another.

His new companions, the Norseners Harald and Bjarne, were the only gain from his trip to Englalond. They had borne themselves well during a difficult journey and showed no sign of disrespect at his sickness.

Nor did they show undue haste to get to Bochum and reap the benefits of being his aides.

'Brother Slew,' Harald said, 'where's the need? An ill hydden does not benefit from hurrying. We'll take it slow and find respite for you somewhere on the road.'

They did. Across the Frisian heath, skylarks trilling overhead, pilgrims making their way to the ports to cross to Englalond, they took possession of a ruined place and stayed there for some days.

Slew remained grey-faced, hunched, unable to hold his food down.

Harald and Bjarne spent those days preying on defenceless passers-by for food and money and favours in lieu of both. When three monks came by they succumbed to the Norseners' wiles enough to go off the road with them.

The brothers, as Slew put it, a mordant humour not entirely

deserting him, killed the brothers and took their black robes for
uniforms. Thus was formed the Order of the Sphere, with the sick
Slew as its head and themselves as its first Brethren. It was meant as
a jest, but when Slew recovered and they continued, the joke became
worth taking seriously.

'What do you stand for?' they were asked. 'In what do you believe?'
Slew did the answering.

'Stav,' he said, 'the ancient art of fighting for what is right and true,
whose symbol, friends, is the CraftLord's Sphere.'

'Stav? Never heard of it. Is it a holy thing?'

'Very,' said Slew.

His two followers suggested to any who stopped that a contribution
of food and money would bring enlightenment to those who gave
with a free heart and win them a better reflection in the Mirror.
Pilgrims give generously to monks bigger than themselves who hold
their staves as if about to use them.

Meanwhile Slew stumbled along the road, a shadow of the Master
he had been.

He blamed the gem, believing that it sucked the life from him. He
wanted rid of it and the return of the peace of mind that he hoped
that parting with it in Bochum would bring. He wanted to forget its
blinding green light and the memories of Springs in his childhood in
the Thuringian forest where he was raised.

When he reached Bochum at last, after a long and fatiguing journey,
he was surprised to find that news of his supposedly secret mission,
and the success of it, had got there before he did. The gem's arrival
at the very heart of the Empire, following so swiftly on the heels of
the Emperor's waking, was almost more excitement than anyone
could bear. People hopped about at the thought of it and could not
stop talking of the hows and the whys and the wherefores and the
everything to do with the discovered gem of Spring.

As in Brum, people immediately wanted to see it. Failing that, they
wanted to clutch the hand of the hydden who had brought it home,
as they thought of Bochum.

'It's only right it's here! Look ... there's no place else in the
Empire so fit to have that gem ... On display of course, that's how it

will be. The Emperor will command that to be done very soon, you'll see . . .'

If people could not shake Slew's hand then touching the hem of his black cloak – or the robe of the Order of the Sphere that he affected to wear sometimes – was the next-best thing.

Failing that, well, there were the Norseners who returned with him, big strong hydden, twins, though they didn't look like it. Harald and Bjarne had believed that following Slew would lead them to something better. They were right. Females knocked on their doors every night. Food was provided free by the Court every day. Life was good.

As for Slew, he kept his door locked and in any case did not sleep where people thought he did. He was sick of sensuality and food, sick to his heart.

'Master,' said one of his servants, 'is there anything we can do?'

He stared, his mind elsewhere.

'Master . . . ?'

'Tell my fellow brothers to come to me.'

Harald and Bjarne came.

'A task,' he said, 'to cure me.'

He sent them to the city where Machtild lived and to where by now she should have returned.

'Tell her I am sick. Bring her to Bochum.'

'We will.'

Slew knew very well what the gem of Spring was and what, by giving it to Sinistral, he might be giving up.

He knew Beornamund's story and how and why the gems had come to be. Like other boys he too had dreamed of what it would be like to find the gems and, bringing them together, see remade the crystal sphere that the great CraftLord had made.

But that dream died when he found himself in the Library of Brum, wending his way through an embroidered story of seasons whose shadows gnawed at his own and made them worse.

Before, they had been just stories, legends and myths. Now they had been made real and it was his own hand that had stolen a gem from someone who needed it. A girl, a woman, an old lady, a crone

. . . her unhappy life had for a time become his own, her arid seasons his as well, her bleak spirit his own. In cheating her he cheated himself.

When he vomited over the side of Borkum Riff's craft into the dark racing sea he had been trying, he knew, to puke out of himself the bile of her sadness, if sadness was all it was. The bitter juice and bits that shot from his mouth and poured down into the racing water were meant to be an end of it.

Back in Bochum, people eyeing him greedily, wanting to touch his hand and hem, wanting to devour him, which only made him feel alone and that he had failed. The sickness was now gone, but that black sadness he had felt in her was inside him still, the memory of her memory churning, his mind struggling, his anger mounting.

Nothing felt the same, all looked bitter; there was no light in what he saw.

Even so, Slew, like the Emperor Slaeke Sinistral, had a dark presence.

When he entered a room, heads turned. When he rose to leave it, conversation hushed and slowed, eyes following him curiously and sometimes hungrily. As if in hope that something of his charisma would become attached to themselves by the mere act of looking.

He was more than just tall and well made; he carried himself as the Emperor did, with natural grace. But he did not have the Emperor's wit, and with that the ability to mask menace with charm.

Instead Slew had a feral menace that Slaeke Sinistral no longer had.

So heads turned when he had his summons to the Hall and the Emperor's presence.

'Come near, Slew,' said Sinistral.

Slew came near.

'Give it to me.'

Slew gave him the pouch.

'It is inside, Lord, but . . . beware, it is heavy on the spirit.'

'Come nearer still.'

Sinistral examined him.

'You look worn, somewhat hollowed out. I take it then that you disobeyed me and looked at the gem?'

'In taking it I could do nothing else . . .'

'Tell me what happened. We can go to a lower level for privacy.'

Panic crossed Slew's eye.

'I prefer to have the Summer sun on my face. I knew too much darkness, Lord, in recovering the gem for you. I prefer the light up here.'

'Then tell me here and now . . . speak low for I do not wish to have to clear the Court. And hold, your mother Leetha will want to hear.'

Another shadow in Slew's face.

'Lord, let me tell you the story by yourself.'

Sinistral grasped his arm and said with quiet anger, 'You dawdled coming back, you kept me waiting, Leetha was sick with worry . . .'

'And I was sick with the gem, Lord. Please, I do not wish to see my mother.'

'The Master of Shadows fears his own mother?'

'Were you never sick at heart, my Lord? Does sickness not make us stronger who survive it? My Mastership will be enhanced by this. But . . . I do not wish to see my mother.'

Sinistral saw the sense in that and yes he had been sick, deep down sick, when he first took possession of the gem of Summer from his mentor ā Faroün.

He saw in Slew an echo of himself and that the gems might be a bond between them.

'Emperor . . . did you ever hear of a lutenist called ā Faroün?'

Sinistral sat back in his throne content. The question was a clever one, or showed luck of a kind worth investing in. He relented.

'I shall see you without your mother. She has her flaws; mine was no better. Did the gem find you or you it?'

When Slew began to answer him Sinistral shook his head.

'Later, outside, underneath the stars, we'll sit and talk.'

'Yes, Lord.'

'And these Brethren of yours, the Order of the Sphere. Is that some kind of joke?'

'It is. Yet people take us seriously. We are listened to, we are followed, people wish to be our followers, my words of unwisdom are written down, and females offer favours to delightfully corrupt us, seeing as we are celibate. Well, my fellow brothers are not, but I am for now.'

Sinistral laughed.

'They'll get tired of it; I did. By the way, Slew, did you manage to raise your gaze high enough on your journey back to notice anything odd about our Mother Earth?'

'In Englalond there were earthquakes that we barely escaped. Humans died more than hydden did. Borkum Riff – he sends his compliments – fears what will happen when the tremors break the seabed open. In Frisia, where I was sick and lay abed and my companions took their pleasures, I had time to listen to the Earth. She is angry and getting more so. And here, in Bochum, in the tunnels, has She expressed Herself?'

Sinistral shook his head: 'Not yet.'

'Do you think she will?'

'She must.'

Later, when he had gone, and the Hall was clear and there was nothing but the echoing fall of dust lit by the dying evening light, Sinistral said, 'You can come out now.'

She slid out from the curtain behind the throne.

'You heard?'

'I did. So he is sick.'

'Why so, Leetha? You understand such things.'

'He knows I did not favour him when young but preferred his brother and mourned his loss. Like someone else I know, a longing unfulfilled makes him ill, which the gem's light exacerbates. He gave it to you without a moment's demur, Lord.'

'He did, my beloved. Let us go and play with it a little.'

'The Remnants will not like us doing so.'

'They can go to hell,' he said with sudden savagery. 'I do not need them any more.'

She looked at him sideways-on, concerned. Such sudden displays of petulance and selfishness were one side-effect of misusing the gem's power.

He looked well, healthy, but like the Earth, he trembled too. His head shook a little and occasionally his 's's were hesitant and, for moments only, he lost the power of his right hand, until, grabbing it with the other, he brought it back to position and life.

His thoughts though were acute, his mind even more able to reach into hers.

'I needed Spring and now I have it. Come, I have a rendezvous with your son and the stars but first . . . beloved . . . help me play.'

'Blut won't like it, Lord.'

Sinistral laughed.

'Blut is already there, waiting, notebook in hand, a natural historian. He'll like it very much.'

They went down to Level 18, where Blut was waiting, having arranged that the seals into the Chamber be undone.

Close-to, the gem of Spring looked at first like that of Summer but darker, duller. For a moment it did nothing, but then whoosh! The light came from it. They let it shine for seconds as it seemed.

'That was fourteen minutes, Lord,' said Blut, 'by my chronometer.'

'And I feel good,' said Sinistral, 'very, very good. Now—'

'Time distorts itself around the gems,' said Blut.

'So does memory.'

That evening the Emperor sat with Slew toppermost, in the lee of a refuse tip over and through which rats scurried squeaking in the dark, on top of which gulls roosted. The feral dogs that roamed these parts might have been a danger but the area around them had been cleared and Fyrd stood discreet guard out of sight.

Above them, all the stars.

'I have the cure for your sickness, Slew. Right here. In this pouch.'

'Spring? I think not.'

'No, no . . . Summer. Take it, hold it, open it, let it shine on you a second or two and it will give back what Spring took.'

There in the dark among the rats, Witold Slew let Summer briefly shine into his eyes.

Sinistral watched the stars and saw them shift, whoosh! Now here, now over there, splaying apart, the moon sliding off to the side.

Two seconds were nearly two hours, in which Slew, bathed in the gem's alluring light, seemed now to find recovery.

'Thank you, my Lord, your Master of Shadows is in good health once more. Tomorrow again perhaps?'

'We'll see,' said his cruel Lord.

They sat, the stars above their heads, the Earth and the Universe very beautiful, all things bright, all things beautiful, laughing together by the tip, rats running riot.

'Again, Slew?'

Again.

The stars slid, the moon shifted and Slew, sniffing at the pouch which held fires beyond imagining, said, 'In Englalond I met a girl, who became a woman, who turned into an old lady who decayed into a crone. She made me sad.'

'Where was she?'

'In an embroidery.'

'By ã Faroün?'

'It nearly took me into its own story.'

'Not nearly, Witold Slew, it did. Now . . . tell me, please, that you brought it with you?'

'I . . . no, Lord, I didn't. I left it there.'

Sinistral rose, anger incarnate.

'You may have left the greater prize,' he hissed, his voice reverting briefly to what it was when he was decayed. 'Because, you fool, the embroidery is a map to universal delights – and the other gems.'

Slew frowned. He had sensed something in the cloth but not quite that.

He felt nauseous.

'You did not say . . .'

The Emperor's mood swung the other way and he smiled. 'I had quite forgotten that it existed until you mentioned it, but now you have . . . well . . . there is time . . . we shall get that too. It alone is reason enough to invade the city of my birth.'

He laughed at the thought.

A city destroyed to win a piece of cloth!

In the background, listening, Blut drew out his little book and made a note. A cloth embroidered. A map that might be a guide to the other gems. Delights. A crone. Blut's eyes glistened as he too looked at stars.

36

VOWS

Cluckett approved of Jack the moment she met him.

And disapproved a short while later when she discovered that he was to take her Mister Stort away from her that very evening.

'But he hasn't even had time to rest his scholarly head upon the herbal pillow I have made for him,' she said. 'He needs rest and respite if he is to do his work.'

'So do we all,' said Jack, who was quickly getting the measure of her, 'including myself. Now listen, Goodwife Cluckett—'

'I prefer plain Cluckett, sir, but I am listening.'

She said this breathlessly, bosom heaving, feeling that though he might be the cause of Stort's imminent departure there was in the service of Stort and his many friends an excitement and a testing of her wyfly mettle that she had never experienced while her husband was alive.

'Cluckett then. I am tired, Mister Stort is tired, and I do not intend to waste valuable time discussing the finer points of Stort's pillows. Nor have I the energy to discuss whether or not he should be coming now. He is essential to our secret mission . . .'

'Secret, sir?' she repeated with suppressed excitement, 'I didn't realize.'

'Yes.'

'And my master is essential?'

'Absolutely. The future of Brum depends upon him.'

'On Mister Stort?' she said, beaming with pride.

'It does, sort of. Therefore—'

'Mister Stort is very wonderful is he not, and so often misunderstood?'

'*Therefore*, Cluckett,' Jack said very forcefully, 'we do not need any further discussion now. What we need you to do while we are resting—'

'Yes sir, that's it, name it! I like a hydden who knows his mind and is masterful in explaining his needs to others, especially Cluckett.'

'Good. Now, we will require such supplies as you judge will give us sustenance for at least three days to get us started. Water we'll find, but a mead concentrate will be appreciated and some kind of biscuit and hard rations needing a minimum of preparation that will see us through the coming days until we are well on our way.'

'That is easy, sir. Regard it as done. You'll need medical supplies I daresay, toiletries, stout twine . . .'

'Twine?'

'For snares, sir. Knives, of course, and plastic bags, small but powerful torches . . .'

'You have done this kind of thing before, I take it.'

'The late Mister Cluckett was a dab hand at living rough and off the land. It goes without saying you'll need a compass each and . . . lucifers and paper of the purpose of ablution.'

'Cluckett, do it and let us sleep.'

'Oh, sir, I shall,' she cried happily as she set to. 'I shall wake you at half past two and have both baths ready . . .'

'Two baths?'

'Rest, sir and don't flurry your mind one second more,' she said, adding in a tone as firm as Jack's had been, though with a different bent: 'Leave it to Cluckett!'

Jack rested better than he had for weeks and had been able, for the first time since Judith's birth, to appreciate what parenthood had meant to Katherine and himself. His journey to Brum had been straightforward enough, but pressured by time. Even then, as the distance increased between himself and Woolstone, he had seen how lucky he was: Judith well and Katherine too. Now he knew he loved them both and was loved in return and lay on a palliasse in Stort's room in a state of pleasurable half-sleep, enjoying these thoughts.

He had expressed some of them during the night to Stort, the two friends prone and in proximity as they had so often been under the night sky the previous Summer, their limbs and minds and spirits relaxed.

Jack fell asleep again, for longer than he thought, for when Stort woke him he was surprised to see he was already washed, brushed and dressed for travel.

'It is nearly four in the afternoon,' he explained, 'but Cluckett advised me to let you sleep and I have done so. Food is ready, a briefing with the others at Festoon's residence has been arranged for six, and no doubt we can make a decision then about when and how precisely we should leave Brum, secrecy being of the essence. Meanwhile, Cluckett has drawn a bath for you . . .'

Jack was up at once and into the small area at the far end of Stort's kitchen that served as a washery.

A thin curtain offered privacy but Jack cared little for that.

'Talk to me while I bathe,' he said to Stort.

'But Cluckett—'

'She's a goodwife, Stort, and I doubt she's prudish. She'll have seen naked flesh before I expect, though rarely any as scarred as mine . . .'

Jack stripped off and climbed into the hip bath she had prepared.

'Goodness, sir,' she said, unabashedly bringing him a hot drink as he soaked, 'those must be the evidence of that grim accident that Mister Stort once told me about . . .'

'They are,' said Jack.

'Let me take a look at your back and neck.'

'There's no more anyone can do,' said Jack shortly.

'There's much that a trained goodwife can always do, if you please!'

She took a look, running her strong fingers gently over his neck and right shoulder.

'You must know the meaning of pain,' she said softly. 'I am so sorry.'

'Well, I . . .'

'A moment!'

She came back with an embrocation of her own devising, rubbed it on him after he had dried himself, and informed him that she had put a jar of it in his portersac.

'Do these scars ever weep? When you are stressed perhaps? As now, for I presume from their state that you have been under some pressure of late?'

'I have,' said Jack gruffly, 'and let's leave it at that. But I thank you—'

'Say no more, sir,' she said. 'Meanwhile, a robust tea will be served in the parlour where your guest awaits you.'

As Jack got dressed and Stort reappeared he whispered, 'What guest could I possibly have?'

'Come on, Jack, time's limited and there's much to do,' said Stort, avoiding giving an answer. 'Make yourself decent, she's waiting.'

'Who's waiting?' he asked, but Stort had wandered off again.

When Jack pushed the parlour door open he was overwhelmed by several potent scents – florid, robust and bold – as of a female no longer young who might on occasion like to be.

'My dear Jack!' Ma'Shuqa cried, enveloping him as she always had. 'Welcome back!'

As he hugged her in return, his hands lost in the layered brocades and silks of her bilgesnipe dress, she added, 'My, you're bigger and stronger than you were. But that's how our Stavemeister should be.'

Stort poked his head round the door, said he had already had tea, did not want more and would leave them to it.

'To what?' said Jack, but again Stort had gone.

'So . . .' he said cautiously as he tucked in to Cluckett's sandwiches and cakes, 'what's this all about?'

Ma'Shuqa came straight to the point.

'There be a matter touchy and hard on which it's my duty as her adoptive Ma to talk plain and speak frank. You know my meaning I think?'

Jack had no idea what or who she was talking about.

'The female whose life you've ruined!'

'Me? What female?'

'My sweet ward, poor Hais, who you traduced and laid waste on life's hard road.'

'Hais?' said Jack, frowning. 'The bilgesnipe girl who . . .'

It all came back and an odd memory it was. He had barely thought of her since the day he and Stort and the others had escaped from Brum with Festoon, at the time when Brunte's insurrection was in full swing and they were in danger of their lives.

Jack had attended a betrothal lunch at which Hais, a friend of Katherine's, was the bride-to-be. He might have forgotten the occasion entirely but for the fact that he unwittingly unloosed a knot – a Cunning Knot as the bilgesnipe called it – which by tradition meant that he became betrothed to Hais. It was so clearly an accident, and he was so obviously needed elsewhere, that he had apologized to the company and to Hais and left. It was true however that for a moment he and Hais had exchanged a glance of the kind that in other, better, circumstances might have led to love. But their wyrd took them separate ways, Jack and Katherine had gone theirs together, Judith had been born, and the matter was surely no more than an embarrassing memory in which no one did anything to regret.

But here was Ma'Shuqa on the warpath.

'That be she I've on my mind, Jack, and have had since that sorry and difficult day you unloosed the Cunning Knot and with it a deal of trouble and tears.'

'I didn't do it on purpose,' he said, 'it came loose in my hand.'

'But now you're spoused and with a babe.'

'I'm settled yes . . .' though 'babe' was not a word he could apply to Judith. She was about as baby-like as a summer storm.

Jack sensed trouble.

'Ma'Shuqa,' he said, 'first, I don't see how *you* fit into this . . .'

She looked outraged.

'Second, I think it's Hais I should be talking to not you . . .'

'Humph!'

'And finally I'm not spoused yet but I expect to be.'

She looked utterly disbelieving.

'Not spoused!'

'No. We were intending to but—'

'Not spoused?' she said again, more quietly.

'Well, of course, we were going to get married sometime but there's not exactly been the time – and now . . .'

She sat back and beamed.

'Well, Jack, lad, you be a one, you really be, and I've been a-thinking all this time, what with Hais weeping and wailing and off her food which is a pity 'cos she's comely and food helps keep her so . . .'

Jack stared at her, puzzled.

'You seem amazed and I agree 'tweren't your fault. Spoused is one thing, the odd child here and there is another, but nary a problem if you're a loving hydden which we know you are, and Stavemeister too, and can support 'em all. Least we expect is a few wild oats sprouting here and there.'

'Judith is not a wild oat, she's—'

'Oh!' said Ma'Shuqa indifferently, helping herself to cake, 'that's her scroungy name is it, Judith? Humph. Not much o' a name in my view, and I can tell you right now that my Hais, bless her, won't go for a name like that when you spouse her, which now you can, and have young, plenty I hope 'cos I like—'

'*Marry* her?' said Jack.

'Got to,' said Ma'Shuqa, 'seein's you loosed the Knot. Loose that one and you tie another, that's the simple fact of it.' Her face darkened. 'Don't tell me you're thinking o' scuffling out of it like wot males often do, because if that's the case—'

There was a knock at the front door and the murmuring of an urgent voice. It was opened, and Stort, looking unhappy and pointing mutely at his chronometer for Jack's benefit to indicate that time was short, announced a second guest.

Hais appeared.

She was as darkly, plumply beautiful as all bilgesnipe females were, dressed in the traditional silks with a warm face and smile. In no way was she a tragic figure.

'Ma'Shuqa,' she said, 'I might have known! This is not your business, it's mine.'

'My sweeterling,' cried Ma'Shuqa, 'be not angry with your would-be Ma! I have good news and true! This rogue b'aint spoused, so he's all yours to 'ave and to hold. Take him! Wed him this evening! Bed him tonight! Ma'Shuqa knows best, she did the same!'

'And where, Ma'Shuqa, is Pa'Shuqa now?'

'He be heroic and lost without his stave!'

'He be a coward and run off more like! Now, I need to talk to Jack and he hasn't got long . . .'

'My spouse weren't never no coward and I'm hurt you put it so,' said Ma'Shuqa, real tears rolling down her cheeks. 'He be heroic to me an' I miss 'im like you missed Jack. It's no good denying that and putting the witters into me with that talk of Pa'Shuqa . . .'

Stort reappeared and pointed again at his chronometer and mimed cutting his throat.

'Five minutes,' whispered Jack unconvincingly. Even Stort could see he needed more than that and retreated once more.

Jack watched Hais boldly telling Ma'Shuqa to leave them be and then, seeing the older female's tears flow, how Hais went to her and held her tight and whispered, 'One day Pa'Shuqa will come home and a hero he'll be I'm sure.'

'He will, he will . . .'

Seeing this, and seeing how kindly Hais treated Ma'Shuqa, how gentle her spirit seemed, and then exchanging a glance with her, as he had so long before, Jack realized that the offence he caused was greater than he had realized.

'Jack . . .'

It was Stort again.

Jack stood up and said, 'Ma'Shuqa, I thank you for your concern. It is well placed and Hais is lucky to have you at her side. But this is not how I wish to talk with her, not with you here or with Stort hovering. And talk with her I must. As she must with me. Now . . . embrace me, wish me well and leave us alone, if only for a moment. Stort, please close the door and I shall come when I am ready.'

'They're waiting for us at the High Ealdor's residence . . .'

'Hais has been waiting for more than a year, so she comes first. A wrong was done to her which I must find a way to put right if I can. Master Brief would not have wished me to begin my Stavemeistership without trying to do so!'

Ma'Shuqa left, Stort quietly closed the door and Jack and Hais turned to face each other, alone at last.

'I don't know what Ma'Shuqa told you, but you are under no vow of obligation to me, Jack,' she said quietly. 'What happened that day was just—'

'It was in the wyrd of our lives that it happened,' said Jack, 'but why I have no idea. Katherine and I . . . you know she is the mother of my child . . .'

'Is that child to be the Shield Maiden, Jack? Is that really true?'

He nodded.

'We think she is, yes. But she's not an ordinary child and she needs no ordinary parenting. I would prefer to be with her now, but Katherine and I felt that for the time being I should be here.'

She came closer and looked up at him.

'You don't have to say any more . . . For us a Cunning Knot and its release means much, but for you, Jack, it means little, and why should it? I just wanted to say that I release you from its bond and wish you well in your love and life with Katherine.'

It was well said and well meant, but as Jack thanked her and said goodbye he was left with the uneasy feeling that the matter was not quite laid to rest.

The route Jack and Stort took to Festoon's residence passed the Library just when it was closing. The Sad Readers were reluctantly trailing down the stairs and Thwart himself was locking the doors.

'He should be there as well, so he's running late like we are,' said Jack, 'which means the meeting is now short of three of us. Excellent, because that gives me a little time!'

They hurried up the steps and greeted the new Master Scrivener.

'Have you someone here who can take a message?' said Jack.

'One of the readers just leaving will,' said Thwart. 'They're always happy to have something to fill their time . . .'

He called one of the Sad Readers back and deputed her to go and warn the High Ealdor they would be a little late.

Jack looked grave as they went inside.

'I just wanted to pay my respects at the spot where Master Brief died.'

They closed and bolted the doors and went down to the Lower Reading Room and from there to where the confrontation with Slew had taken place.

Thwart opened up the obscure corridor in which the ã Faroün material was kept.

The desk had been straightened and the papers that had been scattered were on it.

'I have not filed anything away yet,' said Thwart, 'thinking that Mister Stort would like to help me with that difficult task . . .'

'What's this?' asked Jack, pointing at the embroidery in which the gem of Spring had been hidden. Despite the gloom of the basement its colours were spectacular.

Jack opened it up and laid it across the desk as Slew had done while Stort briefly explained its provenance and meaning.

'Where was the gem hidden?'

Stort said, 'That doesn't matter now, Jack, or rather it does, but this embroidery is rather more than it seems. In some ways I think it's quite sacred. I understood from Brief that ā Faroün embroidered it himself as an act of meditation and contrition.'

'Contrition for what?'

'Things he did in his life which he wished he had not.'

'Like what?'

'He simply said that he made the embroidery to tell the truth in the only way it could be told. Words are unsatisfactory vehicles for certain kinds of truth.'

'Was this the inspiration for the paintings in the Chamber of Seasons?'

Stort shrugged.

'I don't know but . . .'

He darted forward and examined the embroidery more closely.

'That's very strange . . . I could have sworn . . . no . . . no matter . . .'

'What?'

'It's just this embroidery, but it seems to have a life of its own. When we return to Brum from Bochum – assuming we do, of course – I must examine it and ā Faroün's papers in more depth.'

Twilight was falling when the meeting with Feld and the others began. To Jack's relief most of the work had already been done. Feld and Backhaus had various maps and other information about Bochum and its tunnels, while Barklice had got together the essential requirements for light travel and camping.

All had their portersacs ready packed, Stort's as usual overfull and overflowing with a pan, a mug, green twine and his beloved black plastic bin-bags purloined from humans.

Brunte joined them, partly to wish them luck but also because, like Jack, he wanted to look at the famed Chamber of Seasons.

'If the High Ealdor will allow. I haven't been there since . . . well – you know . . .'

They knew.

It was there that Jack had had to wield Brief's stave to stop real hurt being done to Lord Festoon when Brunte tried to arraign and kill him during the insurrection. The moment Brunte suggested revisiting the Chamber a new and interesting possibility occurred to Jack which he decided for the moment to keep to himself.

They took the old lift up to the Chamber, a slow and rackety thing which was so small they had to make three trips of it.

'It has its quirky aspects,' said Festoon, explaining why he was insistent that they bring their gear with them, 'not least of which is the fact that one does not always emerge from the lift on the return journey in the same place where one left. That ā Faroün must have had a wonderfully complex mind!'

Some of them already knew the Chamber, others not. It was octagonal and so large that it felt more like a hall than a room. Its floor was made of polished woodblock and it was lit by a lantern window high above. The eight walls consisted of four with large wooden mahogany doors for each of the seasons, marked Spring, Summer, Autumn and Winter. The walls between were illustrated with images appropriate to each season, one running into the other and telling the story of life and the mortal journey across the Earth for which the seasons from Spring to Winter, or Youth to Old Age, seemed to be the metaphor.

But the Chamber did not offer just a narrative of life.

It was so constructed that it could turn and move, as life did, so that one moment someone thought they were standing looking at images of Winter, the next he was immersed in Summer. As for the doors they were real, as Jack and Stort knew, for last time they were there, two Springs before, they had gone through the door of that season and found themselves magicked to Waseley Hill.

This time on arriving at the Chamber Stort gave them an informal lecture on the frescoes, though in Jack's view he seemed reluctant to go too deep, doing nothing more than describing what they could all see with their own eyes and avoiding questions. Then they paced about the Chamber, separately and together, comparing it with the embroidery in the Library in which Stort had hidden the gem.

'Strange,' said Stort for the second time that day.

'What is?'

Alone with Jack he was more prepared to answer.

'The thing is that it's all very colourful but I'm sure it's not quite the same as I remember it, and I cannot help thinking that the Summer it depicts does not now look summery at all. And what is more . . .'

'What!?' exclaimed Jack, exasperated.

'Well, you see that hill down which the river runs?'

Jack nodded.

'Take a closer look.'

Jack did.

'I see a hill with a lot of vegetation on the lower slopes, a bit more bleak and bare on the top like it would be I suppose.'

'Look carefully at the shadows of the vegetation, and the gulleys and ravines high up. You'll find it easier if you half close your eyes.'

Jack did.

Then suddenly, 'By the Mirror, Stort! Do I now see what you see?'

'Keep your voice down, Jack,' said Stort urgently. 'I've a feeling this is something best kept to ourselves.'

What they had seen was that one of the images in 'Summer' was of a place surrounded not by the beauty of nature but by the ugliness of what humankind does to it – a dark landscape of chimneys, mines, canals and industry.

As the others approached, wondering what they must now do, Jack guessed he had been shown the way forward.

'Gentlemen, the one thing we have not decided is the best way to leave Brum without the whole of the city knowing what we're about, with all the risks that entails.'

'I had thought of that and—' began Backhaus.

'Me too,' said Barklice, 'but—'

Jack held up his hand.

'The answer is right here,' he said.

He stepped to one side and pointed at the great, dusty door above which, inscribed in faded letters of gold, was the word 'Summer'.

'Some of us here will remember passing through the door marked "Spring". It brought us luck and a quick escape. I suggest that now, if we all have our portersacs on our backs and our staves at the ready, we try the door of Summer in the hope that it will send us safely on our journey to recover for Brum the gem of Spring and perhaps that of Summer too.'

With nods of assent it was agreed.

Portersacs were donned, staves taken up, the hands of those staying behind shaken and final farewells made.

'Good luck, my friends!' Festoon cried. 'Good luck!'

Jack turned to the door, tried the handle, which was stiff but eventually turned, and with a great effort heaved it open.

'Gentlemen,' he said, 'after you.'

37

STATE OF MIND

'My Lady,' said Blut, 'he is not himself. Eighteen years was too long, his recovery time too brief, the gem's light perhaps too harsh . . . and now . . . he is . . . *erratic.*'

'Where is he?'

'On Level 18, in his chair, thinking, he says.'

'I thought he had left that behind. *Blut, don't tell me you let him go back down again . . .*'

Others were intimidated by her, he was not.

She had the Emperor's ear, but so did he.

Both were threatened if the Emperor lost his sanity.

'On his waking I had hoped he would focus on what matters. He needs to be seen to rule, not play. But he obsesses. Right now it is about his celebration of the "return" of the gem of Spring to Bochum. It was, of course, a theft, and a dangerous one. One does not interfere with the wyrd of Beornamund's gems.'

'He's been doing that for years with the gem of Summer, Blut.'

'That's another thing. He intends to announce the presence of the second gem and put them on public display in the Great Hall. But you are party to that, Lady.'

'It pleases him that I am. I am organizing a little dinner.'

'The gems are not baubles to be played with at an Emperor's whim—'

'Blut, you go too far.'

'I speak the truth, and if I do not I fail to serve my Lord. He employed me to do precisely that, knowing I always would whatever it may mean. I say, Madam, that the gems are not Imperial toys; they are extraordinary objects with extraordinary powers. For fifteen hundred years they had been kept apart and the gem of Spring has never been together with the others.

'Now your son Slew has brought it here, where the gem of Summer is. This is most dangerous. Slew is sick. My spies in Brum tell me that the finder of the gem of Spring, a scrivener by the name of Stort, was also sick when he touched the gem.

'Now the Emperor is sick again, or at least not the ruler we had hoped. I like not having the gems so proximate. It has danger about it. In fact I think the gems like not to be so used. And now what does my Lord intend? To display them side by side, to show them to the world.'

'What of it?'

Blut shook his head.

'It may be safe. Or it may be like putting a lucifer next to a pile of wood soaked in petrol, and lighting it. Mirror knows what conflagration there might be. I like it not, Madam, not at all.'

Leetha hesitated and then said, 'We shall risk it if he wishes it. Without him we would not be here at all.'

They were talking in low voices, in the Emperor's private quarters in the corridor behind the throne in the Great Hall, beyond the arras there. A shadow fell, a voice spoke.

'How true, my dear, how true.'

It was Sinistral himself, come up from the deep. He had heard it all.

He raised a hand as Blut's eyes widened in alarm.

'Treason perhaps, Blut, but not treasonable. You are right; I employ you to speak the plain truth.'

'Thank you, Lord. You look well but tired.'

'I am well and I am tired. Now let me guess, you were about to say that I have become irrational.'

'I was, Lord. You told me yesterday that you can feel the Earth think.'

'I can.'

'You said that you see in people several of their lives at once.'

'I do ... I see them in Bochum's corridors, hurrying about, doing

things, going in one direction when they should be going in another
. . . I see their different lives all too well.'

'See, not imagine, Lord?' asked Leetha.

She sat down, her garments shot through with the light grey the
Emperor liked. His were black, his blond hair sleeked, his brows
blackened with a paste of lemon, gall and iron rust, his lips paled with
a touch of chalk. She the same.

'I see those lives as plain as brot. Imagine someone is a brot baked
this morning and therefore sliceable. I see them as that brot and I see
them as its slices.'

'In parts, which make a whole? Is that it, my Lord?'

'No, it is not it, Blut, in the sense you mean. The slices are their
different lives, lived in this world, each the result of a different choice.
I decide to execute you for treason and a thousand slices emanate. I
decide not to and another thousand come into play. It is endless, so
naturally I do not see them *all*. Just the interesting ones.'

Leetha pondered this and could see Blut's point. Such visions were
peculiar to say the least, and perhaps a sign that the Emperor might
be less than sane.

'He will tell you, my dear, that I am also, sometimes, sick. I vomit
as does Slew and he believes, rightly I think, it is the gem.'

'He has said as much already, Majesty.'

'Has he now?'

Blut stayed expressionless.

'Does he know, by the by, that to say the Emperor is insane is
treasonable?'

Blut answered the question himself to remind them he was there.

'I do and I should. I drafted that legislation myself.'

'You see, Blut always speaks the truth. If he did not I would have
to have him killed. But as he does, I don't. Truth well told is a very
powerful thing. Encourage it. Now I must go.'

Smiling still, the Emperor went and left them to it.

'And another thing, Lady,' whispered Blut, 'my Lord sits toppermost with Witold Slew your son, the leather pouch in his hand, and
feeds him glimpses of the light of the gem of Summer as if it was an
opiate.'

'What else?'

'He wishes to destroy Brum now he knows it has thrown out the Fyrd.'

'That *is* insane,' she said.

'He has ordered General Quatremayne to assemble a force of Fyrd to cross the North Sea and attack Brum.'

'When?'

'Soon.'

'Anything else?'

Blut hesitated because there was, but how to broach it?

'It is nothing.'

'Let me judge that.'

'The day he submitted to the gem's power and light and was restored, he expressed a fear, irrational I think.'

'I do not recall.'

'He was afraid the long-dead ā Faroün, his mentor when he was a boy, would somehow reappear . . .'

Her eyes went cold.

'Well, my Lady, of late he has woken with that name upon his lips – not at night but when he sleeps in the day. He trembles and whispers that name.'

She raised her hand.

'It is better not to speak it in his presence, Blut. It . . . haunts him still.'

'What does?'

'What happened to ā Faroün.'

'What did happen? If it affects my Lord I should know.'

'It was as simple and stark as it was horrible. The Emperor had to witness the execution of his beloved mentor.'

'Why?'

'I cannot say.'

'You cannot or prefer not?'

'The latter. He was falsely accused of arcane practice with my Lord. You say he has spoken that name?'

'Yes . . . but arcane practice? What is that?'

Lady Leetha did not answer. Instead she said, 'It is a pity you did not tell me this before. I might have soothed him. There is ill-magick in that name. It conjures up bad things, like a spell that brings forth evil.'

'When was this, my Lady?'

'When he was in his thirties and his mentor in his hundreds, his longevity being due of course to his possession of the gem. He was burnt.'

'*Burnt?*'

'Alive.'

'His father forced the Emperor to light the flame. That act, those screams, haunt him still. Hence his nightmares and fear of fire. The gem, the very thing that gives him life, reminds him of that terrible death ... I am sorry he has such worries now. It augurs ill. That name is not good luck.'

Blut, absorbed, suddenly realized the time.

'Forgive me, I am late ...'

'For what, Blut?'

'A meeting with the finest chef in the Hyddenworld.'

'Who made that claim?'

'He himself,' said Blut without a smile, 'but others say the same.'

Leetha laughed.

'You mean the celebrated Parlance, former personal chef to Lord Festoon, High Ealdor of Brum, now a runner of restaurants, a caterer extraordinaire and, in his way, even a healer?'

'The same. I have hired him to create the banquet at the coming celebration of the gems. He is an irritating fellow who affects to speak French but is Brummie born and bred. However, he can cook. As for Brum ... it has a delightfully self-important High Ealdor who has no power, and a very ordinary Marshal, Igor Brunte, who has real control ... and the bilgesnipe of that city are treated with respect. Extraordinary. Were I the Emperor I would investigate the place.'

Leetha stood, turned, her perfume wafting in the air, her dress swinging.

'Perhaps you ought to be,' she said softly.

'I think not, my Lady.'

Blut hurried off to meet the chef.

✳

'My Lord,' he said two hours later, 'my apologies for being late.'

In fact this was not quite the truth.

He *had* been late, Parlance was hard to shake off, but when he arrived to see the Emperor as arranged he was asleep in a chair, a blanket to his chin despite the Summer warmth. He had therefore sat and waited until his Lord, his rest unsettled, tears flowing from a dream, woke up.

So why Blut apologized he did not know.

'What were you doing that made you late?'

'Talking to a chef.'

'Ah, excellent. For the banquet? Talk me through the arrangements.'

Blut sighed, shook his head, pursed his lips and looked disapproving. He produced a file.

'If you would glance at this, Lord,' he said grudgingly, 'it outlines the arrangements that will make it possible for the maximum number of people to see the gems safely, the Hall not being big enough.'

Sinistral read the document in silence.

When he had finished he said, 'I had a dream just now. In fact, I wept.'

'Yes,' said Blut, non-committally.

'Did you hear that shimmer of a change in the Earth's song? Just now, a moment ago, I think. Or was I asleep again?'

'You have been in and out of sleep today, Lord, or as I prefer, in and out of waking. I have heard many sounds while I have been sitting here but their interpretation escapes me as yet. They are very beautiful.'

'They are, Blut. People should take more time to listen to the Earth.'

He leaned forward confidentially.

'I was weeping in my sleep for you, I think.'

'*Me*, my Lord?'

Blut's surprise was real.

'For you. That shimmer I felt was a warning sign that change is on the way. In a sense, change is always on the way, since nothing stands still in the Universe. There is no stasis and people would be happier if they accepted that fact.'

'We have often said as much, but—'

'We?'

'Forgive me. My wife and I. That nothing lasts for ever, least of all such shifting states as happiness and unhappiness.'

'You are a philosopher, Niklas.'

Blut shook his head.

'No, I have simply listened and remembered the things you have said or written in the past. It is a privilege—'

Sinistral raised his hand.

'Please, Blut, do not be the courtier, it does not suit you.'

'But it *is* a privilege knowing you, my Lord. It is a training, Lord.'

'For what?'

The Emperor's eyes were sharp, not mad at all.

'For . . . life, Lord, nothing more.'

'Well, well . . . that shimmer was a warning; my tears preceded it, sensing its coming. Our unconscious worlds are as big as the Universe because they *are* the Universe. I wept because of the command I must now give you – but I fear nothing less will do.'

'Lord?'

'Send away your family to a place of safety.'

Blut stayed silent.

'You do not seem surprised or even alarmed. It is a command.'

'Then I shall, Lord.'

'Now, the celebration . . . it is imminent?'

'In two days' time.'

'Brief me.'

The idea had started with a desire to have a public celebration of the Emperor's 'recovery' at which various medals and awards might be presented to the great and the good in recognition of their services to the Empire over the two decades of his sleep.

Blut had seen at once that such an event would be an organizational, political and diplomatic nightmare, since everyone who was anyone would feel slighted if they were not invited to attend. That was bad enough, but manageable.

But when Witold Slew arrived with the gem of Spring the Emperor added a finale – a public display of the two gems he now possessed, together.

'My Lord, if you do that then the ordinary people will want to come as well . . .'

'And why not? Are not the ordinary people, as you put it, the very stuff and heart of the Empire?'

'They are, of course, but the Great Hall can only accommodate so many . . . and many have a rightful claim to be there, starting with the courtiers. No matter, we have put in place measures to stop most of the invited guests even attending . . .'

'I don't understand.'

'They have invitations, but by the time they have been processed the event will be over. They have the honour of being invited; we have the pleasure of not entertaining them. They will blame the administration, Lord.'

'You mean you.'

'I mean the person I have put in charge. You will need to punish him.'

'Do I know him?'

'Better that you don't know his name . . . It is hard to shake the hand of a courtier you are going to execute.'

'As a matter of fact it isn't. I have often done it but that was before your time. But you're right; I do not need to know his name. Meanwhile, have you seen my new robes? They are magnificent.'

'No, my Lord, I have had one or two other matters to attend to, like security, to stop a revolution; catering, to feed four thousand guests; procurement, to ensure a supply of eight thousand flagons of mead and—'

'Ah! You have not time to see my robes?'

'And then there is the matter of . . . of . . .'

For the first time in eighteen years Blut felt himself losing control.

'Sit down, Blut. You can forget my robes, they will be all right. What matter is it that worries you so much?'

Blut wiped his brow and asked the Emperor's forgiveness for his momentary lapse. 'It is of no real consequence I suppose, but some things drive one beyond breaking point.'

Sinistral was astonished. He had assumed that Blut was unbreakable.

'Enlighten me.'

'It is the chef for the banquet that you ordered us to have.'

'The chef?'

'You said, "Find the best one in the Empire" and unhappily I did.'

'You would. Did he come from the spicelands of Asia, perhaps? Or the succulence of the Arabian littoral? Or is he an expert in the wholesome fare, robust and good, of Americky and the Antipodes?'

'No, my Lord, he comes from Brum, city of your birth.'

The Emperor was pleasantly surprised.

'I don't think of Brum as being the home of good food, Blut. Fatty chips, mushy peas, overcooked meat and flatulent fish and cakes so heavy that they numb the stomach and slow the mind. Or have things changed?'

'One chef has changed them, Lord. A genius of the kitchen arts, a magician of the meat, a star with the sauce, who creates heaven with herbs – I quote his literature about himself.'

'Have I heard of him?'

'I doubt it, my Lord; he emerged into the light of day while you were asleep.'

'His name?'

'Parlance, my Lord. He was the High Ealdor Lord Festoon's chef. Since then he works for the highest bidder, who this week is yourself.'

'And?'

'He is temperamental and demanding.'

'Give him what he wants and praise him.'

'He wants praise from you, not me.'

'Then tell this Parlance that if his food pleases me, his Emperor, I shall personally present him to the Court on the night of the presentation of the gems.'

'Thank you, Emperor. Now . . .'

'My robes?'

'Later, perhaps . . . I have a meeting with the generals to discuss security.'

'Is there an issue?'

'For me, yes. They are more relaxed.'

'You should get your family out of here, Blut, or have I already mentioned that?'

Blut nodded and wiped his spectacles. 'You have.'

'Blut?'

'Lord?'

'I think my hair is falling out.'

'Lord . . .'

'Blut . . . I am terrified and don't know what to do.' He wept.

'Shall I fetch my Lady, Lord?'

He shook his head as Blut wiped his tears.

'No, fetch Witold Slew, I have a new task for him.'

'May I ask what it is? Is it something I might better do? He is a fighter, not an administrator.'

'It is for a fight I need him.'

'Against whom?'

'My greatest enemy.'

'My Lord,' began Blut, much alarmed, 'name him and I shall have him arraigned.'

'I mean myself,' whispered Sinistral.

38

ANCESTOR

The last time Jack passed through a door in the Chamber of Seasons he ended up in the place he needed to be.

This time, as the door of Summer shut-to behind them and the world whirled for a few moments before coming clear again, he was not so sure.

He had expected to arrive somewhere that would take him closer to their destination, which was Bochum in Germany. Maybe on a green road outside Brum heading towards the East Coast; or on the coast itself at any of the hydden ports from where they might make passage over the North Sea; or, if they were really lucky and the Mirror-of-All, which he guessed held the secrets of the doors, decided to be benign they might arrive on the further shore.

As it was they found themselves huddled in a circle on a patch of grass at night, like a small tribe of hunters in prehistoric times, but in what looked, smelt and sounded like a tiny island of wasteland in a vast urban human jungle.

'We stay just as we are,' said Jack at once, for at least where they were they felt safe and protected, as if they had been put there for a reason and that reason had to do with the ground itself.

He alone stood up. His stave felt alive and good in his hand, as if it approved of where they were.

There was little light close by, and even standing up Jack did not attract any. But the sky above his head was lurid with ambient city glow, and whichever way he looked there was no end to the lights of roads large and small, of tower blocks and modern offices, chimneys of industry, high-speed trains, a wide canal and, overhead, the lights of aeroplanes here, there and everywhere.

'It's all right,' he said, 'this is a no-man's-land between a canal and river and we are not overlooked. For now we're safe.'

As well as the endless stretching lights and buildings there was a constant hum of fast traffic, the occasional clackety race of a speeding train, and once at least the sudden shrill hoot of a ship's klaxon from the larger of the two canals.

When Jack had passed through the door of Spring with Katherine, Festoon and his chef Parlance, they found themselves on Waseley Hill, a few miles from Festoon's residence. This did not feel like Brum or even Englalond.

'No point in moving until we've worked out where we are,' said Jack. 'Any ideas, anyone?'

The only one of their party who did not shake his head was Feld.

'Something's familiar about the place,' he said.

'And something else,' said Jack. 'Although we're in the middle of the largest city I've ever known, this particular spot has a good feel to it. Almost as if our kind has been here before.'

Their eyes had adjusted to the night and Barklice said, 'I'll just go and . . .'

Jack nodded to the others to let him go. He knew no hydden as good as Barklice at working out where he was and what direction he should take.

They watched as he walked slowly towards a stone of some kind across the grass.

He reached it, circled it, went close and peered at it, touched it and came back.

'Human. It's got writing on it, but it's not in any language that I know. Stort, you're the linguist, over to you.'

'Feld, go with him. Stort's in the habit of getting lost.'

But Jack was not too worried about that; there was an air of rightness about the place, as if here and no other was where they were meant to start their quest from.

It looked like the Mirror-of-All had, in its wisdom and knowing the nature of their quest, set them down where they needed to be.

When Stort reached the stone he went closer than Barklice had done, Feld at his side.

'By the Mirror,' he cried after only a short examination, 'we're not in Englalond but in Germany.'

Feld laughed with relief.

'We are not just in Germany, Stort, we are in the Rhineland, and in a very, very special part of it. A part I happen to know . . .'

'What's written on the stone?'

'I shall read it,' said Feld. 'It is a sign put up by humans . . . *Hier wurde 1963 bei Baggerarbeiten im Rhein-Herne-Kanal ein Neandertalerrastplatz (180,000 Jahre alt) entdeckt . . .*'

Feld fell silent, Stort stood still.

'What's it mean?' asked Barklice in a low voice.

The two came back.

'What it means,' said Stort, 'is that the ground we now sit on marks a place of great antiquity and holiness. It's a burial ground.'

'Also, we are only a few miles from the entrance to the hydden city of Bochum,' said Feld, 'and I am a fool for not recognizing at once where we are, since I was brought to this very spot as a child.'

'I heard the word "Neandertal" in what you read out,' said Jack quietly. 'Were they not the first of our kind?'

His stave shimmered, its carvings crackling with blue light.

'They were giants-born, Jack,' replied Stort, 'from whom humans and hydden came by blood and by deed. They were the originators of mortal kind and the word you said you heard you did not quite complete. What *"Neandertalrastplatz"* means is a place where one of the Great Ones was buried. Your ancestors were here, Jack, and that's why we were brought here.'

Jack was silent, as were they all. He felt connected to the Earth and to the past, yet very present in the here and now.

'We should not forget,' he said, 'that humans have honoured this spot. Whatever the name of he or she who was buried here their spirit is with us now. Let us honour it for a time before Feld shows us the way to go.'

They stood up in silence, feeling that this was as good an omen as there could be. A giant-born leading them from one of his ancestors' resting place. Their determination to do what they must in the days ahead felt all the stronger for knowing that and seeing with their own eyes that his stave was alive with the power of the past.

'Some say that a spirit will linger about a place, especially a wise one, for many centuries,' observed Stort, 'to give what help it can to those that follow, until a Great One comes along and frees it to journey on, knowing another will see the tasks of mortal kind fulfilled.'

Feld said, in no way lightly, for there was a gravity about the place, the night and themselves, 'Yet I doubt that any spirit would still be here after 180,000 years, unless it was a truly Great One waiting for another just as great.'

'Well,' said Jack, 'be that as it may, we will honour it with fire.'

He found some newspaper in a bin, gave them each a sheet to scrunch up and set a small flame going with a single lucifer. He placed it on the ground and invited them to join theirs to his. 'We keep the flame alive until we all have shared our spirit here. That's the way 'tis done.'

How he knew this he did not know, but he felt driven by the same ancient impulse as he had on the night when Judith was born and he made an offering to the gods.

His flame leapt up as Barklice, next Stort and finally Feld added their paper.

'We honour you,' he said, placing a last ball of paper on the burning ashes of the others.

As he stood up once more, staring at the flame, his stave began to tremble and the flame on the ground, whose life was surely almost done, grew bright, taller, bluer, so much so that they all stepped back a pace.

Then the light began playing about the carving of his stave again, brighter now, crackling louder, jumping from one of them to another, circling their circle until the flame on the ground, higher than they were now, whooshed up into the sky, a wind catching their hair and cloaks, a great flash across the sky, to north and south, until as suddenly as it came, it was gone.

Jack stood transfixed, the others around him in awe.

'We honour you,' he said again, adding, 'A Great One has finally returned home to the Mirror this night. Let us remember him as we seek the gems of great Beornamund, which is now our quest.'

They stood in silence a few moments more before Jack commanded General Feld to take them on.

'I will, Stavemeister, I will!'

Feld explained that the site they were on lay between the River Emscher, a little to their north, and the Rhein-Herne Canal, to their south. These waterways ran east–west and Feld led them eastward, along the narrower Emscher.

It was not what most hydden would call a river at all, but a man-made conduit on a large scale, cleanly landscaped with grassy banks rising sharply on either side and the occasional bridge spanning them, quite high above their heads. The riverbed itself was artificial and looked like an oversized gutter.

It was artificially lit, but not greatly so, and the occasional human who came that way, on bicycle or foot, was easily enough avoided.

They walked fast and steadily, with barely a word said. The night remained clear and not quite warm, and though their position between the two rising banks of the river obscured the wider view, they occasionally caught a glimpse of human structures, factories, and a power station. Unlike those in Brum these were modern, clean-lined, and a few brightly lit in yellows, reds and greens. It was impressive.

From time to time Feld scaled the right bank to get a broader sense of where they were.

'We're not going to arrive at the entrance to the Bochum tunnels until past dawn, so we may have to hide up if the day is bright and our route gets busy with humans, which I think it will. So this might be a good moment to show you something.'

They followed him up to the top of the embankment, from where they could see how vast the metropolis they were in really was.

'It's really a number of human towns joined together: Essen, Bottrop, Gelsenkirchen . . . Bochum is where that group of taller buildings is,' he said, pointing to the south-east.

'The hydden city of Bochum is to the right, under the collieries between that nearer town, Wattensheid, and human Bochum itself. So it's a lot more subterranean than Brum. As for the area straight ahead, there are the tunnels Bochumers do not go near as they are occupied by the Remnants.'

'The hydden not under the Empire's control?' asked Jack, who remembered Feld's briefing. 'But that's a larger area than Bochum itself!'

'Much larger,' said Feld, 'and largely unknown to civilized hydden. Same goes for the area to the south and east of Bochum, over to our left . . . but I'll point that out later.'

Dawn was breaking and they went back down to the river path and journeyed on.

'If we can we'll avoid the Remnant tunnels,' Feld told them as they went. 'They're a law to themselves and it's too dangerous to go there without guides and protection. They're largely uncharted and the Fyrd rarely go into them.

'There have been plenty of attempts to subdue the Remnants, but it's proved easier to take control of a whole continent than those mysterious tribes and their tunnels. There's no one alive who knows the whole system or will ever know it. It's evolved over centuries over hundreds of square miles as humans have successively dug and abandoned shafts and entire collieries one after the other.'

As the sun began to rise Feld increased the pace.

They left the Emscher by way of a rail track that ran east of Gelsenkirchen and then south into Bochum. From that they reached the Huller Bach, a small tributary river of the Emscher which had a course that led them towards the centre of Bochum itself.

The area was a mix of light industry, housing and very rough open ground, occupied by industrial buildings in the past, now mostly gone. It was excellent hydden country but the routes were complex and slow work.

'You wouldn't think that one of the great cities of the Hyddenworld is as good as under our feet,' said Feld, his normal mask of military efficiency giving way suddenly to a boyish grin, 'but in fact, if I can just get my bearings . . .'

He darted up high again, looked about, came down, hurried forward, turned a corner towards a large rainwater outlet pipe blocked against animals – and hydden too it seemed – by a metal grille.

'Nearly in! Stay here . . .'

He hurried up the bank into grass and shrubs and disappeared.

Five minutes later they heard the sound of echoing steps coming towards them and Feld appeared on the other side of the grille.

'Some things never change,' he said. 'It was like this twenty years ago!'

He reached up to the top, then to the sides, and released some swivels.

The grille fell back sufficiently for them to clamber through, but he didn't let them.

Instead he came back outside.

'This isn't Brum,' he said, 'and if you go down there without knowing what's up here you'll be disorientated in minutes. So my friends . . .'

They kept low while he found a high point from which they could survey the surface as the sun rose. It was a wasteland of old workings, torn-down factories, steelworks, the remnants of giant chimney stacks, brush land, almost nothing.

'Bochum lies under that,' he said. 'Now look to our right . . .'

'The south,' said Barklice automatically, 'using the sun.'

Feld nodded.

'What do you see?'

'A security fence.'

'What else?'

'Beyond it?'

'Yes.'

'Nothing but . . . I can't make it out,' said Stort.

'Jack?'

'Just birds in the air . . . wheeling around . . . seagulls?'

'Seagulls and rooks,' said Feld. 'What you're looking at is the biggest open-air tip in these parts. Can you smell it?'

They could: acrid, sweet, filthy, faint.

'That's because the wind's blowing away from us . . . we're lucky. Now, the most important place in hydden Bochum is its Great Hall, from which four tunnels radiate. In those tunnels, with the Hall as the centre, most of the Empire's business is done.

'The Hall reaches the surface right in the centre of the dump you're looking at, but you'd hardly know it. On the ground it's just the footings of a demolished building. Inside, those footings act as the roof, complete with high windows. Humans never go near it. It's fenced off because it's toxic, the dump is used occasionally for ordinary waste by humans in masks. The deep interior where no humans go is where the footings are. So . . . we'll go down into the tunnels here and make our way to one of the big tunnels that lead to the Hall. Hopefully you won't get lost!'

'But we can get discovered?'

Feld shook his head.

'Bochum's no different from any other hydden city except that it's overtopped by wasteland and toxic tips. People come but . . . they don't so easily go. People aren't checked in, they're checked out. So getting in is not a problem . . . and today, from what I heard just now, there's a market or something on. The place is busy. Let's go.'

They went inside, pulled the grille to, and immediately the hum of the human city outside was replaced by the quieter sounds, mainly voices and feet, of the hydden city below.

'I don't have good memories of this place after childhood, so let's make this as short and sweet as we can, Jack. Barklice, give me the charts.'

They moved along the pipe until they found a dry spot.

'Right, this is what they call Level 1. Level 2, the one on which the Great Hall stands, is below us and the entrances are about here . . .'

He pointed to a few spots on the chart.

'As you can hear it's a busy time . . . the days around the Summer Solstice always are. This is the market end of the city, or one of them. Guards keep an eye on things like the stavermen do in Brum, but it's usually free and easy. They'll assume we're buyers from one of the towns nearby. Leave the talking to me.'

'Do they talk English?' asked Jack.

'German and English. This is lower Saxony,' said Feld, 'and Frisia is beyond that. It's as good as the home of English!'

They moved off quickly, tired now, wanting to rest.

There were stairs down, rather dank, but they led to a light, well-lit concourse, busy with people.

'This way,' said Feld.

Ahead was an open gate, but with some bored-looking guards nearby. As Feld predicted, they were only checking people out.

They joined the crowd, reaching the gate together, along with a few others. The guards barely looked up and they passed through feeling immediate relief.

'You see: easy,' said Feld.

There was a crash behind them and a raising of voices. For some reason the guards had closed the gate. The group hurried on, turned a corner and found themselves facing six Fyrd who had formed a line to stop them. Each was armed, two had crossbows cocked.

When they looked behind them there were as many Fyrd again. Armed, grim.

'I thought you said . . .' began Jack.

They turned to the front again.

'Where are you from?' said one of the Fyrd.

'Bottrop,' said Feld, 'just friends out for the day.'

'Yeh,' was the cold reply, 'sure you are. Now, get in there.' He pointed to a side tunnel, its entrance well guarded.

'Things seem to have changed,' said Feld.

39
RESERVOIRS OF TIME

Judith's behaviour suddenly changed.

From hiking in the woods and out on the moors she had spent a few days at home, skulking in her room, glowering at everyone, snappy, and walking down to the village, such as it was.

'What she does there I have no idea, Arthur,' Margaret said. 'I mean what *is* there to do?'

Back in the cottage Judith would sit all day by the guttering, ill-built fire, poking at it.

Then, late one afternoon, she suddenly screamed, literally screamed. Not as a child any more, nor quite an adult.

Something had hurt her, deep down.

When Katherine asked her what was wrong she replied, shockingly, 'How the hell am I meant to know?'

When Margaret told her not to be rude she replied, 'It's the focking fire, it wears a man down,' and laughed stupidly.

That was not a word the Foales or Katherine ever used, and the phrase that followed it was puzzling.

Her behaviour was anger-making and no one wanted Margaret to get angry. It was out of character and the doctor had told her that if ever she had another fall she was to get right back in touch.

Then Judith got up and said to no one in particular, 'Oh Christ, I'll deal with it.'

She left the house and slammed the door.

'What did she mean, Katherine, she'll "deal" with it?' said Margaret in a measured voice.

Katherine sighed.

'I've lost all track of what age she's meant to be.'

'Pubescent, maybe slightly older,' murmured Arthur, looking at a chart, 'I'd say. Not being an expert on teenage behaviour . . . Actually I don't know any more either . . .'

He looked enquiringly at Katherine, who looked delphically back. It was woman's stuff and he wasn't going to ask.

'Yes,' she said finally, 'she's started or something. That's probably why she's so difficult. How do I know? – I'm not much more than a teenager myself, though sometimes I feel like an old woman. And she's a Shield Maiden, which in this case does not help.'

'Ah!' said Arthur, not at all sure he understood but hoping he did because he was not going to ask for details. He smiled ruefully, so did Katherine.

'She just needs time and space,' she said, 'and lots of hugs. And she misses Jack. I do too.'

'Well, all right!' snapped Margaret. 'I still think that kind of behaviour is unnecessary and rude.'

It was evening, already dark, and the still Byrness air outside was alive with the midges that had been keeping them all indoors. The fire, which was needed against the evening chill of June in the high borderland, was guttering as usual.

Katherine said, 'She's probably cross about the fire, and I understand why. It's hopeless. I have stopped trying to work out what Judith means or doesn't mean. I doubt she knows herself, and anyway I doubt she cares. A storm doesn't mean anything. It just is. Judith is like that. She just is. She's gone and she will shortly come back, or not, as the case may be. When she does we'll know what she meant.'

'You sound like Jack,' said Margaret.

'Good! But you—'

'I'm not talking about me,' said Margaret, 'not to anyone. There's no point.'

Margaret had had another fall, two in fact, that morning. She said it was a slip, but the others feared it was something more.

'I'm not going to any doctor here in Scotland; I don't understand a word they say.'

'We're not in Scotland, my love,' said Arthur, 'we're—'

'Well, it feels like it,' she said sharply. 'But it's not me we should be worried about, it's Judith. Where does she learn those words? She doesn't know anyone to teach them to her, it's so . . . so . . . horrible!'

'The radio probably,' suggested Katherine, 'she listens to it in her room.'

Living with Judith was more of a trial for the women than Arthur. Her unpredictability washed over him but they took it personally, though Katherine was becoming more philosophical by the day.

As for the fire, her comment had made him laugh. Also it was absolutely spot-on. She got the phrase 'deal with it', he guessed, from the forestry worker who lived by himself a couple of hundred yards down the road. He was a big, taciturn, brooding man who kept two fierce dogs which tore at the flimsy fence that was all that kept them in as they tried to get at passers-by.

If that man was the source of her vocabulary it was a matter for concern. As for the dogs, that was something else entirely. Arthur had been scared of them until he walked that way to the shop with Judith. To his horror she ran at the fence, banged and kicked at it with her hands and feet, and shouted and snarled at the dogs. Briefly they tried to leap over the fence, presumably to rip them both apart.

But suddenly Judith fell silent and growled, a deep, guttural growl. The dogs stopped barking and then they whined, pleadingly as if trying to find a way to stop *her* climbing over the fence and tearing them with her teeth.

'Bastards,' she said, a word he had pretended not to hear.

They had carried on, and, coming up the road, carrying an axe, they met the brooding man.

He waved at Judith and she waved at him.

'He owns the dogs,' she had said, 'and by the way, his fire works a treat.'

The fact was that even if Judith could be labelled a teenager she was, by any normal standards of behaviour and appearance, an intimidating one. A man of God, meeting her in a country lane, might make the sign of the cross for protection.

She was large and strong and walked in the same hunched-forward way her father did, as if she was about to lift rocks, scatter the enemy, climb Big Ben and hang on with her left hand and arm while holding a screaming human being in her right and eating him, or her.

Her appearance did not help.

To say, as Margaret and Katherine did, that she did not care about it simply was not true. Not that she preened herself in front of any mirror; in fact she had removed the mirror from her room and propped it on the floor of the corridor outside.

'I prefer to be my own reflection,' she said.

Now, after her brief and sweet experiment with ribbons at Paley's Creek, her approach to clothes was strictly utilitarian. Arthur liked it, but then he liked to shamble through life looking dishevelled.

Her growth had been so rapid that almost within days of her birth Katherine had given up on new clothes for her. Charity shops were cheaper and more practical.

Since coming to Byrness she had relied on clothes and shoes borrowed from those in the cottage and on others bought with Arthur's help from a charity shop in nearby Otterburn. This was like no such place Arthur had ever seen. It was full of camouflage trousers and jackets, old military compasses, ancient studded boots, equipment that looked like it had come from a 1960s American war film, pickaxes, collapsible shovels and lengths of brand-new rope.

Judith browsed for two hours, got him to buy her old camouflage trousers, a combat jacket and a few other things.

'Absolutely brilliant!' she said afterwards.

She insisted he stopped the car near one of the forestry plantations so she could go in among the close-growing trees and change. She came out looking like a member of the Special Forces on patrol, which apparently was her intent.

She had no weapon but for a stick she had cut off a tree, thick and strong. To Arthur it looked like a stave.

'Thanks, Arthur,' she said, climbing back into the car beside him, 'now I can disappear in the forest entirely and no one will know I'm there.'

'What do you do up there?'

'Watch the men.'

'Which men?' wondered Arthur nervously.

'The soldiers. Otterburn's the biggest training camp in Britain. They go in as boys, come out as men, I'm told. Anyway, I watch them.'

'What are they doing?'

'Trying to learn not to be seen.'

'Hyddening,' said Arthur.

'If you say so. I listen to them.'

'What do they talk about?'

'Focking this and focking that.'

'Judith . . .'

'Sorr-ee.'

So Arthur knew the full truth about where her swearing came from, but he had promised not to let on so he didn't. But the silent man with dogs had something to do with it as well.

He should not have been surprised that when Judith reappeared soon after storming out about the fire she was carrying a sledgehammer.

'Help me move the sofa back.'

'What . . . ?' began Katherine.

'I told you I was going to deal with the fire. Make it work better. I know what to do. No need to even leave the room. Might need a dustpan and brush as the bits will be too big for the Dyson.'

Arthur herded them into the kitchen, from where Margaret looked doubtful and Katherine amused.

'Make some tea,' ordered Arthur, closing the kitchen door on them while he stayed to watch.

Judith was shovelling the pathetic fire – smouldering logs, spitting coals, unburnt newspaper – into a galvanized bucket. She took it outside.

When she came back in she produced a lump hammer and cold chisel from the voluminous pockets of her flak jacket.

Tap, tap; bang bang *bang!*

Bits of mortar and rock fell into the grate. She put on some workman's gloves, which he had seen before, and knelt down to take a closer look.

TAP TAP *BANG!*

More debris.

She stood up, grasped the sledgehammer, got herself comfortable, looked around to make sure he wasn't too near, and Arthur said, 'You should wear eye protection.'

She held the hammer poised for a moment and then put it carefully back down.

'That's what *he* said. Forgot.'

She pulled plastic goggles from another pocket and put them on, picked up the hammer and positioned herself again.

Arthur backed away to the kitchen door just as Katherine was beginning to open it. He kept his back firmly to it and gave Judith a thumbs-up.

She didn't mess around. Three big blows, which shook the whole house, and then a fourth followed by a final kick at one of the sides and the last of the surround crashed down.

Dust and soot settled, but she hadn't quite finished.

She knelt down again, applied the lump hammer and cold chisel to the fireback, chopped at it and removed it in two parts.

'Right,' she muttered, *'right . . .'*

She worked fast but methodically, carrying the dusty, dirty material outside and piling it by the gate onto the road.

'He'll take it away tomorrow,' she said, 'and build the fire like it should have been in the first place.'

She brought in some bricks, found a rusted griddle from an old barbecue that had been dumped in the garden, and built them in a moment into a makeshift grate to hold coal in the bigger space she had now created.

She took some firelighters, lit them, put kindling on top and carefully put back the half-burnt coals and logs onto the flames.

Arthur had let the kitchen door open again.

The other two were watching.

'Like father, like daughter,' said Arthur. 'Jack loved a fire.'

The fire roared and for the first time in the cottage's miserable existence the faces of the people in the room were made bright and red and happy with warm, radiant, burgeoning flames.

'Fire . . .' said Judith, her mood transformed.

'. . . of the Universe,' added Katherine.

Mother and daughter had rarely been happier.

The only sadness, and it was a deep one, was that Jack was not there to share the moment.

Later she repeated, 'The man down the road'll come tomorrow and fix the surround and things. No charge . . .'

'Who is he?'

'The man with the dogs. The big one's called Morten. Don't stroke him, he bites. He was unhappy when young.'

Margaret shook her head, Katherine laughed.

'And don't light a fire in the morning or he'll not be able to do the work. I'll clear the rest of the mess before I go.'

'Judith, where—?' began Katherine.

'Arthur,' she said, cutting across Katherine with unnecessary brusqueness, the moment of sharing gone as rapidly as the shifting weather of her moods, 'will you come with me tomorrow? I want to look at something. Don't want to be alone.'

Katherine's normal equanimity gave way to a look of hurt.

Arthur glanced at her apologetically and said, 'Of course.'

'We might be gone a couple of days.'

'Er, fine.'

'I've got the gear. It's all planned. It's outside under the lean-to.'

Having Judith was like having a wild and errant son and it was, he suddenly realized, painful but a privilege. He was, he knew, and Katherine knew it too, a surrogate in Jack's absence.

'What time?'

'With the dawn.'

Her eyes were sparkling but nervous.

When morning came she led, he followed.

'Where are we going?'

'Kielderhead Moor via Chattlehope, but after that, well . . . we'll see.'

The names meant nothing to him.

She set off up-valley towards the Catcleugh Reservoir, its wall looming up before them.

'Ugly thing,' he said.

'Focking dangerous,' she said, her grin only a partial one, her eyes very serious.

It was Summer, he supposed, but up there it felt like a time without a season.

The midges cleared once they got into the wind.

He knew how fast she could walk and how unremittingly, but she went more slowly than usual, at his pace he realized, looking round frequently to make sure he was all right and able to keep up. She was looking after him, caring for him, and Arthur felt enormously protected, as if in the arms of a warrior angel.

Their conversation was sporadic, brief, elliptical, yet extraordinarily precise.

'Margaret's not happy here,' he said impulsively.

'Don't blame her. But soon I'll be gone, so it'll soon be over. When I go you can go too.'

'Judith . . .' he began.

She turned back and looked at him and he saw that she was already a long way away from him, from them all. She was young and she was racing on ahead.

'It's all right,' she said. 'A storm doesn't mind being a storm; it's just that it sometimes wishes it wasn't the only one.'

'There are other storms,' he said.

'It's not a storm I want but not to be alone, but there's no one who . . .'

She was going to say 'who understands'.

But she knew she would be wrong.

Her Dad did, sort of.

Stort understood best of all.

She missed him with an ache inside her very being.

'Arthur?'

'Mmm?'

'Have you ever been in love?'

'I am in love.'

'What's it like when they're not there?'

'It feels like something's missing at first, but then as time goes by and you love someone more and more, when they're not there you look at the world and smile because you know they are.'

'Is that what it's like for you and Margaret?'

'Yes.'

'Does it ache at the beginning?'

'If I remember right it does, but that's not love exactly; it's need. That's different. Why do you ask?'

'Reasons.'

A long silence then, just the tramp of feet on the boggy, stony path until they reached a bleak granite building and stopped.

'Chattlehope,' she said, pausing to stare at the black water of the reservoir below to their right. A skirl of light moved across its surface, a reflection of the sky as wind disturbed the water. Bleak as lonely tears.

'Sixty-one men died building that,' she said. 'She will have her retribution, Arthur. But I think there's worse to come.'

What that meant he didn't ask. But he guessed that 'She' was the Earth.

The going was getting tougher and Judith the Shield Maiden, in her army fatigues, was in no mood to talk any more or stop.

'I need a pee,' he said as they broke through the sterile forest trees onto Girdle Fell.

He turned his back to her.

How long does it take a man to relieve himself?

A minute when young?

It took Arthur three, no more than that, with a bit of huffing and puffing and shaking about. Maybe only two and a half.

But when he turned back she was as good as halfway across Kielder Moor, almost out of sight. But she sensed he was wondering because she turned back towards him, holding up her hand to show she would wait.

He couldn't understand how she had got so far in so short a time. In fact she couldn't have done and yet – she had.

'Time shifts,' muttered Arthur. 'She's a mistress of time.'

He eventually caught up with her and then, having turned off the path before Kielder Head, she said, 'We'll take a break, Arthur, to let them see us.'

'Who?'

'The army boys. They're up there in East Kielder Forest, playing about like they do. They put stuff on their faces and stick branches in their hair and in their backpacks so you think you're looking at nature when you're not. It's men pretending.'

They reached a small area of flatter, disturbed ground in the open, and little streams they could hear but not see ran through the peat all about them.

'We're on an old settlement,' said Judith. 'Prehistoric people lived here. Once. Where did they go? What lives did they lead? Eat, you're hungry.' He was.

She gave him rye bread, a chunk of cheese and tomatoes.

'Chocolate to follow. But first . . .'

She offered him soup.

'You'll need it, it's going to get cold once we're through the trees above and out onto Emblehope Moor. After that, when the Summer's done . . .' She stood up. '. . . and Autumn falls . . .' The wind caught her hair. '. . . and we cross into the Winter that is Kielder Forest and all its works . . .'

They had left their lunch break behind them on the moor and she was racing and he beside her, the heath rough on his old legs, the wind cold on his face. Then he was flying. And he wanted to tell her she was loved before she upped and left them all, so she'd always know.

'When we get to Winter, or I do, it'll be bleaker than we've ever known,' she continued.

Judith was holding Arthur's arm so he didn't peel away into the landscape below and get lost in its shade.

'And that's when I don't want to be alone.'

They saw the soldiers crouched and low, covered in white cagoules to camouflage them in the drifts of snow.

Arthur said, 'But it's June.'

'It *was* June,' she replied. 'They can't see us, Arthur, that's the thing. They don't know we're here so it's as well we're not armed except for this.'

It was the stave she had cut, no more than a stick then, now a stout and sturdy weapon as tall as she was.

Arthur frowned, looked at his hand, looked across the moor for something to give him a sense of scale, but found nothing. Had she taken them into the Hyddenworld? Was that what she could already do, even without a henge to help her?

'They're the enemy, not us,' she said, pointing towards the soldiers.

They watched as the soldiers fired clinical sniper shots at a target across the valley, each as calculated as the cut of a surgeon's knife. By their side a spotter, using binoculars, whispered instructions.

An infinitesimal change in the sights. Another round of shots.

The shots were a blasphemy that cut through the tree-ruined landscape that was the dark forest of Kielder.

They landed deep inside the forest's dry and dark sterility.

'Poor trees,' she whispered, touching them as she passed.

She instructed him, 'Touch them, Arthur, they're all alone. Imagine ten thousand of us, our feet in concrete and our arms cut off, standing upright so close that even in a gale the wind sweeping across the moors doesn't reach those inside and you can't move and turn and see who's behind. Imagine! That's Kielder.'

He saw that she was weeping.

'Our Mother Earth feels their pain and I do too. Sometimes I can't bear being all alone and ask, "Why me?"'

They reached the black, black waters of the reservoir.

'Submerged beneath the surface are the huts of the men conscripted to dig this wound into the Earth's surface,' she said. 'Come on, Arthur, let me show you.'

She pulled him unresisting beneath the surface of the waters to feel its cold sterility.

'People looking at the cold surface above us,' she said, 'don't know we're here underneath. Do we exist? I don't think so. Ready to leave? Too soon, Arthur; I want you to get so cold you feel Earth's pain.'

She let go his hand and he touched neither the surface nor the bottom, drifting, turning round and round, hands out, flesh watery white, no longer alive to the world above. He felt the Earth's cold in every joint and muscle right through to his head.

'Judith,' he wanted to say so he wasn't alone down there, 'Judith . . .'

It took two years for the waters of the moors around to fill that great scar, she whispered, her voice deep and blurry with the water.

She carried him out, water streaming off him, from his ears and his mouth and his clothes.

When he looked back the water of the reservoir was gone and there was just the original wound, grey-black, a massive gouge in the Earth's flank.

'See you in two years,' she said, flying away and leaving him to sit and wait and watch the filling-in, his tears ten thousand little streams, and he shivering throughout.

Want to go back to the fire, he wished to say, but he was too cold to say anything.

One night, three nights, two whole years?

He didn't know how long he had been up there when he realized they were finally coming off the moor back into the human world, back past Chattlehope, past the hanging waters of Catcleugh.

When they returned the fire was waiting and ablaze.

'Did you have a nice time?' asked the women.

'We did.'

'He came then, to fix the fire?'

'He took a shine to Katherine,' said Margaret, and they laughed at some secret about all that.

Judith said, 'One more night, then you must go.'

'I was just beginning to enjoy myself,' said Margaret, the flames flickering all over her wrinkled face and hands.

Judith shook her head.

'Got to go,' she said, 'because Byrness is under sentence of death. The reservoir's dam is going to burst. Tomorrow morning . . .'

They packed the car at dawn, locked up the cottage, said their goodbyes to the place and the time and Katherine began weeping. She suddenly understood. Her baby was no more. Her little girl gone. The teenager matured. They were saying goodbye to the place; Judith was saying goodbye to them.

'But Judith . . .'

Judith held Katherine like a woman now, not a child.

Held her like Jack did.

Held her with love.

Katherine wept but Judith did not.

'It was going to be sometime, Mum. Well, it's now. I . . . thank you . . . say thanks . . .'

'I will, I will, I will,' said Katherine.

'Tell him I love him.'

'I will.'

'Mum?'

'Mmm?'

'Am I ugly?'

Katherine held her tighter still. No question could have made her feel more loved, nor more needed. 'You are the most beautiful creature on the Earth,' she said softly, 'and you make me proud.'

'You'll make me cry and Shield Maidens don't cry. Let me go.'

'Your sister did,' Katherine said, 'and you'll learn how to, I expect.'

'Let me go!'

They parted, laughing.

'I'm not coming,' Judith called out to Arthur and Margaret. 'Mum, goodbye. Now go! *Go!* There's no more time. I'm going to tell the man to leave as well and the dogs with him. Too dangerous.'

'Focking dangerous,' murmured Arthur, inaudible but to himself. *'Judith, we should tell . . .'*

'It's in the wyrd of things that you go and they stay, except maybe the man and his dogs . . .'

She turned from them and was gone to tell the man and do whatever it was she was going to do down the coming seasons of her life.

'To north or south, uphill or down?' asked Katherine when Judith was gone.

'Down and away,' said Arthur. 'The sooner we put Catcleugh behind us the better. If we went up that way you'd have to go through Kielder and, trust me, you wouldn't want that. The place looks like a sentence of death.'

Katherine eased the car onto the road, turned downhill, and did not look back.

*

Behind her Judith was already long gone, the man well warned, and Morten happy at her side as she strode back up into the trees.

In their dark shade the Reivers were waiting for her with their dogs.

'Come,' she commanded them, 'your wait is over and you have your queen at last!'

She raced away, Morten followed, and the Reivers galloped behind her to right and left, right across that dreadful, bullied, ruined landscape.

'Look!' she said pointing.

Even a Summer sunrise didn't improve it.

'Look what men have done to the Earth!'

The sun arced across the sky towards dusk.

Far below, winding away down the narrow, darkening forest roads, heading south, the others went, contained in a car, fleeing red rear lights in the landscape, heading home to Woolstone, their task done. Judith watched them go and then looked another way. The Shield Maiden's childhood was over but she was not alone.

'You look ill,' the Reivers said.

'I am ageing,' she said, 'and I have much to do. What season is it?'

'Up here it's always Winter, down south it may be Summer. How would we know? We've never been.'

The Earth shuddered to hear their racing feet and the dread beat of their hearts. It was Herself she heard.

Behind them in the dark that night, the great wall of the Catcleugh Reservoir cracked and the first trickle of water began.

A man had already closed his cottage door, put the key under the mat out of habit, whistled up Morten's son, and began climbing away from Byrness, up the steepest track he knew. The village sat in its sterile darkness, a few lights on, waiting and waiting, nothing to do, fires guttering and the wind ill-tempered off the reservoir.

Silent, a white snake writhing through the dark, the River Rede began to race and grow as the trickle down the face of the dam wall upstream turned into an angry waterfall.

There was a thundering rumble and bang! as earth and concrete broke and the lichen-covered capstones along its parapet moved one from another, the narrow gaps between them widening and widening as the water they'd contained, eager now for freedom, roared out its right to liberty and began its killing spree.

The humans' grip on their world was weakening.

40

HOLY CHARADE

'This isn't what it seems, Jack,' said Feld quietly as the Fyrd led them away. 'Do exactly what they say.'

It was as well he spoke, because Jack was all for resisting and having a fight right there in the outer tunnels of Bochum.

'We'll see,' he muttered, signalling to the others to say nothing, make no protest and for the moment go along with what they were told to do.

'It's just processing,' explained Feld. 'It's what they do when they can't think what else to do.'

They were hurried off the main concourse away from the crowds down a well-lit corridor which looked to Jack like a very large sewage pipe cleaned up, painted grey and floored.

They were taken to an empty room and told they would be locked in there until late afternoon when their processing would begin.

Jack was worried, Feld less so.

'It's about control,' he said. 'We've arrived at a time of festival or celebration and this is their way of keeping people they can't easily identify under control. There are probably a lot of others like us, getting equally frustrated and angry.'

He was right, they were kept locked up until the late afternoon, when the door opened and they were led, firmly but not roughly, into a large space in which a whole mass of people had already been herded, most with portersacs and staves. They were standing about and many complained loudly.

'It's a holding room before they do the paperwork,' said Feld, 'and we're going to have to make some fast decisions. The first is not to look too much like a single group. That way we may be able to split up without anyone realizing we're working together. They don't like groups, they're threatening.'

Jack nodded, looked around, and appraised things.

He had assumed when they were stopped that they had been targeted for some specific reason and no one else had. In fact the Fyrd who had stopped them had left them at once and gone back out the way they had come without talking to anyone or passing on information about them.

At the far end of the room was a harassed-looking seated official in grey garb that matched another, but which was not Fyrd uniform. Bureaucrats.

More people were suddenly brought in, as they had been, and were placed behind them. They were in a queue and it was moving forward, those at the front being asked questions and filling in forms. There were several doors behind the officials, a grille through which Jack could see more, and a double door to the left side through which most of those who had been questioned were filing, irritated and voluble. Some people, forming a smaller group, had been put over to the right-hand side.

'I need to know who these groups are and why they're being treated differently,' said Jack, bringing his own group together, 'and fast. Once we're through one or other of those it's going to be harder to get back and go through the other if it's preferable. Meaning we'll have lost control. Also if we split up we may find it hard to get back together again . . .'

The queue moved forward, more came in from behind, some of whom began pushing.

'Okay, listen. Let these new people come past us; look confused, but stay loosely together until Feld and I have worked out what's going on. Stay with Stort, he's tallest and we can find you quickly in this crowd. Just try not to move forward . . .'

He and Feld filtered out of the queue to right and left, drifting forward towards the front and side.

It was noisy and chaotic and the Fyrd inside the area had given up trying to do anything other than keep the crowd moving.

Jack pretended he was looking for someone he had lost, peering about ahead of him, nodding indifferently to the Fyrd who tried to push him back in the queue and saying, 'Just looking for my brother . . . he's . . . yes . . . yeh . . .'

He did not exactly resist the Fyrd, but he did keep moving forward. Finally the Fyrd left him to it. He glanced across the room to Feld, who was doing much the same. Feld headed towards the people going through the double doors and was able to get a look at the papers they had filled in.

Jack reached the much smaller group on the right side. He saw at once that their dress was better than average, they looked in no way fearful or helpless, and they wanted answers. It was obvious too that some spoke neither English nor German and appeared to be representatives of the places they had come from, like officials or even ambassadors.

He returned at once to the others, just as Feld did.

'A few of them are Bochumers,' said Feld, 'who've got caught up in the Fyrd's net. That's why they're so angry. But most are travellers coming here to celebrate the Emperor's return to normal life. The Fyrd don't want them any nearer the centre. The crowd down there is getting too big.'

'What are the papers they've been given?'

'Coupons for meals and accommodation,' said Feld. 'Look. I've got one, someone dropped it, Mirror help them.'

Jack looked at it.

It was printed, not handwritten, and had a name at the bottom: *By Order of N. Blut, Commander of the Emperor's Office.*

'We don't want to go that way,' said Feld. 'Jack's right, we'll never get back out of there before someone starts asking us difficult questions about why we're really here.'

Jack nodded.

'The other lot are ambassadors or representatives who think they're being treated with disrespect being shoved in here . . .'

Barklice, who had had a little wander of his own, said, 'Also they're panicking because there's a ceremony of some kind. Someone mentioned gems . . .'

'Tomorrow?' said Jack, his eyes lighting with excitement.

'No today, this evening,' said Barklice.

Fewer people had been coming in and the Fyrd guards were beginning to eye them and close in.

'Right!' said Jack. 'We go with the ambassadors . . . Stort, start speaking a language you're absolutely sure no one will understand!'

'Ah,' said Stort. 'Now there's quite a wide choice . . .'

'Don't talk about it, do it. And while you're at it think of a good reason, a compelling reason, why the Emperor should want to see us before anyone else. And give me your portersac, and Barklice your stave. Look important, look . . .'

Stort produced colourful cloths from his 'sac and wrapped one round his head in the form of a turban. The other he draped over his shoulders like some rich potentate.

Jack studied him.

'Not bad . . . but . . . what's this?'

He pulled a piece of branch out of Stort's portersac.

'Ah, that, yes . . . I was going to cut it down and make a catapult out of it . . .'

'Hold it,' said Jack urgently. 'Make it look like an emblem of office.'

'You mean like an official from a religious state perhaps?'

'Everyone else fall in behind him; Feld you take the rear. Do not speak. Leave that to me and Stort. I'm your interpreter, Stort . . .'

One of the Fyrd finally came over.

'Get a move on, you lot.'

Jack looked at him with outrage on his face; Stort ruffled up the material about his shoulders and took up the branch. It helped that he was taller than everyone else.

He ignored the Fyrd and everyone else, muttering to himself in some strange language full of short vowels, conflicting consonants and clicks and glottal stops.

'We here,' said Jack slowly, missing a few words and speaking with an accent, 'for Emperor Hyddenworld great and good!'

'Just move on, sir,' said the Fyrd more politely. 'They'll deal with you down there.'

Jack led Stort forward, bowing as he went.

Barklice ran around like some minor official of Stort's Court and ended up bowing and scraping behind him while Feld did a good job of looking like a bodyguard.

They reached the others in the ambassadorial group as a door opened and they were all ushered into a different room. Jack saw that the other groups, or delegations, were producing various documents.

'Petitions,' whispered Stort. 'We need one.'

'Quick,' whispered Jack, 'give me a reason better than anyone else's. I want to jump this queue before they're inundated with these other people's paperwork.'

For a moment Stort stood still thinking, then an idea came to him, though what it was the others had no idea.

He drew himself up as magnificently as he could, held up his emblem of office as if it was a holy artefact, and murmured to Barklice, 'I'll need paper, ink, a pen.'

The crowd of people around the table was angry and demanding, but Stort advanced so grandly upon it that it was clear he was not going to stop.

'What language were you speaking?'

'Pictish.'

'Where's that from?'

'North-east Scotland. It's one of the Caledonii—'

'Right . . . Make way!' cried Jack, 'for His High Prince and Holiness of the Caledonii!'

He spoke loudly and clearly, and to emphasis the point Feld came to the front and crashed the bottom of one of the staves on the ground. Tap! Tap! Tap!

The crowd parted, the official looked nonplussed, silence fell.

Stort, muttering still, made a small squiggly gesture with his right hand.

'Paper!' cried Barklice. 'Ink! And a pen!'

'For His Holiness,' cried Jack again, while Barklice fawned and made as if to adjust Stort's ethereal dress, and Feld tapped sharply a few more times.

Then, as they saw these items appearing, Jack commanded the official, 'Bring a chair!'

Stort had guessed that there were many there who had never seen a scrivener scrivening and this was what he now intended to do. At the same time, his mind was working fast.

The paper was placed before him.

The ink to its side.

As for the pen, a simple dipping type, Barklice took the one offered, smelt it, bit it as if it might be dubious coinage, dipped it, and proffered it to Stort as a waiter might offer a beautiful glass to the proposer of a toast.

Stort did not dally.

He pulled back a little to give everyone a better view and proceeded to scriven theatrically upon the paper, with many words and scrolls as he went, as if he was producing Holy Writ.

The crowd was suddenly subdued, even in awe.

Feld held his hand up as if to say, 'You can watch but come no closer.' Barklice stood to attention, raised his hands in the air and gazed ecstatically upward, as if witness to something rare and wonderful.

Jack looked at what Stort was scrivening and understood not a word until, bigger than the others so far, he saw something that anyone official in Bochum could understand: N. BLUT. Obviously he had borrowed that from the paper Feld had found and hoped it would impress. It did.

Several officials who had gathered around saw it, pointed at it and whispered in a worried sort of way to each other about it. Stort continued to scriven, dipping his pen frequently, not minding if ink splashed here and there as if the words he wrote were inspired by the fires of faith.

After a few more incomprehensible paragraphs, those around him now so awed that the only sound was the scratching of Stort's holy pen, the name EMPEROR SLAEKE SINISTRAL appeared, bigger than Blut's.

This too attracted comment and consternation and a look of unease came to the officials' faces.

Again Stort scrivened, his pen racing, ink flying, faster and faster until, unable to continue from a sitting position, he stood up, the paper beginning now to move with the violence of his pen such that Jack had to hold it still.

Then came the last name, the crux, Stort's compelling reason to see the Emperor.

He scrivened it, underscored it magnificently and handed the paper to Jack as if to say, 'His Holiness has scrivened, his minion will translate.'

Jack looked at the paper, looked at the last name, got some sense of Stort's purpose and tried desperately to remember exactly what it was that Stort had said about the embroidery in the Library, but it had slipped his mind. Something important, and now very relevant, but . . .

The officials looked at him expectantly.

'His Holiness,' began Jack, 'is here, as are we all, at the express invitation of Commandant Blut for the purpose – and here I summarize – of bringing to Emperor Slaeke Sinistral's attention that we have a message – a greeting – from . . .'

Beads of sweat broke out on Jack's brow, Stort muttered, Feld glared, Barklice lowered his hands and began a curious dirge.

Jack peered again at the last name and light dawned.

Of course! It was the one name that would strike a chord with the Emperor and, if only from curiosity, lead him to think that they might be permitted a moment of his time. He would know he was dead, but that made the message all the more intriguing. That much gained, much might follow.

'We bring a greeting,' continued Jack, 'on the occasion of our great Emperor's recovery to health and his noble discovery of the gem of Spring, from the ineffable, the great, the good and the unsurpassable – ' He paused, not quite sure how the name was pronounced, but did it boldly all the same, ' – the unsurpassable scholar and lutenist ā Faroün!'

Silence fell.

The officials looked at each other in puzzlement.

It began to look as if the absurd charade would not have any effect at all.

But then something remarkable.

One of the officials, remembering his hydden history perhaps, or aware of the great lutenist's work, repeated, 'Ah . . . ā Faroün!'

Barklice called out loudly, as if to a great warlord, 'Save us, mighty ā Faroün!'

To Jack's amazement the assembled crowd, feeling in some way that courtesy to His Holiness demanded it, repeated together, 'Ã Faroün!'

Stort beamed and repeated, 'Ã Faroün!'

Taking the hint, the crowd responded saying, 'Ã Faroün!' again and again, louder still, until very quickly it became a chant that expressed their frustration at being held against their wishes, and, perhaps, disappointment that whatever celebration was under way elsewhere in Bochum just then, they were not part of it.

'Ã Faroün! Ã Faroün! Ã Faroün!'

It had turned into a demonstration.

The officials began to look panicky. It is one thing to use the strong arm of the Fyrd on ordinary folk, but on important people it is quite another, and Stort, and those who now seemed to have accepted his lead, were beginning to look very important and very threatening.

Jack whispered, 'Head for that door, Stort,' indicating one behind the desk. To Feld he said, 'Keep the others close so we don't get split up.'

When the door Jack indicated had opened earlier to let officials in he had noticed that the corridor beyond was better lit than the ones they had come from. More than that, he saw a number of people in official robes hurrying down it in the same direction, some glancing at their chronometers as they went.

Obviously they were going to a special event, and Jack thought there was a chance that it was one at which the Emperor might be present.

Stort drew himself up once more, gazed in a pious yet imperious way at those around him, and without more ado strode, stave in hand, through the door, his friends following, and the crowd of ambassadors and others too.

Officials fell away, one alone running on ahead in a vain attempt perhaps to warn someone of what was happening. At the same time, down the corridor behind them, some double doors burst open and another crowd appeared. This was the larger one which had gone a different way earlier and had somehow got wind of what was going on.

Feld was smiling. He saw a group of tough-looking males carrying staves and had a word with them.

'Friends in need,' he said. 'They'll help us. Better still, they confirmed where we are,' he said. 'Just keep on marching and we'll get to the Great Hall. Couldn't be better, but what we do after that I have no idea.'

'Nor me,' said Jack as they swept along in Stort's splendid wake, his stave like a shepherd's crook, his followers a good deal more like a crusading army than sheep.

41
CELEBRATION

The Great Hall of Bochum was looking its best. The day was clear outside and sun streamed through its high windows in shafts of light through the dry and dusty air. These shifted slowly through the day, their colour changing from the softness of morning to the harsh brightness of midday. By evening they were nearly horizontal once more, lazy pink and orange with the sunset.

Most hydden in Bochum worked in the levels beneath. To them the Hall was both respite and inspiration.

Three wide concourses led into it from west, north and east. These were places of promenade, Court gossip and assignations. At their furthest ends the business of trade and shopping, finance and money-lending took place.

A fourth way lay behind the Emperor's throne at the south end of the hall, hidden by an embroidered arras of silk.

It led to Sinistral's offices and private rooms and to a complex of elevators and moving stairways which enabled him, should he wish, to access any part of Bochum, secretly and fast.

During his long sleep it had been Blut's responsibility to keep these lifts and stairways open and in working order, which had been done with quiet efficiency.

A discreet green door on the left side of the South Wing, as it was known, led into what looked like a plain, empty room. In fact it had three more doors, all entrances to lifts, one of which offered access to Level 18, half a mile below.

None of this was visible on the surface above except for the ruined footings of a former human factory, now the roof of the Great Hall. It was this location in the heart of a massive tip and rubbish dump that Feld had pointed out to Jack and the others when they first approached Bochum.

Hydden were banned from that area of the surface, as were humans by their own authorities. The reason was not just the danger from so much unstable waste and swampland bubbling with toxic gases. The area had been colonized by dogs, now feral, their ancestors the aggressive guard dogs used to control slave labour used in armament factories thereabout during the human war seventy years before.

Their vile progeny, tainted and mutated with mongrel blood, far more aggressive than the dogs that spawned them, roamed the tips in rival packs, drank in the swamps, and fed off the rats and other species that survived in the rubbish.

Once in a while a hydden accidentally ventured into that dangerous place. Unless they were rescued by armed Fyrd, wearing protective suits, their chances of survival after nightfall were nil. The dogs sniffed them out, encircled them, attacked and ripped them apart, their filthy pups fighting for what scraps remained. All that the hydden in the tunnels below knew about their last moments were their screams, echoing and reverberating in the ventilation shafts.

But such terrors were far from anyone's thoughts that early evening.

The Hall was bedecked with Summer flowers which had been cleverly placed around the walls and in stands on the floors, where they caught the light.

The flowers, like the candles that were lit as twilight fell, were My Lady Leetha's idea, she being in charge of the decorative aspects of Bochum's biggest event for years.

Blut had not approved.

Her first demand, for two thousand candles, he had been able to head off on the practical grounds that by the time the last was lit the first would long since have burnt itself out.

'Then, my Lady, there is the most serious aspect, the risk of fire which, as you know, the Emperor is peculiarly sensitive to.'

'Well then, if we can't have two thousand make it one thousand; they will look so pretty.'

Blut had said he would see what might be done and arranged for no more than one hundred candles, tall and thick, to be placed at intervals around the edge of the hall, with two buckets of water next to each one.

When Blut had first taken on the dreadful business of the Emperor's celebration such tedious arguments over minutiae had come close to breaking him. But he had taken it all in his stride, made the decisions as they came, and kept his focus on more important things.

He had even learnt from the experience. He had often wondered what quality above all others set Sinistral apart, such that he had ended up as Emperor. Blut now saw that his secret lay in his management of people, a skill Blut had developed with difficulty and which still sometimes failed him.

At that skill Sinistral had a master's touch, unaffected by his long sleep. He knew how to give praise and motivate those around him. He even calmed down the temperamental chef Parlance, from Brum, who had nearly driven Blut to distraction when he first arrived, with his endless demands for better equipment, better staff and better produce.

The Emperor's offer to give public praise if the banquet pleased him, and a subsequent quiet word between the two in the kitchens, had done the trick. Blut was glad he had not yielded to temptation and sent the chef packing. For now, the banquet over and the courtiers starting to file into the Hall for the presentations, all were singing the little chef's praises.

Blut could at last begin to relax.

The event was going well and the behind-the-scenes work by his own department was making it all seem effortless. An hour more and it would be over bar the shouting, which he had no intention of staying for. Let the younger folk sing and dance – he would retire for the evening to his humble near the surface while the Emperor, no doubt, would find somewhere safe to stare up at the stars.

Blut stood near the throne with Ealdor Vayle, the most senior courtier, checking a few details of the Emperor's imminent arrival at the far end of the Hall and the placing of certain of the more important courtiers as they accompanied Sinistral to the throne. From then on Blut would take a back seat, moving behind the Emperor so that he could prompt him as appropriate; and, too, be able to move forward swiftly and keep at bay any officials and courtiers likely to irritate or overtax the Emperor with their worries and blatherings.

Vayle had the Court protocol at his fingertips, and like Blut knew just how to head off trouble before it escalated, yet not ruffle feathers when he did so.

General Schlotle appeared, the supreme chief of the Fyrd, though one now in the shadow of General Quatremayne, his likely successor. He looked calm and collected.

'All under control, gentlemen, though not without some difficulty in the corridors, there being more people wanting to come to this event than even you predicted, Blut. But . . . we have put in place ways of diverting them, slowing them, such that by the time we have processed them – politely of course – the event will be over.'

'Any dissidence or ill-feeling?' asked Vayle.

'Surprisingly little . . . the mood is cheerful.'

The Hall was now filling rapidly and the hubbub of voices getting louder and louder as the excitement built.

Schlotle had placed Fyrd guards around the room, though not so prominently that they looked in any way menacing.

Two contingents of three, dressed in ceremonial uniform of black and red, stood either side of the throne. Various important officials and ambassadors were to sit in seats that now formed a line to one side.

The normal cord barriers had been removed, and all that stood in front of the throne was the Emperor's stave of office and the two magnificent bejewelled arks of gold in which the gems of Spring and Summer had been placed. The clue to which was which lay in the jewels that encrusted the lids.

One, to the left of the throne, shone green with gems of tourmaline and obsidian, jade and shining emerald. The other, to its right, shone yellow with sapphire and citrine, fluorite and a dozen yellow amethysts.

'Are they to be opened and the gems revealed?' asked Vayle. 'Everybody wishes to know.'

'They are,' said Blut, 'very briefly but not together, for that risks a melding of their light such as no one has ever seen or can imagine. I have advised the Emperor against it but, well . . . he is the Emperor after all. One must hope he does not get carried away.'

'Quite so,' growled Schlotle. 'It's never a good idea to provoke the people to overexcitement, but I think we have the situation very well contained.'

He smiled complacently, having missed Blut's point entirely. It was the gems that Blut was worrying about, not the people.

Trumpets sounded in the main Concourse; the audience in the Hall settled and a hush fell. Schlotle, Vayle and Blut, nodding to each other, went to take up their different positions around the throne. In addition to the candles, and the dying sun, the Hall had been lit by four great gaslights. These were now slowly dimmed, which had the effect of making the very last of the evening light bright on the western windows. As that, too, died the candles took over, their warm flickering light and shadows spectacular on the flowers and decorations.

A few moments later, to another fanfare, the procession arrived, children coming first, dressed in Court uniform, wyfkin next, and then the Emperor himself, flanked by courtiers.

There was nothing formal or serious about any of their faces. They had been instructed by Sinistral to be happy, to talk, to joke and to laugh, to walk into the hall with joy. This was a celebration, a time for joy.

Musicians walked with them, playing the tuble and the hot drone, choristers singing roundels of youth and gaiety.

In the midst of it all, taller than most, more resplendent than any, glorious in robes of sable and black velvet, his hair seeming aflame with the candlelight, came the Emperor himself, laughing, smiling, waving, ever youthful, if now somewhat stiff of step and movement. A step behind, to his left, came My Lady Leetha, her robes a soft, pale echo of his own – plain, pale, flowing and exquisite.

To his right, his own dark stave in his hand, walked Witold Slew, the only grim face there: love, power, strength – these three qualities seemed now at the very heart and soul of the Empire. As they passed down the centre of the Hall the courtiers rose as one, clapping, smiling, joyful.

When they reached the front, four great bilgesnipe, dressed in red, picked up his throne and brought it forward onto a dais between the two arks that held the gems.

Sinistral sat down, all others followed.

Elevated though he was, the arks were higher, and when a spotlight was turned on, their jewelled lids shone bright. Yet Sinistral, youthful as he seemed and strong, shone brighter still and the arks were like stars in his firmament, the whole making a dazzling and awesome display.

The guards receded into shadows and Slew, dressed in black, passed his own stave to the cripple who accompanied him on such occasions and took up instead the Emperor's stave.

The music died, trumpets sounded once more, and Vayle, now standing at a lectern of gold to one side, took over as Master of Ceremonies and began, 'My Lord Emperor, Lords, Ladies . . .'

It was beautifully and gracefully done as awards were made, medals given, jollity sustained, and presentation after presentation greeted with clapping, laughter and pride.

'And not forgetting,' said the Emperor towards the end of the presentations, his strong voice carrying effortlessly to the farthest recesses of the Hall, and there being no hint of his irrationalities or nascent insanity, 'the gentleman who, I believe, has given more pleasure to us all than any other here today! I present to you the great chef Parlance, born as I was in the rebellious and contentious city of Brum, which . . . which . . .'

It was then, as Parlance came forward to accept a scroll of honour, that Blut realized something was wrong.

The clue lay in the Emperor's face, so joyful and confident all evening. He had paled as he repeated himself and there came over him a look of puzzlement and dismay.

He glanced over the guests to the western entrance, by which two Fyrd stood.

Blut followed his gaze but saw nothing wrong.

Yet there it was on Sinistral's face – bewilderment, uncertainty, fear.

Blut glanced at the audience but they had noticed nothing, thinking the Emperor's hesitation was merely for emphasis. But Leetha had and she, like Blut, looked concerned.

'. . . Which,' said the Emperor a third time, cocking his head as if he heard something they could not, *'which . . .'*

There came a running of feet and through the western entrance came a Fyrd, sweating, puffing, desperate-looking.

Discretion would have suited the moment better, but that he did not have. He hurried so fast down the Hall that Blut barely had time to intercept him before he reached the Emperor himself.

Blut grasped his arm and stilled him.

'Well?'

'It's . . . they . . . we couldn't . . . they . . .'

'Who? What?' hissed Blut. 'And keep your voice down.'

'They're coming,' said the guard, 'and there are too few of us to stop them.'

'Who's coming?'

Too late: the Emperor had heard.

He stepped back from the lectern ashen-faced and reached for Blut's arm.

Leetha came to him as well.

'Who's coming?' she said.

'Can't you hear him?' whispered Sinistral. 'Can't you hear?'

For a moment the Hall was silent as the grave, the audience struck dumb by this strange turn of events.

Then they heard the tramp-tramp-tramp of what seemed an approaching army and the curious sing-song chant they uttered as they came.

Ā Faroün! Ā Faroün! Ā Faroün!

The Emperor let out a cry of fear.

Leetha commanded, 'Get him to safety!'

Ā Faroün! Ā Faroün! Ā Faroün!

But as Fyrd tried to grasp his arms he shrugged them off, suddenly fierce, his fear replaced by anger.

'Master of Shadows,' he thundered, 'Leetha, Blut, stand by me! We shall face ā Faroün and kill him or die ourselves!'

Blut whispered, 'You see, My Lady? He veers towards madness.'

To which Leetha replied, 'Perhaps, Blut, or perhaps not. We shall see.'

No one moved, for whatever the state of his mind and the value of his commands, all there wished to stay and support the Emperor.

42
FIGHT

As Jack and the others neared the entrance to the Great Hall, with the angry mob behind them spoiling to disrupt the celebrations, he saw that their situation was serious.

Ahead were four stolid-looking Fyrd, their ironclad staves at the ready and crossbows on their belts.

Beyond them was an audience of well-dressed hydden of both sexes and all ages who until seconds before had been facing down the Hall, their attention drawn to something he could not see from the corridor. Now, hearing the chanting, they looked fearfully Jack's way.

He had Feld to his right and three or four of the tough-looking fighters who had agreed earlier to help them if need be. Now they sensed that real action was in the offing they had come forward resolutely to be near when they were needed.

Stort and Barklice were to Jack's left. He doubted that they would be much use in serious hand-to-hand fighting, but then that was not their role.

'You're the one who knows about gems, Stort, so your job is to grab 'em if you see 'em! We'll protect you, or divert attention from you, while you do.'

But Stort looked put out.

'My dear Jack,' he said stiffly, 'these are some of the holiest artefacts in the Hyddenworld, one does not just "grab 'em". In any case, anyone directly touching them would be ill-advised; they can heal and they can also make you sick and there's no predicting which . . . It took me days to recover from holding Spring for just a few minutes . . .'

Jack grinned. 'Then Barklice will have to lend you a hand!'

'Um . . . I . . . suppose . . .'

'Thank you, Barklice!'

The corridor was lit only by gaslights at shoulder height along the walls, which cast their shadows back and forth in an intimidating way upon the ceiling.

It was evident from the soft hues and flickering light in the Hall ahead that it was lit mainly by candles. They could see some on its far side – tall and elegant, their flames high, the reflectors behind them bright.

Nearer-to, by the entrance they were approaching, the Fyrd were lit from either side, so Jack guessed there were candles there too.

'The audience poses a problem,' he said in a low voice. 'It includes children and their parents among them and we must not cause them harm or put them in danger. Are there other ways out?'

'Two main ones,' said Feld, 'and one behind the Emperor's throne, but his guards won't want that used. Keep smiling . . . as I suggested!'

This seemed an odd command at such a moment but it was not. Feld had explained earlier that the Fyrd were trained not to draw their bows and shoot until they believed there was no alternative. Smiles confused them.

Now they were yards away and smiling still, the chanting ever louder from the mob behind, and the Fyrd looking at each other uneasily, their hands beginning to prepare to draw their crossbows.

Jack slowed the pace, as if coming in friendship, though the chanting gave the lie to that. But every second of indecision by the Fyrd was a second gained.

'I need to know the layout of the Hall and see where the gems are,' said Jack. 'Therefore use your staves to form a barrier and push the Fyrd back so that we have time to see what it is that Stort must do.'

'Halt!' one of the Fyrd finally cried.

Jack suddenly charged, buffeting the nearest backwards before turning his stave to the horizontal. The others did the same and the Fyrd retreated, still unsure what was going on.

Jack stepped back into the protection of the small enclave so created and Stort came to his side. There was shouting, stave thrusts and a couple of crossbows taken from belts, but they stayed calm, trusting that the others would protect them long enough to assess the position.

They saw the throne, the arras behind it, the lectern to one side and the two jewelled arks before it, bright and multicoloured in the candlelight.

'The gems must be in those arks,' said Stort. 'Green for Spring and yellow for Summer. Very original. We must hope they are not locked in some way.'

It was obvious to Jack who the Emperor was: he was tall, blond and exquisitely robed in black. By his side stood a female courtier, in her forties and beautiful, his consort perhaps, in grey silks set with jewels of moonstone, pearls and agate.

In front of them, dressed in black, was a younger version of the Emperor who might easily have been mistaken for his son. No more than two or three years older than Jack himself, but taller, broader and holding a mighty stave of office.

'That's the Master of Shadows, Jack,' said Feld in his ear. 'Take him down and the rest will fall ... But by the Mirror, if I am not mistaken I know him. He is—'

But Feld was unable to finish, for the Fyrd countercharged and the barrier had to be broken if they were to defend themselves properly.

'Stay close, Stort, stay very close . . .' rasped Jack as a Fyrd charged him and he too had to upend his stave and strike a counterblow before he was hit.

A few moments later he heard a scream behind him and felt a sharp slicing burn across the back of his neck and side of his throat. For a moment Jack thought that someone had taken a knife to him and slashed at his neck and throat.

He struck a blow ahead, put one hand to his neck, felt hot liquid and for a moment feared the worst. He turned to see who his assailant was, fearing that Stort must have been struck first, and saw the cause at once. One of the great candles had fallen over, knocking another down. This had sprayed hot wax on him even as fires broke out around both candles. The screams were of courtiers fleeing the sudden blaze.

Jack turned back to the fray, Feld now at his side. There was shouting, grunting, and Fyrd came at them hard and fast.

Another candle fell and flames shot up a hanging nearby towards the high roof and windows above.

'Keep moving,' cried Jack. 'Keep the momentum up! Force them to turn and run . . .'

It was obvious that their arrival came as a total surprise. The Emperor was only lightly guarded and the courtiers around him were middle-aged or elderly. They were unsure whether to stand by him or to turn tail and flee.

Of them all only the Master of Shadows stood his ground, but even he seemed uncertain whether to guard the Emperor or the two arks.

But there was something more, something dark, as if the fight in general and in its individual particulars was happening in air so thick and murky that everything was slowed down and hard to see. At first Jack thought this was merely the smoke from the fires. But then it seemed caused by something more.

While, behind them all, from the corridor, those still marching forward continued the cry *ã Faroün ã Faroün ã* . . . which Jack wanted them to stop because it was ugly to his ears and was beginning to confuse him, as if its simple sing-song syllables were interlaced with evil.

Blut, watching the action from the Emperor's side, knew within moments that this was a fight they could not win: too many, too sudden, too resolute. While at their head was a fighter the like of which he had never seen. Dark, grey-eyed, powerful, with a stave that caught the candle flames and turned them into shards of confusing light. At his side a former Fyrd Blut knew from past times and the recent report of Slew. He was General Meyor Feld, second in command in Brum and as experienced a Fyrd as could be.

And an angry rabble large enough to worry the most secure Emperor.

All here? In the Great Hall?

Schlotle had failed, the system had failed, everything had failed. *He* had failed.

And yet ... something odd. Their leader was slowing and seemed confused, as did the Emperor, as did many of them.

Not Blut.

'My Lord,' he said urgently, 'we must get you away to safety, and the gems too. Order Slew to bring them. My Lord ... while we have this moment to do it ... My Lady, *tell him* ...'

But she too seemed struck still, though whether by that cry of ā Faroün or something else Blut could not say.

'*My Lady* ...'

She turned slowly to him, her face shocked, saying nothing.

Is the world going mad? thought Blut. *Will no one take command?*

Then she spoke, but her normal confidence had deserted her and her voice was thin with fear.

She was looking at Slew, who was looking at the intruders' young leader as she said, 'He knows ... he remembers ... he *knows*, Blut. May the Mirror help them!'

'Knows *what?*' demanded Blut, stepping forward to take up the gems himself and then hustle his Lord to safety. 'Help me!' he commanded a courtier next to him. 'I speak in the Emperor's name!'

Jack's moment of strange slowness, when his mind seemed invaded by dark worms of dismay, was brought to a halt by Feld.

He had warded off another Fyrd, a stand-off was approaching as if no one quite knew what was happening, and he said, 'I know that face ...'

'Which face?' whispered Jack, struggling to drag himself from the heaviness the name ā Faroün put into him.

'The Master of Shadows. His face ... I know it. He is the one who killed Master Brief. *He's* the one!'

Jack felt shock.

'*He* killed Brief?'

'He did.'

Stort heard it and with a cry tried to run forward and avenge his mentor, but his stave flailed uselessly in his scholar's grasp.

'No!' said Jack. 'Not you, Stort ... it is for me to deal with him.'

Then, as if time had speeded up again and the thick air dispersed, Jack stepped forward towards Slew, whose eyes were filled with hate and the light of the flames that now rose round the Hall, where the fallen candles were.

He said calmly, 'You want the gems your carelessness and Brief's stupidity gave me? Then take them . . .'

Jack tensed, expecting a body thrust from his stave. But Slew simply moved it slightly to one side so that it formed a shadow as he did so, and then another when he moved it back such that Jack could not see his feet or legs or read his intent.

His feet darted one way, then another, and the stave arced out of darkness so fast that Jack could not raise his own stave to deflect the blow that suddenly came.

Bang!

The blow hit the side of his face like a hammer and then . . .

Bang!

Another from the other end of Slew's stave to his ribs . . .

And bang! to his head again and Jack was falling, flying, staggering back into empty chairs as Feld began coming forward to help him.

'No!' cried Jack, his ears ringing, his head in thundering pain. 'No! Leave him to me.'

While behind Slew, the Emperor seemed to have come to his senses. He had raised his arms to right and left to stop his own people going to Slew's aid.

'Let them fight!'

'But my Lord, the gems, the fire, your safety . . .' said Blut.

'I am alive, Blut, never more so . . . It is the Master's task to fight on my behalf and, it would seem, this young hydden's desire to challenge him on behalf of . . . whom?'

'Brum, it seems, my Lord. They are citizens of Brum.'

The Emperor laughed, looking around with such command that all those of his Court remaining fell back.

As for Lady Leetha, she still seemed in shock.

She turned to the Emperor saying, 'You must stop them, Lord, please stop them . . .'

'No,' said the Emperor, 'I will not.'

While Feld, understanding Jack's wish to fight on his own and thinking perhaps that this way fewer would be hurt and if right was on their side the gems would be theirs, held their own people back.

The cry of *ā Faroün* died, the roar of the curtains of flame took its place, as Slew, still smiling, waited for Jack to come forward again.

'Take them,' he said, stepping to one side of the arks. 'They are yours . . .'

His stave turned in the air, shadows formed about it, whirling about him, hiding where he was, his whereabouts confused by his laughter, which seemed like shadows too.

Bang!

And Jack reeled.

Bang!

And he spun round, his stave turning in the air above him. Thrust!

And one of his ribs cracked and pain shot through his body, sudden stabs of pain from rib to side, from rib to lung, from rib to his upper back.

Pain!

Jack knew pain, his boyhood had been lost to pain, and it held no more fear, nor any power over him.

He reached his hand and arm through it . . . and began to wield his stave as he should.

Thrust! Bang! Twist! went Slew's ironclad but each move was now parried by Jack.

Then on through the blows that followed until Jack caught up his spiralling stave and rose into its power and let its spinning turn carry him off and away to safety.

Shadows?

He knew their meaning and their seductive darkness.

He reached his other hand up, flipped his stave into an attacking position, shifted in the air, and turned the ancient carvings that Brief had honoured all his life towards the flames around the room.

Shadows?

Jack laughed as the carvings caught the light, fractured it into a thousand shards of brightness that spun out like starlings seeking the shadows with which Slew surrounded himself, breaking them up, revealing his feet once more, his legs, his arms, catching his dark cloak in their shining beaks and ripping it to shreds so that he was utterly exposed.

Bang! and Jack's blow caught him on the neck.

Bang! and the next hit Slew on the arm and broke it.

Thrust! And the third took him in the groin and Slew screamed and whirled away, his last shadows fleeing, his hair streaming, his eyes fearful, his stomach sick.

Bang! and his head began to bleed, one eye to swell, his beauty to be destroyed as he fell onto the floor near the arks which, pushed and buffeted by his body, began to sway.

Jack did not hesitate.

He went in for the kill, and stood over him, the end of his stave raised over Slew's throat.

'For Brief,' he said coldly, 'five minutes of whose life was worth yours in its entirety.'

'Noooooooooooooo!'

It was Lady Leetha, running past the Emperor and to Slew's side, her jewels torn and tumbling from her chest, her arms raised against Jack's stave.

'He is my son.'

Jack's eyes were cold and black as the agate she had worn, which now lay in the dust.

To right and left the jewelled arks swayed.

He reached a hand to still them, first one, then the other.

'Your son killed a much-loved hydden to steal the gem whose possession you now celebrate. Why then should I not kill him?'

He raised his stave higher.

Tears came to Leetha's eyes and her hands and arms fell slowly to rest on Slew's chest and shoulder as he groaned.

'Because he is your brother,' she whispered. 'Because of that.'

Jack stood staring down at them, unable to make sense of what he heard, unable to believe into whose eyes he gazed, unable to think.

Leetha helped Slew sit up, Jack backed off.

Slew staggered to his feet, his stave clattering on the ground, his pale smile returning.

'He doesn't remember, Mother, he was too young. Let him then have something to remember me by next time we meet . . .'

Slew opened the ark that contained the gem of Summer and reached inside.

He found what it was he sought and sighed.

He seemed suddenly to gain strength, his eye to heal, his face to glow with health as light suffused him for a time and dazzled them all. Then, closing his hand upon the gem, he quelled the light.

He took his hand, a fist now, out of the ark and held it high.

'You can take the other one as you will,' he said, 'but this I give freely to my brother . . . for – ' he laughed a bleak, ill-intentioned laugh – 'for letting me live.'

He offered his clenched hand to Jack.

'Take it,' he said.

Jack, confused by all that was happening, silently offered his hand.

Stort pushed forward past Feld, 'No! Jack! Do not touch the gem . . .'

It was too late.

Jack took it, fell back at the shock of it, steadied himself as Slew turned away, shaken by the fight, made weak by the gem. Jack opened his hand, shook his head in puzzlement, slipped the gem into the pouch Stort proffered and said shakily, 'I'm all right, I think I'm all right.' Perhaps he was, but he looked dazed and seemed unable to think clearly, or to know what to do next.

It was Feld who took final command.

'Stort, get the other gem and its pendant. *Now.* Barklice, help him. You others, form a protective ring around us; I am not convinced that Jack is well and we need to get him out of here.'

Stort and Barklice took the other gem from its ark without a single word from the Emperor, who simply stood and stared and seemed not to care.

Leetha went to his and Slew's sides. She stared at Jack, horror-struck and guilty, but he did not look at her. He was too dazed, too confused.

'Right,' said Feld, maintaining the initiative, '. . . and where now?'

The fire had taken hold in the area where they had come in. The hall had emptied through the other entrance but that was now filling with Fyrd, summoned to help and beginning to look threatening. The strength of the opposing forces, having gone one way, now swung back to the other.

But there was one person there who had barely moved at all from beginning to end of these events, having taken refuge behind the arras. He now emerged.

He was small, he was bold and he was Parlance, the most famous chef in the Hyddenworld.

'*Ah, Messieurs Stort et Jacques!*' he cried, unruffled by the mayhem all about. ''Ow good to see you again. Zis way!'

He moved back quickly behind the heavy arras to an open door there. Feld pushed Jack through and Stort and Barklice followed, and as Blut shouted a command to stop them Barklice crashed it shut and bolted it.

'*Parlance?*' said Jack unbelievingly.

The diminutive chef was dressed in his work clothes, his knives at his belt and his huge chef's hat upon his head. The medal that the Emperor had awarded him earlier was on his chest.

'It is *moi*,' said Parlance, 'but forget the *politesse*, your lives are at stake. They are slow now, but soon they will be fast. You will go that way . . . and I will tell them you went *this* way . . .'

'That way' was up some stairs and round a corner out of sight.

'There is a door,' said Parlance almost urgently, 'take it for it leads to *la liberté*, but have a care, there are *chiens méchants* out there . . .' He shrugged philosophically. 'But paupers cannot be choosers, *n'est-ce pas?*'

'Aren't you coming?'

'Ah *non!*' said Parlance, sadly, 'I 'ave a soufflé awaiting my attention!'

'Well . . .' said Jack, suddenly hesitant.

Something was dawning on him.

If Slew was his brother and that woman was Slew's mother then she must be his mother too . . .

The door they had bolted was now being battered by heavy feet and staves and could not last many seconds more.

'Quick *mes braves*! Shoo . . . *shoo!*'

Which Jack and the others did, their heads full of questions, but in the knowledge that the gems were safely in Stort's possession.

'*À bientôt!*' cried Parlance, running towards the bolted door and affecting, as it gave way just as Jack and the others disappeared, to be trying to open it himself.

'*Ah! Messieurs et Madame!* I am so short I cannot reach zis bolt! But quick, you may still catch *les monstres* from Brum, they 'ave *disparu* down zos stairs . . .'

They charged in the direction he was pointing, Slew at their head, Blut following behind.

Parlance, having made sure that Jack had made good his escape and no one was looking, darted up the stairs and closed and bolted the door through which they had gone up to the outside world.

That done, the chef checked his chronometer and headed back down the stairs towards the Imperial kitchen, mopping his brow.

43
EVENING

When Katherine and the Foales had got back to Woolstone Margaret still felt unwell. Next day Arthur took her for a check-up in Oxford. Katherine wanted to do the driving but Margaret preferred to go with Arthur alone.

Until the last year she had never been unwell in her life. It had always been Arthur, and always she who looked after him. Now it was his turn to look after her and it felt right that way.

They had been married nearly half a century, had good times and bad, and they had reached the point where, for some things, words were not needed.

This was one of them.

The falls had given due warning of Margaret's decline. The seriousness with which their doctor took them, his insistence on more frequent tests and check-ups, and the pills she was prescribed for blood pressure told them both that things would never be the same. But what spoke loudest of all was that she no longer wanted to do very much, or walk, or even garden.

Death held no fear for her: she had had a good life and was tired now and beginning to let go. There was fear of loss but not of death itself, and for her visit to the doctor Margaret wanted no one else but Arthur with her.

'You can have a rest my dear,' she told Katherine, 'have a sleep. These have been hard times for us all.'

The appointment was at ten in the morning, so they left at half past eight. Arthur called home at eleven to say things had been delayed and they were doing other tests.

'Is everything all right?'

'She's so tired, Katherine,' was all he said.

Tired was what Katherine was too, but a sleep-in she could not do. She was restless, irritable, and it was the first time she had been alone and in the house since Judith was born.

She missed Jack and Judith terribly with a pain like no other she had ever known.

Distressed, she got up and felt the house all oppressive around her and went out to stand on the crumbling patio and listen to the garden and the chimes . . . In fact, she told herself, it was the first time in years she had been alone in Woolstone. Maybe the first time ever.

She caught a glimpse of a tall, thin, haggard woman in the glass wall of the conservatory: clothes dowdy, hair lank, posture stooped. A defeated woman. It took her a while to recognize herself.

She looked through her own reflection on into the conservatory to where her mother had lain bedridden and hurting for so long. The last time, the only time she could remember her parents alive, together and normal, was that day they picked up Jack in the health centre in North Yorkshire. Her Dad's face was now just a photograph with no connection with real memory. Her mother was different.

'Mum,' she said aloud . . .

Mum, I'd like to talk to you.

Mum, I don't know what happened.

Mum, I did everything wrong.

Mum, I'm numb inside and out.

Mum, why did you leave me alone?

She went back inside and up to her room.

No, friends, no one to talk to.

First Mum, then Judith gone like a bad dream that came and went and left devastation inside my heart.

Jack's gone, he's gone and he was my rock and I fear he may never come back.

Everyone's gone, nothing and nobody left. Purposeless and drifting.

She wept for the sense of the loss of them all.

✳

An old birthday card stood on her desk near the window.

It was from her old school friend Samantha, who had moved to Hong Kong when her Dad's work took him on a contract there. After that, Australia. She had never come back, but they exchanged cards and emails and she knew all about Jack coming into Katherine's life.

When they went into the Hyddenworld Katherine stopped replying to Sam's emails, which piled up in her inbox until space ran out. When she had come back to have the baby there had been no time to clear her emails or write to Sam. Anyway, what was she going to say? What *could* she say? To anyone else it would make no sense.

Katherine had a telephone book with friends' numbers in, but she had so few friends it was nearly empty. She had no mobile yet. No time or inclination. She went back online and found a file with Sam's old emails and the one with her contact details in Australia.

What was the time there?

Ahead or behind? She couldn't remember and she didn't care.

'Sam?'

It was an old woman at the other end of the line. Maybe her mother.

'I'll get her. Who shall I say . . . ?'

But Katherine couldn't get her own name out.

'Sam! It's for you. I don't know. No. Female. Yes.'

Then, to Katherine, 'She's just coming . . .'

'Hello?' said Sam.

Katherine sat breathing, then not breathing, silent and not quite silent.

'Hello . . . ?'

Sam's voice, gentle like it had always been. Back then it was like that, before all this.

Before.

'Sam?'

'Yes . . .'

'Sam . . . I . . .'

'Katherine?'

'I . . . Sam . . . I . . . I . . .'

Katherine did not cry easily. She had certainly never cried like that, not like *that*. She cried like she would never stop. She wept. She howled like a small broken animal that has no one and nobody.

'Katherine, whatever is it?'

Her voice was caring and she was crying too, for in Katherine's tears she heard the cry of the world.

'It's something bad isn't it?'

'Yes . . . but . . . I . . . c . . . can't . . . oh, Sam, I can't . . .'

I can't say it because no one can know, no one can ever know, and it's not bad it's worse than that it's . . .

'Look, Katherine, I'm going to ask you questions like we used to when we couldn't get something out or we were too embarrassed. Remember? I ask, you answer. Easier that way.'

'Okay.'

'Are you missing your Mum?'

'Yes. But it's not that.'

'Is it to do with men?'

Sam's voice smiled and then stopped smiling.

'No. Worse.'

'Jack? He's . . .'

'Not Jack, it's . . .'

That's a revelation, thought Katherine: it's not Jack.

'Okay . . .' Sam was thinking. 'You're pregnant.'

Silence then, what was there to say? Utter, utter silence.

'Worse.'

'Your . . . you . . .' and Sam thought about the long silence and what its reasons might have been. And why her friend was calling now. And what was worse.

'You had a baby?'

'Yes.'

'And . . . he . . .'

'She.'

'She . . . ?'

'Yes.'

And that was the worst, that lie which wasn't a lie exactly.

Yes, she died.

She was never my baby at all.

She . . . I don't know what she was, what she is . . . and I don't know what to think or what to feel.

Katherine wept uncontrollably.

'I don't know what to do . . .'

Sam wept too.

'And something else . . .'

Was this it? Was this at the root of her grief or was it all of it? She didn't know.

'It's Margaret Foale . . .'

'She's . . . like . . . your adoptive mother?'

'I think she's dying, Sam, and I don't know what to do . . .'

When they were finished Katherine felt hollowed out with loss and grief, for her mother, for Jack, for Judith and for Margaret. But for the time being there were no more tears to cry.

The phone rang, it was Arthur.

'They're keeping her in overnight, more tests. I'm going to stay. Are you all right?'

'I'm fine, Arthur, fine. Give her my love. And Arthur . . .'

'Yes.'

'Good luck. I'm thinking of you both.'

'I . . . it's not easy, Katherine. Growing old is not easy. It doesn't creep up on you like they say. One day you wake up and it's hit you like a ton of bricks. Like today.'

She went out to the scullery, found her walking boots and put them on. The day was warm with sun and clouds, and she went out the side door, down through the garden, round the henge, over the barbed-wire fence and across the fields towards White Horse Hill. She wore jeans and a T-shirt and as she went she realized she had not locked the door. She had never had to before. There was always someone there.

The chimes will protect the house; they always have and always will.

She strode the familiar paths as she often had with Jack and with Arthur, breathing the scented Summer air, enjoying the sound of skylarks and the Summer flowers, scabious and knapweed, rough and ready things she liked.

The chalk turf was her turf, the slope up the escarpment steep, the presence of her beloved Jack very real, but he was not coming back. She could grieve, grieve for them all. Tucked away in all those feelings and the tears and her talk with Sam were tiny seeds of relief, of freedom, of visions of a wider world.

She climbed and climbed, right past the White Horse, on past the Iron Age earthwork and then down the slope to the gate onto the Ridgeway.

She stood where she and Jack had stood once and told each other that one day they'd just set off and head east and then north, along the Ridgeway, then onto the Peddar's Way, on for ever, together, like they were meant to be.

Not in this life it seemed.

Margaret and Arthur came back that night while it was still light.

'She wouldn't stay,' grumbled Arthur.

'Tests, tests, tests!' said Margaret. 'Your mother Clare always said she knew better than the doctors and now I know what she meant. You look peaky.'

'I am, a bit. What did Mum mean?'

'That if you listen to your body it'll tell you what it needs.'

'What's yours need?'

'To die, more or less. It's old and wearing out and it's been a hard few years.'

Arthur scowled and said, 'Going to the study.'

'At least our bed'll be comfortable,' said Margaret.

'Damn silly. All the way there and all the way back.'

'I'll bring you tea.'

'I'll bring you whisky,' said Katherine.

When he was gone Katherine said, 'So? What *is* wrong?'

'Heart. Angina, and probably worse. Katherine . . .' She drew her chair nearer, 'I do not want to linger on a couch like your mother did and I don't intend to. She didn't either but she had no option: she had to see you into some kind of maturity, God help us all. All day today, made to feel helpless in the car and then the hospital, I wanted to be up on the Hill like I used to when I was your age. What did you do?'

'I spoke to Sam in Australia, I cried a lot and I went for the walk you wanted to do but couldn't.'

'Well, what to say? Tomorrow promises to be fair.'

'We can drive up the Hill and park.'

'We can leave the damn car right where it is and walk. I'll make a picnic.'

They all made one next morning, adding the bits they liked.

'My early tomatoes,' said Arthur.

'They still look green, my dear.'

'Muesli bars,' said Katherine.

'Get stuck in my teeth,' said Arthur.

'Cheese and chutney sandwiches,' said Margaret, folding tinfoil around them.

'Soggy,' said Katherine.

'Well, there it is, dear, that's what I've made!'

They were always the same, their picnics. Each to his or her own, their plaints affectionate, their food, despite the gripes, always completely consumed.

'You're not walking,' said Arthur.

'I am,' said Margaret. 'Tired I may be, and a little in pain, but I'm walking like I always have. You wouldn't have it any other way.'

'You shouldn't,' said Katherine.

'But I must, you see, I must.'

They went slowly, nearly meandering, chattering their way along the old much-loved paths, happy to see the White Horse resplendent, a tired old lady, a vigorous old man and their adoptive granddaughter.

Margaret was slower than she ever had been and grey-faced; Arthur attentive, Katherine watchful.

They knew it was the last time, each moment hard but more precious for it, an old lady saying goodbye to the corners and places of woodland and stile, bramble and gorse that she and her partner in life had always loved.

'Katherine, it was a blessing when you came into my life,' said Margaret suddenly, giving away the tenor of her thoughts. 'However terrible the circumstances, I was given a gift. One day you'll see that Judith is a gift as well, despite everything.'

Somehow they reached the top, the world spread out all summery at their feet. They lay listening at leisure to the buzz and the hum of a July day.

'Englalond,' murmured Arthur. 'If I smoked a pipe I'd smoke it now.'

'I'm glad you don't, darling. Jack is a gift as well. Life is a gift. Every precious moment.'

'It is,' said Arthur, his wrinkled, freckled hand reaching to hold hers.

Katherine thought *Jack . . . you and I have a very long way to go to get to where they are but we've started now and we can try. Come back, my love, come back soon.*

'Listen,' said Margaret.

They listened.

'What?'

'I thought I heard the chimes.'

'And I thought I heard horses' hoofs,' said Katherine, sitting up alarmed. Great horses' hoofs across the heavens. A brief hint of thunder.

Getting home was difficult.

They had to walk on either side of Margaret on the steep bits going down.

'Oh, oh, oh!' she said. 'And once my legs were elegant, now they can't even hold me up.'

'I should never have let you come out in the first place,' said Arthur, 'but then I never could say no to you. Bloody silly. Stubborn.'

'Huh!' said Margaret. 'You or me?'

'Both of you,' said Katherine, 'both of you.'

Over the barbed-wire fence with difficulty, round the henge, a brief pause by the chimes, up the lawn to the house.

'Oh, I'm glad to be back,' said Margaret, 'help me to a chair . . . yes, here in the conservatory.'

They did, and glanced at each other when she was settled.

'You stay with her, Arthur, I'll fetch tea.'

He looked bleak and sad because, Katherine guessed, he thought they had just finished the last walk up the Hill that Margaret would ever have.

'Did you enjoy that?' she heard him say.

'Very much, my dear,' replied Margaret, 'so very much.'

She was asleep by the time Katherine came back.

'She'll have something when she wakes up,' said Arthur.

So they had tea quietly, saying nothing as they watched the light fade on White Horse Hill at eventide.

Until night fell and Arthur helped Margaret up to their room.

Katherine sat for a while in the dark of the conservatory but she felt restless and uneasy.

Outside it was dark, the night winds fretful, the chimes uneasy. She walked across the lawn, feeling the dark as Jack sometimes did, but he did it better and more naturally than her. Reaching the conifers she did not go inside the henge.

'Never again,' she whispered, 'I never want to go back. This is my home, this my world. I'm sorry, Jack, I'm so sorry, but I want you to come back to the human world. I want to be . . . normal, I need you to be here so that we . . . we . . .'

She didn't know what they might do when he came back. She just wanted her Jack to find the way home and she prayed that he would, as once, not so long ago, at that same spot, Margaret had prayed for Arthur's return.

Now all was changed but the feeling was the same: the longing, the hope, the despair.

'Come home, my love,' she said.

44

DOGGED

The moment Jack and his friends raced up the stairs to escape from the Great Hall of Bochum and the doors were shut behind them they knew where they were.

It was the rubbish dump underneath which, Feld had pointed out when they arrived, most of civilized Bochum lay.

There was a foetid smell about the darkness they were in, a slithery, oily, acrid feel to the air which caught the backs of their throats and made their eyes feel prickly. Though the drifting clouds above their heads were lit from beneath by the myriad lights of the vast industrial landscape within which they stood, at ground level all was dark and shadowy and hard to make out.

Worse, the ground felt unstable and it was easy to slip or stumble.

'Over here,' said Jack, pulling out one of the torches Cluckett had packed for them. The ground was covered with rubbish in and out of which rats ran, scattering as they came and following after them.

'Stay together and stay close!' he ordered, 'because we're not going to have time to start searching for each other in this lot if we're to get away before the Bochumers realize which way we've come.'

He felt shaky, but strong enough to lead. He put it down to the foul air.

The path they were on was no more than an animal track, and it continued round the edge of the building they had been in. To their right were the windows which inside were high up, but now they could look in.

They could see that the fire had taken hold, the flames beating against the glass.

'Crack!' went one window, followed by a rush of air from outside it.

'Crack!' went another, just ahead, the pulling of sucked air so strong it threw Barklice off balance.

If they could have moved away from the building they would have done so, but the ground sloped up steeply to the left and was impossible to climb, being no more than a mound of filthy, ill-smelling rubbish of all kinds, in all stages of decay.

They started to run, Feld in front now, his stave at the ready in case they met anyone, and Jack behind, ready to defend the rear. The fire in the building to their right was getting worse by the moment, more windows cracking and the heat becoming intolerable. They could hear shouting inside and water shot up at them. Someone was already taking command.

Feld stopped abruptly at a gap to the left and Jack caught up.

'We need to get away from this fire . . .' he said.

Crack!

They darted through the gap and found themselves in a wide space, the mounds of rubbish all around so high that they could not see human buildings in any direction, just the lurid clouds above.

Some of the tops of the mounds were now lit orange by the flames behind them, like mountains at sunset. But at ground level it was still hard to make anything out.

'What now?'

'You're the route finder, Barklice,' said Jack.

The verderer clambered up the nearest mound, cursing the rats as he went. When he reached the top he looked about, his form lit red on one side and a silhouette on the other, with smoke drifting the way he pointed.

He slithered back down and said, 'Short of climbing up a mound of this stuff every five minutes the only way we're going to get a bearing to take us out of here is to follow the drift of the smoke and hope the wind isn't flukey and doesn't change direction.'

Jack nodded, looked behind, saw no one in pursuit but for the reflective eyes of some creature of the night, and off they went, Barklice now in the lead.

It was ten minutes later that Stort said, 'I don't want to worry anyone but we're not alone out here . . .'

He stopped and pointed, first to their right and then to their left. The eyes of the kind Jack had spotted before had increased in number. What creatures they were it was impossible to say, for they hung back in shadows too deep to betray their form.

'There are none ahead,' said Barklice, 'so let's just hurry along and hope they're harmless and more scared of us than we need be of them.'

Stort however gulped audibly enough for Jack to hear.

'Well?' said Jack in a low voice, for something was on the scrivener's mind. 'Please don't tell me you've lost the gems.'

'No, they're safe inside my jerkin,' said Stort, 'but they are not my present concern. I am thinking about what Parlance said as we fled out here. He mentioned *chiens méchants*. It's French for dangerous dogs, plural. Meaning more than one. It seems to me that those staring eyes represent a lot more than one.'

'They might be rabbits,' said Jack.

'Rabbits have a pleasing and cheerful roseate colour to their friendly eyes,' said Stort. 'These eyes are dirty yellow and mean green and I saw a pair earlier that were cruel blue.'

'Rabbits!' said Jack firmly. 'Now let's—'

There was a throaty growl to their right, and a preparatory snarl to their left. The eyes were closing in.

'Hurry,' called out Jack to Barklice, '*hurry!*' for when he looked behind he saw that the eyes were closing in from that direction too.

All hydden know that when dogs are on the prowl, hurrying is not the best strategy. But this was not a promenade in Brum.

This was in swirling, smoky darkness, with a stench to the air and the dreadful sound of the first pattering of a pack of dogs, sniffing and snarling as a prelude to attack. Dawdling was not an option, nor was mere hurrying. The eyes were getting closer, the forms of their pursuers ever clearer, as the snouts and tails, claws and muscled flanks of dogs behind, to right and to left began to show themselves.

'Run for your lives!' shouted Jack and run they did.

On, and on, the pack chasing in pursuit, barking and snarling, weaving in and out of the mounds of rubbish, running across their path ahead, snapping at their heels and hands and calves from every side.

Running until their breaths grew shorter, their chests tighter, the pack closer.

'Jack,' cried Barklice suddenly, 'they . . . they're *herding* us.'

It was suddenly plain that they were, for they had veered from the bearing the drifting smoke above their heads had given them, round a little, then a little more, then on and on and then right again until, barely able to run any more, they almost fell through a narrow gap in the rubbish and found themselves in an open space, dogs all about, circling them, snapping at each other, closing in on all sides. They were in a canine killing field.

The best they could do was back themselves to the nearest mound of rubbish, hoping that in amongst it somewhere there might be a line of retreat. But such gaps as there were – dark little avenues barely a foot wide and ending in more walls of waste – went nowhere.

Worse still, the fire they had first run from was suddenly near again, the walls of the Hall no more than a hundred yards away.

'They've brought us almost back to where we started!' said Feld.

They turned to face the dogs which, stepping forward here and then over there and then suddenly at the side, were impossible to deal with singly or together. One got hold of Feld's stave, its teeth splintering the wood as it nearly wrested it from him.

Another leapt at Barklice and was only driven back by a blow from Jack's bigger stave.

They formed a semicircle, warding the dogs off, each trying to work out a strategy between running for it and getting caught or staying as they were and being worn down and eventually turned to dogs' meat.

'The thing is,' panted Stort, 'they're not coming any closer . . . just near enough to keep us trapped here and . . . well.'

He jabbed ineffectually at a snarling dog, loosening his grip on his stave which, at once, was pulled from his grip altogether into the main mass of the dogs. They attacked it ferociously, tearing its hard wood to shreds, chewing its splintered parts as if they were meat.

'Which is what will happen to all of us if we stay here much longer,' said Barklice.

'All we can do,' said Feld, 'is to run and hope for the best!'

'Agreed?' said Jack.

Barklice nodded and said, 'You choose the moment, Jack.'

'And yet,' said Stort, who, now he was without a stave, had been forced to take a position in a small gap in the rubbish behind them, 'we might just ask before we run what is it the dogs are waiting for? In my studies of the canine tribe I think I can safely say that all have a leader, an alpha male, and looking at these beasts it is a puzzlement they have not got one. Anarchy rules among the dogs of Bochum it seems . . .'

He had no sooner said this than they saw, at the rear of the pack, a commotion among the dogs which rapidly turned into a fight between rival groups.

'Our moment may come when they are sufficiently distracted,' said Jack. 'Be ready for my call!'

But not yet. On either side the dogs kept watch on them, punishing the lightest movement with snaps and snarls, while in front of them the dog fight quickly turned into an unequal battle for the leadership of the sort Stort had suggested was to be expected.

A thickset, muscular pit-bull terrier, the evident leader of one of the tip's more brutal tribes, was ranged against a taller, broader beast of a dog with fine Labrador blood, the leader of a rival gang. But this dog, more intelligent-looking, his coat a fiery ginger, was bleeding from its flank and the loss of blood had weakened it. What was more, it was handicapped by having to defend an injured dog that was barely more than a pup, but with the same ginger hair.

The thickset pit bull crouched low, its teeth bared and its small evil eyes narrowed, and moved in for the final assault. The bigger dog did its best but it could not defend itself and the pup, which they guessed was one of its own.

'The last,' said Barklice quietly, pointing beyond the dogs to the shadows where lay the pitiful spectacle of a bitch and three more pups, all torn and dead.

The end of the fight for dominance was swift. The bull terrier lunged in fast, grabbed the leg of the pup before its father could save it and tossed it squealing over its head to where its followers began tearing it to death.

Jack saw their chance and shouted, 'Run!'

Unfortunately it was just at this critical moment that Bedwyn Stort happened to look behind himself, no doubt thinking that perhaps there might be a route out that way after all. So when he heard Jack's sudden cry he ran instinctively – in the wrong direction.

The gap was indeed another impassable cul de sac, and as he charged into it and got stuck the others fled quite another way. When Stort emerged he was horrified to see the last of them, Barklice, disappearing round a corner into darkness, many of the dogs in pursuit, while he was left alone facing, what?

He stared in horror at what stared at him.

It was the defeated dog.

His last pup had been torn to death . . . his mate and their other young were lying dead beyond. Once the leader, he was sidelined now. He was big, square-headed, huge-clawed, his eyes hazel and clear.

He saw the trembling Stort and, no doubt, saw a chance to redeem himself.

His nearly beaten spirit found then some last vestige of aggression and will. He turned and growled at his former pack, its members already trying to sneak away, tails between their legs, flanks shivering in defeat. They stopped, turned, waited and watched.

Could he still find a way to show his strength?

He thought he could, growled low, hackles rising, teeth showing, and advanced slowly towards Stort. The other dogs, even the great pit bull, stopped to stare. A kill, especially of hydden, was always worth the watching.

He growled again and came forward faster, smelling fear.

It was a situation from Stort's worst nightmares.

'Help!' he whispered, his throat constricting. All he could do was bend down and retrieve a short spar of his broken stave and hold it in front of himself with a shaking hand.

The big dog speeded up, his great feet thundering on the ground, his snarl already nearly victorious.

Stort backed way, realized his bit of stave would not serve, and all he could think to do was heave off his portersac and hold it as protection in front while he squeezed backwards into the gap behind.

'Help!' he whispered again, but no help came.

The dog, puzzled by the portersac, slowed, its former followers bunching up behind, trying to squeeze round it and be the first to sink their teeth into Stort's freckled flesh.

But their erstwhile leader was big, his shoulders broad. He had not been their leader for nothing.

He shrugged them off, snarling and sniffing as he did so, the scent of Stort a welcome one as his teeth tore great lumps out of the portersac. Stort, pushing his way backwards into the constricted space, utterly trapped, no help in sight, the scene made worse by the billowing flames of the Hall nearby, pulled his portersac up closer.

It was then, in what seemed the last moments of his life, that he spied that pocket of his 'sac which Cluckett had thoughtfully labelled 'For emergencies'. If this was not one of those, Stort would never after know what might be.

He opened the pocket and pulled out its contents one by one.

Twine, useless.

A small bandage. Was Cluckett mad?

A spoon. 'I think not,' muttered the desperate Stort.

A clothes peg. Stort laughed madly.

The dog pressed nearer still.

Then more of the same from the pocket, trivia and trinkets, all useless in the emergency Stort now faced. He dug deeper still, and threw what he found into the air crying, 'Useless, Cluckett, no good at all!'

Until there was nothing left, nothing to pin his hopes on except . . . except . . . right there at the bottom, what was this?

A piece of paper? She was not just mad but insane!

He pulled it out and stared in astonishment.

It was an envelope and written on it, in his own hand, was the number 63.

He felt hot breath upon his legs as the last of his 'sac begin to disintegrate and the doggy tongue licked about as if in search of the best place to bite.

'What is this?' cried Stort, holding the envelope to the light, unable to remember what was in it or why . . . or why . . .

It was his sixty-third attempt to achieve the near-impossible – a powder which, if wafted in the face of a dangerous dog, will cause it to retreat, turn tail and run. Such, at least, had been the hope. With that, and with a dramatic devil-may-care gesture, he tore the envelope open and scattered the anti-canine powder into the jaws of the beast he faced.

There was a strange moment of puzzled silence which communicated itself mysteriously to the entire snarling pack behind, which also fell silent.

Then the dog swallowed what Stort had thrown at him, envelope and all. It gulped strangely and fell back a step, licking and chopping its jaws as if it had just consumed an ice-cream sundae and wished to get the benefit of what remained.

Then something odd: a dreamy look came into the great dog's eyes. It looked about as one who has seen the light but has temporarily forgotten where it is. Then, spying the eyes of Stort, who stared at him almost from the same level, the dog looked upon the scrivener in a way no creature, animal or mortal had ever looked at him before, not even his own mother: it gazed at him with utter devotion, total loyalty, fierce pride and terrifying protectiveness.

Then without more ado it leapt at Stort who, bemused by a range of expressions which naturally made no sense to him, thought his end had come. Two great clawed paws settled on his shoulders, but instead of bites he suffered something nearly as bad: the licking of a new and eager love.

Doggy love.

Love beyond any love another mortal may know.

Love as great as the great Universe itself.

By comparison the embrace of Ma'Shuqa, which had at the beginning of Summer very nearly caused the death of Stort, was a mere peck on the cheek.

'Aaagh!' he gasped. 'Oh . . . help!'

His powder, it seemed, did not have the power to disperse at all, but rather to engender immediate, uncontrollable adoration.

Then Stort felt a painful bite on his shin.

One of the other dogs had thrust in its nasty, snivelling snout and was chewing at Stort's leg.

'Ow!'

Then, as he struggled to fend off the big dog another smaller one bit the other leg.

'Ow!'

Then an ankle!

'No! *Help!*'

Help?!! The big dog heard it and seemed to think: *Is my master under attack? Can it be that another dog dares to threaten him?*

Such, or something like it, were the thoughts that lumbered through the canine's brain.

It ceased licking Stort.

It stared into his eyes and seemed to say, 'Leave this to me!'

It turned like a trained athlete, torn though its shoulder was from its earlier fight, and it growled.

The other dogs backed off at once.

It looked back at Stort for clear instruction.

Master, what shall I do? Only tell me, I shall obey!

Stort understood.

'Well,' he said, 'I suppose . . .'

The other dogs moved aside and the big bull terrier reappeared.

'Um . . .' continued Stort, 'perhaps you could . . .'

The bull terrier moved forward fast.

'Kill!' cried Stort.

The dog launched itself off at once, now a canine army all by itself, its shoulder no longer seeming to hurt at all.

Kill? Your wish is my command!

It dived in, grabbed the murderer of its mate and pups, shook it about as Cluckett might shake a duster at Stort's front door on a Friday morning, and then tossed it away, its lifeless body falling into shadows.

Stort was getting the idea.

'Heel!' he cried.

The great beast came to heel, blood dripping from its maw. It looked at Stort in expectation of a pat or two, which it duly got.

'What's this?' said Stort, realizing that the dog had a collar. The dog was or had been owned by a human and it had a name.

Stort read the metal tag aloud: *Georg Friedrich Händel*.

'Strange name,' said Stort, 'distantly familiar, but plain Georg will do!'

At this utterance, Georg's happiness was complete, his identity returned. It looked up at Stort with pride and pleasure for a job well done, it bent its head a little as if to say 'What next?' and when Stort began walking the way the others had gone, it trotted behind him, its head not much below Stort's, but its position a respectful two paces behind.

Stort spoke his thoughts aloud, as was his habit: 'I wonder where the others might be?'

Georg took this as a command, ran forward a little, sniffed about in the rubbish a good deal, and then having found a scent, looking back to see that Stort was following, he set a fair pace forward, twisting and turning through the maze of the rubbish piles and leading Stort confidently on.

Jack and the others were in dire straits.

They had realized they had lost Stort, and with him the two gems; it was too late to go easily back, for they were pursued by too many dogs to fight.

They slowed down, hoping that the dogs would disperse, which rather mysteriously they did, and then very cautiously they headed back. But the fire in the Hall had died, the wind had grown as flukey as Barklice had feared, and with no moon or stars showing it proved nearly impossible to get their bearings. They had wandered and wandered until, despair and tiredness overtaking them, they stopped.

'All we can do,' said Jack judiciously, 'is to rest a little, wait for dawn, and hope against hope that the gems in their pouches may still be found . . .'

A growl, deep-throated and threatening.

A great dog's face peering round the mound at the base of which they had stopped.

'More dogs,' muttered Barklice as they all stood up to fight once more.

The dog stood proud, looked back the way it had come to what they thought must be its fellows. Instead Bedwyn Stort appeared, a majestic, heroic silhouette against the clouds, the gems safely on his person.

'I feared for a moment I might have lost you,' he said, before pointing at Georg and speaking words he thought he would never hear himself say: 'Don't worry about him, he doesn't bite.'

Of their five-day escape from Bochum and Germany a good deal was afterward said.

The truth was simple.

Stort proffered the gems in their pouches for the dog to sniff and said softly, 'Now . . . find a way to get us home.'

No challenge, not even that one, was too great for Georg. He cocked his head, peered about a bit, sniffed again and seemed to get in touch with something beyond himself because he offered up a howl to the very Universe itself.

He went to Jack and then to each in turn.

Then back to Stort, biffing him with his head as if to say, 'Trust me, I know where to go.'

He headed south out of the city, by forgotten railway tracks and closed collieries, by Alten Bochum and Wasserstrasse, from the south by Weitmar and Haarl . . . through woodland and sward, and down to the old River Ruhr.

There they found a craft by following Georg's questing gaze, and headed upriver for mile after mile.

Only one thing troubled them as they went. It was Jack. With each day that passed he grew sicker, until a day came when they noticed blood on his shirt and jerkin. His old burn scars were opening up.

'We must get you safely home,' said Stort. 'I fear it may be because you touched the gem of Summer. Some it helps and some it harms . . . We must make sure these open wounds do not become infected.'

'Did not Cluckett provide us with an embrocation against such an eventuality?'

He dug around in Jack's portersac and found a small jar of the remedy the goodwife had packed. Stort applied the balm liberally.

'This should keep the infection at bay even if Jack's spirit does not yet improve. It took me a good while to recover mentally from exposure to the gem of Spring.

He was right.

Another day passed and Jack got worse.

'Stort . . . I can hardly walk . . . I'm sorry . . . I . . .'

From that moment on they took turns to carry his portersac and his stave and to help him along.

Georg the dog seemed to understand and hurried his pace. Until, resting by day and travelling by night, they reached the valley of the Loermecke River and the prehistoric limestone caves there. Georg grabbed Jack's jacket as if to say, 'Come with me, giant-born, the Great One among your Neandertal forebears lived here once. As he led you to Bochum so shall he guide you back to Brum.'

So as they came, did they go, the carvings of Jack's stave calling up the crackling blue light of the ancients as it had before.

Into the caves they went. Georg stopped at the entrance to wanly watch them go. Head to one side, a sound of sadness, his life bereft, his new master leaving.

Stort looked at Jack and ill though he was he looked at Stort and nodded.

They turned into the timeless tunnels of the cave as Stort called with new-found love in his voice, 'Come on then, come on!' and Georg, his great spirit surely touched by his ancient forebears too, followed after the master he would always love, protect, honour and obey.

45

COMING OF AGE

In the last days of July the Earth grew still again, the days calm. A quiet, warm Summer briefly reigned. Balmy morning winds and a curtain moving gently at the open window, which was the first thing Margaret Foale saw when she woke up.

'Arthur . . . ?'

'Yes, my love.'

'It is so beautiful, the Earth.'

'She is.'

Margaret was slow now, tired, giving way.

The house was at peace again after the noisy, violent, fractured, secret raising of Judith to be the Shield Maiden, which had taken them all to the edge of themselves and Jack away again.

They all missed him as they missed Judith, both bright stars in their quiet firmament.

'Arthur, can I take her anything?' wondered Katherine downstairs. 'Tea? Breakfast? Anything?'

He shook his head, unable to sit down, fingers fretting, wishing there was something he could do but knowing there was nothing.

'She's fine, she's happy, she's looking at the view from our bedroom window. She loves to lie and stare out now. The White Horse resplendent, galloping who knows where.'

They went up to her and sat on either side of her bed, holding her hands.

'We were wondering where you think the Horse is going,' said Arthur.

'To the ends of the Earth,' Margaret replied. 'Now, I think I ought to sleep a little.'

The White Horse was the last thing Margaret saw, waking to it one morning, whispering to Arthur to stay with her, hold her hand, because she felt tired, so tired, and . . .

'It is so beautiful . . .'

She held his hand and with the other reached for the Horse, to touch it, to stroke its great mane, reaching through the window, through the light Summer breeze, reaching out at last as her friend Clare had reached before her.

'I wanted to see her ride it, Arthur, I want to see Judith ride but you can, you will . . . she will be . . . it is . . . so . . .'

She fell silent, her hand falling still on the blankets.

Arthur held her, Katherine moved softly about downstairs.

She stirred closer to him and said, '. . . so beautiful,' and was gone.

In the days following, busy days when the world went on hold with grief and Katherine saw Arthur through the worst and they feared they were the last in Woolstone House, the last of all . . . Katherine knew that Judith had come home.

'She's here, Arthur, she's here . . . I can feel her near, being with us.'

'Being with *you*, Katherine. That's what children do when their parents need them: come home. It's what they do. It's their true coming of age when they see they have a role to play. It's the moment of paradox when they can say goodbye and parents can be free and their love is deeper than it has ever been.'

'But I was never a mother . . .'

He said, quite sharply, 'Never say that, never. You made her and carried her and gave her birth. You are her mother. She has no other, you're the one.'

'I never talked to her, never shared the moments a mother's meant to share except . . .' She smiled and blinked back tears. '. . . except once when we put ribbons in each other's hair and flew upon the wind.'

Arthur shook his head and said, 'It isn't over, your job with her. If she's here . . .'

'I know she is.'

'If so, then go and find a way to talk to her, she's probably as fearful as you are. But she's come home when you need her maybe that's because she needs you too. Go and talk to her.'

'I don't know how to.'

'I think you do, you had the best of teachers – your mother Clare. You could start with the chimes. Those damn things are always tinkling away in a know-all kind of way. Talk to them. Maybe Judith will hear you there.'

'I . . .'

'I often do when I tend my tomatoes and find that someone's been stealing them . . . is it you?'

She laughed and shook her head. 'Wouldn't dare,' she said.

'We all have to start somewhere with our grieving,' said Arthur, 'it's the living's new beginning. Not my words – Margaret's. Go and talk to your daughter; truth travels furthest of all when it comes from the heart. It'll reach her.'

'I miss Jack,' said Katherine simply.

'Then tell her,' he said. 'Who better to comfort you?'

So Katherine did, out in the garden, under the trees, whispering her words to lost Judith, saying she didn't know what she should say but she'd try. Wresting the truth from herself and letting her see her cry for Jack.

That same pagan Summer, which started with tremors and storms in May and was ending with quiet in July, was a time of change in the tunnels of Bochum too.

The fire that started in the Hall on the night of the aborted celebration had caught hold and raged through the tunnels for a time.

The Emperor, once so decisive in his rule, was suddenly ineffectual and able only to wander about and say, 'Disperse! Disperse! It isn't worth it.'

Insanity was the whisper of those days, as the Court tried to recover itself and find a new direction: 'The Emperor is insane.'

'Disperse, dispersal, my Lord?' wondered Blut. 'What do you mean?'

'The end of Empire, when people leave the comfort of what they know.'

'Anarchy?'

Sinistral shook his head.

'Freedom, Blut. I have seen one fire too many now and this one marked the beginning of the end of days. The gems are gone, I can no longer rely on Summer – and never even had a chance with Spring – to prop my ageing body up. Though I shall try my best to live and even do more things. Am I not, for my age, still young?'

Blut could not but agree.

'Who needs Summer when they have themselves, Blut?'

The truth was that Sinistral's exposure to the light of Summer, and his dalliance with the light of Spring, had given him back the bloom of youth, for a time. But he was stiff and seemed less quick, less sure than before, though Blut thought that he denied it and made excuses.

'My Lord, if only you had given the order to grasp hold of that hydden from Brum . . .'

'The one you say is named Bedwyn Stort?'

'Slew thought that was he, yes. If you had let us grasp him we could have stopped him doing what he did.'

The Emperor laughed.

'I like the idea of tyrants "grasping" their enemies, Blut. You have a delicate touch with language. Most of us would say "kill them" or worse. But grasp . . .'

Blut stared him down, unamused.

'I could not see him clearly,' said the Emperor. 'The smoke . . .'

'My Lord . . .' sighed Blut.

'I was dizzy.'

'I think not.'

'He was taller than me.'

'True.'

'And it seemed to me that he had about his face, his presence, the look of what I might call prophecy. I stole the gems, he looked like their true Bearer. Seeing that, how could I deny him possession of the gems even had I wanted to?'

They were in the Chamber of Sleep where, since the fire, Sinistral had taken to coming to listen to the rain, which had returned. And to sleep.

'But don't worry, Blut, it's only for a little while. I am deciding what to do and who should take my place.'

'My Lord, that's absurd.'

Now, days later, they were talking about Stort and the gems and Sinistral's life and Blut was writing it all down.

'So . . . I said to you before that I see people's lives in slices, their different parts, past and present, sometimes future too. He was, is, far more worthy than myself to take the gem of Summer. It has been poisoning me for years. Now I am free of all that, though not the guilt.'

'For what?'

'My mentor ã Faroün would not give the gem to me. I told a lie to my father about the greatest hydden I ever knew. I told him he had been untoward towards me, I need be no more specific than that.

'My father ordered that he be burnt and being clever made me light the flames and watch. In his death was the beginning of my own. Its prolongation with the gem has been a torture. Just punishment I think.'

Blut was silent and his pen fell still.

'Have you sent your family away?'

'They leave tomorrow.'

'Good timing, Blut, very good. I fancy things will get hot round here.'

He laughed, genuinely amused. Blut did not see the joke.

'Now listen. I am getting up from this chair, while I still can. It is so comfortable I could fall asleep again and not wake up at all.'

Witold Slew emerged from the shadows. His wounds had healed and he too looked healthier and more free.

'My Lord,' he said, 'you asked me to attend.'

'I did. To whom do you owe your fealty?'

'Yourself.'

The Emperor shook his head and said, 'No, you owe it to my office and through that to the Court and Empire. The Emperor's wish is your command, is it not?'

'It is, Lord.'

'Blut, bear witness to that.'

'I do.'

'So, fetch me a candle, one of you, and set it in a holder that it will not blow out.'

They did.

He got up and pointed to the farthest darkness of the Chamber.

'I am going for a little walk from which I doubt I shall return. My final command, Slew, is that you do not follow me but stay here and serve who you must. From this moment on that is not myself, for I declare that I am Emperor no more. There! I said it! Now there is no more to say.'

'Lord . . .' said Slew.

'Lord . . .' whispered Blut.

'Really, trust me, there is no more to say.'

He held the candle towards the dark and said, 'Listen to the rain! Is it not beautiful? But what are you both waiting for? You have work to do. Go, Blut. They await you.'

'Who?'

'Vayle, Schlotle, Quatremayne and their minions. Decisions to make, work to do. By you, not me. Goodbye, Blut, we shall meet again, but by then I may be as I should really be – old.'

He reached a hand to Blut who, nonplussed, took his.

A strong grip, confident, youthful.

'My Lord, please . . .'

'Goodbye Blut.'

He turned away from them.

'Lord,' said Blut, 'I . . .'

Sinistral waved his hand dismissively and did not look back.

'Listen to the *musica*,' they heard him say as he stepped from the protection of the canopy into the rain. '*Listen!*'

Blut watched him go, history on the march, an era passing.

'He sounds happier than I've ever heard him sound,' he said.

Insanity or the sanest of them all?

He did not know.

'Come then, Slew, we have work to do.'

They returned to Level 2 and found the Court and its officials in the ruins of the Hall, its roof open to the sky, the stench intolerable, gulls flying squealing up in the human world, rubbish on the floor, and rats beginning to colonize.

The throne was there, a little burnt, dusty, but still in place and unoccupied. Blut looked at them, smiled, shrugged as if in reluctant surprise and, seizing the moment, sat down.

'Well, gentlemen and lady, we have some decisions to make.'

'Difficult decisions,' said Vayle.

'Retirement for me,' said Schlotle, 'once we're on our feet again.'

'And you, Quatremayne?'

'With your permission I think that nothing's changed in the wider sphere, just delayed that's all. Come the Autumn we should invade Englalond, Lord, and crush so-called fabled Brum. Sack it. Lay it waste.'

Blut gave no response.

'Schlotle?'

'He's right, my Lord.'

'Vayle?'

'A wise decision which the courtiers, when they return, will support, Majesty.'

He turned to Leetha, whose eyes were red. She had already said her goodbye to Slaeke Sinistral or, more accurately, he had said his to her.

'My Lady?'

'Leave Brum until you have seen it with your own eyes. That was *his* way on anything that mattered. See it for yourself . . .' she paused awhile before adding with due emphasis and a glance at the others, 'my Lord Emperor.'

Blut considered this and nodded. Had power ever passed so peacefully? Was *this* Sinistral's final legacy? He leaned forward and she came confidentially to him.

'Plain Emperor will do,' said Niklas Blut, ruler of the Hyddenworld.

'Emperor?'

'My Lady?' he said.

'I came for the Summer and the Summer is nearly done. Now I shall leave.'

'You were ever the ruler of your own life,' he said. 'We would have it no other way.'

She laughed, as did the others, whose mirth was joined by the screaming of gulls.

'The dynasty of Sinistral is over,' said Slew, beating the floor with the Emperor's stave, 'let that of Blut begin.'

They looked at him to see his response.

He took off his spectacles and wiped them clean, pondering.

'On reflection . . .'

'My Lord?'

'I think that perhaps . . .'

'Emperor?'

'We citizens of Bochum and the Empire . . .'

'Yes . . . yes, Lord?'

'Owe a debt of gratitude to the citizens of Brum, brave defenders of liberty, bold travellers through the centuries, traders and chefs as they are.'

Silence.

'Would you not agree?'

Slew's hand grew a little firmer on the Emperor's stave, and he looked at the courtiers and officials in a way that might have given some to take a moment's pause and agree that the old must give way to the new.

'Therefore,' said Blut, in a calm and measured way, 'the first command of my rule is that an envoy be sent to Brum at once to convey greetings of friendship and respect and to say . . . to say . . .'

'Lord, what must the envoy say?'

'That I, Blut, Emperor of the Hyddenworld, will visit Brum in person when Autumn comes to . . . to . . .'

'My Lord, what will you do?'

'To grant them the freedoms which by dint of a treacherous insurrection they already have but which we in our magnanimity now recognize etcetera and so forth and signed by me.'

'Yes, Emperor.'

'Did someone write that down?'

There was an uneasy silence. No one had.

A twinkle came to Blut's eye.

'It seems an Emperor needs a scrivener,' he said. 'Where in our great Empire may the best be found?'

'In Brum, Emperor,' Leetha said, 'I'm sure they will oblige and provide us with one.'

'Thank you, my Lady, I trust they will.'

So still, the Earth, those last days of Summer, waiting as She was for things to be as they must be before the Autumn came. Quiet Summer evenings, abundant life, sorrow for what She had done, the deaths caused, the tragedies in the night, dams breaking, waves racing, the drift towards the end of days.

Meanwhile . . . the Shield Maiden, when would she come of age?

My Lady Leetha, climbing through the old Thuringian trees, seeking someone she could not find, accepting of what had happened in Bochum but glad to be out of it all once more, said, 'Where are you, Modor, why do you hide? I saw him, I really did. I saw him!'

'Did you?' whispered the breeze in the thicket not far from the top, where the wise Modor lived.

Wise but not always happy. Still, when Leetha came to see her, well, that was fun.

'So, you saw him?' she said.

'I did.'

They sat on fallen trees, supping stew with good rough brot.

'You're still unhappy,' said Leetha, who rarely was.

'I have been, I will be, for a while. It is not natural to be alone.'

'Where is the Wita, the Wise One?'

'Not here. He came, he went. Jobs to do.'

'How long has he been gone?'

'Decades, I think,' she said, before adding, to change from a painful subject, 'So you saw your son?'

'How long, Modor?' persisted Leetha.

She had never seen the Modor look so sad or so alone.

'I can't remember when I last felt his touch. I miss him every moment of my old life, every single moment. As he does me, I'm sure.'

'So why isn't he here?'

'Jobs to do,' she said again. 'Now . . . tell me . . . what did he look like, this Jack of yours? He was handsome when a boy.'

'He is handsome now. They all were, the ones from Brum. You should have seen them coming into the Hall, him and his friends, staves at the ready, fighting the Fyrd, leading a crusade.'

'What friends were those?'

Leetha wrinkled her brow.

'There were four, I only know the names of two. Feld, who once served as a Fyrd in Bochum, and the famous Mister Stort.'

'Ah, I've met him once or twice and more. In fact, I met Jack *and* Stort not long ago, at Paley's Creek. Probably the other one was Barklice, a verderer who is rather extraordinary in his way.'

'You know everybody, Modor, and remember everything.'

'Which is a curse. It is better to forget, there is bliss in that.'

'Well, anyway, I saw him and I stopped him hurting Witold Slew.'

'You mean your son.'

'If you want to put it that way. I prefer to call him Witold Slew.'

'How is the Emperor?'

'He is Emperor no more and therefore happier than he was. Now . . . I do miss *him*. Modor?'

'Mmm?'

'Will you ever die?'

'Not yet, my love, I'll be here for you until the Mirror calls you home.'

'Will my sons be safe?'

'I cannot tell you that,' whispered the breeze in the old thicket where My Lady sat, whispering to herself, 'I cannot tell you that.'

'Arthur, will you come with me to the henge? I think she's there. I'm sure she is. Maybe I could see her in there, maybe she can hear me there?'

'I think she hears you everywhere . . . and no, I won't. That's a journey you must make yourself, mother to daughter. It's not very far, Katherine, it's just down the garden, by the chimes, between the two biggest trees . . .'

'I'm frightened.'

'That's reasonable enough, it's a frightening thing to do, talk to someone without barriers. Now listen, I think a walk up to the Ridgeway would be good for us. Clear the cobwebs, that kind of thing. Early start, picnic, but not where we had one before, further along. Before the end of the month. New beginning, Autumn coming, *that kind of thing . . .'*

He left her to it and Katherine, glowering at the noisy chimes, went to the conifers and said, 'I'm not coming in! I'm not coming back to the Hyddenworld! You'll have to talk to me here!'

She was smiling, almost laughing, but then the laughter faded.

The henge was empty and Judith gone.

She sat down, her back to one of the trees, patient until, dusk falling, Judith returned. Just like that.

'It's so odd,' said Katherine calmly, 'but you look older than I do now!'

Judith, dressed as roughly as ever, boots and all, looked tired and in her late twenties. 'I *am* older, ageing faster, but it's not quite what you think. I see things differently.'

'How is it then?'

'I run the lines, I sing my way, I swim the deep waters and I grow a thousand shoots. Time is different, but I feel my age, I feel time going. The Earth is quiet right now, but not for long. Mum?'

'Yes? You still call me that?'

There was such sweetness in being able to say that.

'Tell me about you and Dad.'

'What do you want to know?'

'Things. What comes to mind. How you met him.'

'Oh.'

They sat through time itself, talking like that, Katherine knowing this was it, her last time with her daughter. Now, that moment, which was everything. Until by the end, when it was dark, she felt free as a bird, her loss and anger washing out, lost somewhere in the grass, gone. She felt empty of all that.

'Mum . . . ?'

'Yes, Judith.'

'What's it like being loved?'

'Like . . . like . . .' Katherine laughed, unable to answer.

'Do you know Bedwyn Stort?'

'Of course I do. He is the best of hydden and he has a gift beyond all others. He makes others happy.'

'Tell me about him.'

Katherine did.

'Some more.'

Katherine told some more and they both laughed. 'He does things wrong but in doing that he does them right. Why do you ask?'

'He said he felt me move in your stomach.'

'Womb. He did.'

'He stared at me as if he knew me.'

'I suppose he does.'

'Is being loved knowing that someone knows you, really knows you?'

'A bit, I think. Why?'

'I think *he* knows me and . . . and I think I know him. It helps when I feel lonely. I used to cry for loneliness.'

'And now?'

'Now too, but it's not been so bad since I met him. I think of him there when I was inside you, from the beginning of time, and I feel better.'

'I think of you too. So does Jack, I'm sure. Tell me, Judith, when I was talking to you by the chimes, did you know?'

'Yes.'

'Could you see me?'

'It's not like that. I just know. It just happens. Like running the line, and racing the Reivers. Did that dam burst in Byrness?'

'Yes, I'm afraid it did. People died. We would have died if you hadn't made us leave.'

Judith shrugged.

'But I couldn't save Margaret, could I? I can't do very much as a matter of fact. Mind you I am not exactly the Shield Maiden yet. I need to let go of some things. Attachments . . .'

Katherine felt a pang.

'How can I help others if one hand is tied to someone or something else? That's why I've come back, to find out how to leave.'

Katherine smiled.

'Makes sense,' she said.

'Meanwhile . . . all I can do is just nudge things along, feel things, do what She can't do, try to stop her doing what She can do! Some hope . . . Mum. Sorry.'

'I'm sorry too.'

'Mum . . .' she reached out but then, as Katherine tried to touch her, she was gone just like that, running the line.

Then she came back.

'I can't love him. Stort. Not ever . . .'

'Why not?'

'Time is against us, and his mortality. How can we ever scale the mountains of time between us?'

'Then all I can say is that I hope for both your sakes one of you will find a way.'

'Hmm,' murmured Judith, unsure of that.

Then she really was gone, running the line, over the Hill, up by the Horse, a star in the sky.

46

TO SUMMER'S END

They came back towards the end of July of that year when Summer was not itself and might never be again, and found themselves in a great circle of standing stones.

All of them but Feld knew exactly where they were.

'Avebury,' said Barklice with relief, looking up towards the downland scarp above them. 'If we can get him up there and onto the Ridgeway it's only twenty miles to Woolstone . . .'

Jack was sick to heart and body, the open wounds of his old burns infected, his blood seemingly poisoned. He was pale and delirious, sweating one moment, shivering the next.

They knew the cause, which was the gem he touched, but not the cure, though in his delirium Jack himself thought he did.

'Let me touch the gem of Summer again. It made Slaeke Sinistral young, it will do me . . .'

'No, Jack. It made you ill, not well.'

'Please.'

'No.'

'If you don't . . . I'll . . .'

'I will not, Jack,' said Stort, 'and you're too weak to make threats. I bear the gems for the Shield Maiden alone.'

They made a stretcher from branches taken from around the henge and portered him up to the Ridgeway, taking it in turns to share the carrying. It wasn't easy and Feld did more than the other two.

The only one among them who found the going easy was Georg

the dog who, discovering there was life beyond a rubbish dump, was joyous in all he did.

By evening they had got halfway to White Horse Hill.

'Where are we?' said Jack, so weak he could not stop his head rolling from side to side.

'Nearly home,' said Stort.

'I have no home,' cried Jack dramatically, tears in his eyes, 'nor family, nor anything . . .'

'You have Katherine, Jack,' replied Stort in a measured and sensible way.

But Stort knew he was thinking of Bochum and the female – he had no other name for her – who claimed Slew was Jack's brother, which meant she was their mother.

'Jack . . .'

But he was asleep again, grey-faced.

'Perhaps we should have gone back, Feld. We should have found out the truth of his past, for therein lies something of his sickness.'

'Through those dogs? I think not, Stort.'

Next day they hurried on, Jack no stronger.

'We need a miracle,' fretted Barklice.

'Perhaps,' said Stort.

Long though the day was, it was dusk before they got within reach of the Hill and Woolstone, but too late to go all the way.

'Another half mile on from here is a place I know which will do to shelter him.'

'Its name?'

'Wayland's Smithy, after the old god Wegland.'

Stort looked relieved.

'I have heard of it. It is a place of sanctuary, a burial place of warriors. You should have mentioned it before, my dear Barklice!'

But as they approached it, huffing and puffing as they went, Jack grey and still, they were very surprised to catch the scents of food and mead and to see, glimmering on the tall trees there, the light of a fire.

'Travellers,' said Stort, 'who may not be friendly.'

They put Jack's litter down and Stort stayed with him while Feld and Barklice went to investigate.

Georg pattered about, restive, sniffling at Jack's things, looking for food in Stort's pockets, staring at them, head to one side, hoping for something, as dogs do.

'What you need, Jack, is Katherine and love. That's all. It's a pity we couldn't get to Woolstone tonight. It's not that far, White Horse Hill is already within sight.'

Georg's eyes stared, his mouth open, his tongue hanging out as he panted and thought.

Was this a command? Did his master wish him to do something? He thought perhaps he did. In fact he knew he did. But what?

'Maybe, if we get you settled up here somewhere,' continued Stort, 'then tomorrow I could . . .'

Georg knew then what he must do, though the place was strange, the scents new, the night mysterious. He delved into Jack's possessions once again, snuffled about, and then had another thought. He ran around, found what he was looking for, clamped it in his jaw and before Stort could stop him he was off into the night.

'Dogs!' said Stort. 'He'll soon come back . . . but meanwhile, peace and quiet, Jack, home cooking, stillness, such as I never had when I returned to Brum. Not a crowd, or festivity, or any . . . any . . .'

He heard voices, he saw lights, he heard music and he stood up, his mouth opening in astonishment.

'Or any excitement. You don't need that!'

But excitement was exactly what was coming towards them along the Ridgeway from the direction of Wayland's Smithy.

'Er, Jack, are you awake?'

Jack groaned.

'No,' he said, 'I'm not.'

'Are you perhaps a little better?'

'I am worse.'

'Could it be that you could entertain some visitors?'

'Here? In the middle of the Ridgeway? Are you mad?'

He sounded better.

Whoever it was approaching them, candles in hand, they must be friends, for Feld and Barklice were at their head, smiling.

But then they stopped, and it was not they who came forward but a solitary individual, known to Stort but whose presence there that night, had he tried a thousand times, he could never have guessed right.

She loomed towards them, purposefully, and Stort's heart missed a beat.

'Um . . .' he began.

She came nearer still, her bosom preceding her.

'Er . . . can that possibly be . . . ?'

'Good evening, Mister Stort, I am glad and relieved to see you well,' said Cluckett before her eyes narrowed and she said in a way that would not be denied, 'Now, sir, show me the patient.'

Stort knelt down by Jack and said, 'We've found a goodwife, she'll tend your wounds . . .'

Jack gripped his arm.

'A goodwife?' he said faintly. '*Here?!* Why? How?'

And then, with mounting horror, 'What's her name?'

'Cluckett,' said Stort.

'Kill me first,' said Jack.

Stort smiled and shook his head.

'No, Jack, she wants you alive.'

They had all come to White Horse Hill together, Pike, Brunte, Backhaus, Ma'Shuqa and even Lord Festoon and many pilgrims besides. They had set up camp at Wayland's Smithy and when Feld had arrived they were starting a feast.

'We are keeping old traditions alive, Stort,' said Lord Festoon, 'and making this pilgrimage to give thanks, as we folks of Brum always have.'

'For what?'

'Why, my dear fellow, hasn't anyone told you? An envoy was sent from Bochum. We have been pardoned for the insurrection and won our liberty in perpetuity and for all time. The Emperor Blut himself is coming before long to give thanks for what you and Jack did . . . it is a most happy time.'

'What did we do?'

'I do not think that this new Emperor likes gems. He was glad you took them back. Now come and feast . . .'

Stort declined. Jack was genuinely ill and he wished to keep him company. Cluckett had seen to it that his wounds were cleaned and dressed and he was in a place of quiet and sanctuary, away from the crowd.

'I am gratified to see you have applied the balm I gave for his scars very well, Mister Stort, without which I very much fear—'

'. . . that he might have died,' said Stort sombrely. 'I am – we are – very grateful to you.'

Cluckett flushed with pleasure at this unexpected praise and said, 'I am glad you think so, though I fear your friend may have found my treament just now somewhat rigorous. Needs must, Mister Stort, needs must!'

'How long will his recovery take?'

'In the normal course of events it could be weeks, likely months, probably years. But now I've given him a tonic, and bled him, and poulticed what needed it, and drawn out the sweats and . . .'

Jack groaned, a deep abiding groan.

Stort went to him.

'Has she gone?' he said. 'Did you by happy chance knife her in the back, cut her up and bury her where she can never be found?'

'No, Jack, I didn't, and be careful or she'll hear you.'

Stort returned to Cluckett.

'And then I put my thumbs in his back and thighs to speed up the recovery and tweaked his joints and did the jerks, which gets things going I can tell you! All he needs is the comfort of his spouse's touch and he'll be as right as rain in the morning.'

'You mean Katherine?'

'That's the one!'

'And I thought he was dying!'

'You stick to your work, Mister Stort and I'll stick to mine if you please. What he needs now is a good night's sleep, but I have my doubts with these folk about he'll get it . . .'

But in that she was wrong.

For the pilgrimage had been a long and hard one and they had only arrived earlier that day. Come the midnight hour, when the church clocks in the Vale struck midnight, all were asleep, even Jack, even Stort himself.

*

But down in the Vale, a little way on from the end of the pilgrim road and on its far side, across a stream and over a meadow, under a strand of barbed wire and through a henge, a dog ran. It dropped the object it had been carrying outside the conservatory doors of Woolstone and howled.

Katherine woke at once.

It howled again.

She opened her window and saw nothing at all but the moon over White Horse Hill.

The dog howled a third time and she heard Arthur get up, go downstairs and open the patio door.

'You heard it?' she said, coming down.

'I found this,' said Arthur, 'just outside.'

It was Jack's stave, formerly Brief's. It sparked and crackled with blue light.

She dressed quickly as if for a very long walk.

The dog barked again.

'Do you want me to come?' said Arthur.

'This is something I need to do alone,' she said. 'His stave will protect me.'

'Where exactly would you say you're going?' said Arthur. 'And when are you coming back?'

'Into the Hyddenworld,' she replied without hesitation, 'I do not know when I'm coming back.'

She held him tight, knowing that now he would be alone in the house. But that did not feel wrong at all. He needed time alone, as she and Jack now did.

'Soon,' she whispered, 'we'll come and get you. But for now . . .'

'Off you go!' he said.

With the stave in her hand she passed through the henge and into the Hyddenworld like an adept.

'Easy,' she said to herself, but the walk afterwards was hard. She finally reached Wayland's Smithy at two in the morning. The dog woke Stort and, yawning, he came and found her.

'Where is he?'

'I wondered where the dog went to ... ah, thank goodness, you have his stave. He's over here.'

'Is he all right?'

'Mirror knows,' said Stort, 'yesterday he was dying, today he might outwalk the lot of us ...'

She went to him where he lay on the ground and put her arms around him, he fearful that it was Cluckett with another cure until she kissed him.

When he knew it was not, he held her as tight as he ever had.

'I love you,' he said.

'And I you,' she replied.

It was dawn three days later on White Horse Hill and Jack and Katherine were up there, waiting for the sun to rise. All the others bar Stort had set off back to Brum and they were about to leave.

Stort was on the far side of the hill, standing alone in the wind.

Each had their way of saying farewell to the past and of greeting the future.

'She's still here,' said Katherine quietly. 'She's waiting, I think.'

'I think she is,' said Jack. 'But time to let her go, to be herself.'

They were not talking about Margaret, whose spirit had gone now, far ahead. It was Judith of whom Katherine spoke.

She had hoped for some sign or other, but she didn't know what. Something that told her her daughter was free, if not of life's hurt then of childhood. Her freedom would be Katherine's too.

'I'm frightened for her,' said Katherine.

'And ... ?' said Jack.

'And for myself.'

'We have a whole life to live and already we've done so much.'

'Yes,' she said, but it didn't feel that way.

'She's here,' whispered Katherine later, shivering a little with the chill of the dawn. She stood up.

'I wish I could see her one more time before we leave for Brum.'

'Look!' said Jack. 'There, down in the combe.'

He pointed at the wraiths of early morning mist that gathered beneath the Hill, swirling, waiting for the sun to chase them away. It was down there that Judith, little more than a child, had raised her hands and arms in joy at discovering the Earth.

'We're ready to go,' said Jack.

Still Katherine lingered, hoping.

'She's so alone,' she said.

'No,' said Jack, '*you* think you are. But you're not, you've got me and we've got us!'

He grinned at her.

'Stort'll catch us up,' said Jack. 'He's resting and thinking like he does, let him be. He too wants to say goodbye. Now . . . let's go. We'll take the Ridgeway for a while and then drop back down to the pilgrim road for Brum. We know it well enough.'

Moments later the sun finally showed and they stood to honour the moment. The mist had shifted and was suffused with light.

'It's always so beautiful when the sun first catches it,' said Katherine.

Westward, the other way along the Ridgeway, the trees were still dark and the great copse of beeches that surrounded Wayland's Smithy, the barrow on the horizon, was dark against the waking sky.

They stood shoulder to shoulder.

No real point in hurrying.

This was what living was for.

A patter of feet, light and fast, and a grey shape raced across the sward before them and chased mist across the down.

'Morten,' said Katherine, recognizing the dog from Byrness. 'Judith must be near. Maybe we'll see her after all.'

They waited in the silence of the dawn.

Stort was resting because he had got up in the deep of the night, packed his 'sac and left it under the hawthorn on the Hill ready for the off next day.

Then he trekked down through the dark to Woolstone, stood in the henge, went to the chimes. There was something he had done which he had regretted and so he had come back to undo it.

It was the chime Judith gave him, the day they ate tomatoes, which, being superstitious, he had hung back up.

He knew the one but . . . though he looked hard with a light on them all, it wasn't there.

He felt a pang of disappointment and shook his head. Moments come and then they go and a hydden should grasp a gift when it is given, with a glad and welcoming heart.

'Next time . . .' he murmured, but there might not be a next time. Of course there'd be a next time! That's the way to think!

Suddenly he could feel her. Right there, very near in the garden, then out across the downs, racing, running, flying, circling, finding for herself where she should be and where she must go, summoning up first light.

The chimes sounded, he shone his light on Arthur's tomato plants, cherry-red and ripe.

He bent to try one and knew at once she was right there, wanting to give him one.

Did he pluck, did she give it? He didn't know.

It was cool but full of taste, a burst of Summer in his mouth.

The chimes trembled and even as he looked in the dawn light they shifted and changed, one going, one coming, and a new one right there before him . . . yet old, it looked old, though its sound was young.

He looked closer and knew it was the one she had given him.

A gift when it is given . . .

He left it where it was. It was not for him to touch the chimes. He sensed her laughter, turned towards her, and felt her race away up the Hill. He followed and, reaching the tree and his portersac again, sat down and fell asleep.

What finally woke him was Georg, restless and eager. He sat looking about, tail swishing, as if expecting a visitor.

'We'll see what we see,' said Stort, watching the sun rise, glimpsing Jack and the others but not going near. He wanted these last moments alone as, he was sure, did they.

The White Horse was just out of sight, below the fall of the slope.

'Go on!' he said to Georg. 'The sun's rising, go and chase wraiths!'
Georg did, as happy as could be.

Stort got up.

The Hill was deserted, the combe below swirling with mist, the sun not yet quite high enough to reach right down.

He walked to the flat area of grass above the Horse, the fort rising behind him.

Georg, who had disappeared, raced suddenly at him, right past and off again, ears flapping.

Stort stood with nowhere else to go.

He took out the gems, thinking he might just leave them for her, somewhere on the chalk carving of the Horse, in the centre of its eye perhaps.

Another dog raced by, grey and beautiful, utterly benign, silent in the morning, its feet barely touching ground, flying, turning, exquisite.

'You're near,' he whispered, 'and now I'm suddenly trembling because I won't know what to do.'

'Hello,' she said, from where she stood, over by the Horse, down a little. 'Hello, Bedwyn Stort . . .'

He dared to look.

She was a girl before, now she was a woman, tall and strong: the Shield Maiden. Her dark hair held the sun, it lit her eyes and robe and was warm and golden between them.

'Hello, Judith,' he said, aware that that was who she always would be to him, if to no one else. 'Hello again.'

'I saw you this morning by the chimes,' she said.

'I knew you were there.'

'I wanted us to run together in the henge like we did.'

'You always can with me,' said Stort. 'I'm not much good at that sort of thing but, well, with me you always can.'

'You're my . . . friend,' she said.

He felt a pang of longing and regret. Friend was not what he wanted to be, but what else can a Shield Maiden ever have but that?

'I am,' he said. 'I always will be.'

'Yes . . .' she said, also unable to say more.

She too felt regret because of what could not be.

I love you, Stort, she wanted to say but she could not and never would. The love of a Shield Maiden is for all not one.

'Until the end of time,' said Stort. 'I'll be your friend and call you by your given name, Judith.'

I love you, she told him with her whole being.

And I you, Judith, he replied.

Their longing was the whole world's and their silence a hundred thousand words of love, not one of which could ever be spoken out loud.

Their dogs raced back and forth, here and there, down and up, so beautiful, his dog and hers, weaving a pattern of love across the grass, down in its hollows, over the Horse's lines, through the mist and back out of it. It took Stort's breath away.

'I don't know what to say or do,' he said at last.

'Nor I,' she said, 'and I'm meant to be the Shield Maiden!'

The last of the Summer breeze was in her dark hair, the first colours of Autumn in her eyes.

He wanted to go to her but didn't know how.

She too, to him, but it felt too far.

Far, far down, in the combe beneath them, their dogs raced and turned, weaving the mist into shapes that turned and wove into yet more. Turned and rose as if the Earth Herself was sighing.

Rose up as if from the dark western sky.

As if from the pale east, turning, the shape changing as the dogs, spirits of the new morning, wove the sunlight and the mist into something that made distant thunder, a Horse's hoofs, the Earth turning beneath them as they came.

It was then the great White Horse came to her and knelt down for her to mount it for the first time.

'I think,' said Stort, trying to see her where she was, which wasn't easy that morning, not easy at all, 'I think . . . that it must be time . . .'

He took the pendant from his own neck and went to her. She leaned down towards him as he put it over her head.

'And this,' he said, offering the gem of Summer, 'is for you to put in its right setting because I don't know . . . I'm not . . .'

'You place it there,' she said, 'for there is no one else. You can touch them without harm.'

She looked at him as he at her, near and far, here and over there, down by the grass, up in the sky, into each other they looked.

He took the pendant in his hands with the chain around her neck and carefully placed the gem of Summer where it must be.

She laughed then, sitting up, reins in one hand to steady the White Horse, reaching to him with the other.

'I have something for you too,' she said. 'Come near.'

He came closer, the Horse stilled, she let go the reins and slipped the golden thread that held the chime he had left where he thought it should stay, over his head.

'There,' she said, tucking the chime inside his jerkin, 'there, Bedwyn Stort and . . . don't ever part with it again!'

'I won't.'

She took up the reins again, the hoofs of the Horse restless, but still she lingered.

'What?' he said.

'Did you notice that I am getting older? Tell the truth.'

'No, I didn't and I don't. You are most beautiful to me.'

'But I'll get older and older still . . .'

'And I'll never see it because . . . I . . . I must not say . . . I think . . . I wish . . . I am a fool.'

She laughed again and said, 'That's the last thing that you are.'

The White Horse reared and readied.

Stort stood back, the wind of the morning wanting to drive him away, the sun wanted to burn him, the mists confuse him.

The world turned and he reached after her as the Horse rose up. Though she seemed to reach as well their hands did not quite touch, though they finally reached to each other right across the sky.

Not yet, the wind said, *but sometime, always . . .*

'For ever,' said Bedwyn Stort, his hand feeling the chime she had given him, his dog come back to heel alone.

'Look!' whispered Katherine, taking Jack's arm.

The sun had risen high enough to touch the White Horse and make it come alive.

'Look!'

The White Horse rose, its Rider on its back, the light of Spring and Summer on her breast, in her hair the first colours of Autumn.

'Did we really make her, Jack?' Katherine said. 'Look where she goes!'

They stood and watched Judith ride through the sunlight and the morning until she was gone and Stort came to them.

'Well,' he said, 'we three again, not including the dog.'

Georg raced on ahead.

'We have a trek to make,' said Stort, 'things to do and much to discuss. Agreed?'

'Agreed,' said Jack.

They set off together as the first winds of Autumn began to worry at their feet.

ACKNOWLEDGEMENTS

With special thanks to Jackie Brockway for whose support, help, encouragement and occasional kicks through the writing of this story I shall be eternally grateful.

We very much hope you enjoyed *Awakening*. If you have a comment or query about the book or series, write to the author directly at *william@williamhorwood.co.uk*. Readers can join his emailing list for news of future events and titles on his website: *www.william horwood.co.uk*